## A MOMENT OF PASSION ... AND BETRAYAL

"I think we should go back," Jesse said.

Annabel nodded. "Of course. You certainly don't want to make little Sarah mad. You've got to be the dutiful husband. If Sarah says sell your bike, sell your bike. If she wants you to entertain twelve kids like a clown, then do it. If—"

Jesse grabbed her, only intending to shut her up. But when he looked down at her, he knew she had won. She had been whittling away at him from the very beginning. She had made him doubt himself, and Sarah, and everything he thought he should be. He grabbed her hair and tilted her head back. She slid her hands up around his neck. Her fingers were cool and silky.

Later, he would look back and try to convince himself that she was the one who initiated the kiss, that she pulled his head down and pressed her red lips to his. But at the time, it was all blurred. Maybe she initiated it, maybe he did. All he knew was that he was finally touching her, kissing her, his tongue was in her mouth and it felt better than he'd ever imagined. . . .

# TWICE
# IN A
# LIFETIME

## CHRISTY
## COHEN

BANTAM BOOKS
New York Toronto London Sydney Auckland

TWICE IN A LIFETIME
A Bantam Fanfare Book/August 1993

FANFARE and the portrayal of a boxed "ff" are trademarks of Bantam Books,
a division of Bantam Doubleday Dell Publishing Group, Inc.

ISBN 0-553-56298-3

Published simultaneously in the United States and Canada

Bantam Books are published by Bantam Books, a division of Bantam Doubleday
Dell Publishing Group, Inc. Its trademark, consisting of the words "Bantam Books"
and the portrayal of a rooster, is Registered in U.S. Patent and Trademark Office
and in other countries. Marca Registrada. Bantam Books, 1540 Broadway, New
York, New York 10036.

PRINTED IN THE UNITED STATES OF AMERICA

RAD     0 9 8 7 6 5 4 3 2 1

*For my parents,*
*all four of them,*
*who will understand why*

# Twice in a Lifetime

# 1

J ESSE B EAN RODE up the bike path that bordered the
    river, made one loop around the jewel-like lake in
front of the hotel to cool down, and then saw her. She was
jogging, just a flash of blue behind the aspens, but he immediately knew it was Sarah. She seemed to sense his
gaze on her and stopped abruptly. She hesitated, looked up
at the hotel as if eyes were watching, and then emerged
from the trees.

Jesse got off his bike, took off his helmet, and tried to
slow his breathing. He'd been cycling for two hours at top
speed, whizzing past fir trees and cottonwoods with their
first buds of spring, but that was not what took his breath
away. It was Sarah. She sucked the air right out of him.

He hadn't expected to see her this morning. It was
barely dawn and, from what he remembered, Sarah was
usually a late sleeper. Jesse had hoped to be showered,
dressed in his tuxedo, with his wife, Annabel, firmly plant-
ed on his arm when they had their first meeting in fifteen
years. He had hoped to have some time to prepare, to
come up with a few nonchalant things to say, to be armed
and ready to look at Sarah as if she were nothing, as if all

they'd gone through and been to each other no longer meant anything to him.

But now, caught off guard, all of his plans disintegrated. His heart pounded. Last night, he had hardly been able to sit still while he imagined Sarah arriving at the hotel with her husband, Patrick. He could picture Patrick telling Sarah that this day would be a reunion of family and friends, a chance to put the past completely behind them. Patrick did not have a capacity for bitterness and even after all these years of knowing him, Jesse still marveled at the differences between himself and Patrick. He wondered how they had ever been able to be friends.

All last night, he had pictured Sarah and Patrick in their room, cuddling before they fell asleep, laughing in the darkness, not thinking of him at all. He had tossed and turned and then got up long before dawn to ride as hard as he could until his mind cleared.

Now, Sarah walked toward him slowly. She had hardly changed at all. Her hair was still that same shade of blond, with just a few strands of gray. She had not gained or lost any weight that he could discern. Her face was the same, she walked with the same step. Though he knew she was miles from the ingenuous girl he'd first met and fell for, she would always be young and idealistic to him. If he simply closed his eyes to his surroundings, to what day this was, he could almost imagine them back in time, married again, happy, just starting out on their great adventure.

Sarah reached him. Her eyes were wary, but even so, Jesse smiled. Despite everything, it was good to see her. She and Patrick lived in Boston now, had a life that did not require his presence at all. He had his own life, too, with Annabel, with his store, with his cycling. It was amazing, really, how completely they had been able to cut each other out of their lives. The one thing left linking them was the children. It was why they were here today, because two of their children were getting married.

Jesse extended his hand and was surprised when Sarah took it. Her hands were warm from jogging. He had forgotten how small her fingers were.

"Long time no see," Jesse said at last.

Sarah hesitated, then laughed. He laughed, too, and the

knot in his stomach relaxed. This would be all right. It seemed as though lifetimes had passed since their marriage exploded. Did she forgive him? Did she still think of the past? Was she happy with Patrick?

Jesse had so many questions and yet he knew he would never ask any of them. The time for talking had long since passed. She let go of his hand and he fidgeted with the gears on his bicycle.

They stood there in awkward silence while Jesse racked his brain trying to remember the casual things he had planned to say. Then, because his mind was blank, and because he could not pass up the only opportunity he would probably have to be alone with her, he reached out and touched her cheek.

"You're beautiful," he said. She was. In her jogging suit, with sweat on her forehead and no makeup, she was as beautiful to him as Annabel was in all her makeup and fancy clothes. He was surprised that she didn't pull away. Surprised and pleased.

"Our daughter's getting married," Sarah said.

Jesse dropped his hand and nodded. "Yes. Adam's a good man."

Jesse rubbed his forehead. He didn't like to think about Adam and Carolyn. This was their wedding day, and there was hardly any way around thinking about them, but Jesse still did not have to like it. He remembered first meeting Adam when he was three years old. He was energetic and outgoing, always more Annabel's son than Patrick's. For sixteen years, he had been Jesse's stepson. Now he would become his son-in-law. God, it was all so confusing.

He looked back at the hotel's private lake. In the early morning, the sheer coating of ice around its edges made it look like a perfect white diamond. Adam and Carolyn had sent him postcards of this place, when they had first decided to have their wedding here, but he hadn't expected reality to match up to photographs.

Originally a lodge that had been built in the 1880's on the valley floor with the Rocky Mountains as a backdrop, the world-class hotel retained much of the character of that building. The timber frame had been reinforced almost invisibly with twentieth-century hardware; the old stone fireplaces in the lobby had been painstakingly removed and then rebuilt with stronger mortar. The rooms were all furnished with authentic antiques and equipped with wood stoves.

But it was the grounds that drew the praise, that brought the celebrities and awed the critics. In front of the entrance to the hotel was that diamond lake that had just recently thawed with the April rains. Six swans, two black and four white, skimmed the surface, blurring the perfect reflection of pine trees and aspens and, even farther off, the jagged snow-covered edges of the mountains. Beyond that were the gardens, just now bursting with the first colors of springtime. Purple and blue crocuses were bunched in thick, showy masses beneath the trees, and the daffodils had somehow been forced up early, to smear the landscape with yellow. And everywhere, there were gazebos and bridges and ponds and waterfalls and fish and ducks and birds, so that it was like a tamed wilderness, a part of nature, yet removed from all of the hardships of it.

Jesse thought of all this rather than his daughter marrying Annabel and Patrick's son, or his divorce from Sarah, or the awful day when he found out that Sarah had married Patrick. He couldn't think of any of that without cringing, without wondering how their lives had gotten so entangled.

It had started out so well. They had just been two couples. Best friends. Jesse and Sarah, and Annabel and Patrick. But then they had stretched the boundaries of their relationships, tested the unforgiving limits of marriage.

Today, he would be forced to remember what had happened. Annabel would be there, by his side, while Sarah would stand beside Patrick. How strange that would be. For the first time, they would actually have to look at each other face to face, see what they looked like with opposite partners. So many years and they had somehow managed to avoid really looking at each other.

He glanced at Sarah. She was looking back at the hotel, as if they were being watched. All at once, the feelings, the weight of the past, hit him. He stepped forward, reached out his hand again and then dropped it.

"Sarah . . ." He looked at her, his first love, his first

wife. He thought of Annabel asleep in his bed and Patrick asleep in Sarah's. Though he wanted to say everything, he knew he could say nothing. Long ago, in an assault of words and treachery, everything had already been said.

Annabel opened her eyes slowly. Every joint in her body ached. The best hotels always had the worst beds. The downy, body-forming mattress was apparently considered the height of luxury, but what she really needed was that hard-as-nails bed from home that supported her back.

Annabel reached over for Jesse, but she knew before her hand fell through the empty space that he would not be there. When had he ever been there in the last couple of years? She didn't know why he didn't just sleep out in the garage, his arms wrapped around that damn bicycle instead of around her. That machine was more of a lover to him than she was.

Annabel looked over at the clock. Seven-fifteen. She could hear people thumping around in the room upstairs. A bird chirped outside her window. God, she hated the morning. She hated everything about it. Coffee and morning shows and quick showers and getting dressed for work. If she had her way, she would sleep straight through until noon and wake up to hot sunshine and soap operas and a day already half over.

She sat up. She stretched out her long back, her black, permed hair falling past her shoulders. Her spine ached like an old woman's. She thought of her son, Adam, waking up in his house with Carolyn beside him. What would they say to each other on this morning of their wedding? Would they talk about their parents, all four of them, and how it had taken a wedding to bring them back together again? Would they worry about the awkwardness that was bound to occur between the four of them? Or were they so thrilled to be getting married that they didn't care about anything but each other? Annabel clenched her teeth, knowing the answer. Carolyn and Adam thought only of each other, of getting married, of spending a lifetime together. Their optimism about love was both touching and sad.

Annabel thought briefly about the quick, emotionless

wedding vows she had made to Jesse. Then she thought back to the day she and Patrick married. The vows had been overshadowed by floral arrangements and seating charts. Annabel had tried to make absolutely certain that everyone had a good time, that they danced and drank and ate enough, that they would go home and tell their friends that Annabel and Patrick Meyers had had the world's classiest wedding.

Annabel smiled sardonically. She had come a long way since then and she was glad. Why would anyone want to be young again? Youth was like a prison sentence. Yes, there were parties and passions, but there was horror too. Chills and hangovers, love gone bad, friendships lost. Every feeling, every jealousy and betrayal was blown way out of proportion, doubled, tripled, until you could hardly walk beneath the weight of so much emotion.

Annabel closed her eyes. Was she mature enough to face Sarah and Patrick again? She was forty-seven years old. She'd had two marriages, raised a son, finally found a career. Did that mean she could no longer be hurt? Did that mean that she could face this day, face Patrick, her ex-husband, face Sarah, her ex-friend, and not feel that same gripping of her heart, the guilt, the jealousy? If she was so mature, then why was she still looking for forgiveness? Why was there still this crazy hope inside her that the four of them might somehow become friends again?

The truth was, she didn't know what she would feel when she finally saw Sarah and Patrick again. Somewhere in this hotel, they were waking up together, probably smiling at each other, sharing a good-morning kiss. The thought of that still did things to Annabel's heart. Because no matter how long she'd been married to Jesse, no matter how much she loved him, no matter how little Patrick meant to her now, she would always think of Patrick as her husband. He was the one she chose first. And there was something magical, something precious about anything that came first. All these years, she had been trying not to think about the fact that Jesse chose Sarah first, that Annabel was merely someone who filled up the empty gap in his life created when Sarah left.

Annabel threw off the covers. Enough. She had promised herself that she would not get emotional or introspective. She would just be. She would smile for her son and pretend that it didn't bother her in the slightest that he was all grown-up and getting married. She would not say one word about the girl he had chosen to be his wife. Annabel had promised him she would be a model of restraint.

She stood up and walked to the window. When she pulled back the curtains and looked out, she caught her breath for a moment. There was no finer picture than what lay beyond her window. First the lake and the swans, then the gardens, then the aspens and firs, and then, finally, the rugged, snow-covered Rocky Mountains, surrounding it all like a protective father. Because Carolyn and Adam lived alone in Denver, Carolyn had made most of the arrangements for her wedding herself. Annabel couldn't help but be impressed. Carolyn and Adam would take their vows in one of the gazebos, next to a small waterfall. The guests would sit in white chairs lined up on the grass and then they would move inside to the lobby and restaurant for a sit-down lunch and dancing. It was exactly the kind of wedding Annabel would have wanted for herself at Carolyn's age.

Annabel was about to step away from the window when she saw a bicycle glide onto the path through the hotel grounds. She knew instantly that it was Jesse. She could spot him in a crowd of bikers. She knew the tilt of his head, the black nylon pants and wind jacket, the light blond hair streaked with gray that escaped his helmet. She watched him circle the lake once, winding down his workout. He'd probably been out for hours. For as long as she'd known him, Jesse had been a man of few but intense passions. She remembered when his focus had been football and he knew every player on every team, and the statistics surrounding them. Before that, it was motorcycles, riding them, tearing them apart and putting them back together. And for a while, for the worst while, it was Sarah.

She saw his head turn toward the trees and she followed his gaze. A figure in blue was walking toward him. It took a moment for Annabel to recognize the origins of the tingling in her spine. Jesse stopped riding, stepped off his bike, and removed his helmet. The figure slowed its step and moved hesitantly toward him.

Annabel gripped the curtains tightly. She squinted and could make out the figure's straight blond hair, parted on the side, her not quite plump but certainly no longer thin physique. She knew the exact brown shade of her eyes. She could picture the intensity in Jesse's face, although he had his back to her.

The two of them came together. Annabel watched Jesse extend a hand to his first wife, to Sarah. Sarah hesitated for a moment and then took it, looking up into Jesse's eyes. Annabel had always been jealous of Sarah's petite size, the way she seemed like a child to be protected while everyone assumed that Annabel's height made her strong enough on her own. Jesse must have said something funny because Sarah laughed.

As if Jesse were aware of Annabel watching and knew exactly what would hurt her most, he reached out and touched Sarah's cheek. It was a gesture Annabel had watched him make back when he and Sarah were married. She had waited for over fifteen years for Jesse to tenderly touch her own cheek that way, but he never had.

Annabel kept waiting for Sarah to pull away, to do something, anything to make the point that he was no longer her husband, that these were actions for married people, not ex-lovers. But she let him touch her.

Annabel turned away from the window and stomped to the bathroom. She turned on the tap and splashed cold water in her face, as if she could wash away the images she'd just seen. Without bothering to dry off her face, she walked back to the window and pulled back the curtains. Jesse and Sarah were gone.

Five minutes later, Jesse opened the door to the hotel room. Annabel was sitting on the edge of the bed, her face dry, her composure intact. She'd had too many years of practice not to know when to hold her tongue.

"How was your ride?" she asked.

Jesse smiled. Annabel gripped the bed covers.

"Good. Ready to face the day now."

He whistled as he went into the bathroom. A moment later, the sound of the shower drowned him out.

Annabel walked back to the window. She looked out on the stunning scene but did not see it. She was thinking of the irony of life, of how she had been pegged all these years as the formidable one. Yet, in the end, despite Annabel's treachery, Sarah had grown strong. And in the dust kicked up by Sarah's sweetness, Annabel was left struggling for air.

Annabel stood very still, thinking of today, of her son's upcoming wedding, and then, because she couldn't help herself, because it would be a day for remembering, she thought back to how it had all started. A straight switch, they had called it. Two couples swapping partners as if they were nothing more than goods to be bartered with. But, of course, they were more than that. It had been so much more than that.

# 2

*1972*

ANNABEL DEPOSITED ADAM on the swing and gave him a good push. Then she sat down on a bench to watch him. He delighted in this playground, only three blocks from their house in a northeastern suburb of Seattle. It boasted four swings, a slide, a sandbox, and a minimum of three screaming children and their devoted mothers.

Annabel glanced down at her nails. One of her longest had chipped.

"Damn," she said, reaching into her purse for a file. Her hands were shaking slightly in the cold March morning air. At least it was dry. They had had eight continuous days of cold, hard rain until this morning, when the clouds finally made the leap over the Cascades and left the Puget Sound area crisp and clear, at least for an hour or so until the next storm moved in.

Annabel started repairing her nail. Someone sat down beside her, but Annabel didn't look up. The last thing she wanted was conversation.

"Excuse me," the woman beside her said.

Annabel pressed her lips together and pretended she hadn't heard. Dozens of times before women had attempted conversation with her in this playground and every time she had been bombarded with baby-formula recipes and diaper-service advice and complaints and praise for pediatricians. Never, ever, had she heard a single word about the real world outside of child rearing.

Adam was her son, but he didn't consume her. She still had thoughts about politics, about that moron Nixon, about art, about the latest movie, about love, about marriage, about life. According to these playground mothers, with the birth of a child, a woman's ideas about everything except feeding schedules became irrelevant, useless. Annabel simply would not stand for it. Let the rest of them devalue themselves. She knew she was still worth something.

The woman beside her cleared her throat.

"Excuse me," she said again. Very slowly, Annabel raised her head. Beside her was a very young woman, not far past twenty, with an infant wrapped snugly in a blanket in her arms. The woman had brown eyes and straight, shoulder-length dark blond hair, parted on the side. She was pretty, in a very suburban, girl-next-door kind of way.

"Yes," Annabel said.

"I was just wondering which one is yours." The woman gestured toward the swings. There were four children now, vying for the best swing or leader status on the slide. Adam swung happily where she had left him. A larger boy had taken on pusher duties.

"The dark-haired one," Annabel said, although inside she was thinking, *He's not mine and I'm not his. Why does everyone bind us together like we're one thing?*

"I thought so," the woman said, smiling. "He looks just like you."

Annabel nodded and went back to her filing. She knew much of this was her own fault. No one had gotten her pregnant but herself. She had been the one who didn't put her diaphragm in four years ago. Just once, she didn't want to hassle with it. She had been certain she was safe. She'd just ended her period a week earlier; everyone knew that it was impossible to get pregnant at that point in her cycle.

But it wasn't. One moment's lack of caution and Adam was conceived. Of course, Patrick was thrilled. What man didn't want a son? And he didn't have to do a damn thing to help raise him. Just come home every night to Adam's squeals of delight, lift him up once on his shoulders, then escape to his study, his work, and return the boy to Annabel.

All the way around, it was a raw deal. Hormones almost ruined her. First the curl relaxed in her hair and Annabel was horrified. She'd lived her whole life with long, luscious, naturally curly hair; it was her trademark. The hairdresser thought she should wait until after the birth to get a perm, so Annabel had to live nine months with the flattest, dullest hair imaginable.

Second, she bulged out like a watermelon. After Adam was born, it had taken her six months of one hundred sit-ups a day and brisk walks around the neighborhood to get her figure back.

Third, Patrick and her doctor had practically begged her to breast-feed, but she would have none of it. No way was she going to get saggy, blue-veined breasts like her mother had. It wasn't that she didn't want the best for Adam, but even after his birth she could not reconcile the vision of him sucking on her with that of Patrick's seductive kisses. Did no one else notice the incongruity? How did women mesh the two sides of themselves, the sexual and the motherly? If she had to choose, Annabel would always go with her sexuality. She didn't make excuses for herself. She had always known what she was, where her strengths lay.

She loved Adam. She looked up and watched him swinging, happy. She smiled. He could do that, make her smile just by being. She was not sorry she had him. She was only sorry that by having him, she was made into something less in everyone's eyes but her own.

"My name is Sarah Bean," the woman said. "My husband and I just moved in down the street."

"That's nice," Annabel said, without looking at her. She finished one nail and moved on to another.

"We just love Seattle. We were living in Spokane when we first got married, then Jesse got the job at Boeing and we moved out here."

Annabel put the file back in her purse and looked up. Even she had her boundaries of rudeness.

"Annabel Meyers," she said. Sarah smiled widely and Annabel allowed herself a small smile in return. She wanted friendship too, yet she felt an opposing need to turn away from it. It had both rewards and demands, and she wasn't sure which was more powerful.

"Do you live around here?" Sarah asked.

Annabel nodded. "Over on Handon."

"We're just a street down, on Juniper. I loved the house as soon as I saw it. Built back in 1935, but really solid. The previous owners did most of the renovations."

They both fell silent. Adam decided he'd had enough of the swing and started crying. Annabel stood up and went to him.

"Come on now, none of that," she said, picking him up. He was a solid chunk in her arms now. She still remembered him as an infant; small, almost featherweight.

"Go home," he said, burrowing his face into her neck. "Want to go home." Annabel nodded and walked back to the bench. She picked up her purse.

"Nice meeting you," she said to Sarah.

"May I walk with you? I really need the exercise."

The look on her face was so forlorn that Annabel could not refuse. She herself had lived in the Seattle area all her life. Her parents were here, her two brothers, her friends from childhood. She could not imagine suddenly finding herself alone in a new place.

"Of course."

Sarah stood up, rearranging the baby in her arms. Annabel had yet to ask about the child, as most mothers did right away. The truth was, she had no interest in other people's children.

"She's six months," Sarah said, providing an answer to the unasked question. "We named her Carolyn, after my grandmother."

Annabel looked down at her as they started walking, but she did not say the requisite "She's so pretty." She set Adam down beside her and took his hand.

"What does your husband do?" Sarah asked, to fill the void.

Annabel pressed her lips together again. This was the other safe topic of mothers; a husband's references and qualifications.

"He's a scientist," Annabel said.

"Really? That's fascinating. What does he study?"

Annabel stopped suddenly and turned toward her. Sarah took a step back.

"To tell you the truth, I don't know exactly. Something about cancer, but I can't be more specific than that. I know he makes a good salary and pays the bills, that's all. And as for Adam, he's three years old, we have a good pediatrician, he's toilet trained, and aside from an occasional ear infection, we haven't had any major problems with him. Does that answer all of your questions?"

Annabel knew, the moment she started talking, that Sarah would cry. She could see her face falling with every word, yet she could not stop herself. She was just so tired of all the prattle, the niceties, the nonsense. She was here too, dammit! Was she invisible, or merely a source of information on her husband and son, the ones with real value? Didn't anyone give a damn about what she had left to contribute? For three years she had been bringing Adam to this park and putting up with it. For three years, but not a second longer.

"Look, I'm sorry," Annabel said, reaching out and then dropping her hand. Adam had started to whine beside her and she didn't know whose tears to dry first.

Sarah shook her head.

"It's all right. I was being intrusive, I know. It's just that I'm new here and I haven't met anyone. Jesse is gone so much and Carolyn takes so much out of me and—"

"Look, forget it. Let's go to my house and I'll make us some coffee. Okay?"

Sarah nodded and they started off again. Annabel knew she was a fool to invite her home, but she couldn't have a lonely, miserable woman on her conscience. They finally reached her house and Annabel found her key. She quickly herded everyone inside.

Sarah had dried her eyes and was looking around. Annabel couldn't help showing a bit of pride.

"It's a turn-of-the-century house. Original glass and

staircase. The heating system's a mess, but we live with it. Those new tract houses can't hold a candle to this."

"It's gorgeous," Sarah said.

Annabel smiled and went into the kitchen. She shooed Adam off to his toys in the corner. Annabel put the coffee on, then returned to the living room. Sarah was still standing by the door, holding her daughter.

"I don't have to stay," she said. "Really. It's not as bad as I made it sound."

Annabel stepped forward before she had a chance to stop herself.

"Of course you're staying. It'll do me good too to have some company. Conversation with a three-year-old has its limits."

Sarah smiled so widely again that Annabel laughed.

"You really are lonely," she said.

"You can't imagine."

They walked back into the kitchen and Annabel poured them each a cup of coffee. Carolyn had fallen asleep in Sarah's arms.

"You can lay her down in the bed upstairs. It's the first room on your right."

"Thank you."

When Sarah came back, Annabel was staring out the window. A light rain had started falling again.

"I knew it wouldn't last," she said.

Sarah shook her head. "I love the rain. Everyone told us not to come here, that the rain would get us down, but so far that's been my only consolation. I love to listen to it tapping on the roof at night."

"You just moved in?" Annabel said.

"Yes. Two weeks ago. We've been living in an apartment out near Boeing for about a month."

"I can't imagine leaving everything you know behind."

Sarah fingered the rim of her cup.

"I thought of it as an adventure. I loved Jesse so much and there was some opposition to our marriage. This was kind of like an elopement, only we had Carolyn too."

"What kind of opposition?" Annabel said.

"The usual. My parents didn't like his looks, or his cigarettes, or his motorcycle riding. They forbade me to see him and I sneaked out. He was too quiet for their taste, too much of a loner. They thought he was a hoodlum." She laughed and the sound was like trickling water. Annabel had never heard anything quite like it and she felt a jealous twinge at its uniqueness.

"Was he a hoodlum?"

"No. Well, not completely. He left home at sixteen and supported himself with odd jobs. When I met him, he was living with friends and not working at all. He was one of those leather-jacket guys you see hanging out on the street corner. He took my breath away."

"So you married him."

"Yes. When I was nineteen and Jesse twenty-four. There wasn't much my parents could do to stop us by then. All of their restrictions had only driven us closer together anyway. They didn't come to the wedding though."

They were silent, while they each thought of their own weddings. Annabel had a smile on her lips.

"I almost wish my wedding had been like that. Something dramatic and romantic. But it wasn't. It was exactly how it was supposed to be. I picked my colors and chose my bridesmaids and we danced and everyone told Patrick he was the luckiest man in the world."

They looked at each other and then both started laughing.

"Is he the luckiest?" Sarah asked.

"Some days. Other days he's the unluckiest. Depends on my mood."

She poured them each more coffee and they listened to the rain as it came down harder. Adam walked up to them with his Lego creation.

"See, Mommy," he said. "It's a car."

"What kind of car?" Annabel asked.

"A fast one," he said, running it over the table.

"Not on the table, Adam. Race on the floor."

"Can't," Adam told her. "It's a spaceship now." He zoomed off into space, running around the room with his rocket. Annabel shook her head.

"How did I get myself into this mess?" she said, more to herself than to Sarah.

"You're good with him," Sarah said.

Annabel looked at her. No one had ever told her that before. They all said that she was too young-looking to be a mother, that she had retained her figure well, that she kept herself as beautiful as always. But those who knew her well always had that skeptical look on their faces when she came into the room with Adam in her arms, as if she alone had flunked the maternal-instinct test.

"Really?" she said.

"Yes, really. Not too firm and not too lenient. That's a hard balance."

Annabel smiled.

"Would you and your husband like to come for dinner tonight?" she asked suddenly. "I've got a huge roast that can easily feed four."

Sarah looked away.

"I feel like you're taking pity on me," she said.

Annabel reached out to grip Sarah's hand for a moment.

"Honestly, I'm not. It would be nice for me and Patrick to have company. It's been a long time."

Sarah stood up.

"Then I accept."

Annabel walked with her upstairs to fetch Carolyn.

"There's only one condition," she said.

"What's that?"

"No diaper talk. I don't give a damn what kind of talcum powder or baby wipes you use. Got it?"

Sarah laughed and scooped up her daughter.

"Got it."

Sarah looked across the table at her husband, Jesse, willing him to talk. It was so important to her that this dinner go well, that they make a good impression. He had his friends at the office, he had people to talk to. He had no idea how badly she needed a friend.

But the more she willed him, the quieter he became, as if in defiance. He poked at the roast Annabel had made, swirled his potatoes around on his plate, acted as if the conversation did not include him. Sarah looked from

Annabel to Patrick, trying to see what they were making of him.

"Tell me more about your job, Patrick," Sarah said, hoping she wasn't talking too much.

"There's not too much to tell," Patrick replied.

Sarah studied him. He was what she had expected a scientist would be, but not the man she would pick out in a crowd as Annabel's husband. Sarah had been awed by Annabel in the playground today. She had no idea where she got the courage to talk to her, except maybe from the loneliness that had become the biggest part of her in the past month. Annabel was the kind of woman Sarah could only dream of being. She was breathtaking, with her black curly hair that swirled around her pale skin, her hazel eyes, her modellike body, tall and thin yet curvaceous.

Yet Sarah had managed to begin a conversation with her, and after she made a fool of herself by crying, Annabel had shown herself to be quite approachable. Now, as she looked at Annabel's husband, she wondered what had brought them together. He looked the part of the intellectual: his sandy hair was out of place, as if he had much weightier matters on his mind than combing it; he wore his wire-framed glasses on the tip of his nose; his brown eyes had a kind of faraway gaze to them. Sarah wondered how much he knew, what it must be like for Annabel to talk to him, to hear his ideas. She imagined the mental stimulation must be terribly sexy.

"Science is anything but glamorous," Patrick said. "It's mostly tests and more tests and analyses. The university just got a grant, so at least we don't have to worry about funds for a while."

He smiled at her and Sarah smiled back. She had felt a camaraderie with him from the moment she walked through the door, when he had taken her coat and held both of her hands in welcome, as if they were old friends. He had looked right at her as he spoke, crooned over Carolyn, given every impression that he understood everything, all the long days when the phone never rang, the lonely nights when Jesse stayed late at work, trying to make a good impression, the endless weekends when Jesse was out working on his motorcycle and she was left alone, going crazy with the sound of Carolyn's cries.

"And you, Jesse?" Annabel asked. "What is it you do at Boeing?"

Jesse looked up, a little startled. Sarah gripped her fork tighter as she watched him. With her, when he could spare the time, Jesse was gentle, magnetic, passionate. But with others, he was often uncommunicative and downright rude. He answered in monosyllables, he offered nothing of himself, he retreated behind those baby blue eyes and shut himself off.

Sarah's word could not convince everyone that there was more to him than leather jackets and Harleys and stony silences. Her mother did not give a damn that he was gorgeous, that his sexy eyes and the way he towered above her made her heart pound. Her father had gone as far as locking her in her room to keep her from him. But in the end, Sarah had triumphed. She kept crawling out of the window until she reached an age where they had no more control over her actions. She had chosen Jesse over them and that was the end of it. Only recently, in the quiet of her house, had she realized just how much she had given up.

Now, just this once, Sarah hoped for something more, for that quality that her parents had probed for again and again in him and never found. She needed Jesse to be warm, to show his humor, to make some gesture, however small, of friendship.

"Not much," Jesse said. "Sales."

Annabel looked across the table at Patrick. Her mouth turned up at the edges.

"My father's in sales," Annabel said. "He's made a good living off it."

Jesse nodded and went back to his food. Sarah resisted the urge to kick him under the table.

"How about you, Sarah?" Annabel asked. "Any career goals? Or are you going to be like every other mother around here and give up your life for your children?"

That, at last, got Jesse's attention. He lifted his eyes from his plate and stared at Annabel head-on.

"Is that what you're doing?" he asked her.

Annabel showed only a moment's hesitation before answering.

"Only temporarily," she said. "Not for a second longer than I have to."

They stared at each other for a moment longer and Sarah felt a little queasy. But then the feeling passed and Jesse looked at her.

"How about you, babe?" he said. "Any career goals?"

She knew he was teasing her, but she ignored it.

"As a matter of fact, yes. I want to be a teacher. I know I won't be able to get to it until Carolyn is older, but I'll get to it."

Annabel clapped her hands.

"Bravo, Sarah," she said. "Don't let these macho men push you around."

"Hey, now wait a minute," Patrick said, but Annabel was laughing, not listening. She stood up and cleared away some of the empty dishes.

"We'll show them all," Annabel said only to Sarah. "You wait and see."

Sarah helped Annabel with the dishes. As she passed Jesse, he pulled her down and kissed her. Sarah was startled by the intensity of his kiss and she pulled away quickly, embarrassed that Patrick had been there to see it.

When Sarah reached the kitchen, she heard laughter. And not just any laughter: Jesse's. She was so amazed, she dropped the dishes in the sink.

"Quite dangerous," Annabel said softly.

"What?"

"Your husband. He's got that look about him. I can see why your parents were so worried."

Sarah smiled. Suddenly, she felt nineteen again, when her heart was possessed completely by Jesse. It had been so easy to walk out on everything she knew, everyone she loved. She remembered how every heartbeat, every thought, every moment had been devoted to Jesse. She remembered burying her head in his jacket, breathing in the smoky, sultry scents of him.

Just now, when he had kissed her, it was like going backward, losing herself all over again. His lips could be so hard, they left their mark on her. She touched her lips with her fingers.

"I love him," she said.

Annabel looked away, as if she didn't want Sarah to read her thoughts.

"Yes," she said quietly. "I can see why."

# 3

JESSE PULLED INTO the liquor-store parking lot and cut the engine on his Harley. He felt the eyes of a woman walking out of the store on him and he looked up and gave her a wink. She bowed her head, a smile on her face, and Jesse thought, *There goes another one.*

He walked into the liquor store and picked out a bottle of cheap Burgundy. This was his job, to bring the wine. He wasn't quite sure how this chore had been bestowed on him, but he didn't mind so much. This place was on his way home from work and he knew if he left it up to Sarah, she'd show up with some sissy Chardonnay he could barely swallow.

He walked over to the hard-liquor aisle and picked up a bottle of tequila. He was in a party mood. He'd just reached the end of his six-month probation period at Boeing and his boss had rewarded him with a raise. Not much, not even a dollar an hour more, but something. It would pay for the tequila and wine, at least.

He took the bottles to the counter.

"A pack of Marlboros," he said.

The old man behind the counter found the pack and Jesse paid him. He walked out, stuffed the bag of booze beneath the straps on the back of his bike, and hopped on.

He jumped on the starter and revved the engine loud four times. Then he backed out and took off down the street.

He loved these last five minutes before he reached his neighborhood. He came in the back way, through the pines, where the developers were just now thinking of putting in tract homes. It sickened him the way they just came in, ripped out the trees, and built up a row of look-alike three-bedroom homes in various shades of brown. Sarah told him if it bothered him so much, he should get involved, go to the council meetings. Sarah still thought the world was changeable.

Jesse cleared his thoughts out, fired the engine up to fifty, and enjoyed the ride. He rarely wore his helmet, no matter how much Sarah pestered him about it. The wind rushed past his ears, cars flew past him in a blur of lights. He leaned into the turns at the last minute, so that he fell more than he had to. He put his foot down to graze the road and felt the heat scour another millimeter of rubber off his soles.

He got hooked on motorcycles early, after test-driving a couple of friends' Triumphs. He got his first bike when he was sixteen, a 1958 BSA, in mint condition. It took all his savings and a loan from friends, but it was worth it. When his parents refused to let him ride it, he packed his bags and went where no one gave a shit what he did.

He crashed with friends until he was able to scrape enough money together to move in with a roommate. When he got short of cash, or quit a job he hated, there was always a buddy he could turn to who would take him in, until he found another job and got a new place.

The gang all laughed at him for finishing high school. They figured once he ran out on his folks, he should cut out on school too, go all the way with his new freedom. His parents had turned their backs on him completely after he left. He could have dropped out then and there and they wouldn't have said a word. But he didn't. He wasn't an idiot. He wasn't going to work in burger joints for the rest of his life.

He graduated from high school and graduated from fast food. He was good with his hands and he found a job in a TV repair shop. Then after that, a quick stint in a mo-

torcycle shop. Then roofing and factory work and construction. He didn't stay long. He went into them all with
high hopes, but came out of each of them feeling bitter
and deceived. A boss would promise him a raise in six
months and not deliver. Or a job that was supposed to
teach him something about carpentry was really nothing
but getting coffee and stacking wood.

There were times when the money ran out completely
and he had nothing. A couple of nights he slept on the
street rather than turn to friends again. It wasn't so bad.
He felt daring, sliding into his sleeping bag beneath a tree
in the park. He was too young to realize there were dan-
gers in the darkness.

But, he never spent more than one night under the
stars. The next morning he always managed to find a job.
Only once had he resorted to anything extreme. It was just
a small-time liquor-store heist; he didn't even get away
with much money. He'd felt a rush of excitement and
pride at pulling it off, but that quickly faded to something
close to regret, and he knew he wouldn't do it again.

He didn't think about it much now. He had never told
Sarah. He'd done what he had to do and he wasn't
ashamed, but he knew she would not see it that way.

He might have lived on the fringe forever, going from
one job and friend to the next, if he hadn't met Sarah. At
first he hadn't realized how special she was. She was not
a part of his crowd. She was friends with a girl who
thought it made her look cool to hang out with the bikers.
Sarah came along a few times. She was so different, so . . .
soft. Before long Jesse was hooked.

He had known her parents would hate him. For Sarah's
sake he might have been willing to try to change, but Sarah
never gave him the chance. She turned into another person
altogether when her parents forbade her to see him. Their romance became a hundred times more precious because it
was illicit, every kiss a thousand times more erotic. Jesse
sometimes wondered what would have happened if Sarah's
parents hadn't forbidden their love. Would the relationship
simply have run its course and fizzled?

Instead they had married in a cloud of protest and then
moved to Seattle. Jesse was legitimate now, much more so

than Sarah's parents ever would have believed. He had a job in sales, for God's sake. On the days when he made sales calls, he actually had to wear a suit and tie.

But at least he had his Harley. The BSA had lasted him a good ten years and was still good for a nostalgic trip around the block. He worked on it whenever he got the chance. The Harley, however, suited his image now. There were so few statements to make now that he was an adult, and he was pleased that he'd managed to hang on to this one. The Harley branded him a tough guy, even still a little rebellious. His boss hated the very sight of it, but he couldn't fault Jesse when he was doing so well on the job.

Jesse took the last leg of the windy road and then reached the borders of his neighborhood. He slowed down. He wasn't going home. This Friday night was the Meyerses' turn. For four months now, they'd been trading off dinners every Friday after work. Annabel and Sarah got together earlier in the day to set things up, then he and Patrick showed up to make the drinks and carve the roast. It was the kind of evening he'd always assumed he'd hate. It reminded him of his parents and Sarah's parents and every old couple he'd ever scorned. He could never understand why they didn't go out. What the hell was so appealing about a Friday night at home?

And yet, just look at him now. Actually anticipating this night, the way he could kick off his shoes, drink as much as he wanted, laugh a little. It was unsettling how quickly and unnoticeably he had become what he'd always despised.

He hadn't known what to make of Annabel and Patrick that first night they met. When he got home from work that day, he'd found Sarah rummaging through her closet like mad, as excited as he'd seen her since they moved out here. She told him about her day, about finally meeting someone at the playground. She'd already made plans for dinner that night, for Christ's sake. Then she said the woman's husband was a scientist.

"Shit," was all Jesse could think to say. "What the hell am I going to say to a scientist?"

"I'm sure he's very nice," Sarah said.

Nice, maybe. But certainly boring and snooty as hell.

Jesse had thought about refusing to go, but when Sarah got all teary-eyed, he couldn't refuse her.

"And this Abigail person?"

"It's Annabel," Sarah said. "She was a little frightening at first, kind of distant and unapproachable, but then she really seemed to warm up."

"Sounds like a great couple."

"Oh Jesse, please."

So he went. He didn't say much. It wasn't his style to gab and ask questions he didn't care about the answers to. His only surprise came when he walked in the door and was immediately struck by the one thing, the most important thing, that Sarah forgot to mention.

Annabel was gorgeous. Not pretty the way Sarah was, but a drop-dead knockout. She was almost as tall as Jesse was, and thin, with breasts pressing against her sweater in a way that made him stare. Then there was that hair. He'd always thought of himself as a man who preferred blondes, but there was something so erotic about that blackness, the tight ringlets that framed Annabel's pale face. Jesse had felt himself harden as soon as he looked at her, but then Sarah took his hand and the feeling subsided.

After a few glasses of wine, everyone loosened up and he was surprised to find he was having a good time. He and Patrick moved into the family room to watch a basketball game. Every now and then, Jesse heard Sarah's and Annabel's laughter coming from the kitchen.

Sarah asked the Meyerses over for the following Friday, then Annabel reciprocated, then they simply fell into this alternating, weekly dinner-party pattern. Now, as Jesse turned onto Handon Street, he found himself eager to reach the house, to walk in without knocking, the way Patrick had told him to, as if he belonged there. To see . . . Jesse stopped without completing the thought.

He pulled up in front of the house. It was Victorian style, painted in cream and pink and light blue. It was more feminine than handsome, more suited to Annabel than Patrick, but then it was obvious that Annabel was the one who ran the show.

Jesse unstrapped the bag of wine and tequila. He took

a cigarette out of his pocket and lit it. He walked to the door and let himself in.

Three-year-old Adam ran toward him, a G.I. Joe in his hand.

"Hey," Jesse said, grabbing him with one arm and scooping him up. Adam laughed with delight and then squealed when Jesse tickled him.

"Stop! Stop!" Adam said, laughing until tears ran down his cheeks. Annabel hurried out from the kitchen thinking something was wrong. She smiled when she saw Jesse.

"Torturing my son again, I see," she said.

Jesse put him down and Adam held up the figure in his hand.

"See, Jesse, it's G.I. Joe," he said. "Dad got it for me."

"Cool," Jesse said.

Adam ran off into the other room.

Annabel came toward him. Jesse took a drag of his cigarette and threw out the smoke as a screen.

"What kind of wine?" As she took the bag her hand grazed his. She pulled out the bottles of Burgundy and tequila.

"You have no taste, Jesse Bean. You know that?"

"That's not true," Sarah said, coming around the corner. Jesse let his breath out as she slipped into his arms, unaware that he'd been holding it. He squeezed her and smiled at the curves he knew so well. She was always in a good mood after these dinners. He thought about what he was in for much later tonight. "He chose me."

"True. True," Annabel said, stepping back. It had been like this from the very beginning, Jesse realized. He hadn't paid much attention, but it was hard to miss this constant realignment of positions, moving in when someone was out of the room, then retreating when they returned. It was all harmless, of course. Everyone did it. A little flirting never hurt anybody.

"Patrick's in the den," Annabel said. "I think it's baseball tonight."

Jesse kissed his wife's cheek then walked into the den. Patrick was already set up in his chair, watching a Giants-Dodgers game.

"Two to one," he said. "Those damn Bums are ahead."

Jesse smiled and sat down in the chair beside him. He finished his cigarette and looked around for an ashtray.

"Use that crystal thing Annabel got from her mother," Patrick said.

Jesse ground out his cigarette on the inside of the crystal vase and then settled in.

Annabel brought them each a glass of wine.

"Hey, where's my tequila?" Jesse asked.

"Confiscated."

As she walked out both Jesse and Patrick watched her go.

"Where the hell did you find her?" Jesse said, half in admiration, half in disgust. Patrick laughed.

"She found me. My friends were throwing me a party after I got my master's. Someone brought her as his date and she decided she'd rather be mine. I never even knew what hit me."

After watching the game for a while in a companionable silence, Patrick asked Jesse: "What about you and Sarah? She find you or you find her?"

Jesse lit another cigarette and offered one to Patrick.

"No thanks. Could never tolerate the stuff."

Jesse scratched his head. "I don't really know exactly," he said, blowing smoke up to the ceiling. "It was like Sarah was just there, one of the crowd. The other girls were all over me, but she kept her distance."

"We all like the one we can't have."

"Yeah. She was different. Softer. I felt like I had to take care of her."

The batter for the Giants got a fastball down the middle and hammered it out of the park. Patrick jumped up.

"Woo-hoo!" he said. "Did you see that? Four hundred feet, easy. It's two to two, boys. That'll show the Bums."

Sarah walked in.

"Come on. Dinner's on. Stop watching your silly games."

"They're not silly," Patrick said. "Baseball is a thinking man's game."

"Of course it is."

She slipped her arm around Jesse. He dipped his nose

to her head and breathed in the scent of her. He still felt he needed to take care of her. He wondered, briefly, what it was like for Patrick not to have to take care of anyone but himself.

Later that night, after the mix of wine and tequila had made the four of them first giggly, then talkative, then downright nauseous, Jesse and Sarah decided to walk home and leave the motorcycle in the Meyerses' driveway.

Patrick, watching them go, kept calling out, "My friends! My good friends! Don't be strangers!" until they disappeared around the corner. Annabel pulled him back inside.

"You're being an idiot," she said, reaching past him to bolt the door. He lifted his eyebrows as she raised her sweater over her head.

"It's just that I'm so hot," she said, revealing a lacy white bra beneath. Patrick reached out to touch her, but she eluded his grasp. She spun around the room, somehow managing to keep her balance. Patrick had always admired her ability to hold her drink.

"No, that won't do it," she said, swaying in some kind of hypnotic dance. Patrick ached for her. She unclasped her bra, then slid it off.

Her breasts slipped out and seemed to glow in the light. She had the whitest skin; he doubted that she had ever tanned it, even as a child. It was milky, with large, dark brown aureoles around her nipples. Patrick had to force himself to breathe.

"Hmmm," Annabel said, running her hands down her hips. She was still wearing her jeans. She moved her hands over the front of her thighs and Patrick's eyes followed her motion. "Yes, still a bit hot."

She unzipped her pants, slipped out of them, and tossed them at Patrick. He was just quick enough to catch them before they hit him in the face. He threw them aside. She had been wearing no underwear beneath her jeans. She moved her hands up over her stomach, then to her breasts.

"Yes, that's it. Much better."

"God, Annabel," Patrick said. She looked at him. She

walked very slowly toward him, never taking her eyes
from his face, while his eyes could not help traveling all
over her. When she was within touching distance, she took
both of his hands in hers. Her skin was hot to the touch.
She grazed his fingertips across her stomach then lifted
them almost to her breasts. She closed her eyes slightly
and smiled.

"Tell me, who would you rather have. Me or Sarah?"

Patrick finally raised his eyes from her breasts and
looked at her face.

"What?"

"I just wanted to know who you prefer. Sarah's so . . .
good. You know. So motherly. I could be that way too, if
you want me to be."

She skimmed his fingertips over the erect tips of her
nipples. He squeezed each nipple between his fingers and
Annabel moaned.

In an instant, he had her on the floor. His mouth was
all over her; he wanted to claim every inch of her. She
pulled at his pants and underwear, finally getting them
down to his knees. Then he was inside her, pushing up
into her, every sense in him overloaded with Annabel's
touch and smell and taste. He came inside her violently,
while she still thrust herself up to meet him. A moment
later, she came too, the way she always did, dramatically,
with every muscle in her body tensed, and a strangled
scream in her throat. He collapsed on top of her.

When he finally rolled off her, he noticed that her
clothes were everywhere and he was still twisted in his
pants. He listened for any sounds of Adam upstairs, but all
was quiet. He looked over at Annabel and saw that she
was smiling, a triumphant look on her face. He knew she
had waged some kind of battle with him and she had won.
She had waged similar battles over the years, each one always some test of his love for her. He didn't know what
she was afraid of, or why he had to keep proving himself
to her.

He leaned over and kissed her lips softly.

"You are the only woman for me," he said.

She nodded, appeased for now.

•    •    •

When they arrived home Jesse put Carolyn to bed. He knew better than to mix drinks, but they had run out of wine and the tequila he'd bought was all they'd had left. He had thought about protesting, but then he thought, *What harm can it do?*

Sarah walked up the stairs unsteadily, gripping the handrail. Jesse met her halfway and helped her up. He laid her down in bed.

"It's spinning," she said, gripping her forehead. "Jesse, make it stop."

"I can't, babe. It'll stop tomorrow."

"That's too late," she said, tears slipping out of her eyes. "Oh God, I feel sick."

She got up amazingly fast and ran into the bathroom. A moment later, he heard the unmistakable sounds of her vomiting. He walked in and patted her on the back.

"That's the way," he said, knowing from experience that it wasn't pretty, but it sure as hell made you feel better. When Sarah was done, he got her a glass of water.

"Lie down again," he said. "It won't spin as much now."

She lay down in her clothes and Jesse took off her shoes. He sat down on the bed beside her.

"You're a party animal," he said, smiling.

"Don't make jokes. I was just trying to keep up with you and Annabel. Where did you learn to drink like that?"

Jesse shrugged. "The streets, I guess."

She closed her eyes.

"Still spinning?" Jesse asked her.

"Yes, but not as bad."

He sat with her for a few minutes, until her breathing evened out. Then he went back downstairs and sat down on the couch.

He didn't know how much the rest of them would remember about tonight. Sarah, probably almost nothing. Annabel too. But Patrick hadn't been too drunk. And Jesse was never too drunk to forget.

They had eaten dinner and polished off the wine. The talk was nothing special then. Just movies they'd seen, the news, jobs. Then they moved to the living room, opened the windows on the warm summer night, and brought out the tequila. They sat on opposite couches, Jesse and Sarah on one, Annabel and Patrick on the other.

There was something about it, each of them with a shot glass, daring the others to match what they could swallow. It reminded Jesse of his youth, not so long ago, when how much you could put down was a measure of your stature.

Every bet to take another drink drew a laugh. Annabel said something outrageous and they were all roaring. They were best friends, thick as thieves on this warm night, sharing their secrets. Annabel started it all by telling them that Patrick wasn't her first or even her second. Patrick seemed surprised only for a second, then he burst out laughing with the rest of them.

"Who were the others?" he asked her.

"Some of your classmates from college," she said. "We had a go-around one night. I wanted to see if I could tell the difference, so I had them blindfold me. Then they came in, one after the other."

Only Sarah looked shocked and the rest of them kidded her about that. Jesse didn't know if Annabel had been serious or not.

Then it was Patrick's turn. He couldn't think of anything to say, so Annabel goaded him.

"Come on, lover boy, I know what you're capable of. Tell us about your fantasies. Give us one deep dark secret."

Patrick looked at each of them and that was when Jesse realized that in those moments after the tequila settled into their bloodstream, they had stopped being married and had become instead only four very drunk, consenting adults. The boundaries between them had blurred. It made him realize how little marriage could mean, if you let it.

"You don't want to know," Patrick said to Annabel. She looked back at Sarah and Jesse and smiled.

"Don't think I can take it, huh?" She stood up and leaned over Patrick. As she bent over, Jesse's eyes scanned her rear, smoothly outlined in blue jeans. Sarah giggled and Jesse took her hand.

"I can take anything," Annabel whispered to Patrick. She kissed him hard and Jesse saw Patrick's tongue enter her mouth. He felt himself getting hard and he rested his free hand over himself, to hide it.

When Annabel pulled away, they were all silent. She still bent over him and Patrick looked straight in her eyes.

"Sometimes when we're making love, I have this fantasy that I'm with two women," he said. "One good and one bad. The bad one's doing all these incredible things to me and the good one lets me do whatever I want to her."

"Oh goodness," Sarah said and took another shot of tequila. Jesse still watched Annabel's body. He thought he saw her arm twitch.

"And which one am I?" she said.

Patrick showed off his perfect smile.

"The bad one, of course."

There was only a slight hesitation, and then Annabel burst out laughing. She collapsed beside Patrick and soon they were all laughing. They had long ago taken their shoes off and now they were slouching way down on the sofas. Jesse looked down and noticed that all of their feet mingled on the floor. He could make out one of his between Patrick's and Annabel's.

"Now you two," Annabel said.

"No way," Jesse said. Annabel got up and came over to their couch. She sat down on the far side of Jesse and wrapped a finger around a lock of his hair.

"Come on, Jesse boy. Sarah can't know everything about you. Tell her something exciting."

Jesse glanced over at Sarah. She was watching Annabel twist her finger around his hair as if it were the most natural thing in the world. Still, Jesse shifted away from Annabel and then she returned to her own couch.

"Sarah knows about my past. I was the bad boy in Spokane."

"Very bad," Sarah said.

"What was the worst thing you ever did?" Annabel asked. Jesse shook his head.

"No way."

"Come on," Annabel said.

"You all could turn on me and I'd end up in prison."

They all pounced on him then, wanting to know what he'd done. They pulled him off the couch and onto the floor. Pretty soon, they were all sitting together, in a circle. He couldn't tell whose legs or arms were whose.

"You've got to tell us now," Patrick said. "You've got a captive audience."

Jesse shrugged. "Fine. None of you will remember tomorrow anyway." He took a deep breath. "I robbed a store is all. When I was broke and living on the streets. I wouldn't go back to my parents and ask for help, so I borrowed a friend's gun and held up a liquor store. I got six hundred dollars. And on the way out, I shot up the windows for good luck."

They were all quiet.

"You're making that up," Sarah said.

"No. You asked for it. Now you know."

"I'm calling the cops," Annabel said. They all looked at her and then she smiled. The tension broke and they laughed.

"You're serious, aren't you?" Patrick said.

"Yeah."

"Shit."

"I'm not sorry," Jesse said. "I didn't hurt anybody. That store had insurance. Sometimes you just have to do what you have to do. I needed the money."

Sarah was looking at him as if she didn't know him. Jesse reached over and put his arm around her shoulder.

"Come on, babe. Lighten up. It was a long time ago. It's not like I've lived a life of crime. It was a one-time thing."

"I can see that happening," Annabel said, looking at him. "I wouldn't say I would never do it, if it came to that. I think all of us would do whatever we had to do to survive."

"Exactly," Jesse said.

Annabel looked over at Sarah.

"Now, sweet little Sarah," she said. "There's got to be something simply awful you can tell us."

Patrick poured the last of the tequila into Sarah's glass and she downed it. She cocked her head.

"I'm trying to think . . ."

It was while they were waiting for Sarah to think of something bad that Jesse felt Annabel's finger slip up beneath his shirt. It traced his spine and every now and then the fingernail bit into his skin. Jesse looked over at Annabel, but she kept her eye on Sarah. Just that one touch was setting his nerves on fire, but he could not stop it without calling attention to it. He took Sarah's hand and Annabel dropped her finger away.

"I borrowed a jacket from a friend and then told her I lost it because I wanted to keep it for myself," Sarah said. "Does that count?"

They all looked at her and then fell back against the couches, laughing. Fifteen minutes later, too unsteady to drive, Jesse and Sarah left for home.

Jesse closed his eyes now. He remembered the feel of Annabel's finger on his back. She was drunk, he knew that. Yet she wasn't so drunk that she didn't know what she was doing. And he couldn't deny that it felt good. Even a fingertip was different in every woman. Sarah's fingers were gentle and loving, even passionate, but they were Sarah's. They would always be Sarah's.

Patrick was right when he'd said Annabel was the bad one. Jesse knew he should stay away from her. But she was fun too. She made them all laugh. She was a good friend to Sarah. There were a hundred reasons to stay friends and only one to break away.

Jesse stood up and went back upstairs. He took off his clothes down to his underwear and climbed in next to his wife. She mumbled something as he slipped his arm over her stomach.

There was no harm done tonight, though perhaps they'd all be a little embarrassed tomorrow. He found himself looking forward to next week. He smiled a little as he wondered if Annabel would try anything with him again.

# 4

ANNABEL HEARD THE doorbell from her bedroom upstairs and ran down the stairs quickly. She laughed at herself a little, remembering the times, just a few months back, when she had pretended not to be home. Sarah had started coming by in the afternoons for coffee and conversation and Annabel had hidden with Adam in her room, turning his silence into a game.

She wasn't certain why she did it, exactly. Perhaps because Sarah was still new to her, and she wasn't always certain how to act. And also because solitude was so simple, without any rules to follow or games to play, while friendship meant you had to smile and be nice and listen to things you might not want to hear. Friendship, usually, meant that you had to pretend to be somebody you weren't.

But that was a few months ago. Change came gradually. First, Annabel found herself listening, really listening, when Sarah spoke, instead of looking past her shoulder and daydreaming. And when she started listening, she realized that Sarah was actually quite interesting. She played the role of the mousy wife, but there was substance to her underneath. She was articulate. She could make Annabel laugh.

Those afternoons of conversation, and their shopping

trips, and walks, and picnics with the kids, became something to look forward to rather than to dread. Sarah always listened and responded, a much better reaction than Annabel usually got from Patrick. She didn't offer advice for every problem, the way Patrick did. She just took the words in and nodded, or gave Annabel a quick tap on the shoulder and moved on.

After a few weeks, Annabel stopped pretending she wasn't home. A few more weeks and she was hurrying to the door.

Sarah did not require much. She was not like the friends Annabel had had in high school, who giggled constantly and talked only of movie stars and boyfriends and what dress they would wear on their dates. And Sarah was not a replica of those women on the playground, who could not see past their children. Sarah had ideas, ideas nobody had been interested in until Annabel came along. Once she started asking her about them, it was as if the lid came off and everything poured out. Sarah would find herself out of breath after hours of discussion on life and love and art and politics.

Annabel stole a quick look at herself in the mirror at the bottom of the stairs. She saw no flaws, which pleased her. Adam was asleep and Carolyn could sleep almost anywhere at any time. It would be just the two of them.

She opened the door. Sarah walked inside with a sleeping Carolyn in her arms.

"You have no idea how lucky you are with her," Annabel said.

Sarah laughed. "She makes up for it when she's awake."

Sarah took her upstairs to the bedroom while Annabel went into the kitchen to make coffee. Ten minutes later, they were sitting at the dining room table, the steam rising up from their coffee, and the warm scents of the summer afternoon coming in through the open window.

"You look good today," Annabel said, meaning it. Sarah had pulled the left side of her hair back and secured it with a clip with a pink rose on it. She was wearing a denim skirt and white blouse that hid what few flaws there were in her figure.

Sarah smiled widely and Annabel laughed. Being friends with Sarah was like having a little sister, something she'd always been bitter about being denied. Brothers had been of no use to her. She wasn't interested in joining them in their basketball games out by the garage. She hated the slimy frogs and disgusting spiders they brought into their bedrooms to dissect. They were both younger, so they didn't bring home any eligible men she might be interested in. They were a waste, really. A complete and total waste.

But Sarah was different. She yearned for advice and Annabel yearned to give it. When she was just with Sarah, Annabel felt perfectly at ease. There were none of the games to play to get what she wanted, the way there were with Patrick. There were no undertones of sexuality, the way there were with Jesse, or any other man. There was hardly any competition, because Annabel already knew she was prettier. With Sarah, Annabel came the closest she had ever come to being exactly who she was. Just Annabel. No facades, no masks, no games. She was surprised to discover that there was an Annabel, that there was substance beneath all the makeup she wore.

"You look good too," Sarah said. "But then, you always do."

Annabel did not deny it. She nodded slightly, accepting the compliment. She was not conceited about her looks. No one who spent an hour and a half in front of a mirror every morning blending eye shadows and rearranging curls could be conceited about her looks. Annabel knew that she made the most of her appearance. It was her strongest suit, and she always played it.

"Jesse asks me what we talk about every day," Sarah said.

"And what do you tell him?"

Sarah blew on her coffee. The aroma of jasmine from the backyard wafted in around their noses.

"I tell him I honestly don't know. We just talk."

"Men don't get it," Annabel said. "They don't know how to talk."

"Don't you and Patrick have conversations like this? I figure since he's so intellectual . . ."

Annabel laughed.

"Don't confuse scientific with intellectual. He knows about cancer cells and virology, or whatever the hell he calls it. But ask him about the state of the economy or how he feels about equal rights or racism, and the man draws a complete blank. He exists on one level."

Sarah looked at her.

"But you love him?" It was half a question, half a statement. Annabel sipped her coffee.

"Yes. But that doesn't blind me to what he is and isn't. You love Jesse, but you've got to see that he's entirely selfish, going to work all day, then coming home and barricading himself in your garage, working on that silly motorcycle of his. He doesn't have a clue that you might be tired, that you might need him."

Sarah was quiet and Annabel realized she had gone too far. It was so easy to talk with Sarah, she sometimes forgot that they were not exactly alike. Sarah had illusions about what her life *should* be like, and in particular what Jesse *should* be like. Listening to her talk about how good Jesse was, how much he loved her, it was obvious that Sarah was not seeing things for what they were. Jesse was a man of great passion and fire, but romantic and tender he was not. Sarah was confusing nineteen years' worth of romantic fantasies about marriage and knights in shining armor with three years of the reality of a husband who was more concerned about the shine on his fenders than how happy he made his wife.

Annabel, on the other hand, had no such illusions. Patrick was certainly flawed, and she was not afraid to point that out to anyone who would listen. He was stuffy to the point of boredom and much too logical. He didn't know how to fight with her; he either gave in and walked away, or called her dramatic and was perfectly calm until she exploded. He was too obsessed with his work and too casual about her. He never combed his hair or cleaned his glasses until she pointed out what a mess he was.

Assuming that everyone thought and acted as she did was often Annabel's downfall. It just seemed completely unreasonable that there could ever be any other way than hers. And yet, in the five months she had known Sarah, she had not heard one word spoken against Jesse. No man was *that* perfect.

"I'm sorry," Annabel said, reaching out and squeezing Sarah's hand. Sarah shook her head.

"Don't be. You're right. I do see that. But it's nothing I didn't know going in. Jesse has always had other interests. I was just so glad to be in his life at all . . ."

Annabel wondered what it must be like to lose yourself the way Sarah had lost herself in Jesse. Annabel was so distinct from Patrick. He did his thing; she did hers. It worked, yet she wondered what she was missing. Did it feel good or bad to love like that?

She was just about to ask when one of the children starting crying. They looked at each other as they listened, then they both said, "Adam."

"Can we switch kids?" Annabel asked.

"Believe me, you wouldn't want Carolyn, not when she gets into one of her moods."

Annabel went upstairs and got Adam out of bed. She hated this part of it, having to interrupt her life to accommodate Adam's. She hadn't thought it through before Adam was born. She had assumed that she'd somehow manage to squeeze him into her schedule.

She took him to the bathroom and sat him on the toilet and made sure he did his business. How degrading motherhood was. It wasn't about nurturing. It was about stooping over to clean up poop and spit-up and smashed bananas on the floor.

For a moment, as she watched her son unravel the toilet-paper roll until the paper was all over the floor, Annabel was utterly defeated. Intellectually, she knew this would all end and Adam would grow up. But right now maturity seemed an eternity away. There was only this stink of the bathroom, and temper tantrums, and sticky floors, and dirty clothes, and earaches, and . . .

Adam finished, but didn't want to wipe his bottom. Annabel took a deep breath and did it for him. She could not reconcile this image with the fantasies she had for herself, of someday being someone, doing *something*. Adam had turned her into a bottom wiper. She doubted very much that that qualified her for anything.

She pulled Adam's pants back up and took his hand. She was halfway down the stairs when the feeling came on. It was like a rushing between her ears, a need for speed and excitement and danger, a yearning to break out of this life, if only for a moment. She hurried into the kitchen.

"Let's go for a drive," she said to Sarah. Her eyes were wide and fiery, she knew. She had had too many days of the same thing: preparing food, doing dishes, cleaning the house, chasing after Adam, fighting with him, washing him, bristling at his cries. Sarah looked up.

"Why? Do you need something from the store?"

"No. I need to go, get out of here. Let's get a little crazy."

Sarah hesitated and Annabel resisted the urge to shake her, to wake her up. *Live a little,* she wanted to shout at her. Then, as if she really had said it, Sarah smiled.

"I'm in," she said.

They drove the back roads to Snoqualmie. It was a Wednesday afternoon, no one was out, and Annabel took the straightaways at eighty miles an hour and the hairpin turns at fifty. Adam laughed from the back seat and Carolyn slept on in her car seat. Sarah put her feet on the dashboard, rolled down the window, and let the wind rush through her hair.

"You're crazy!" she shouted. Annabel had turned the radio to a rock station and the squeal of electric guitars filled the car. Annabel turned the volume up as loud as it could go and they could barely hear each other when they shouted. Annabel took another quick turn, skidding a little, and laughed.

"Only now and then," she shouted back.

Sarah closed her eyes and tried to anticipate the turns. The only time she had ever driven fast was with Jesse, back in Spokane, on his motorcycle. But even then, they couldn't have been going more than seventy and Jesse had slowed down at every turn, looking around for cops.

Annabel had no such qualms. Speeding tickets were the last thing on her mind. Sarah opened her eyes when a new song came on. She watched Annabel sing along with

Bob Dylan, the wind thrashing her perfect curls around her face. Sarah laughed out loud and Annabel reached over and turned off the music.

"What?"

Sarah shook her head.

"I don't know. I'm just happy. Free."

Annabel pulled over to the side of the road. She opened her door.

"You drive," she said.

"It's your car . . ."

"I don't give a damn. Drive."

Sarah felt a rush of adrenaline surging through her. She got out and hurried around to the driver's side. She strapped herself in. Adam was chanting behind her, "Go. Go. Go. Go."

Sarah looked over at Annabel.

"You heard the boy," Annabel said. "Go. And don't pussyfoot around. I want to feel some speed."

Sarah laughed. She reached over and turned on the radio, loud. Then she peeled out of the shoulder, kicking up dust and skidding. Annabel let out a shout.

"That's my girl!" she said.

Sarah pressed down hard on the gas. They were laughing and singing all the way to the town of Snoqualmie where the road hooked up with I-90. Sarah gave it one more push of gas, one more tiny breath of freedom through the tiny town and then they heard the siren. Annabel reached over and turned off the radio while Sarah pulled to the side of the road. They looked at each other once, as the sheriff got out of his car, and then they both burst out laughing.

Jesse shook his head. He and Patrick were sitting at the counter of Jesse's favorite bar. Jessie had a Tom Collins in front of him, Patrick was sipping a beer.

"A ticket," Jesse said.

"Not just any ticket," Patrick told him. "Going eighty-five in a thirty-five-mile-per-hour zone. Annabel said the sheriff gave them a twenty-minute lecture about endangering the life of their kids."

"Shit," Jesse said. He downed his drink in three swallows and asked for another one.

"They get crazy when they're together," Patrick said. "You'd better tell Sarah to watch out. Annabel likes to cut loose once in a while."

Jesse smiled.

"I can understand that. I'm just surprised Sarah does."

They were quiet then. A baseball game was playing on the TV jacked up in the corner of the room. They watched it for a while. Patrick cheered when a Cub squeezed home the go-ahead run.

"I thought you hated the Cubs," Jesse said.

"Not when they're playing the Dodgers."

They watched the game and Jesse felt the tension slip from his shoulders. This hour after work was the hardest. He was still wound up, still thinking about sales made and lost, and he needed a little time to relax. Sarah didn't always understand that. She wanted him to come straight home and help her with Carolyn. She got angry when he went out with the guys or headed into the garage and his bike.

She was less angry when he went out with Patrick. She liked the idea of the two of them spending time together, becoming friends on their own the way she and Annabel were. Jesse had been hesitant at first. He didn't think he and the scientist had much in common. He'd been wrong.

They both liked a stiff drink after work. And sometimes a game of pool. If a baseball game was on, they could watch that.

They didn't talk much, and that suited them both fine. Jesse would probably never be able to relate to Patrick when he was in his starched white lab coat, but after hours, he was just one of the guys. He didn't put on any airs.

Jesse had had plenty of friends while growing up in Spokane. They raced together, smoked together, stirred up trouble together. But when he left, he didn't miss them. It had never been like that.

Sarah thought he must be lonely. She didn't understand; he didn't get lonely. He didn't have the capacity for it. He could be completely alone on this earth and it wouldn't matter. People, generally, just got in his way. When he met someone on the highway while he was riding, it infuriated him that they were breaking up his view. The men he worked with were merely competition. The people he sold to were only a commission.

He didn't dislike people. He simply didn't care about them. So it was funny, really, that he enjoyed being here with Patrick. They had no ritual, the way Annabel and Sarah did. Jesse would simply call him up at the lab, ask him if he was interested in a drink, and then they'd meet here or at one of the other bars Jesse knew so well. Or Patrick would call, tell him he couldn't handle Annabel right away after work, and they'd meet. They had come together maybe a dozen times now. Sarah always asked him what they talked about and she couldn't understand when he said nothing.

"You mean you don't talk about anything important?" she asked him.

"No. I mean we don't talk."

She didn't get it. And she said he didn't get it. What the hell. He liked Patrick's unobtrusive company and he thought Patrick liked his. He didn't know about Patrick's history or too much about his job or his feelings or any of the things Sarah and Annabel knew about each other. All of that was garbage anyway. He knew the kind of beer Patrick liked and that he hated the Dodgers and loved the Giants. What else was there?

"Want to shoot some pool?" Patrick asked him.

Jesse smiled and led the way to the table.

Patrick was working in the lab when the phone rang. Usually, one of the student assistants got it and Patrick was irritated when it kept ringing. He looked up at the clock, saw that it was six-thirty in the evening, and realized they had all gone home.

He went to the phone and picked it up.

"Patrick Meyers," he said.

"Mr. Meyers, this is Elaine Povick. I'm a nurse at Memorial Hospital. I'm afraid there's been an accident."

Patrick's heart went cold. Yet he answered in the same, calm voice as always.

"My wife?" he said.

"No. A Mr. Jesse Bean. Nothing life-threatening. He asked me to call you instead of his wife. He said he didn't want to worry her."

"I'll be right there," Patrick said.

He made the drive to the hospital in ten minutes. He went into the emergency room and a nurse led him back to Jesse. He was sitting up on the bed, a few cuts on his face, and a bandage over the right side of his forehead. His knuckles were bandaged up too.

"The Harley," Patrick said.

Jesse flashed him his smile.

"You got it."

"Sarah's gonna kill you."

Jesse started laughing as the doctor walked back into the room.

"I see the crash didn't affect your humor," he said.

"Nah," Jesse said. "It just taught me not to look at pretty girls in convertibles while I'm trying to make a turn."

The doctor chuckled and looked over Jesse's cuts.

"I'll want you back in six weeks to take out those stitches in your forehead," he said. "And put that ointment on three times a day. If there's any sign of infection, you need to come back in."

Jesse nodded.

"Try to stand up," the doctor said.

Jesse did so, wincing a little when his feet hit the ground.

"You say you were wearing your helmet?" the doctor asked.

"Yes, for once. Hell of a lot of good it did me. I fell on my side and the helmet took the first blow. Then it came off and that's when I cut my face."

"Well, you're lucky. I don't think you suffered a concussion. I could keep you overnight, but I take it you've got your partner here to help you make up some story for your wife."

Jesse laughed.

"You got it, doc."

"All right. You can go. Take it easy for a few days and call if you've got any problems."

"I'll take care of him," Patrick said.

He put his arm around Jesse's waist and helped him to his car. Then he went around and got in on the driver's side.

"Pretty girls, huh?"

"Gorgeous," Jesse said.

Patrick laughed and started the car. By the time they reached Jesse's house, they had the story all worked out.

Patrick pressed the doorbell and Jesse put on his best imitation of a drunken stupor. Sarah opened the door.

"Oh my God," she said. She pushed Patrick aside and grabbed at Jesse. She pulled him in, asking over and over again what had happened. Jesse said nothing. He was doing a very bad imitation of a drunken smile.

"He had a little too much to drink," Patrick said. Sarah still crooned over him and Patrick could see she was hurting him with her probing.

"There was a fight," he said.

Sarah turned around. Her eyes were round and scared, and Patrick couldn't meet them directly.

"A fight?"

"Afraid so. Some guys were giving Jesse a hard time about his bike. Seems they wanted to ride it. He didn't even know what hit him. They were on him before I could even get in there to help. Luckily the cops came fast and it was all broken up before any real damage was done. I got him to the hospital right after. The doctor said he'd be fine."

"No real damage?" Sarah said, turning back to Jesse. She looked at his face and then down at his knuckles. "You call this no real damage?"

"Don't hurt," Jesse slurred. Patrick turned away to hide his smile. No one really sounded like that when they were drunk.

"Don't talk," Sarah said softly. "Let me get you up to bed."

She guided him to the stairs.

"If you need anything," Patrick said, seeing himself to the door. Sarah looked back at him.

"You've done enough already, haven't you?"

"Ah, don't be mad at Patty," Jesse said.

"And that's enough out of you, Jesse Bean," Sarah said.

Patrick met Jesse's eyes quickly and could see the humor in them.

"Good night, Sarah," Patrick said, opening the door.

"Humph," Sarah said, walking Jesse up the stairs. Patrick pitied the poor guy. It was going to be a long night.

# 5

❦

SARAH CROUCHED DOWN at the edge of Lake Washington and dipped her fingers into the water. It was icy cold and the surface had taken on the gray color of the sky. She stood up again and looked around the lake. The pines and firs hugged the shore like thirsty animals and then climbed the hills that disappeared in the clouds. Sarah noticed more homes partly hidden in the trees than she'd seen the last time she was here, a few months earlier. There were more cars on the road around the lake, more stop signs, a new market and restaurant. Still, once you took the turnoff and entered St. Edward State Park, it was like leaving civilization behind and grabbing the last remaining chunk of nature. This was her favorite place. Especially on a cold, wet day like today.

She turned around to see Carolyn chasing Adam around a tree. She smiled. He was so good with her. He was almost five and lightning fast, but he pretended to trip and fall so Carolyn, at one and a half, could feel she was gaining on him. She laughed loudly every time he slipped and the sound drifted out over the lake and up into the clouds.

Annabel was sitting on the bench of a picnic table, watching her. Sarah felt as if her secret were written all over her, yet no one, not even Jesse, had said anything.

Sarah wasn't quite sure what she'd been waiting for these past two weeks. The perfect moment? The instant when Jesse was looking into her eyes, loving her the way he was supposed to? When she found out she was pregnant with Carolyn, she hadn't waited for anything. The moment she knew, she shouted it to the world.

She walked back to the picnic table and sat down opposite Annabel. Annabel was still watching her, studying her, and Sarah laughed.

"What?"

Annabel shook her head. "I don't know. Something's different."

Of course Annabel would sense it. She seemed to know everything about Sarah, just by looking at her. It was scary and comforting, all at once, being known like that.

Sarah looked over at Adam and Carolyn. They had stopped running and Adam was holding Carolyn's hand, taking her down to the water.

"They make a perfect couple," Sarah said.

"First loves never last."

"Jesse was my first love."

"Sorry, I keep forgetting you have the only storybook romance left."

A light mist began to fall and Annabel pulled her scarf up over her hair. Even now, in the rain, she looked perfect. Jeans, with a blouse, then a sweater, then a long gray raincoat over that. Sarah glanced down at her baggy khaki pants, frilly sweater, and Jesse's coat she'd borrowed. She'd known Annabel for more than a year now. Some of her style should have rubbed off already.

They fell into a companionable silence. It had taken months for Sarah to realize that she didn't always need to make conversation. At first, her silences with Annabel had been torturous, and she struggled to fill them with inane chatter. But then, once she grew more comfortable with Annabel, she found that words weren't always necessary. They could fix dinner together for their Friday-night get-togethers without speaking. They could walk and listen to the wind through the trees and be perfectly content. With Annabel, Sarah found that she could just be, she didn't have to try to impress. Annabel was not interested in small talk or pleasantries. It was a relief, Sarah thought, to finally know someone who cut right to the heart of an issue.

"I'm pregnant," Sarah said suddenly. Annabel's mouth hung open for a moment, then she came around to Sarah's side and hugged her.

"Congratulations."

She sat down beside her and Sarah leaned her head against her friend's.

"I haven't told Jesse. I don't know why."

"Does he want another one?"

"I don't know. We've never talked about it. We never talked about it before Carolyn came along either, but back then I was just so sure of . . ."

"Of what?" Annabel said, turning to look at her.

Sarah bit her lip. She'd lived by an unspoken rule: she could never discuss marital problems with anyone but Jesse. If her parents had taught her anything, it was that a marriage was a marriage, a singular, self-contained entity. Problems were solved from within. Her parents never fought in public, never berated each other in view of another soul, including Sarah. It gave the illusion of perfection.

Annabel had no hesitations telling her the things Patrick did wrong. She often described, verbatim, their arguments and accusations. She both condemned and applauded him. But not once since they'd become friends had Sarah opened up about her fights with Jesse. It was vitally important to her that everyone think they were blissfully happy. Whether they actually were or not was secondary.

But this was different. This wasn't about a fight or anything Jesse had done wrong. This was about a feeling she had, a kind of trepidation. Annabel was her best friend. They spent every other day together. And she was not like the friends Sarah used to have, activity friends, she called them. The kind who were there if you were going shopping or out to dinner. There had been friends for exercise and friends for eating, friends you took to the mall, and friends who were always up for a movie. Annabel was just there, for no reason. If she couldn't trust her with her secrets, she couldn't trust anyone.

"Nothing's changed," Sarah said. "I know Jesse still loves me and God knows I love him as much as ever. But when he comes home from work now, it's different. We still have dinner, he still plays with Carolyn, but I don't feel I have all of him. He keeps a part of himself sealed off. Do you know what I'm saying?"

Annabel stood up. She walked a few feet toward the water where Adam and Carolyn were sitting on the sand, digging. She kept her back to Sarah as she spoke.

"Yes, I think I do. You're not quite sure what he's thinking anymore, or if he's thinking about you at all."

"Yes, that's it," Sarah said. The feeling had come on slowly, so slowly that she hadn't even realized she was experiencing it until a month ago. Jesse had settled into his job and even gotten a promotion. He had made friends at work, went out with them occasionally. On the weekends, he still spent hours in the garage, fiddling with his motorcycle.

He was still Jesse, yet he wasn't. Every now and then when he kissed her, she peeked through her lids and saw that his eyes were open. Sometimes, when she was speaking, she stopped in the middle of a sentence and he didn't even notice. He used to compliment her on her cooking, her cleaning, the way she'd rearranged furniture or painted a room a new color. Now, he simply took for granted that she would do all of those things. He had his job, she had hers, and there was no need to acknowledge that both of them did them well.

"I feel like . . . I'm becoming invisible to him," she said softly. Annabel laughed bitterly. She turned halfway toward her, but Sarah could not see her eyes.

"You are becoming what every wife becomes," Annabel said. "Familiar. Jesse knows you'll always be there when he comes home. He has no doubt that you'll have dinner on the table and Carolyn bathed and ready for bed at eight o'clock. You've never once shaken him up or changed the game plan, so his life is completely predictable."

Sarah watched Annabel standing there, her posture erect, her head high and proud as always. She knew, of course, that Annabel would never be predictable. Annabel had told her about the times she'd met Patrick at the door naked, or sent him a message at work to meet her at a fancy hotel, after she made arrangements to send Adam to her mother's. Annabel was not the type of person to fall into a routine. She was imaginative; she seemed to have no trouble finding ways to spice up her life.

"I can't change," Sarah said, looking away. Sometimes, when she got too close to Annabel, when they got to the heart of their feelings, she felt this intense pressure weighing down on her. Its force was dizzying, almost paralyzing. It was so obvious, she didn't know why it had never been said aloud. *Sarah was not good enough.* She did not dress as well as Annabel or tell jokes as well or please her husband as well. Sarah loved Annabel. She made her laugh and was there whenever she needed her. But there was no mistaking it; Annabel was better than she was. They both knew it. Annabel was not mean about it, but it was no secret that she thrived on it. She loved to give advice and take compliments and bask in the glow of superiority. Sarah simply pretended that it didn't bother her.

"You can," Annabel said. "You must. If you love Jesse, you have to wake him up. Do something different. Go a little crazy. I know you've got it in you."

Sarah looked at her. Did Annabel know something she didn't? Why did everyone assume that she had a dark side, a wild side, like Annabel? Was it a necessity, to be both good and bad? Was it not possible to be only good— reserved, conservative, quiet? Except for marrying Jesse against her parents' wishes, Sarah had never done a "bad" thing in her life.

"What am I supposed to do now that I'm pregnant again?" Sarah said.

"Come on, it's not a death sentence, though God knows I'll never do it again." Annabel ran her hands over her still thin hips. Sarah's had widened after giving birth to Carolyn and had never returned to their former size. She kept battling her weight, struggling to keep it five pounds over what it had been before Carolyn.

"Listen," Annabel said, smiling her wicked smile that could only mean she was plotting something. The rain came down harder and she started gathering their things together. "This is what you do. Find a sitter for Carolyn, even if it's only for a few hours. Be gone when Jesse comes home and then knock on the door about half an hour later, when he's good and worried and realizing just how devastating life would be without you. Tell him you're taking him on a date. Take him to dinner. Order oysters. Find a hotel with a Jacuzzi in the bathroom. Seduce *him*, for a change."

Sarah turned away. It was awful sometimes, being known so intimately, so easily, as if she were not complicated in any way. It didn't take a genius to know that Jesse always instigated lovemaking. Annabel knew it. Patrick probably knew it too.

The kids ran back to them, laughing in the rain, wanting to stay until they were soaking wet.

"It's too cold," Sarah said to them, picking up Carolyn. She felt her stomach tighten as she did so, and she thought of the new life inside. Out of all their differences, Sarah thought this was the one that differentiated her from Annabel the most. The presence in her stomach felt good to her, right. Annabel had told her point-blank a while back that if she got pregnant by mistake, she would abort it. Annabel lived for herself. Sarah lived for Jesse, for her children. As they ran to the car, the clouds opening up and dumping rain on them, Sarah couldn't help thinking that Annabel was the one who had gotten the better end of the deal.

Jesse knew, as soon as he opened the front door, that something was wrong. It was too quiet. Carolyn's toys were all stacked neatly in the corner, instead of being scattered everywhere the way they usually were. No lights were on. No smells of pot roast or chicken came from the kitchen.

He threw down his jacket and briefcase and hurried into the kitchen. He searched the counters and refrigerator door for notes, but there were none. He turned and ran upstairs. He flung open every door, but the rooms were all empty. He was halfway down the stairs again when a range of possibilities hit him. They'd been kidnapped. Or

Carolyn was hurt and Sarah had taken her to the hospital. Or Sarah had left him and taken Carolyn with her.

She was always home. That was understood. He went to work, she stayed home. That was how it worked. There had never been a time when he was home and she wasn't. Only something drastic could have pulled her away.

He turned and ran back upstairs. He went straight to the closet and looked at Sarah's clothes. They all seemed to be there, although he couldn't be sure. He had never bothered to look before. He shook his head. He was being ridiculous. Though it was out of the ordinary, she had probably just gone out to the market or over to Annabel's. He picked up the phone on the nightstand and dialed the Meyerses' number. Annabel picked up on the second ring.

"Hello," she said.

"It's Jesse. Is Sarah there?"

"You sound upset," Annabel said. "Is anything wrong?"

"I just need to know if Sarah's there."

"Uh . . ." She hesitated and Jesse gripped the cord.

"Tell me, Annabel. Don't lie to me."

The silence on the other end of the line was deafening. Jesse was about to slam down the phone and run over there personally when she spoke.

"She's my best friend," Annabel said softly. "You've got to understand. I told her I'd cover for her."

Jesse felt his head start to pound. He hadn't paid attention to Sarah lately. He knew that. But it was hard to feign passion in a passionless relationship. He still loved her, still wanted her, but every time he had fantasies of making love or going a little crazy, Carolyn waddled in and climbed between them or Sarah got that maternal look on her face that smashed sexuality to bits.

They had become their parents. God only knows how it had happened, but it had. He gave her those little pecky kisses when he left in the morning and came home. They made love no more than once a week, though he wanted it every night and she knew he wanted it every night but went right on pretending she was oblivious to his needs. They could have been brother and sister, for all the passion in their relationship.

Jesse did his best to pretend he was happy with the state of his life. He did his own thing. He went out with his buddies. He worked on his Harley. He watched football. Sarah hadn't said there was a problem. They went on as they always had; he going to work, she taking care of the house. If it was ordinary, predictable, dull, he tried not to think about it.

"I need to know," he said.

Annabel sighed. Jesse could hear Adam shouting in the background.

"Promise me you'll never tell her I told you. It would kill our friendship."

"I won't tell her."

"Promise me, Jesse."

"Fine," Jesse said abruptly. "I promise. Now tell me."

Annabel hesitated once more, then plunged in. "We were at the park earlier today and Sarah told me how unhappy she was. She said you weren't there for her anymore; you took everything she did for granted."

Jesse was silent. He couldn't deny it. He didn't think it was totally true, but he couldn't deny it.

"A while back," Annabel went on, "she met a man at the playground. He was divorced and was trying to make it up to his son by taking off time from work to be with him."

Jesse gripped the phone tighter.

"Go on," he said.

"Well, they met and talked. Nothing ever came of it. But she was so hurt, Jesse. You should have seen her. She said if you didn't pay attention to her, someone else would. So I guess she took this man up on his offer to go out. She asked me to cover for her if she wasn't back by the time you got home. I was supposed to tell you she had some errands to run or something. I don't know where they went, but I'm sure it's perfectly harmless. Lunch maybe and nothing else. I think . . . I mean, I know she still loves you."

Jesse looked at his knuckles gripping the phone. They were bone white. He glanced around the room, but he didn't see it. Funny, he'd always thought if either of them was going to have an affair, it would be him. Even now, when it was all laid out before him, he didn't think Sarah was cut out for it. He just didn't think she had it in her.

"Are you sure?" he managed to say. His voice came out raspy and tired. He loosened his grip on the phone.

"Yes, Jesse. I'm sorry. Please, please don't tell her I told you."

"I told you I wouldn't."

"Maybe you just shouldn't say anything. Let this blow over."

"Yes, maybe."

"Jesse, I think you should go out. Get out of the house. Go get a beer and give yourself some time to cool off. You don't want to be there, waiting for her to come home. It will drive you crazy."

"Maybe I'll do that."

"Do it. And who knows? Maybe she didn't go. Maybe she just needed to get out of the house for a while."

"Goodbye, Annabel," Jesse said. He hung up the phone. Everything was still quiet. Jesse wondered if he would cry, but he could feel no tears coming on. The funny thing was, he was not sad. He was angry, more at himself and this man who had no doubt pushed himself on Sarah than at Sarah herself. And he was also, strangely, relieved. There had been this pressure on him from the very beginning, as though he alone had to prove that marriage was worth something. Now, he could be like all the other bruised and battered souls. He could stop trying to make what he and Sarah had into something special.

He gripped his hand into a fist and thought of slamming it against the wall, but then whatever anger he'd had subsided. He went downstairs, grabbed his jacket, and walked outside. He hopped on his motorcycle and took off down the street. He had a full tank of gas and he intended to use every drop of it.

He turned the corner onto the main highway just as Sarah pulled up into the driveway. She was dressed in her best dress and nervous as a schoolgirl. Still, she thought Annabel was right. A night of romance with her husband would do her good. Carolyn was over at the sitter's and didn't have to be picked up until eleven o'clock. She had made dinner reservations at a French place Annabel had recommended and booked a room at an exotic hotel for a few hours. A change of scene, a hotel made for exactly this kind of thing; it made her smile with excitement.

She got out of the car and took a deep breath. She didn't see Jesse's bike, but she assumed it was in the garage. She walked to the door and knocked.

Two streets away, Annabel stood on her patio, listening to the sound of Jesse's motorcycle speed past onto the main highway behind their house. Patrick had called to say he would be late, Adam was busy doodling at the kitchen table, and she was alone.

She hadn't known she would do it until the opportunity arose. She honestly had had only Sarah's welfare in mind when she made the suggestion that she take Jesse to a hotel, spice up their love life.

But then she heard Jesse's voice on the phone.

It all became so clear in that instant. No friendship ever compared to the rush of making a man want her. Annabel had felt that rush with Patrick. It was what made her want to marry him, actually, the fact that he had been harder than most men to catch. The games, the flirting, the tingling in her body when a new man brushed past her; these things had a force all their own. How could she be expected to think straight when she was feeling something so intense, so good? If she could, she thought she'd spend every day with a new man, making him want her in the morning, thrilling at the unique touch of him in the afternoon, and then gorging herself on sex with him at night. Then the next day, she could start all over again, with someone new.

Annabel knew she was bad. She had always known it. She had slept with five different men besides Patrick since their marriage. Men she'd met in the park, in the neighborhood, wherever. Patrick didn't suspect. It would probably never occur to him that Annabel might cheat. And if it did, he would not understand that it was not about the sex, but more about the chase, the hunt, the killing. That was what she lived for, making men want her. It was like the very best drugs and booze, an intense, orgasmic high that rushed through her when a man's eyes were riveted on her, when his fingers reached out, trembling, for her breasts.

She thought that her friendship with Sarah was different, that it meant something. But in the end it had come down to a fight between friendship and sex, and sex had won out again. Sarah made her laugh and listened to her problems and comforted her, but it was all on a human scale. Jesse pressed those buttons in her that triggered euphoria. And he was the biggest prize she'd ever gone after, married, to her best friend even. There was just no competing with the thrill of that.

She hadn't been sure things would go her way. A thousand things could have gone against her. Jesse might not have left the house after he talked to her and Sarah might have been able to convince him what she was really up to. Jesse might still tell her where he got his information. But she didn't think so. He was proud. He probably wouldn't even confront Sarah with what he knew, or thought he knew. It would just be a seed there, for him to think about. And even if he did accuse her and Sarah denied it, how would she explain away the hotel bill she had put on her Visa? She might try to tell him about the evening she had planned for the two of them, but it wouldn't sound right. Sarah was not the kind of wife who booked a cheesy hotel by the hour.

Annabel smiled. She couldn't help it. She knew that if Sarah found out what she had done she would lose the best friend she'd ever had. Yet, sadly, that sacrifice was worth it to her. She wasn't proud of herself. She didn't even understand herself. Why did men matter so much to her? Why had she been given an overdose of sexuality and been denied all the softer traits, like loyalty and trustworthiness?

She did not like what she had done. The moment she hung up the phone with Jesse, she thought, *Oh Sarah. What have I done?* Yet she had done it. And she would do it again and again if it would make Jesse turn to her, see her, want *her*. She would push Sarah out of her mind. She would put on a smile and act nonchalant when they were together. And when Sarah was gone, she would not remember their talks and the laughter and the speeding ticket or anything that might let the guilt seep in. She had always been this way; why should she change just because Sarah was her friend?

Jesse was one of a kind. There was no denying that. He had been on her mind since day one. Sarah had been ashamed of his silences, the scowls on his face, but Annabel had found him incredibly erotic. Sarah was no match for him. She didn't even begin to tap into his sexuality. It was a tragedy to let all of that magnetism be wasted.

Annabel had made a few moves in Jesse's direction, gauged his reaction. He responded to her, that was certain. She could feel his eyes on her when she moved through the room. He prickled when she touched him. But then he always turned back to Sarah, as if he had to remind himself that he was married. As long as good little Sarah was there, he would never stray.

But what if good little Sarah wasn't so good? What if there was a doubt about her in his mind? Pushing all the self-recriminations aside, Annabel felt as if she'd won a major battle by outmaneuvering the enemy. She was confident that she would not be found out. This whole plan depended on her understanding of men like Jesse. They were proud, volatile, loyal. Jesse would keep his word. It would be beneath him somehow to admit to Sarah that he hadn't figured out her indiscretions on his own, instead of having to hear it from Annabel.

He and Sarah would reach a standoff. This wasn't enough to break them up, Annabel knew, and Annabel wasn't even sure if that was what she wanted. All she knew was that she wanted him. He had taken over every fantasy. He was the man she dreamed about. And once she started dreaming, there was no stopping her. Sarah or no Sarah, Annabel would have him.

Sarah had washed off her makeup, ripped her fancy dress off her back, and polished off three glasses of wine. She looked up at the clock every minute. She picked up the phone beside her, then replaced it. The police had said there was nothing they could do until twenty-four hours had passed.

Carolyn was asleep in her bed. Sarah had driven over to the baby-sitter's an hour ago, at eleven o'clock, and picked her up. Before that, she had called Annabel and every other person she knew to see if they had seen Jesse. No one had.

The wine numbed her a little, but could not kill the fear. He was dead. That was the only explanation. Jesse knew how she worried about him, how she could not stand for him to be even five minutes late. Every conceivable form of death flashed through her mind, most centering around his motorcycle being smashed beneath a logging truck or semi.

She looked up again; it was twelve twenty-nine. It couldn't be only hours ago that she had pulled up into the driveway, ready to surprise him with an evening of romance and lovemaking. It seemed like days, months ago. She had knocked on the door and then, when she got no answer, walked inside. She'd called out his name, searched the rooms for him, then finally looked in the garage for his motorcycle. When she found it gone, her heart started pumping madly and she got on the phone.

She called Annabel first.

"Is Jesse there?" she asked, without a greeting. There was only a moment's hesitation.

"No, Sarah. Should he be?"

"Oh Annabel. I did everything you said. I made the reservations and showed up half an hour after Jesse usually gets home. But he isn't here. Maybe he got upset when he found out I wasn't home and went looking for me. I should have left him a note."

"Of course not," Annabel said. "Every man needs to worry a little bit. And if he is out looking for you, he'll come back soon. Don't worry. Jesse can take care of himself."

"Call me if you hear from him," Sarah said.

"You know I will."

Then Sarah made the rounds of Jesse's coworkers. No one had heard from him since he left work at the usual time. Sarah called the police, but got no help from them.

"A man has to be missing for twenty-four hours before

we start looking for him. He's probably just out getting a beer."

Sarah slammed the phone down and paced up and down the length of the house. Now it was nearing one o'clock in the morning and all Sarah could think about was a life that would mean nothing if Jesse was not in it. How would she even function? How could she possibly give birth to another child, raise it, make a home for it and Carolyn without Jesse by her side?

A crash sounded in the street. Sarah jumped up and ran to the front door. She threw it open. Jesse's bike lay in a heap beneath the garbage cans he'd set out on the street that morning. He was stumbling to his feet. Sarah felt her breath come back and tears of relief sting her eyes.

"Thank you, God," she whispered.

Jesse looked up.

"Kinda crashed," he said.

He swayed as he walked to the door. Sarah reached out to steady him, but he evaded her. He walked inside. He looked at the wine glass and the mess of clothes and tissues on the floor.

"Worried 'bout me, huh?"

"Yes, Jesse. Very much. Where were you?"

He laughed. "Wouldn't you like to know, missy. Same place as you, prob-ly."

"I've been here, waiting for you to come home."

He laughed again and then the laughter turned to coughing. Sarah patted him on the back, but he ducked away.

"Nah. Don't do that. One's enough for tonight, don't you think?"

"I don't know what you're talking about."

" 'Course you don't, sweetcakes. Me neither. Don't know nothing."

Sarah watched him as he stumbled through the room. He walked to the refrigerator and took out a beer.

"You don't need that," Sarah said.

Jesse turned around quickly. His eyes had shifted from a drunken haze to violent clarity. He slammed the beer down on the counter and marched up to her. He grabbed her wrist roughly. Sarah cried out, but he didn't release her.

"I'd say I can have anything I want, just like you," he said, remarkably clearly. Sarah tried to pull away, but he gripped her tighter.

"Jesse, please," she said. "What's wrong? What's going on?"

He glared at her and then the intensity faded and he let go of her arm. He went back for his beer and opened it, and then his words slurred again.

"Nothing's wrong," he said. "Ain't nothing wrong."

He walked past her with the beer in his hands. Sarah reached out to him then dropped her hand. He was angry. That much was clear. Perhaps because she wasn't here when he got home. If she could just explain what she'd been planning.

"Earlier, I was going to—"

He stopped and all was still. Sarah could not even see him breathing. He had his back to her and his blond hair grazed his shoulders. She took one step toward him, then stopped. It wouldn't make sense now. It wasn't something she would normally do and he would sense that. God, why had she listened to Annabel? She could not become like her in one night. If she had only gone on as always, just told Jesse about the baby. They would have drawn closer together again naturally.

"It doesn't matter now," she said. "Not when you'd let me worry about you the way you did tonight. How could you do that?"

Jesse turned around. He was smiling, but his eyes were hard.

"Because I don't give a fuck," he said. "I wanted to go out, so I went out. You weren't here when I got home, so you were exercising the same right. We're even."

Tears slipped down Sarah's cheeks. He had never been anything but kind to her. He seemed like a different person all of a sudden.

"How much have you drunk?" she asked.

Jesse took a long swig of beer, never taking his eyes from her face. She felt his hatred of her just as she'd felt his love a few hours ago. She wanted to throw herself into his arms, make him explain all this to her, but as she came toward him, he stepped back.

"Not as much as I need to," he said.

"Jesse, please."

He turned and walked up the stairs. It seemed to Sarah that if she didn't touch him now, pull him back to her, she would lose him. It was like living in a nightmare with no rules, where everyone knew what was going on but her.

"What did I do?" she called after him. He stopped suddenly. His shoulders sagged. He looked much older than twenty-eight.

"It doesn't matter," he said, without looking around. "I realized that tonight. It really doesn't matter. I was putting too much stock in it. It's my fault, really."

"Putting too much stock in what?" Sarah said, crying. She tried to come up the stairs, but again he kept moving away from her. "Why are you doing that? Why won't you let me touch you?"

Jesse did not respond. He reached the top of the stairs and walked into the bedroom. Just before he closed the door, Sarah shouted, "You can't just walk away from me like that. I'm pregnant."

Jesse turned back and looked down at her.

"Who's the father?"

Sarah felt a rush of anger, but then it dissolved into tears. She had never been able to hold her rage long enough to express it. No one even knew she had it in her.

"How can you ask me that? What did I do to make you hate me so much?"

She crumpled onto the stairs and sat sobbing into her hands. She kept waiting for Jesse to give in to her tears, the way he always did. At any moment, he would be beside her, his arms around her shoulders. She kept waiting and waiting, and then finally she looked up. Jesse had closed the bedroom door and dipped out the light behind it.

# 6

P ATRICK MANNED THE barbecue. Smoke from too-greasy hamburgers shot up into his eyes, but he kept his head down and the spatula hopping. Occasionally, one of his friends from the university came by, patted his back, said, "Good job, Pat," and he smiled.

He heard Adam laughing and he looked up. He was in the middle of the water-balloon race. He had a huge, gyrating blue water balloon in his hands and he was running as fast as he could across the grass to the finish line. He was gaining on the leader, but just before he reached him, the balloon burst and spit water out all over him. Adam collapsed on the ground, laughing.

Patrick looked around the park for Annabel. She had not wanted to come, of course. These once-a-year picnics for the research staff at the University of Washington were dreadfully boring for her. She didn't want to socialize with these "stuffy old farts." Never mind that most of Patrick's coworkers were graduate students or young scientists like himself. Annabel had made up her mind about them long before he even got the job and that was that.

Patrick searched all the playing fields and benches, but he could not find her. She had done the same thing last year, and the year before—disappeared as soon as she saw an opening. Patrick had hoped things would be different this time, but that was only wishful thinking. Annabel had been her same, grumpy self in the car on the way over this morning.

"What am I going to do all day?" she had said.

"What all the other women do. Talk. Join in the games."

"I hate those stupid games. You act like a bunch of fools, running backward and doing somersaults. It's ridiculous."

"Ridiculous," Adam repeated from the back seat. Patrick glanced back at him and smiled.

"Then I guess you'll do what you always do," he said. "Sulk and act like you're better than everyone else there."

Annabel turned away. Patrick gripped the steering wheel more tightly for a moment and then relaxed. He usually didn't say anything. He didn't like rocking Annabel's boat; she could turn the smallest disagreement into a major battle. But this time, Patrick couldn't help himself. They always went out with Annabel's friends, saw Annabel's type of movies, went to Annabel's favorite restaurants. Patrick claimed a mere eight hours every year for his own friends, his own kind of fun. He didn't think he was asking for too much.

"You can be such a bastard," Annabel said, not looking at him.

"Bastard," Adam repeated. "Bastard. Smashtard."

Patrick repressed a smile.

"Don't repeat everything your mother says."

"Pashtard. Flashtard."

Patrick looked over at Annabel. "Now see what you've done?"

He smiled at her, but Annabel was not amused.

"I just want you to appreciate what I'm doing for you. I'm sacrificing a whole day for these stuffy old farts and I'll expect some kind of reward later."

Patrick pulled into the parking lot. Annabel moved her hand onto his knee as he parked.

"Couldn't you just ask for jewelry or furs like other women?"

Annabel smiled and slipped her hand up his leg.

"I'm not like other women," she said, squeezing him once and then getting out of the car.

That was an understatement. Annabel was the most extraordinary woman he'd ever met. He remembered the first time he saw her, standing beside his friend and her fiancé, Tom, at Patrick's college graduation party. She had caught his eye, casually left Tom's side, and never gone back. When she reached Patrick, she touched his arm.

"I wonder why Tom never introduced us," she had said. "I'm Annabel."

Her perfume had engulfed him and Patrick searched the room for Tom. When he couldn't find him, he looked at Annabel again.

"I think he wanted to keep you to himself."

She laughed and Patrick felt the first twitching of his heart that years later, he still wouldn't be able to shake.

"No man can have me to himself," she said.

Annabel never explained why she left Tom and came to him that night. It couldn't have been his looks or intelligence. Tom was the more attractive man and Annabel never showed much interest in his intellect. He never knew why she stayed interested in the following months, when he told her he was loyal to Tom. Unless that was the reason—he tried to resist her and she was a sucker for a challenge.

He never fully understood how she managed to change his mind, how she whittled away at him with her laughter and caresses until he hardly knew himself anymore, until she was all he thought about. By the time he proposed, their marriage seemed inevitable, and she accepted nonchalantly, as if she'd expected him to ask for months.

The only thing he did understand was that there was one way to keep a woman like Annabel, and that was to never show your feelings. Tom had shown his and lost her. Patrick, from day one, had kept his intensity hidden, and so she never knew how much he loved her, how much her touch thrilled him. She still wasn't sure of his love for her, and so she kept trying to win it.

Patrick and Adam teamed up on the three-legged, father-son race. Adam was almost six now and came up past

Patrick's waist. Still, their legs were such a mismatch that they ended up crawling most of the way down the field. Patrick laughed so hard, tears streamed down his cheeks. His glasses fell off twice and they scrambled all over to find them. They crossed the finish line in last place.

"Sorry, son," Patrick said, falling onto his back with Adam on top of him.

"That's okay, Dad," Adam said. Patrick looked up at his son. He had Annabel's hazel eyes and black hair. But he had Patrick's slim mouth and pointed jaw. And he had Patrick's temperament, thank God.

"Where's Mom?" Adam asked. Patrick sat up and started to untie them.

"I don't know. I think—"

"She's with her brother," one of Patrick's graduate students said. "I saw her when I was getting the cooler out of my car. They said they were going to get a drink, to catch up on all the news."

Patrick nodded and looked away.

"Yes, I heard he might show up," he said, because after all these years, he knew how to make a show of things, to cover up for her.

"It's amazing how brothers and sisters can be so different, huh?" the student said. "Not even the same hair color or eyes."

Patrick looked up. The student was watching him, waiting for him to come clean. Even he knew. They all knew. Annabel was not difficult to read, though she thought she was fooling everybody. Patrick had known what she was like the day he met her, but as soon as she touched him, everything but the stroke of her fingertips ceased to matter.

Patrick had known, the day he proposed to her, that he had been cornered, that Annabel had made him love her. For some reason, a scientist fit into her plans, and he was the one she would have. He had always known that he was no match for her, that she had desires he couldn't come close to sating. But he had believed, however naïvely, that she loved him, that that would be enough. He had thought his love for her would balance out everything.

"Yes," he said. "Annabel doesn't look anything like either of her brothers."

The student nodded and went away. Patrick watched him take a friend aside and whisper. The rumors would start circulating now.

Patrick got himself untied from his son and stood up. He thought of Annabel's brothers, still on vacation in Hawaii. In fact, they had just received a postcard from the two of them and their wives this morning. Annabel had to know her story wouldn't hold water with him, yet she didn't care. Patrick thought back to all the times Annabel had flirted at parties, not caring if he was in plain sight of her. He had never called her on it. Maybe he was a fool, believing their marriage vows meant something, believing that Annabel loved him. But if he said something, confronted her, he ran the risk of losing her and he wasn't ready for that possibility. He didn't know if he would ever be.

One thing he did know was that Annabel liked games. Freedom only appealed to her when she was denied it. Life satisfied her only when she lived on the edge, when every second brought an element of danger.

"Dad? Dad?"

Patrick looked down at Adam. Despite all his doubts about their marriage, he and Annabel had created this incredible child. It was easy to believe that Adam made up for everything.

"What is it?"

"Aren't Uncle Rob and Uncle Larry in Hawaii?"

Patrick nodded. "Yes. I think that man just got it confused, that's all."

Adam looked at him, not convinced. Patrick wondered if it ever occurred to Annabel that her behavior might touch Adam. Did she ever think of how it would affect him, or what he might think of her if he knew what she was up to? Did she ever think of anything other than getting what she wanted, no matter what?

Patrick took Adam's hand and led him back to the picnic tables where a woman was doling out ice cream. Adam jammed his way into the crowd of children and happily took a bowl. He went straight to the hot fudge and drenched the ice cream with it.

Patrick sat down at a table away from the crowd. He could feel eyes on him and he didn't feel up to making excuses. He didn't know how far Annabel had gone. He had never let himself imagine anything past her harmless flirting, a quick brush of her hands across a strange man's shoulder, a drink, talk with no substance behind it. He was a man of science. He dealt in reality. Yet in this one area he hypothesized that if he didn't think about what he feared most, it simply wouldn't be. He could control the circumstances with his mind. He could set up a boundary and Annabel would not cross it.

He had watched her with Jesse. She had her eye on him, that much was certain. Just how much Sarah noticed, Patrick couldn't be sure, but Annabel was certainly not making a great effort to cover up her cat-and-mouse game. Whenever it got too bad, Patrick turned his head away and thought, *She loves me. She left Tom for me. She's my wife.* But when he turned back, Annabel was no more wifely than before.

Adam came up beside him and dived into his ice cream sundae. He had squirted a mound of whipped cream on top of the hot fudge and now he slurped it up. Patrick couldn't help smiling as he watched him.

"Mom will be back soon," Adam said, as if sensing his thoughts. "She's never gone too long."

Patrick nodded and looked away. It was true. Annabel was never gone too long. She always came back to them. But did that make up for leaving in the first place?

Annabel did not come back to the picnic until six o'clock that evening, when most everyone had gone home. Adam was tired and cranky and was not interested in any more of Patrick's games. He did not want to play on the swing or the slide or in the sandbox.

"I want to go home," he said, again and again. "I want Mom."

Patrick looked off in the distance and saw a dark shape taking form across the grass. He knew it was Annabel

even before she came into focus. She was swaying a little
and not rushing her steps.

"Mommy!" Adam said. He got up, his exhaustion forgotten, and ran across the field to meet her. She did not
open her arms when he got to her, but merely let him hug
her. They reached Patrick a few minutes later.

"I told her all about the races," Adam said. "And the
water balloons and the egg toss and the sundaes and . . ."

"Where have you been?" Patrick said. He felt the anger stirring in him, but he held it down.

"At the bar down the street." She slurred her words
only slightly.

"With your brother?"

Annabel raised her eyebrows and then laughed.

"Oh that," she said. "I just didn't want to start a scan-
dal with all you goody-goodies. It was just a man I met,
that's all. He offered to buy me a drink. But I couldn't say
that. You know how everyone gossips."

"Are you telling me all you did was drink with this
man for the past eight hours?"

Annabel looked him in the eye.

"Of course. And he didn't stay that long. There was no
harm done, Patrick. You had your kind of fun and I had
mine. Case closed."

She reached down for Adam's hand. Patrick thought
over his options. He could run up to her and slap her face
the way his hand longed to. Or he could shout at her, force
her with words to tell him the truth, the whole truth for
once. Or he could bottle up all his anger, take her word for
it, and go on as he always had, with a beautiful wife who
sometimes strayed, but who other times loved him magnif-
icently. He could close his eyes and see only what he
wanted to see. He could play the fool, especially in
Annabel's eyes. Because he knew that was what he was to
her, a fool she could lie to and cheat on without even an
inkling of guilt or fear or remorse.

Patrick took a step toward her. His hand ached and he
wanted to grab her, drag her down in the dirt, scream at
her that he was better than this. He wanted to let go for
once, tell her all that he'd been feeling, every emotion
she'd stirred in him, from ecstasy to fury to pain. He

wanted her to see that he was more than a scientist; he was a man, he could love and hate with the best of them.

But then Patrick saw her face, the eyes that would mock him if he said too much, felt too much. Again, as always, he stuffed his feelings down inside himself, and said nothing. This would blow over, like every other episode in their married life had blown over. He picked his jacket up off the table and they started for the car.

Annabel sat on her bed, painting her toenails a vivid shade of red. Adam had started first grade yesterday and the house was deliciously quiet. Annabel had walked him to school this morning, then come home and gotten back into her nightgown. She took a cup of coffee, the latest issue of *Vogue*, and her nail polish upstairs and turned on the radio. She looked at the clock; it was not quite nine yet. She had five and a half wonderful hours of solitude ahead of her.

She was on her middle toe when the doorbell invaded her private world. Annabel closed her eyes, willing the intruder away, but the bell kept ringing.

"Go away!" Annabel shouted.

"Annabel, it's me!"

Annabel closed her eyes. Sarah. Since that night she'd spoken to Jesse on the phone, being with Sarah had not been easy. On the one hand, she wanted to hear about their marriage, about Jesse, and whether or not her tale of Sarah's possible infidelity had had any effect on him. But on the other hand, Annabel could barely meet Sarah's eyes. Annabel would have to turn away and tune her out to stop the guilt from getting to her. She hadn't expected to feel it so strongly. That had never happened before.

"I'm busy, Sarah. Maybe later," Annabel shouted. It would be easier this way, to just avoid her. It was quiet for a moment and Annabel could visualize the tears puckering in Sarah's eyes. She was looking around, wondering what to do.

"Annabel, please!"

Annabel shoved the brush back in the nail polish bottle and sighed. She remembered now why she usually avoided friendships. They cut into her own time, they interrupted her life, they demanded so much emotion and energy. They made her feel things that she didn't want to feel.

Annabel stood up and walked down the stairs with her toes in the air. She reached the front door and opened it. As she had expected, Sarah was crying. Annabel looked around for Carolyn, but she was not there.

"I found a sitter," Sarah said. "I needed a break."

That, at least, was something.

"I guess you better come in," Annabel said. Sarah walked in and Annabel went back up the stairs. She crawled back up on the bed, looked over her toes, and decided she'd have to start over again. She picked up the nail polish remover, a few cotton balls, and wiped her toes clean.

Sarah hovered by the bedroom door. She played with the lint on her sweater. Annabel thought about helping her out, asking what was wrong, but she just didn't have it in her today. Sarah had no idea of the seesaw emotions she whipped up in her. She thought Annabel was one hundred percent on her side.

But she wasn't. Not anymore. They had been friends for over two years now. It was a record for Annabel, staying with someone, male or female, for that long. Patrick didn't count. He was a peripheral item; she forgot about him until he came home and reminded her they were married. The rest of the people in Annabel's life had come and gone on her schedule, coming in when they aroused her curiosity, and then exiting when she had tired of them.

Not Sarah. Sometimes Annabel desperately wanted her to go away, and other times she couldn't wait another second to be with her. Since that episode with Jesse, things had only gotten more confused.

She knew she had no right to her feelings for Sarah, not after what she'd done, so she tried to let them go. At times she was successful, especially when Jesse was around. Then, her priorities were very clear. Jesse was what mattered. All it took was one look at him to erase all traces of guilt from Annabel's soul. He was worth it. He gave her chills with his eyes. She could only imagine what his body could do to her.

At their weekly parties, Annabel concentrated less and

less on Sarah and more and more on Jesse. If anyone noticed, they didn't say anything. Sometimes Annabel thought she was the only one who ever noticed anything.

It was only at times like these, when it was just Annabel and Sarah, that there was any ambivalence. There would be a moment of friendship, a shared laugh, a confidence given, and then the next minute Annabel would be stealing away information on Jesse, in the hopes that she could use it to her advantage later. It was all too confusing. She was afraid she might betray herself, show both her hands.

So Annabel tried to avoid these situations as much as possible. She made up excuses for not being able to go out, or have Sarah over. If Sarah would just take the hint, Annabel was certain the guilt would release its hold on her.

Sarah ran her hands over her seven-months-pregnant stomach. She had bloated out all over, not just in her stomach, and she was quite unattractive. Poor Jesse, Annabel thought.

"I think my hormones are making me crazy," Sarah said finally. When Annabel said nothing, she walked to the edge of the bed and sat down. Annabel sighed, waiting for her weight to stop moving the bed so that she could continue with her toes.

"Everything Carolyn does makes me crazy and Jesse, well . . ."

Annabel looked up. "Jesse?"

"It's the same," Sarah said. "Not as bad as it was, but not any better."

"Did you ever figure out why?"

"No. Neither one of us said anything after that night. We pretended nothing had happened."

Annabel nodded and Sarah went on.

"He went crazy with his bike for a while, riding it over Highway 203 every night. Then it seemed as if he used up all his energy for that and he started getting more into football. He doesn't go out as much now, but he spends all his time reading the paper, looking over the stats. It's like he lives for Sundays."

Annabel smiled. "Football," she said.

"Yes, but not what you think. I could stand it if he just wanted to sit around all day Sunday and watch it, but he goes beyond that. He lives for it. He dreams it, I think."

Sarah looked out the window.

"First it was the bike," she said quietly. "Now it's this damn game. It's like he has to have something to hold on to."

Annabel did not raise her eyes as she spoke.

"Why not you?" she said.

She could sense, more than see, the tears in Sarah's eyes. It was strange. She sympathized like any friend would. A part of her felt what Sarah felt, was hurt because Sarah was hurt. She wanted to reach out, soothe her, tell her everything would be okay. Yet another part of Annabel wanted to smile and shout in triumph. She was both friend and enemy. She could see all the plays from both sides of the fence.

If she had been strictly evil, it would have been easier. She used to think she was. She walked away from an engagement with Tom at that party years ago and set her sights on Patrick. She had agreed to marry Tom because he was studying finance and she knew he would make a lot of money someday. But she wasn't passionate about him.

Strangely enough, she'd been passionate about Patrick. Financially, she knew he would also do well, but it was his black or white outlook, his rationality, his morality, that intrigued her. He was so drastically different from her that she couldn't resist him. His attempts to keep their relationship platonic, for Tom's sake, only set her mind on him more. She got him to marry her even though she knew they weren't suited to each other. And consequently, in the years since, she had cheated on him without a moment's hesitation.

Yes, she had been strictly evil then, but now there was something in her that hadn't been there before. Sarah, with her sad eyes and open arms, had sparked it, and Annabel hated her for that. She did not want this uneasiness inside her. She did not like knowing that she would go on doing the things she did in spite of the guilt or love Sarah inspired. She had been much happier when she was less aware of herself.

Sometimes it occurred to Annabel that not everyone was like this, so torn between good and evil; that, in fact, Sarah was not like this, or Patrick, or Jesse, or anyone she could think of. And that, actually, made her smile, because more than anything, Annabel wanted to be different.

"Have you ever thought that even though Patrick loves you, he's not in love with you anymore?" Sarah asked.

Annabel finished off the first coat on her toes and set the polish away. She leaned back against the pillows.

"No," she said. "If anything, I'd say Patrick was in love with me but he doesn't love me."

Sarah shook her head.

"Ever since that day when Jesse didn't come home until late, things have been different. There's been a distance between us. At first it was awful, but then Jesse started being Jesse again. He touched me again. He said he loved me again. But it was different. He looked at me differently, like I was the one who had changed."

"Maybe you did."

"No, of course not. That's the thing about me. I never change."

"Then Jesse did," Annabel said.

She held Sarah's eye for a moment, and in that moment, it was as if Annabel could not breathe, as if she were at the bottom of the ocean struggling for air. Her lungs contracted, there was a shooting pain through her chest, but then, just as quickly, it released her. Sarah looked away. The moment had passed when Annabel could have said something, made some gesture of condolence, or even come clean. She knew, sadly, that that was the last battle her conscience would wage. It was just no match for the rest of her.

"I fell in love with him because he was the antithesis of me," Sarah said quietly. "I think that was why he loved me too. But now it's all wrong. Lovers can be opposites, but spouses and parents should be similar. We're supposed to be a united front, but we're not anymore."

Annabel reached out, but then dropped her hand.

"You analyze too much," she said.

"I can't help it."

"You've got to help it. Stop it. If I thought things through as much as you do, Patrick and I would be divorced by now."

Sarah smiled.

"He loves you, though," she said.

"So? We're opposites too. We disagree on just about everything, but luckily he lets me have my way."

"I let Jesse have his."

"If you think about it," Annabel went on, grabbing the nail polish bottle again and starting on the second coat, "the ones who are similar are you and Patrick and me and Jesse. Maybe we married the wrong people."

She laughed and Sarah joined in, but Annabel's heart was racing. She looked up through her lashes at Sarah's face, but she saw no realization come over her, no real comprehension of Annabel's words.

"Oh Annabel," Sarah said. "You're such a kidder."

Annabel smiled and said nothing.

# 7

THEY SAT IN the back booth at the Foghorn, a steak and seafood restaurant down on the waterfront. Jesse and Sarah on one side, Annabel and Patrick on the other. Every five minutes or so, Sarah excused herself to go to the bathroom and they all laughed.

"I'm nine months pregnant," Sarah said, when she got up for the fifth time. "It's a wonder I can get up at all." She waddled slowly toward the rest room.

"She does that all night long," Jesse said. "And of course I've got to help her get out of bed, so I'm up all night with her."

Patrick laughed.

"When Annabel was pregnant, all she did was eat. Ice cream, chocolate eclairs, anything fatty. How much did you gain, honey? Fifty, sixty pounds?"

Annabel jabbed him in the ribs with her elbow and Jesse chuckled.

"No weight talk around the girls," he said. "It's illegal. How about those Redskins, though?"

"God, did you see that game?" Patrick asked. The waiter came and asked them if they wanted a bottle of wine and Annabel quickly picked one out. He brought it back and poured three full glasses, and then refilled Sarah's glass with water. Patrick went on about the last-second field goal that had won the game for the Redskins, but Jesse was not paying much attention. He was seated across from Annabel and it was easy to look at her without anyone noticing what he was doing. The place was dark and, after waiting at the bar for close to an hour until a table was ready, they were all, except for Sarah, well on their way to getting drunk.

Annabel had pulled the left side of her hair back with a clip, and the black curls flared out around it. Jesse's eyes were drawn to the place where her ear met her cheek. She had a freckle right beside her lobe.

"The Cowboys are coming on, though," Patrick said. Jesse nodded. Annabel lifted her wine glass to her lips, leaving an imprint of red there. Jesse raised his eyes to hers and found her looking at him. She smiled. He felt the barest of touches against his leg.

Sarah came back to the table.

"Sorry," she said.

"That's okay, babe," Jesse said. He was feeling indulgent toward her tonight. He always felt that way when Annabel was around, as if he were making up for something. "Let's order."

Jesse looked over the menu, but it was hard to concentrate when he had the warmth of Sarah on one side of him and the fire of Annabel across the table. He looked over at Patrick. He was studying the menu diligently, seemingly unaware of the undercurrents. Did he know how good he had it? A woman like Annabel whenever he wanted her. That hair falling all around him, that flat stomach, her scent enveloping him.

Sarah leaned closer to him as if sensing his thoughts and Jesse put his arm around her. He was not angry anymore, not the way he had been that night when she was supposedly with her man friend and he went out riding. He had taken the bike up to one hundred miles an hour. Then he flipped off the headlights and cut a black path through the trees. And all the while his mind was trying to picture Sarah with another man, but he could come up with no images to substantiate it.

He could barely talk to her during the following days. Sarah was crying all the time, trying to make it up to him.

She was always home when he called and got back from work. She never made excuses to try to get out of the house. If she was having an affair, she sure wasn't having a very good one. He could see that his bitterness was killing her.

The funny thing was, as the days passed and his rage started to ebb, Jesse found himself happier than he'd been in a long time. That night had been a turning point and he had walked away with more power than ever before. He had a right to things all of a sudden. There wasn't that burden anymore of having to be perfect, of playing by all the rules, of doing things the "right" way. Sarah had cut loose, so he could too.

At first he took nightly rides along the back roads. After seven or so, the highways to the mountains were empty and he savored the feeling of being the only man left on earth, with a road ahead of him that stretched on forever. Sometimes he took the turns at seventy miles an hour, but other times he wasn't in it for speed. He was in it for the blankness it gave him, the way he was absorbed into the motor, the wheels, the road, the trees, the sky. The sound of the engine penetrated his body until he could no longer hear it. The road became so familiar, he didn't see it. His hands melted into the handlebars until he could no longer feel them. And then, magically, it was as if he weren't even there, as if he had completely ceased to exist for an hour or two.

Then the guys at work got him interested in football. There was a pool every week, twenty-five cents per game and you got to pick the last numbers in the score. Jesse just had a knack for it, somehow. He won most of the money every week. He started reading the stat sheets in the paper, to get a better feel for it. He moved the television closer to the couch so he could flip between channels and games. He felt himself falling into it, the way he had fallen into his obsession with his bike, like it was a warm, moist hole that closed in behind him. It wasn't a sensation he wanted to stop. Sarah had Carolyn and soon this new baby and her man in the park, and Jesse had his bike and football. He didn't think he was being all that unfair.

Now, as he glanced over at his wife, that intense anger

he'd felt that one night was all gone. He wasn't sure what he believed. Maybe she had done it, maybe she hadn't. Maybe Annabel was crazy and had gotten the story all confused. The truth was, it didn't matter. What did matter was that there were no more illusions. Sarah wasn't a perfect wife and Jesse didn't even have to try to be a perfect husband. He could relax. He could make a few mistakes too.

He stretched his foot out under the table and ran it down Annabel's leg. He saw her stiffen and then slowly raise her eyes. They looked at each other. Jesse could not read her expression, but there was no doubt that her eyes reflected her desire for him. Here was a woman with no qualms. He had known that from the start. She didn't give a damn if she fucked up her marriage. Jesse thought she'd probably been fucking with it from the very beginning and Patrick just hadn't paid any attention. Jesse felt Annabel slip off her high-heeled shoe and then slide her stockinged foot up inside his pants leg. Still, she held his gaze. Jesse was hard as stone beneath the table.

"The prime rib looks good," Patrick said. Annabel finally turned to him, but she did not stop touching Jesse's leg. She managed, somehow, to slip her toes up beneath his knee and across the lower side of his thigh.

"Yes, and the shrimp."

Jesse had never felt anything like it. She was barely touching him, yet he wanted to explode. He grabbed Sarah's hand and pushed it down on himself. She jerked a little and she looked stunned, even rather afraid. Jesse smiled at her.

"You feel okay, babe?" he said. He pressed her hand down harder as Annabel's foot slid over his skin.

"Yes. Fine," she said. She tried to pull away, but he held her there. As Annabel lifted her leg, Jesse tried to calculate how close they were and what it must look like beneath the table, this mismatch of various arms and legs.

The waiter came back and asked them if they were ready to order. Sarah slipped her hand free and turned away from him. He could see the blush suffuse her neck and face and Jesse smiled. He looked over at Annabel again. She dropped her foot away, but still held his eyes.

Jesse gulped at his wine and imagined himself leaning across the table to kiss her, as if it were nothing. Something must have shown in his face because Annabel smiled.

"And you, madam?" the waiter asked her.

Annabel ordered and Sarah whispered in Jesse's ear.

"What was that all about?"

Jesse shrugged.

"I just want you, that's all. It's been a while."

He ordered a well-done steak and then sat back in the booth.

"Do you think the Rams have a chance?" he asked Patrick.

"What, are you kidding?"

Jesse noticed Sarah and Annabel looking at each other, but he could not read their expressions. Either Annabel was a hell of a pretender, or Sarah just wasn't opening her eyes. Still, Sarah was the one who kept up this friendship. She couldn't blame him for a little harmless flirtation when she was the one shoving Annabel in his face.

They walked out of the restaurant two hours later, everyone leaning on Sarah to hold them steady.

"What a bunch of boozers," she said and they all laughed.

"You're jus' jealous," Jesse said. Sarah was on the left of him and Annabel on the right. He couldn't tell whose hands were whose.

"Hey, where's Patty-Poo?"

They all laughed and then Patrick stuck his head out from the other side of Sarah.

"Here I am," he said.

Jesse doubled over, laughing. When he caught his breath, he pointed at him.

"You shouldn't be der . . . der-unk. You're a goddamn sci-tist."

Patrick was laughing too and between the two of them, they were practically pulling Sarah down. She slipped out of their grasp and they hooked up with each other, their arms around each other's necks.

"I love you, man," Jesse said.

"I love you too."

"Oh God," Annabel said, moving over to Sarah. "They love each other now."

Sarah laughed. She had drunk only water not only for the baby, but for herself. She didn't need a repeat of that night she'd spent running to the toilet. She and Annabel stayed where they were, watching Jesse and Patrick stumble down the street, still clinging to each other.

Annabel linked arms with Sarah and they started off after them. Annabel had put down as much as the men, but she still walked straight and spoke clearly.

"How can you drink so much and not get sick?" Sarah asked.

"Don't know. The genes, I guess. I feel it in my head, but not my body. I talk on and on like an idiot, but then, that's not much of a change." She laughed and then stopped abruptly. "Practically everyone on my mother's side is an alcoholic, you know."

"Really? Don't you worry about it happening to you?"

"No. There're other things to worry about."

The men were singing now, gathering stares from passersby.

"How embarrassing," Sarah said.

"Oh, let them be. They're just having fun. It's good to see Patrick cut loose. He's such an old fart."

Sarah giggled and clung tighter to Annabel as they came out beyond the warehouses and shops and the wet breeze off Puget Sound hit them square in the face.

"You're so much fun, Annabel," she said. "You make me smile."

Annabel stopped suddenly. She turned Sarah toward her.

"I'm an ass," she said.

"No, you're not. You're sweet and—"

"Oh Sarah, don't," she said. "You'll make me deny it and then the booze will set in and I'll say things I shouldn't."

"You're my best friend and I just want you to know—"

Annabel let go of her arm and looked away. There were tears in her eyes.

"What?" Sarah said. "What did I say?"

Annabel shook her head. She took a deep breath and then dried her eyes.

"Nothing. It's just the wine. Come on, let's catch up to the morons."

She started to walk away, but Sarah pulled her back.

"Why don't you believe in yourself?" she said. "You won't let me say nice things to you. You do that with Patrick too. You turn away whenever he tries to be kind."

"I'm not meant for kindness."

"You are. You're not just your looks, you know."

Annabel stared at her. Up ahead, Jesse and Patrick had stopped and were shouting at them to hurry up. Annabel lifted her hand to Sarah's cheek.

"I'm too drunk," she said, her eyes tearing again. "It makes me feel too much."

"Why is that so bad?"

"Because it makes me realize you're my friend." The tears slipped down Annabel's cheeks. She moved her hand to Sarah's chin and held it firmly.

"You watch out," Annabel said.

"For what?"

"For everything. Open your eyes wider. You're missing so much." Then she leaned forward and kissed Sarah on the mouth briefly before turning and running toward the men. Sarah watched her go. Both Patrick and Jesse opened their arms to catch her. Sarah felt her stomach turn as they both kissed her cheek.

Sarah walked slowly toward them. She tried not to dwell too much on Annabel's drunken words or the sight of Jesse's hand around Annabel's waist. Her eyes were open and she was not such a fool that she did not take these things in. But what she chose to believe was something different. And she chose to believe that Jesse loved her, that Annabel was her friend, that this baby would come soon and draw her family closer, that everything would be okay.

When she reached them, Jesse stopped a pair of tourists walking along the wharf. Jesse took the camera from Sarah's purse and asked them to snap a picture. They stood there for a moment, Sarah, Patrick, Annabel, and Jesse, before Jesse laughed.

"Oops," he said. "Wrong partners."

They quickly changed places and Jesse slipped his hand around Sarah's large waist and Patrick whispered something in Annabel's ear. The tourist snapped their picture and gave them back the camera.

Jesse was out on his bike somewhere when Sarah went into labor. It was different this time than it had been with Carolyn. One moment Sarah was fine, and the next the contractions came hard and fast and there wasn't time to breathe between them. Sarah crawled to the phone and called her doctor. Then she hung up and dialed Annabel's number.

"Annabel," she said. "It's here. You've got to help me."

Annabel and Patrick were over five minutes later. Sarah had slipped to the floor by the phone. There was water and blood all over her legs and the carpet. The pain was too intense for her to move anywhere. Carolyn was sitting in the corner, crying.

"It's okay, honey," Annabel said to Carolyn. "Adam's here to play with you." The little girl sparkled up as Adam came around the corner, his cache of toys in his arms. The two of them went up to Carolyn's room to play.

Patrick knelt down beside Sarah.

"Can you put your arms around my neck?" he said. Sarah nodded, but when she went to hold him, the pain gripped her again and she had to let go. Patrick pushed his arms beneath her and picked her up anyway. He swayed a little as he got to his feet, but then he got a firmer grip on her. He looked over at Annabel.

"You'd better stay here with the kids. I'll take her to the hospital."

Annabel nodded.

"Not to worry, Sarah," she said. "I've got it all under control. You'll be fine."

Patrick walked out to the car with Sarah in his arms.

"There's something wrong," Sarah said.

"Of course there isn't. Just try to relax." He set her down on the passenger side and then ran around and got in. He started the engine.

A contraction came on strong again, right on top of the last one. Sarah gripped the edges of the seat.

"It's not right," she said. "It's not."

Patrick whipped out of the driveway and drove quickly toward the hospital.

"Breathe, Sarah."

She tried to, but she couldn't catch her breath. It felt as if her body would explode with the pain. With Carolyn it had been painful, but nothing like this. She could feel the movement with Carolyn; she could understand the sense of the contractions. This was different. There did not seem to be the right amount of weight bearing down on her.

"Oh God, Patrick," she said, every muscle in her stomach and back cramping. Patrick looked over at her and then pressed all the way down on the gas. In five more minutes, they were at the hospital.

Sarah tried to step out of the car, but her legs buckled. Once again, Patrick slipped his arms around her and picked her up. He moved as fast as he could into the emergency room. The nurse there took one look at Sarah and called for a wheelchair.

"Come on, let's go," she said.

She wheeled Sarah toward the elevator, a clipboard in her hands.

"You are?"

"Sarah Bean," she said through clenched teeth. "I already called Dr. Jacoby. He's on his way. We filled out all the forms last week."

The nurse nodded. They went into the elevator and the nurse hit the third-floor button. She looked over at Patrick.

"Mr. Bean, you can wait upstairs. We'll keep you informed every half hour or so, maybe more."

Patrick looked down at Sarah. He didn't correct the nurse. He took Sarah's hand and she held on to him tightly as another contraction came on.

The doors opened and the nurse hurried them toward the delivery room. Just before they wheeled Sarah away, Patrick bent down to her.

"It'll be fine. I'm right here."

Sarah tried to smile and then was gone.

• • •

Jesse got home three hours later. He hadn't ridden like that for weeks and the fresh air had done him good. He parked his bike in the driveway and walked in the door.

He was assaulted at first by noise, and then by alien smells. The radio was on loud to a rock station and he could hear shouting coming from upstairs. Then the strong aroma of garlic tickled his nose and he went around to the kitchen.

Annabel was at the stove, stirring some kind of pasta sauce. For a moment, Jesse thought he was walking in on some kind of dream, playing out a fantasy he'd surely held in his mind. But then Annabel turned toward him, her face hard and angry, and he knew it was real. She walked past him and turned off the stereo.

"What's going on? Where's Sarah?" Jesse said.

Annabel turned back toward him, her hands on her hips.

"You do realize your wife is nine months pregnant, don't you?" she said.

Jesse's heart stopped. He took a step toward her.

"She went into labor?"

"Yes. And not a very good one. The baby was breech."

"Oh God," Jesse said, taking another step toward Annabel, then back toward the door, then back toward Annabel again. "Is she all right?"

"The doctor thinks so. Patrick just called. They struggled with it for an hour or so and then they had to do a cesarean. There were complications."

"Oh God . . ."

"The baby wouldn't come down. She started to hemorrhage. They had to make some choices. Whether to get the baby out or stop the bleeding."

Jesse snapped out of his daze and grabbed Annabel's arm.

"How is she?"

"Alive," she said, glaring at him. "She kept screaming at them to take the baby first. She lost a lot of blood. Patrick was there. They thought he was you and they were worried she would die and he should be with her.

He said it was the most horrible thing he'd ever seen in his life, all the blood and her screaming and clinging to him."

Annabel related all of this calmly, as if it were just a news item in the paper, but her eyes were red and angry. Jesse looked away from her.

"You should have been there," she said.

Jesse nodded.

"Your wife almost died and where the hell were you? Out riding your damn motorcycle. Do you know what a selfish bastard you are? Sarah lets you get away with it, but not me."

He turned back to her and gripped her arm again.

"She's my wife," he said.

"She's my best friend."

Jesse watched her. There was no hint of insincerity. She was not pretending. Was this the real Annabel then? Or was the real one the woman who touched him whenever Sarah had her eyes turned?

"I have to go," he said, walking toward the door.

"She's sleeping," she said. "Patrick's with her."

"She's my wife," he said again, as if it needed repeating. "What about the baby?"

"A boy."

Jesse nodded. He turned the knob on the front door. There were tears in his eyes when he turned to look back at Annabel.

"I love her, you know."

Annabel bowed her head. "I know."

Jesse walked past the nursery first. Baby Boy Bean was in the front, sleeping. Jesse looked at him and could feel nothing but resentment. This child he hadn't even wanted had almost taken Sarah from him. He turned away.

He walked to Sarah's room and opened the door. The light was off. He stumbled toward the bed and then felt a hand reach out and grip him.

"Jesse?"

It was Patrick's voice.

"Yes, it's me."

Patrick stood up and pushed him back toward the hallway. They went outside into the light.

Jesse looked at him. There were dark circles under his eyes and his hair was mussed. His glasses sat at an awkward angle on his nose.

"How is she?" Jesse asked.

"Sleeping. The hemorrhaging made her weak and then, of course, all of the drugs they had to use to stabilize her . . ." Patrick ran his hand through his hair and looked away.

"How did she handle it?"

"Mentally, great. You should have been there. The doctors wanted to focus on her first, but she wouldn't let them. She wanted that baby. More than anything in the world she wanted that baby."

Jesse closed his eyes.

"Physically though, it was a trauma to her body," Patrick went on. "The doctor said she'll be sore for a while. It was like she went through fifteen rounds with a heavyweight. She's weak as hell. And, of course, there's that gash in her stomach."

Jesse tried to smile, but it was no good. Everything felt strange, turned around. He knew he should be grateful, but all he could feel was this overpowering resentment. These were things Patrick should not know.

"I was there, you know," Patrick said. "When they took the baby out. They thought I was you and Sarah said she wanted me. It was incredible."

Jesse looked away. He clenched his fists.

"Just as long as she's okay," he said.

"She's tough. You married one hell of a lady."

Jesse finally looked up at him. He resisted the urge to punch that admiration out of his eyes. Instead, he merely said, "Thank you."

"You want me to stay?" Patrick said.

"Of course not," Jesse said, too quickly. All he wanted was to get into that room, hold Sarah's hand, let her know that he was there.

"Okay. Just wondering."

Patrick turned and started down the hall.

"Hey," Jesse said. "Did she ask for me?"

Patrick turned around. He took off his glasses and wiped the sweat out of his eyes.

"It all happened so fast and she was pretty out of it, Jesse. With all the pain . . ."

He let the words trail off and Jesse nodded. He turned and walked into his wife's room.

# 8

❧

PATRICK PUT THE cell slide under the microscope. He was looking for any sign of abnormality, any hint of malignancy in the otherwise healthy cells of a high-risk female. The subject's mother, sister, and cousins had all developed breast cancer. She herself was thirty-five, childless, ripe for developing it herself.

Patrick closed one eye and focused in on the tissue. He did not see the black-topped benches all around the room or the plastic racks filled with test tubes on top of them. The see-through glass shelves, with their bottles and jars and Reynolds Wrap disappeared. He tuned out the hum of the refrigerator, and did not smile at the cartoon on top of it which read, "After decades of research, the doctors find the cause of cancer is the rats themselves!"

Patrick tuned out the music someone was playing in the lab across the hall, the graduate students shuffling around him. Even, for a moment, his own thoughts. He became only a mind and an eye hoping once again for that breakthrough, that sign. But he knew, as soon as he began looking, that it wasn't to be. Everything was as it should be. There was nothing to differentiate this cell from that of any other woman less prone to breast cancer.

Patrick slid his chair back and closed his eyes. His assistants quieted as they walked around him, thinking he was asleep. A moment later he heard the door close and all was silent. He opened his eyes.

It was one-thirty in the afternoon and he was alone. He'd been studying a whole cache of these cells since eight this morning. He hadn't really expected to find anything. He had more sophisticated tests to run. But when things got stuck, the way they were now, the way they were almost every day, he liked to go back to the basics, start at the beginning. It was entirely possible that something had been overlooked.

A classical genetic molecular biologist. That was the title on the door. He'd gotten his PhD in molecular biology seven years ago, at the age of twenty-four. He'd been here, at the University of Washington, characterizing the nature of normal cells and cancer cells since then. For the first few years, when he was accumulating data, learning things for himself, he thought he was getting somewhere, making progress. But now, as he looked around him, he realized that he was really no further along than when he started. He wasn't even a baby-step closer to finding out what made cancer tick.

It was only a small relief to him that the grant for this project had been extended. Of course, if it hadn't been, it would have meant he was out of a job. But he was certain he could have found something at another university. Cancer scientists were few and far between. He even had a dream, albeit a farfetched one, of working under Michael Potter at the National Cancer Institute, or Robert Weinberg over at MIT.

The money was just a small relief because it was only the work that mattered. So many of his colleagues worked at their own pace, or rushed to get published before someone else beat them to it. It was all about politics and tenure and notoriety. But for Patrick, it was about lives. It was about his own mother, who had died of ovarian cancer at forty-six and who never got to see her grandson. He had watched her waste away. That was back before they even attempted to stave off death with radiation and chemotherapy. His mother had sat in bed every day, listening to Patrick read to her, smiling and saying she was fine, just fine, even though she could barely hold her head up, or reach to the nightstand for a glass of water. Then one morning, after his father left for work, Patrick went into her room and found vomit all over her nightgown and his mother dead. That last image, the indignity of her death, still haunted him. She had been such a proud and vital woman, before the cancer.

This job was not about the money he made. It was about all the men and women who were going along just fine, thinking they had years left to play out, when suddenly the rug was pulled out from under them. It only took a second for a doctor to say, "You have cancer. There's not much we can do."

Patrick had seen people go from healthy to dead in less than four months. He'd seen the misery of chemotherapy and radiation treatment torture a man for years. He'd seen it all, and he wanted it all stopped.

Patrick rubbed his eyes. He could not admit to himself that he was not getting anywhere. There had to be some other avenue he hadn't explored yet. This last grant was given for the study of high-risk but healthy cells. Was there something inherently different in high-risk people that might trigger the onset of cancer? A precancerous cell amid the healthy ones, perhaps? A lower level of white blood cells? Benign tumors that might turn malignant later on? An unusual intolerance of sunshine or saccharin or smog or some chemical? For three of his seven years here, Patrick had been studying this question. He had stacks of research. He dreamed experiments, new approaches. He had long ago stopped wishing that his dreams might focus on something other than his work. He would have liked to dream about Annabel or Adam, but when he closed his eyes, it was always science that dominated his subconscious, that stole his mind until the dawn.

Patrick stood up suddenly and walked to the phone. His mind had bottomed out. Too much concentration and he couldn't think anymore. He started to dial his home number, but then he hung up the phone and started over. It rang only twice before she picked up.

"Sarah?" he said.

"Patrick, it's you. I swear, you're more concerned about me than Jesse is."

Sarah laughed and Patrick smiled.

"Not just you. It's my job to look out for my godson. How is Sam?"

"Loud," Sarah said. "He can move mountains with those screams of his. He's making up for Carolyn being such a good baby."

"Walking yet?"

"Patrick, please. Give the boy a break. He's only five months old."

"Don't put those kinds of restrictions on my Sam. That kid's a doer. An original. You'll see. He'll be a noncon-formist."

Sarah was laughing and the pressure behind Patrick's eyes lifted. Ever since that night in the hospital, Patrick had felt that it was his responsibility to watch out for Sarah, to cheer her up. Their bond was formed in an instant, when she gripped his hand through her convulsions, when she looked up at him before she lost consciousness and said, "Patrick. You're here." He had held her hand tighter and said, "Of course I am. I'll always be here." And he had meant it.

He called her at least once a week, to see how she was doing, how Sam was. Jesse could only do so much and Patrick was the only one who knew exactly how much Sarah went through to have Sam.

But she had healed quickly. She was ecstatic to have a healthy boy. Patrick found that it hardly took any effort at all to make her laugh. With Annabel, it was always a struggle. She had a more sophisticated sense of humor. Her own jokes were sarcastic, often biting. She was not amused by the little things that happened to him during the day, or gossip he'd overheard in the hallways.

But Sarah was. It took so little to make her happy. Talking became as much a pleasure for Patrick as it was for her, and he realized that he had stopped calling for her welfare, and was doing it for his own.

"What are you up to?" Sarah asked.

Patrick leaned against the wall of the lab and looked around. He felt more at home here than anywhere. Yet sometimes he hated the work tables, the microscopes, the warm rooms, the gene schematics and plasmid drawings on the walls. Everything offered so much hope in the beginning, but then day by day, with inconclusive or even outright refutable data, all his hunches and dreams died.

"The usual," he said.

"Patrick, tell me."

Patrick smiled. It was so strange to hear those words. *Patrick, tell me.* Annabel did not pry. She did not push to get to the heart of him. If he said, "The usual," she took him at his word. Patrick wondered what it must be like for Jesse to have Sarah so interested in his life. Did he welcome it or bristle at her questions? Patrick got the feeling that he bristled, that he did not enjoy exposing himself in any way.

"It's just that I'm not getting anywhere," he said. "I've always thought I was on the right side. It seemed like the secret of cancer had to rest in the genes. What else would explain why it runs in families?"

"And now you're not so sure?"

"Hell no. Maybe the virologists over at MIT and NCI have it right. They take everything down to the dish, break something as complex as cancer down to a single virus. But at least they're getting somewhere. They've got results."

"You get results too. Your work helps theirs."

"Does it? Sometimes I'm not sure. It's frustrating as hell. I've followed every hunch. I've analyzed every bit of data. And we're no better off than when we started. We still know that people are prone to cancer, that it runs in families. But I have no idea why. I can't pinpoint it."

Sarah was quiet for a moment.

"And that's your job, to pinpoint it?" she said finally.

"Yes."

"And what happens if you find that out? What if one day you find this one cell or chromosome that is the cause of cancer? Then what do you do?"

Patrick stopped for a second.

"Then we study it," he said quietly. "We learn where it comes from. We try to learn how to prevent it from causing cancer."

"But what if you can't? What if it's just there? What if it's not something you can remove or fix?"

"Sarah, what are you saying?" Patrick said, rubbing his head.

"I don't know, really. Except that I realize how personal this research is to you. And I think that maybe you're on the wrong end of it. You're killing yourself looking for causes instead of for cures."

Patrick was dumbstruck for a moment. Since that day seven years ago when he walked out of the classroom and into this laboratory, he'd done nothing but study the causes of cancer. It had never occurred to him to do anything else. It had never occurred to him that there was anything else to do.

"Patrick? Patrick?" Sarah was saying.

"I'm here."

"I'm so sorry. I shouldn't have said that."

"Yes you should have. If you meant it."

"But it came out wrong. I don't think what you're doing is insignificant. My God, people are alive today because of men like you. You devote your whole life to making other people well. All I meant to say was that for you to be happy, maybe you should focus on another angle, so that you might get better results. Or at least feel like you're in the thick of the battle and not on the fringes."

It was amazing how quiet it was all of a sudden. As if his ears had turned inward, and all he could hear was the stillness of his mind. Patrick stood up straight. He felt a long-repressed but familiar energy burn through his body. It was the same excitement he'd felt in the middle of a lecture, when a professor mentioned some theory that had yet to be explored completely. Or when he was studying for a test and the answers came easily to him, and he realized that he had, at last, absorbed the information instead of just momentarily memorizing it. Or when he first got his hands on the equipment in the lab and he thought, *My God, I can make a difference, if not for my mother than for somebody. I can do something.*

"Oh Sarah," he said, because there didn't seem to be anything else to say. She was quiet, yet he felt as if she were standing next to him, offering him support. "You understand. You're the only one who does."

"Annabel does too," she said, loyal till the end. "She might not express it, but she believes in you."

Patrick bit back a retort. Love did not blind him. Every day, he wished for a show of support from Annabel, and every day he was disappointed.

"I have to go," he said. "I didn't mean to burden you with my problems."

"It's not a burden. I like to hear about it. Jesse doesn't like to talk about work and all I've got to talk about are the kids."

"Now you're the one who sounds down."

She laughed, but not very convincingly. "No, just tired. I keep promising myself that I'll get out of the house and do something, but then the time comes and I'm too exhausted."

"It will get better."

"Someday," Sarah said.

This was when Patrick hated the phone. He wanted to reach out, comfort her, but he was prevented from doing so by the distance that separated them.

"I'm sorry, Sarah," he said.

"Don't be. There's nothing to be sorry for. This is what I wanted. Two kids. A boy and a girl. I just need to adjust, that's all."

"I'll call you again soon," Patrick said.

"I know you will. Goodbye."

Patrick looked around the lab again. He thought of what he'd been doing, the good, hard, important work. And then he thought of what he might do. There was even less of a chance of succeeding in the search for a cure than there was in the search for a cause. But then he thought about how much more it would mean if he did succeed. And how good it would feel to come to the lab every day, hungry for answers and fresh with new hope.

Annabel slipped downstairs while Patrick was in the shower. She glanced at the clock as she went by, saw that it was twelve-thirty in the afternoon, and then quickly looked away. She opened the cupboard above the sink.

"Mom, what are you doing?"

Annabel slammed the cupboard shut and whirled around. Adam stood right behind her.

"Nothing. Getting ready for the party. That's all."

"Oh. Can I bring my Hot Rods?"

"No, Adam. It's Carolyn's party. I'm sure Aunt Sarah will have lots of fun games for you to play."

"It's gonna be stupid," Adam said, stomping to the table and sitting down. "Carolyn's just a baby."

"I thought you liked Carolyn."

"Not anymore. All she ever wants to do is play with her stupid dolls. I'm in first grade now, Mom."

Annabel smiled and looked away.

"Of course. I'd forgotten you're all grown up now."

Annabel looked back once more at the cupboard and then went to her son.

"Well, maybe you could help the little kids with the games. You wouldn't actually have to play them. You could be the emcee."

"What's an emcee?"

"A leader. You'll be the one who runs the show."

Adam smiled and jumped off the chair.

"Sounds good. Where's Dad?"

"Taking a shower. We'll go as soon as he's ready. Why don't you go upstairs and play until then."

Adam turned and ran upstairs and Annabel waited until his footsteps stopped above her. She listened for the shower. It was still on. She hurried back to the cupboard and took out the bottle. She wasn't sure if she had time to get out a glass, so she just unscrewed it and took a long swallow. It burned her throat, but then it warmed her stomach, going down. She listened again, and then took another gulp. She screwed the cap back on and put it away.

She gripped the edge of the counter and smiled. Patrick didn't like to see her drink before a "respectable" hour, but what did he know? She needed a little help if she was going to get through a three-year-old's birthday party. And it wasn't like she was getting drunk. She just needed a little push, a little sip of whiskey to warm her bones.

Her rationalizations made, Annabel opened her purse and took out the mouth spray. She squeezed the trigger a couple of times and the whiskey was masked with mint. She walked to the bathroom and looked in the mirror.

She had left all of her hair down, and now that she had been growing it out, it fell a quarter of the way down her back. She'd rimmed her hazel eyes with black eyeliner and put on dark red lipstick. She was wearing a low-cut sweater and body-hugging skirt. She was not at all dressed for a child's birthday party, but then again, that was not the reason she was attending.

All that mattered was that Jesse would be there. Sarah had been too worn out looking after both Sam and Carolyn to get together. The four of them hadn't had dinner for close to a month now. Annabel was surprised by how much she missed talking to Sarah, but she was stunned by how starved she was for the sight of Jesse. She missed grazing his arm as she walked past. She missed smiling at him across the table. She missed feeling his eyes on her.

She missed their games. She wanted them back and then some. Patrick was calling Sarah all the time now, as if they were best friends. "I'm the godfather," he'd say when Annabel questioned him about it. He must think she was an idiot. No way were they talking about Sam for half an hour. When Patrick called Sarah in the evening, Annabel could hear his laughter coming from the den like blades slicing straight through her ears.

Annabel said nothing, though. She didn't complain. She never once acted jealous. She simply took it all in, packed the resentment into one compartment, and turned her attention to Jesse. If Patrick had no qualms calling Sarah, then why should Annabel hesitate pushing her flirtations a little further? The boundaries between the four of them were getting hazier all the time. She doubted that anyone would even notice if she crossed them.

The shower stopped and Patrick called down to her.

"Be ready in ten minutes."

Annabel walked back to the cupboard and took out the bottle again. One more swallow. A little extra courage never hurt anybody.

Sarah walked up and down the table, adding scoops of ice cream, refereeing fights, drying tears. She got to Carolyn, at the end, and saw that her new party dress was already ruined. There were chocolate ice cream and punch stains all down the front of it.

Sarah heard Sam crying in the other room. She waited for the sound to stop, for Jesse or Annabel to take care of him, but no one comforted him. Sarah stood up straight.

"I'll be right back," she said to the dozen or so children around the table. "Adam, will you watch everyone for me?"

Adam, at the other end of the table, stood up and smiled.

"I'll be the demcee," he said.

"Yes, you be the demcee."

Sarah walked into the living room. Sam was in his playpen, screaming at the top of his lungs. Sarah picked him up and felt his hot tears against her shoulder. Where was Jesse? And Annabel? Why wouldn't anyone help her?

The front door opened then and Patrick walked in.

"Sorry it took so long," he said, racing in with a grocery bag. "I got everything you asked for. More chocolate ice cream and a new pin-the-tail-on-the-donkey board. I'm sorry Adam ruined the first one."

Sarah shook her head. Sam was finally quieting and now it was Sarah's tears that started up. This party was a disaster from the very beginning. She'd been falling asleep when she wrote out the invitations last week and she messed up the dates. Two of Carolyn's friends showed up yesterday. Then Jesse had to work overtime this morning, so he wasn't around to help her set up. She got up only half of the balloons and streamers before the waves of children showed up. Sarah had expected that at least some of the mothers would stay around to help, but not one did. They all dropped their prettily dressed children off with a smile that said "If you let one drop of cake stain this outfit, I'll sue."

Annabel and Patrick arrived on time, but Annabel was in no mood to play with a dozen children. She wandered through the house, asking too many times when Jesse would be home. Patrick and Adam were Sarah's only salvation. Patrick lined the kids up for pin-the-tail-on-the-donkey and didn't even flinch when Adam tried to put the donkey poster up on the wall himself and ended up ripping it.

It was Patrick who suggested they do things backward.

"Give them food first and then we'll play the games. I'll be back from the store in ten minutes."

He kissed her cheek and was gone. Jesse got home five minutes later and, after waving hello to the kids, promptly disappeared with Annabel. Sarah was going to kill him. Just as soon as she found him, she was going to kill him.

Patrick looked down at her.

"It's not that bad," he said. "I've had worse parties."

Sarah smiled.

"You have?"

"Sure. On my twenty-seventh birthday, Annabel decided I was an old man and needed some revitalizing. She invited all my friends from the university and then hired a stripper."

"Oh no!"

"Oh yes. You should have seen the looks on their faces. And Annabel just walked around smiling, as though we did this sort of thing all the time."

They walked into the kitchen, laughing.

"Where is Annabel, by the way?" he said.

Sarah put the ice cream away.

"With Jesse somewhere. They disappeared as soon as Jesse got home. I guess they're not interested in a kiddie party."

Patrick looked through the door to the dining room. The kids were still eating the ice cream. Adam was walking around the table like an army sergeant.

"That was not very nice," he said.

"Well, Jesse will tell me that this was my idea and he never asked to be involved anyway."

Patrick took the donkey poster out of the bag.

"I'll hang it up this time."

He started to walk out of the room, but Sarah caught his arm.

"Thanks, Patrick. I don't know what I'd do without you."

He smiled and walked into the dining room.

"Hey kids, look what I've got!"

They all cheered and followed him outside.

Jesse and Annabel turned the corner and walked down a block of recently built tract homes.

"I hate them," Jesse said. "You can't tell one from the other."

Annabel looked them over. "Yes, but there's something comforting about the nice lawns, the way everything's so well tended. In our neighborhood, it's one way or the other. Either the owners totally remodel and make it sparkling, or they let it go to pot."

"Our neighborhood's got character," Jesse said.

They had been walking for fifteen minutes. When Jesse got home from work, he took one look at the parade of messy children in the house and grabbed Annabel's hand and led her outside. He had intended only to get a breath of fresh air, but when Annabel started walking, he followed.

The sun was out, but the late fall air was still cold. Jesse looked over at Annabel, shivering in her low-cut sweater.

"You shouldn't have worn that," he said.

"I know."

Jesse looked around once—no one in this neighborhood knew them—and then slipped his arm around her shoulder. She snuggled next to him.

"Thanks."

Jesse could feel every curve of her. Her breast was pressed against his chest. Her leg brushed his as she walked.

"Sarah's probably pissed," he said.

Annabel laughed. "She'll get over it. Besides, Patrick the knight will save her."

Jesse looked at her.

"Have you noticed they've been talking to each other a lot?"

"Of course. Patrick calls her from work. And sometimes at night. He's too honest not to tell me. He says he's just looking out for Sam, as though he feels responsible for him."

They were quiet and Annabel pressed herself closer to Jesse. He dropped his hand a little on her shoulder. An inch or two further and he could touch the silky skin of her breast.

"Do you love him?" he asked.

Annabel stopped suddenly and Jesse dropped his hand. She turned and stared at him.

"What do you think?"

Her eyes challenged him and Jesse took a step closer to her.

"I think you don't give a fuck about him. Maybe you did when you married him, but it didn't last long. Now it's me you're after."

Annabel tossed back her black hair and laughed.

"God, what an ego. You think a little harmless flirting means I'm hot for you. No wonder Sarah needed a change of pace."

Jesse grabbed her face in one hand and squeezed. He watched tears come to her eyes as he increased the pressure on her jaw, but she didn't cry out. He was only inches from her when he spoke.

"Sarah did not cheat on me," he said. "You got the story wrong."

He pushed her away and started walking back toward the house. Annabel took a deep breath and came after him.

"What Sarah did or didn't do isn't the point," she said, when she reached him. "She's not the one who's unhappy."

Jesse glanced at her, but kept walking.

"You're saying I am?"

"It's obvious, Jesse. Little Miss Perfect Sarah isn't all that exciting. Especially for a man like you. I'll bet that's why you have to ride your Harley all the time. To replace all the passion you gave up when you married her."

Jesse looked up over the houses, to the silhouette of Mount Rainier in the distance.

"I sold the bike," he said. "Two weeks ago."

"My God, why?"

Jesse stopped again.

"Because Sarah asked me to. And because, no matter what you think, I love her."

They stared at each other for a long time. The wind was cool and Jesse watched the gooseflesh prickle Annabel's skin. He didn't know who he was trying to convince more, Annabel or himself.

"I think we should go back," Jesse said.

Annabel nodded. "Of course. You certainly don't want to make little Sarah mad. You've got to be the dutiful husband. If Sarah says sell your bike, you sell your bike. If she wants you to entertain twelve kids like a clown, then you do it. If—"

Jesse grabbed her, only intending to shut her up. But when he looked down at her, he knew she had won. She had been whittling away at him from the very beginning. She had made him doubt himself, and Sarah, and everything he thought he should be. He grabbed her hair and tilted her head back. She slid her hands up around his neck. Her fingers were cool and silky.

Later, he would look back and try to convince himself that she was the one who initiated the kiss. That she pulled his head down and pressed her red lips to his. But at the time it was all blurred. Maybe she initiated it, maybe he did. All he knew was that he was finally touching her, kissing her, his tongue was in her mouth and it felt better than he'd ever imagined. He ran his fingers through her hair, the yards of it, the curls. He swam in her smell, nothing like the flowery scents of Sarah, but something muskier, sultrier. He felt as if he were drowning in it.

He pressed himself against her hard. He could feel her teeth against his, her bones jamming into him. It was as if he wanted to take her into himself, swallow her up completely. Yet she wanted to do the same to him and they were fighting for superiority. Jesse had never had to fight for anything with Sarah. She gave in without argument. Everything was different with Annabel. It was intoxicating, dizzying, being with her.

He slipped his hands down her back, up under her sweater, to her skin. He sighed and then worked them into her skirt and down over her butt. And still, always, he was kissing her, she was kissing him. Her hands were as wild as his, exploring him quickly, demandingly, trying to get it all in in one shot.

Finally, breathlessly, they pulled apart. Annabel's hair was wild around her face. Her lipstick was gone; her lips bruised red. She pulled down her sweater. Jesse wiped the lipstick from his mouth. He looked around, to see if anyone had been watching, but he noticed no one.

He looked back at her. He was dazed. Later he would understand all the repercussions of that kiss, but for now he could only look at her and marvel at the ecstasy of being on the verge of discovering a new woman, with curves he'd never touched, passions he hadn't even tapped. He could not feel guilt or regret when his heart was beating so fast, when the scent of her still lingered on him. He could not think at all of Sarah; it was as if Annabel had the power to make her disappear.

"Come on," she said, taking his hand and leading him back toward the house. He followed her like a man without any will. He kept looking down at their hands, her white one, his darker. Even the bones in her fingers were different, exotic. He lifted her hand up to his mouth and kissed it.

She smiled and then disengaged their hands as they came around the corner onto Jesse's street. She ran her fingers through her hair, fixing it. She looked over Jesse, wiped one last smudge of lipstick from his mouth and straightened his shirt. Then she tilted her head back and smiled.

"Shall we go in?" she said.

Jesse wanted to hold her back, kiss her again, but the curtains were pulled back in the house and someone might see. He nodded and followed her inside.

# 9

JESSE WAS WORKING late, the kids were asleep, and, not for the first time, Sarah was lonely. She wandered around the house, trying to find something to do. She had cleaned earlier that day and there were no specks of dust to interest her. She picked up the novel she'd been reading, but it hadn't yet caught her attention. She flipped through the *TV Guide*, but there was nothing on but a parade of silly sitcoms and depressing dramas.

She tried not to dwell on the fact that this was her life now. Competition was heating up in Jesse's office, as it was everywhere. The economy had taken a nosedive, recession was the latest buzzword, and, in Jesse's department, the ranks of salesmen had been thinned out. Everyone was trying to prove he was indispensable to the company, to nab those few commissions left.

Jesse stayed late and worked on the weekends, anything to get a jump on the other guys. Too many nights lately, Sarah wandered around the house, bored, without anyone to talk to or anything to do. Jesse had sold his bike, but he filled the time he used to spend riding it either with work at the office or football games. Sarah felt better about his safety, but beyond that, nothing had changed. She was still alone.

She moved the wedding photo of her and Jesse back a

quarter inch on the shelf. She ran her finger over Jesse's face, down his blond hair that was longer back then, resting on his shoulders. He had a reserved smile on his face, what he thought a married man should look like. That was the thing about Jesse; he had all these set ideas about what things should be like instead of just letting them be.

Sarah turned away and walked to the phone. She dialed Jesse's number at work. He answered on the second ring.

"Jesse Bean."

"Hi, it's me."

He hesitated for a moment and Sarah gripped the phone tighter.

"How late is it?" he said.

Sarah glanced at the clock. "Ten to nine."

"I told you I wouldn't be home until ten. Is there a problem?"

Sarah sat down on the chair beside the phone.

"No. I was just lonely. I miss you."

"I miss you too, babe, but I've got to get this report out by tomorrow morning. The longer we talk, the later I'll be here."

Sarah blinked back tears. If Jesse's work was his passion, the way Patrick's was, Sarah might have understood why he put it ahead of her. But the truth was that Jesse hated his work. He hadn't actively pursued his job. He certainly never dreamed of being a salesman when he was younger. He just fell into it. A friend told him about the opening, Jesse applied, got the job, and they moved out here. Sales was not his life's work. Jesse still didn't know what he wanted to be when he grew up. Sarah wasn't sure if he wanted to be anything.

The job was just something he did because he was supposed to and he had to pay the bills. Every morning, he stepped out of bed and said, "Another goddamn day."

So when he chose work over her, it was as though he placed her at the very bottom of the bucket, beneath the scum that he hated. She'd always thought she would be first with him. It was amazing, really, that she'd gotten things so wrong.

"Of course," she said. "I'll let you go."

"Don't wait up," Jesse said. "I might be later than ten."

Sarah hung up and dropped her head in her hands. She cried until her tears ran out and her stomach hurt. Then she raised her head and looked around her house. It was all she had hoped for, yet it meant so little when Jesse was not here. During the day, with the kids, she could pretend everything was fine. She played with them, cooked their meals, acted like any other wife and mother. But at night, with the silence of the house enveloping her, things were different. The loneliness of her life couldn't be denied.

Sarah turned back to the phone and dialed another number. Sometimes he stayed late too, working on a new culture or experiment. Sarah tried not to be too hopeful, yet she still sighed in relief when he answered the phone.

"This is Patrick Meyers," he said.

"It's Sarah," she said, and then burst into tears again. She barely heard Patrick's voice on the other end, trying to soothe her, telling her everything would be okay.

"I'm sorry," she said finally, when she had calmed herself. "I didn't mean to do that."

"It's all right. You needed to."

"It's all I do now, it seems."

"You're tired," he said. "Two kids in the house all day can wear anybody out."

Sarah wiped away her tears.

"I understand that. But there's more to it. I feel like there's no reason for me to be here."

"Of course there is. What about taking care of the kids?"

"That's different. I'm talking about me personally. Does my life matter? What do I contribute on my own, just as Sarah?"

Patrick was quiet for a long time. Sarah thought about how easy it was for them to talk now, how they had dropped the usual pleasantries months ago and were able to get right to the point. It was the kind of relationship Sarah used to have with Annabel. But since Sam was born, Sarah hadn't been up to socializing very much. The most she could accomplish were these phone calls, with Patrick.

"Maybe you need to do something," he said. "I realize it would be impossible for you to get a job now, but you could at least plan something for when the kids are in school. What is it you want to do?"

Sarah rested her head against the wall.

"Teach," she said simply. It was all she'd ever wanted. It wasn't very creative or awe-inspiring, but it excited her. It felt right.

"Teach what?"

"Kids. Elementary school. It's the one thing I think I'd be really good at."

"Then that's what you'll do. As soon as Sam's in school, you can go back to college and get your degree."

"But that's not for another four years."

"So? It's something to look forward to. Something to get you through the days until then."

Sarah smiled. She found she did that most easily with Patrick. She and Annabel hadn't gotten together on their own for weeks now, and if they had, comparing her hectic, baby-filled life to Annabel's more relaxed, selfish one wouldn't bring about many smiles. Jesse, on the other hand, only confused and frustrated her. She didn't know what he wanted from her, if she was holding on too tight, or letting him slip through her fingers.

But Patrick was easy. Simple. His words didn't have double meanings, like Annabel's did. He didn't hold himself back, like Jesse. He simply was.

"What about you?" she said. "What do you look forward to?"

Patrick sighed. "I don't know. I've been thinking about what you said, maybe going into another field. But I don't see how I can do it. I'm so entrenched in this project, in this university. It would be like starting over."

"But you're not happy," Sarah said.

"You make it sound simple. But it's not. I've got a family to support. I can't just pick up and go like a single guy in his early twenties can."

"I don't think Annabel would want you to sacrifice your happiness for her."

"Are we talking about the same Annabel?"

Sarah laughed, though she knew she shouldn't. She felt

as if it were her duty to defend Annabel, yet sometimes that wasn't possible. Annabel was selfish. She came right out and said she was selfish. How could Sarah defend what Annabel herself admitted, even flaunted?

"Well, if you could do anything you want, what would you do?"

Patrick thought for a moment and then answered.

"Go to MIT. Study immunological cures for cancer across the hall from Robert Weinberg. Trade my information on the immune system with his on virology. Be on the cutting edge of research rather than in the rear, working on some project that has little or no meaning."

Sarah was quiet. She could feel Patrick's passion through the wires. It sparked her own. It made her feel as if they were kids who had not yet learned that the world had limits.

"I think you should do it," she said quietly.

"Sarah, I can't."

"Why not? Send your résumé to MIT. Call the director. Talk to this scientist you admire so much. Let them see your passion. No one can resist that. And if that means taking your family to Boston, then take them to Boston. I'm sure they'd rather move somewhere you'd be happy than stay here and watch your dreams die."

They spoke for an hour longer. Sarah couldn't stop herself from confiding in him, about Jesse's absences, her apathy, the way she wandered around the house like a woman lost. He was such a good listener. He didn't condemn Jesse, nor did he defend him. He concentrated only on Sarah's side of it, gave her suggestions, or just told her he was there if she needed him.

And he told her about his life, about his nights spent mostly in his den, reading or watching television. About how he and Annabel came together briefly, even passionately, but then parted again and lived their own lives. About his days in college and how optimistic he used to be about his future before everything became such drudgery.

Sarah heard the key turn in the lock and she glanced at the clock. It was five minutes to ten. She cut Patrick off in mid-sentence.

"I'm sorry. Jesse's home. I'd better go."

Patrick picked up on the panic in her voice.

"Sarah, it's all right that we're talking. There's nothing unfaithful about talking to another man."

"I know. I'm sorry."

"Don't be sorry. I enjoyed this."

Jesse came through the door.

"Me too. Goodbye."

Sarah hung up the phone and waited for her husband. Her palms were suddenly sweaty, though there was no reason for them to be. Still, when Jesse asked her who she'd been on the phone with, she told him it was one of the women she'd met at the playground.

Annabel sat in the restaurant, already on her second glass of wine. Business men and women were coming in and out, hurrying on their lunch break, downing vodka martinis to help them through the rest of the afternoon, and Annabel felt a quick stab of envy for their lives, the quick pace, the importance written on their faces. She had always talked about doing something important someday. Now that Adam was in school, she could get a job. But once the thought rushed in, it rushed back out again. It could only be part-time and she didn't want to shortchange herself. Better to wait until she could take the plunge into the working world completely.

She recognized, vaguely, that she was making excuses. But she tried not to dwell on it. She had an image of herself as driven and ambitious, and she liked the fantasy. Enjoying her freedom for a few more years wouldn't hurt anything. She still had time to get out there and make something of herself.

She finished her second glass of wine.

"Waiter," she said. She pointed to her glass and the man nodded. He took it away and, a couple of minutes later, brought back another full glass.

Annabel sat back and sipped her drink. Sarah had called yesterday to ask her out to lunch. The call had caught Annabel off guard; it had been weeks since Sarah had come out of her homemaking/mothering exile long enough to talk to Annabel. She seemed to get her fill of socializing by talking to Patrick. But yesterday the phone rang, just like always, and Sarah was talking, just like always.

"We have to get together," she said. "It's been too long."

Annabel had sat down at the kitchen table and wrapped the phone cord around her finger. Sarah's retreat into motherhood had come at a perfect time. Annabel hadn't had to face her since Carolyn's party, since the kiss. She didn't even have to bother to hide anything.

Yet the sound of Sarah's voice instantly summoned up the image of Jesse. Jesse's lips and hands and the smell of him. If she closed her eyes, she could still feel him, still taste him, even after the weeks that had passed since the party.

"I'd like that," Annabel said carefully. She could not sense hostility in Sarah's voice and she knew she wasn't a very good liar. Her heartbeat slowed its pace a little. There was no way Sarah could know.

"Great. How about tomorrow? We can go to Shafer's. I'll get a sitter."

So there Annabel was, waiting for . . . what? A scene? Tears? Anger? Shouts of betrayal? She'd wondered, over these past few weeks, if the reason Sarah stayed away was because she knew about the kiss. Annabel knew she should call her, find out for certain one way or another, but for once her courage failed her. She'd simply rather not know.

Annabel did not pretend to have a righteous reason for what she'd done. She knew damn well there was nothing righteous about it. But then, being morally upstanding had never been what she wanted.

She looked up and saw Sarah come through the door. She looked well, much better than she had at the party. She had gotten most of her figure back since Sam's birth, although there were about five extra pounds padding her. Still, she was smiling today, and dressed in a sunny yellow dress. Annabel exhaled. It was obvious that Sarah didn't know.

Sarah reached her and kissed her cheek.

"Sorry I'm late," she said. "The sitter didn't show until ten minutes ago."

"It's okay."

Sarah looked at her glass of wine.

"Good, you already got a drink."

The waiter came and Sarah asked for a ginger ale.

"Come on, Sarah," Annabel said. "How often do you get out of the house in the middle of the day? Live it up."

The waiter hovered at the table. Sarah debated for a moment and then shrugged.

"All right. A white wine, please," she said. The waiter left and Annabel studied her. She really did look well. Much more relaxed than she had at Carolyn's birthday party. By the end of it, she had looked ready to collapse. It was enough to convince Annabel once and for all that one child was more than enough.

"How long have you been waiting?" Sarah asked.

Annabel sipped her wine. "Not long. Five minutes."

Actually, thirty. She had been unusually nervous about this meeting. She thought she should come early, get a drink, or two. The wine would help her mask her emotions, play it cool.

"Are you feeling okay?" Sarah asked. "You look a little pale."

"I'm fine. You're looking better, though. I thought that party would kill you."

Sarah laughed and Annabel felt the tension easing in her stomach. It was funny. She hadn't thought about Sarah once when she was planning her attack on Jesse. She hadn't thought about her when she and Jesse were walking, or when they kissed, or even, really, when they returned to the party and pretended everything was as it had always been. Because as long as Jesse was there, he was all Annabel thought about. He made her crazy, stole all her thoughts away until he was all that was left.

But now, one-on-one, it was different. This was the essence of her relationship with Sarah. This was when they connected, when Annabel felt that pull of friendship. With just the two of them, Annabel felt the stirring of guilt, even perhaps of regret.

"It started out as a disaster," Sarah said. "But I think the kids ended up having a good time. Adam was great. What a ham he is."

Annabel smiled. This, at least, was safe conversation.

"He'll either be an actor or a politician," she said. "Maybe both."

"He's so good with Carolyn."

Annabel nodded. The waiter brought Sarah's white wine and they ordered. When he left, Sarah reached over and squeezed Annabel's hand.

"I'm so glad we're doing this. I haven't been myself lately, I know. I didn't think about how hard it would be to have two kids in the house. Carolyn's at the age when she needs so much attention. And Sam is still so helpless. It's like I can hear them crying even when they're not."

"God," Annabel said and Sarah laughed.

"I make it sound horrible, don't I?"

"Unlivable."

Sarah shook her head. "It's not. I mean, it is, but I do it. I don't really mind when it's happening. Only after, when I realize weeks have gone by and there's been nothing in my life but kids."

"How did the women used to do it? The ones with eight, nine kids and a farm to run and butter to churn and husbands to feed."

"God only knows," Sarah said. "The only thing that keeps me sane is thinking about when they're older, when they're both in school. Then I'm going back to college."

Annabel sat back in her chair. She had always encouraged Sarah to be her own person, to pursue her own interests, but they had never talked about anything as concrete as college. She looked in her eyes and saw a spark there she'd never noticed before. She was jealous of it. She should be the one with that spark. She looked at Sarah's posture, less stooped than she remembered. When had all these changes occurred?

"When did you decide this?"

"Oh, I've always dreamed of it. But I didn't really think about it for a long time because I was afraid it would never happen. But then Patrick . . ."

Her voice trailed off and Sarah looked down at the table. She busied herself placing her napkin on her lap.

"Patrick?" Annabel said.

Sarah shrugged. Annabel watched a blush creep up over her cheeks. Annabel gripped her wine glass tighter. She took a big gulp and finished it.

"Nothing, really," Sarah said. "He and I were just talking about careers the other day. What we'd really like to do someday, that's all."

Annabel caught the waiter's eye again. He hesitated for a moment and then removed her glass.

"Another please," Annabel said.

The waiter nodded and left.

"And what does Patrick want to do?" Annabel said.

Sarah would not meet her eyes. Annabel thought of her kiss with Jesse, but then the image blurred and the players switched to Sarah and Patrick. She could see them standing out in the cold, Patrick's arms around her, bending down to kiss her. She could actually feel the pangs of betrayal run through her. She grabbed the wine glass from the waiter when he brought it.

"I'm sure he's told you," Sarah said. "He's just been so frustrated in the lab lately. He's thinking of changing to another field of research. Maybe immunology."

Sarah finally looked up and their eyes met. Annabel forced the anger down inside her. She smiled.

"Of course he told me. In fact, we had a long discussion about it last night. I told him whatever he needs to do, that's fine with me. As long as he's happy."

The lie was so obvious that Annabel looked away. Sarah hesitated a moment and then the waiter relieved the tension. He brought them each a salad and warm sourdough bread. By the time he left, Annabel had regained her composure.

"When Jesse and I were walking during the party," she said, sliding a red fingernail around the rim of the glass, "he mentioned not exactly being happy with his life either."

Sarah looked up. She dropped her fork back on her plate.

"Really?"

"Yes, really. You know, Sarah, you shouldn't have made him sell his bike. It was a part of him."

"I didn't make him. He knew I was never thrilled with his riding in the woods. He could get hurt and I wouldn't know where to look for him. It was his decision. I think after missing Sam's birth . . ."

"Yes, of course," Annabel said. "But Jesse seems at a loss right now. The job means nothing to him, really. Just a job. Jesse's the type of man who needs something to hold on to."

Conversations around them went on easily. Annabel picked at her salad and watched Sarah pick at hers. The smile was gone from her face. She moved stiffly, hesitantly. Annabel had completely forgotten that she and Jesse had shared a kiss. The only betrayal going on here was the one between Sarah and Patrick. Their friendship, their conversations, seemed more intimate than any kiss.

"I'm glad you know Jesse so well," Sarah said finally.

"The way you know Patrick."

"Annabel, I—"

Annabel drank the rest of her wine and stood up.

"I just remembered an appointment I have." She opened her purse and took out a twenty. "This should cover it. Thanks for the invite."

She grazed Sarah's cheek with her own and walked out of the restaurant. As soon as she was out of sight, she started running. She ran until she couldn't breathe or think or feel anymore.

Jesse stared down into the crib at his son. Sam was remarkably quiet, not even crying when Jesse laid him down. He toyed with the ear of his stuffed bear and then pulled it into his mouth.

Jesse smiled at him. He had felt cut off from Sam in the beginning. He almost hated him for a while, for putting Sarah through what he did. But once Sarah came home from the hospital and they got back to normal, the anger disappeared.

Now, as Jesse looked at him, he felt a love much stronger than any he'd felt for Carolyn. Carolyn had always been Sarah's child, Sarah's daughter. But Sam was Jesse's. He had the same indentation in the middle of his upper lip, the same square jaw. And whenever Jesse came home, his eyes lit up. He ran to him as fast as his pudgy legs could take him.

Jesse bent over and picked Sam up. He smiled as Jesse tucked him into his chest and swayed him back and forth. Here, all of Jesse's thoughts disappeared. There was only Sam. His baby smell, his blond hair, his attempts at speech, his gurgles.

He heard the door open behind him and the floor-boards creak. Jesse stood up straighter, but did not turn around.

"Are you coming to bed?" Sarah asked.

"In a minute."

He waited for her to leave, but she did not. Jesse turned around.

Sarah was wearing her white cotton nightgown, the one that hung precariously to the edges of her shoulders, the one she knew never lasted on her body for longer than ten minutes if he had any say in it. Jesse looked her over, saw her nipples through the sheer fabric, and then looked away.

"Don't wait up," he said. "Maybe I'll do a little paper-work."

Sarah rested her head against the door. He heard her sniffle once. Jesse squeezed Sam a little tighter and the baby laughed.

"Are you going to tell me what's going on?" she said.

Jesse laid Sam back in his crib and spent a few minutes rearranging his toys, tucking the blanket up beneath his chin. It felt as if there weren't enough air in the room, but he knew that was only his imagination. Finally, he turned back toward Sarah.

"Let's go out," he said. They left the room and Jesse looked back once more at his son. If only he could stay with him all the time, he'd be safe. Safe from his wife, from thoughts of Annabel, from guilt, from himself. He closed the door. Sarah stood in the hall, staring at him.

"Well?" she said. She had controlled her tears and turned them to anger. "What did I do?"

"You didn't do anything, Sarah," Jesse said quietly, walking past her into their bedroom. She had turned down the bed and lit candles on the nightstands. At any other time in their marriage, he would have been all over her. He had always wanted sex much more than she was willing to give it to him. But for now, Jesse ignored the suggestion and went into the bathroom. He shut the door.

"You've been like this for weeks now," she said through the door. "Do you think I don't notice when my husband won't touch me?"

Jesse flushed the toilet and opened the door. Sarah was crying again; she couldn't make up her mind whether she wanted to be sad or angry. He reached out and touched her cheek.

"I'm touching you now."

Sarah shook her head and pulled away. "Not like that, and you know it. You won't make love with me. I never had to initiate it before."

Jesse rubbed his forehead. Again, he felt as if he couldn't breathe. He walked past Sarah and out into the hall.

"I need something to drink," he said. He walked down the stairs and into the kitchen. He found an opened bottle of Burgundy in the cupboard and poured himself a glass. Sarah walked into the kitchen a moment later.

"Is it because I haven't lost all the weight?" she said.

It was so ridiculous, Jesse laughed.

"Of course not. You're as beautiful as you've always been."

"Then what is it?"

Jesse gulped down the wine. How could he explain himself? He wasn't even sure what was going on in his own mind. Except that since he'd kissed Annabel, he couldn't come close to Sarah. It wasn't that he didn't want her, but when he reached for her, he felt Annabel's skin, when he kissed her, he kissed Annabel's lips. The rest of the day, he easily put Annabel out of his mind. He could even stop the guilt, tell himself that it was a one-time thing and there was no harm done. But as soon as he got close to Sarah, the feelings came back, Annabel's voice came back.

He looked at his wife. She was beautiful. As gorgeous as Annabel was, it was Sarah who moved him, who touched not only his body, but also his soul. She was soft and completely feminine, more seductive than Annabel at her most exotic. Annabel reached only the surface of him, his nerve endings, his flesh. Sarah reached deeper inside and got to the heart of him.

He set the wine glass down and stepped toward her. Without thinking too much, he took her face in his hands. He bent down and kissed her, squeezing his eyes shut, his mind shut, and concentrating on these lips he knew so well. He opened his mouth and touched his tongue to hers. She tasted like toothpaste and he pulled away and smiled.

"I've just been tired," he said. "There's not a damn thing wrong with you."

Sarah smiled hesitantly. She lifted her hand to his shoulder and ran it down his arm.

"Can we go upstairs?"

Jesse felt an unusual hesitancy, but he said yes. She took his hand and led him up the stairs. It was strange, her wanting him, and not the other way around. It reminded him of Annabel.

Sarah pulled him into the bedroom and closed the door. She stood before him, the nightgown slipping down over one shoulder.

Jesse went to her, hurrying, trying to rush before his mind betrayed him. He kissed her hungrily, rubbed his hands all over her, and then pushed her down on the bed. He slid her nightgown up to her stomach and she fumbled with his pants. When she had them down, she searched for him.

He was hard until she touched him, and then he knew it wouldn't last. All his desire went out of him. He tried kissing her harder, touching her breasts, pressing himself against her, but all the while his penis grew soft in her hands. They said nothing, but he could feel her tears on his cheek. Finally, she pulled her hand away.

"Oh Sarah," he said, holding her. She squeezed him tightly, not asking why. Jesse tried to think up some excuse, but his mind was blank. He could see Annabel's face clearly, her red lips, her hazel eyes laughing at him. It was as if she were in the room with them, standing right over them, triumphant. Jesse held Sarah tighter.

"I love you," he said. "I swear I love you." His voice

was too urgent, and Sarah dissolved into sobs. They clung to each other like children and after a while Annabel's face disappeared and it was just the two of them again.

Sarah went about planning Jesse's surprise thirtieth birthday party as if her life depended on it. She went to three gift shops before she found the right invitations. She called one of the secretaries out at Boeing and got the addresses of Jesse's closest friends there. She got a recommendation for a caterer and chose each item on the menu with precision.

This would be perfect. She wasn't quite sure why it was so important, she only knew that it was. She had made a mess of Carolyn's party, and she recognized the mistakes she'd made. This time, she would delegate the work, get someone else to cook and clean up. She would only have to get Jesse there and then watch his face light up when he saw the trouble she'd gone to for him. Then, maybe, everything would be all right.

She called Annabel the night before the party.

"Will you and Patrick come over at five?"

"Sarah, we said we would. Stop worrying."

It had been tense between her and Annabel, but Sarah chose to ignore it. She had asked Patrick not to call her anymore, knowing that it bothered Annabel. And since then, Annabel had seemed to return to her old self, with only a hint of animosity now and then when Patrick's name came up.

The distance between them bothered Sarah, but she could not dwell on it. Annabel was important to her, but it was Jesse who mattered most. His coolness, the way he slept on the very edge of the bed; these things were like life and death to her. Every time he pulled away from her, she felt sixteen again, when she wasn't sure if she had him, when he still dated other girls. She yearned for him. He consumed her thoughts. He was like a mystery all over again, and she had to unravel him.

Still, she needed Annabel if this party were going to succeed. She and Patrick would organize the guests and the caterer and have everything ready when Sarah and Jesse arrived.

"This just has to work," Sarah said to her. "I can't believe how nervous I am."

"Why? It's just a party," Annabel said.

But the truth was, it was not. Ever since that night in the bedroom, when Jesse couldn't make love with her, this party had taken on a major significance. It was tied together, Jesse loving her, wanting her, her ability to surprise him. Annabel had been right years earlier when she said Sarah had stopped being a mystery to him. But now, if she could just do something unexpected, be more exciting, show him that she would still go to great lengths for him, she was certain she could turn him around.

"I know it's just a party," Sarah said. "I just want it to go well." Things had changed between her and Annabel now. Since their lunch, Sarah had been careful with her words. She no longer told Annabel her feelings, for fear that they would be misconstrued. It seemed as if everything were changing, and not for the better.

"Don't worry about it," Annabel said. "We'll be there. I'm sure Jesse will be surprised."

Sarah hung up, went over her lists of things to do again, and then sat back in her chair. Carolyn was building her blocks and then screaming when Sam knocked them down. Jesse was at work. The party was tomorrow night. Sarah felt both anticipation and nervousness gripping her stomach into knots. She knew it wasn't that big a deal, yet it was. Things were going to fall into place tomorrow night. One way or another.

# 10

Annabel circulated the room, making sure everyone had a drink and knew what to do when Jesse and Sarah arrived. It was strange and exhilarating to act as hostess in Sarah's house. As if, for a moment, they had switched lives and responsibilities. Almost as if Jesse were hers, and not Sarah's.

Every now and then Patrick showed up at her side, but Annabel always managed to extricate herself. He ruined the fantasy. He exasperated and infuriated her with his talk of work, of his phone conversations with the scientists at MIT. A week or two ago, when he brought up the subject of possibly getting a job at MIT and moving to Boston, she had refused to even discuss it with him. Then, two days ago, he went ahead and contacted the cancer research department at MIT anyway. He had waited until just before they were supposed to leave for the party to tell her.

"You what?" Annabel had said to him. They were standing in their bedroom. Annabel had just barely managed to wiggle into her skin-tight sequined dress. Patrick walked around the room in his dark blue suit, more nervous than she'd ever seen him.

"I said I called the MIT Center for Cancer Research. I was just feeling things out, letting them know I was interested. If not now, then at some point."

For a moment, Annabel thought he was joking. But the look on his face and the nervous way he tugged at his jacket denied that. She put her hands on her hips.

"I told you I didn't want to move," she said.

"And I told you I'm miserable. Don't you understand? This is what I do. I'm at the lab most of the day and the rest of the time I'm thinking about what I want to be doing there. It's my whole life. How can I go on working on these inconsequential experiments? I've got to find something that has more meaning."

Annabel turned away. It was either that or lunge at him. She couldn't remember when she'd felt so angry. Patrick had never defied her before. He had never challenged her or put his own needs above hers. It was why they worked together. She had to have things her way and he always gave in to her.

Since the day they got married, Patrick had been only background material in her life. She didn't dwell on that fact. She didn't look at other marriages and want what they had, a more equal partnership. This relationship, up until now, had suited her fine. She had the security of marriage, a husband who brought home a steady and commendable salary, a house, nice clothes, and the freedom to run her life exactly as she saw fit. Patrick's part in it was actually quite small.

"Annabel," he said, coming toward her. She whirled around and glared at him.

"I cannot believe you would go behind my back like this."

"I didn't go behind your back." Patrick took off his glasses and wiped them on his shirt. "It's nothing really. There isn't even a job opening. I just wanted them to know my name. It's just something I had to do."

Annabel walked past him, digging her heels into the floor. She was unsure what to say. She had little experience fighting with Patrick, especially when he was fighting back. She turned around and looked at him again, as if to make sure that this was really the same man she'd been married to for over seven years.

"This is because of Sarah, isn't it?"

"What?"

"Oh, don't give me that. You two, with your little chats every day, telling each other to go after your dreams. You tell her more than you ever tell me."

"We don't talk every day," Patrick said, looking away. "And I only tell her things because she listens. You don't."

"Oh fine," Annabel said, waving her arm. "Put me down now. How long have you been comparing me to her?"

"Annabel, please," he said.

Annabel walked out of the room. She pounded down the steps and past the baby-sitter who looked up at her anxiously. Adam started crying, but Annabel ignored him. She walked into the kitchen and poured a hefty glass of whiskey. She drained it in one swallow and poured another one. Patrick came in behind her.

"You're scaring Adam," he said.

"Too bad."

"You're my wife."

"You could have fooled me."

Annabel was disgusted to feel tears in her eyes. She didn't feel sad, yet her voice broke and she was acting like a needy wife. Patrick tried to touch her, but she pulled away. She breathed deeply until the tears disappeared.

"You knew who I was when you married me," she said.

"I've never complained."

"That's what you're doing every time you turn to Sarah. You're telling her and the whole world that I'm not good enough. I don't listen enough."

Patrick closed his eyes.

"I don't call her anymore. We decided—"

"Yes, you two decided. Just like you decided to call MIT and Sarah decided to be a teacher. Don't you think both of you are deciding these things with the wrong people?"

The baby-sitter managed to get Adam to stop crying. She took him out to the swing set in the backyard.

"You're right," Patrick said. "I'm sorry. I acted on impulse making that call. I don't usually do that."

Annabel finished the second shot of whiskey and looked at him.

"No, you don't."

"Can you try to understand how important my work is to me? Sometimes it's all I think about for days. I've got formulas running around in my head, ideas, theories. If I could just get into another field, a more advanced lab, a—"

"Okay," Annabel said, holding up her hand. "You win. You've already made the call."

"It could take years to find an opening in Boston."

Annabel nodded. This time, when Patrick slipped his arm around her, she didn't pull away.

"I love you," he said.

She looked up. "Do you?"

"How can you say that?"

Annabel shrugged. "Why not? I think you married me because I was pretty, because I excited you, because I was everything bad that you'd always shied away from before. You didn't care what I was inside. And now you do."

He pulled her into his arms.

"Annabel, no. Why do you do this to yourself?"

For just a moment, Annabel pressed herself into his chest, tried to drown in him. But she knew she couldn't. She couldn't drown in anyone. It was her greatest strength and worst weakness, to be so self-sufficient. She pulled away.

"I've never made excuses for myself," she said. "I know where my strengths are and where they're not."

"There's more to you than you give yourself credit for. Just look at your relationship with Adam. He adores you. And your friends. Sarah. Think of all the times you've helped her, been there for—"

"Stop it," Annabel said. "Just stop it. You don't know what you're saying."

She walked out into the backyard and called to Adam. He waited for her to smile, and when she did, he ran into her arms.

"You be good now," she said.

"I'm always good, Mom."

Annabel laughed. "Yes, you are. Good night."

Now, half an hour later, they were here at the party. Patrick kept trying to talk to her, but Annabel had put him out of her mind. She had downed three glasses of wine on top of those two shots of whiskey and she couldn't care less whether he went to MIT or not. She only knew that soon Jesse would be here. He'd take one look at her in her dress and forget Sarah. It would be payback time.

Sarah had met Jesse at the bar.

"Just a quick drink," she said. "In honor of your birthday. I couldn't get the sitter for longer than an hour."

Jesse had accepted her explanation with a smile, but he knew what was going on. He had known from the very beginning. He'd heard people whispering around him in the office. Conversations stopped when he came into the room. And then, when Sarah stepped outside with the kids the other day, the caterer called to confirm the menu.

Now, as they pulled up into the driveway, Jesse did his best to act normal. He got out of the car and went around to open Sarah's side. No one had thought to park down the street, so the place was jammed with cars. What did everyone think he was, an idiot?

Sarah hung a little behind him as they walked to the door. Jesse played along, found his key, and opened the door.

"Surprise!" they all said. Jesse jumped back and did his best imitation of a delighted fool. He looked back at Sarah and she was smiling and clapping. He hadn't seen her so happy in weeks. He slipped his hand behind her neck and kissed her.

"Thank you," he said.

Her eyes lit up and Jesse wished he could send everyone home. The memory of his kiss with Annabel was finally fading. He was sure he could get on with his life now. And the first order of business was making love with his wife.

But it wasn't to be. Everyone crowded in on him, wanting to know if he had suspected. Someone put a drink in his hand and Jesse gave in to the party. Sarah slid past him to check on the food, but he grabbed her arm. She was surprised for a second, and then she smiled at him. He pulled her close so he could whisper in her ear.

"Later," he said. He grazed her ear with his lips and he

felt her shiver. Jesse felt wonderful all of a sudden. As if everything had fallen into place. Reluctantly, he let her go.

Jesse drank the beers everyone plied him with and talked to his friends. The music was loud, a few people were dancing; it was a good party. Jesse looked around the room and his eyes fell on Annabel talking with a man in the corner. Her dress was obviously chosen for one effect only; to give a hard-on to every man in the house. It was silver and shimmery, hugging every curve. The top of her breasts burst out over it and the skirt came only to mid-thigh. He wondered how she moved in it, or breathed in it.

She turned a little and their eyes met. He tried to stop himself, but his eyes fell to her breasts, to the dark, moist spot between them. He lifted his eyes again and she was smiling. He looked away.

A woman from the office asked him to dance and he accepted. It was a fast song and he still remembered some of the moves from high school. Another woman took her place, and then another, and pretty soon there was a whole crowd of people in the living room, dancing. Jesse kept drinking while he was at it. He hadn't had anything to eat since lunch, and he could feel the mix of beer and vodka and whatever someone put in his hand going straight to his head. By the seventh dance, all his inhibitions were gone. He was strutting all over the floor, picking up other men's partners, swinging them around. Everyone was laughing.

He caught Sarah's eye once. She was hanging back near the kitchen with the caterer. She was the only one who was sober, but she was smiling and laughing, having as good a time as everyone else. Jesse winked at her and then he was lost in the crowd again.

By eleven o'clock, he had polished off more than a dozen drinks and was searching for more when Annabel appeared at his side. He hadn't spoken to her yet. He had caught glimpses of her dancing, her hips thrusting this way and that. She ran a finger down his arm.

"Is it my turn now?"

Her voice echoed in his brain and Jesse knew he was as drunk as he'd ever been. Her body shimmered and rippled like water. Her finger on his arm prickled every nerve ending. The scent of her skin intoxicated him. She had a drink in her hand and she offered it to him. He finished it, the room spun a little faster, and then he set the glass aside on a table.

Jesse tilted his head and listened to the music. It was a slow song now and he smiled at her. She was looking even better than when she came in. Her hair was mussed and he could see the beads of sweat on her chest. She swayed a little, or maybe he did. He pulled her to him.

They drifted among the other bodies. Annabel laid her head on his shoulder. Her arms were tight around his neck. Jesse put both arms around her waist and then couldn't resist moving his hands down over her butt when he thought no one was looking.

He was reeling. The music was inside his head; Annabel seemed to be inside his body. He couldn't tell where he ended and she began. He could hear other voices, but it seemed as if they were coming from his own head. He felt detached, invisible, as if he could do anything and no one would notice.

Annabel moved and her breasts skimmed his chest. He looked up at her. There was no one else in the world but her. He didn't think there had ever been anyone else in the world but her.

"We're not kids," she said, or that was what he thought she said. He was beyond drunk. He was flying. His skin was on fire. He touched Annabel and her body melted in his hand. It had been so long since he'd made love. Too long. Another moment without it and he thought he would go mad.

"No."

"They'll never know. There's so many people."

Jesse nodded. He knew there was something else he should be thinking about, but he couldn't put his finger on it. Everything was a blur except for getting this dress off Annabel as quickly as possible. It was in the way of his hands. He wanted to slip his finger down between her breasts, lick the sweat off her. He would have done it right there, started kissing her, touching her, if she hadn't pulled away and stopped him.

Annabel smiled and took his hand. She looked around and then hurried him toward the front door. She pushed him outside and then looked back again. She closed the door and smiled at him.

"No sign of Patrick or Sarah. We're clear."

Then she laughed and they ran to her car. She opened the door and they crawled into the back seat. With the windows rolled up, there was only the smell of leather and Annabel's perfume. Jesse reached for her, but she pushed him away.

"Wait," she said. Jesse didn't know how long he could. He felt eighteen again and Annabel seemed an experienced, older woman. Very slowly, she slipped her hands around her back and found the zipper. She pulled it down and the top of the dress fell off her. Her breasts slipped out, and Jessie groaned.

He leaned forward and took one swollen nipple in his mouth. Her skin was hot and she tilted her head back. Jesse had never felt anything like it. It was as if her own pleasure were transferred through him, as if he were feeling it doubly. He moved his mouth to the other breast and her hands slipped up through his hair.

"God," she said. Her fingers worked the buttons on his shirt, then his pants. He pulled at her dress, ripping it slightly in his haste to get it off. When she was naked, he pulled her down so she was lying on the back seat. It was a tight fit, her head was pressed into the door, her knees raised slightly, but she didn't seem to notice. Jesse wedged his legs on either side of her and looked her over.

It was incredible to have this different, exotic woman beneath him. Like being a virgin again. Like every pleasure was new.

Starting from her head, he slid his hands, fingers spread wide, down over her. Her skin was so smooth, so cool. He could see the gooseflesh rising where he touched her, and the rest of her body lifting toward his hands, anticipating his touch. He had such power over her, something he never had with Sarah. Sarah submitted, she even enjoyed it to a point, but not like this. She did not let go completely. Her body didn't hunger for his touch. She didn't gasp at every feather stroke. She didn't say "Please. Please," again and again, as if she couldn't stand the wait.

The windows fogged and they were sealed off. Every

noise out of Annabel's mouth echoed in his brain. She barely touched him with her fingernail and it felt as if ten women were touching him. He looked down at her. She was watching him. She didn't close her eyes the way Sarah always did, as if ashamed of what they were doing. Annabel wanted to see everything.

She slipped her hands up his thighs and Jesse's legs shook. She worked her fingers back over his buttocks, into his crevices. She pushed him back into the door and crawled toward him. She kept her eyes on him, holding him in her gaze even as she took him into her mouth.

"Annabel," he said. He grabbed her hair, felt those dark, silky curls fall all over him, touch him like feathers. He pushed himself up into her and she didn't pull away. His ears were ringing. He wondered if time was moving at all, or if it had stopped just for them. She took him deeper and deeper, until he couldn't stand it.

He lifted her up and pulled her to him. When she kissed him, he could taste himself. Her tongue searched out his mouth and Jesse knew he was lost. Sarah could not compete with Annabel's fingers that knew exactly where to rub, her moans that told him he was the best lover she'd ever had.

Jesse sat her down on top of him and then she did the rest. She pressed herself down on him, taking him all the way in.

It was ecstasy. She was warmer, wetter, than Sarah ever was. She was kissing him, her tongue in his ear, then on his neck, in his mouth. She was everywhere and Jesse was nowhere, and all the while she thrust herself down on him, doing all the work, giving him every ounce of pleasure. He wanted to hold back, but he couldn't. It was too good. He felt the tingling coming on, and then the shock waves, and then the pleasure shot out of him. He wrapped his arms around her, clung to her, felt his body spasm again and again, like never before. Sarah brought him to the top, but Annabel took him over. She kept pressing on him, squeezing him as he came, and the waves would not stop. They kept surging through his body, one after the other, and Jesse clung to her.

When it was over, when Jesse could breathe again, he

slipped her onto her back and, in quick, brutal jabs, rammed himself inside her until she came, more intensely than he had. She scraped her fingernails down his back. Her legs tensed and jerked around him. She called out his name, she screamed, and Jesse felt more powerful than he ever had.

He raised himself up on one elbow. The car was hot now and steamy. They were both pressed into the door, their legs slipping down below the front seat. There was no tenderness, as there usually was with Sarah. There were no words of love.

Annabel looked up at him and started laughing. Then Jesse did too.

"My God," he said.

A few minutes earlier, Sarah had begun looking for Jesse. A few guests had left. Someone had turned the music down. It was a quarter to midnight and things were winding down.

She went upstairs and checked the bedrooms. She knew he'd been drinking a lot. She should have insisted that he eat something. Knowing Jesse, he'd drink until he fell over.

He was not upstairs and she went out into the backyard. A few guests wandered around, despite the chilly night, but no one had seen Jesse.

"Probably threw his back out doing those dances," someone said and laughed. Sarah smiled and went back into the house. Patrick was in the kitchen, helping the caterer clean up.

"You don't have to do that," Sarah said.

Patrick shrugged. "I don't mind."

"Have you seen Jesse?"

Patrick hesitated a moment before moving a few more dishes to the sink.

"Not for a while."

"Where's Annabel?"

Patrick looked at her. For a moment, she didn't understand the implication of the look. She hadn't even linked the two of them together when she asked where they were. But the look on Patrick's face sent a chill through her.

"What are you thinking, Patrick?"

"Nothing."

Sarah grabbed his arm.

"Tell me."

"Nothing, really. I just saw them dancing, that's all."

Sarah dropped her arm. He was being ridiculous, of course. Jesse had danced with everyone. It was his party. He was supposed to. And if Patrick had seen anything, it was the alcohol in Jesse's system.

"How long since you've seen Annabel?" she asked.

"About half an hour."

"And Jesse?"

"The same."

Sarah tried to slow her body down, but it had a mind all its own. She ran out of the kitchen and into the living room. The crowd had thinned out even further and there was no sign of either Jesse or Annabel. Someone walked in the front door and Sarah's hopes rose. But it was only Barney, a friend of Jesse's from the office.

"Forgot my coat," he said. He found it in the closet and then looked over at Sarah. "Great show out there."

Sarah's body stopped abruptly. She felt Patrick behind her. His hand slipped into hers.

"What show?" she said.

"Haven't you been out front yet? The windows are all steamed up so no one knows who's in that car, but someone sure as hell is having a good time. You can hear that woman moaning down the street."

He laughed and walked out the door. Sarah took a step forward, but Patrick stopped her.

"Don't, Sarah."

She looked back at him.

"It's not them. It couldn't be."

She walked through the living room and out the front door. Her mind had to force every step. *Left foot forward. Now the right one. Left. Right. Keep going. Nothing to be afraid of.* She saw the car in question, the steamed windows. She looked back at Patrick. He was right behind her. It was his and Annabel's car.

"It's still not them," Sarah said, more to herself than to Patrick. She walked closer, willed the woman's voice not to appear, and it was silent. Barney was just kidding. She was almost to the car door when she heard laughter.

Sarah stopped. She could not take another step. If she just turned and went back into the house, she would never have to know. Jesse would show up later, probably drunk out of his mind. He'd have a major hangover tomorrow and then everything would be all right.

She turned around, but Patrick was already past her. He reached for the door.

"Patrick, no," Sarah said. But it was too late. He pulled it open.

Jesse and Annabel were lying on the back seat, naked. They looked up, still smiling, not yet understanding that they had been found out. Sarah looked first at Annabel, on her back, and then at Jesse, on top of her, obviously still inside her.

"Sarah . . ." he said, but Patrick slammed the door on him. Sarah looked back at the house, but knew she wouldn't make it in time. She ran to the street and knelt down over the gutter. She vomited three times before she was empty.

# 11

❦

SARAH STOOD UP from the gutter. She heard Jesse's voice coming from the car, then someone shouting. She thought it might be Patrick, but when she turned, he was right beside her. She looked up at him. In the darkness, his face was pale and ghostly.

"I have to go," she said.

He nodded. His eyes were dazed, as if he did not understand what he'd seen. Sarah took a step toward him, but then the car door opened and Jesse threw his leg out.

"I'm sorry," she said, and then turned and ran. She ran as fast as she could, the way she used to run as a child, fast enough that the wind stung her eyes, her feet slammed against the pavement, and the houses were only blurs as she passed. She stumbled now and then, struggling against her high heels. She waited until she turned the corner and then she stopped. She took off her shoes and threw them in the street. Then she took off running again.

She didn't know where she was going. She didn't care where she ended up. Carolyn and Sam were at Mrs. Colby's until tomorrow morning. She would get them then, decide then. For now, she just had to keep running.

She made it all the way to Paddington Park before her lungs gave out. She bent over, gasping for air. Her legs shook from the effort and she collapsed onto the grass. It was wet and seeped through her dress, but she hardly noticed.

When she could breathe again, she rolled over onto her back. Above her were the branches and leaves of a maple tree, and beyond that the three-quarter moon and a few stars. Sarah looked at all this and was calm. She wasn't crying. There was only the need to get the air back into her lungs, to relax the muscles in her legs. She did not deny what she'd seen, what it meant, what she'd have to do, but for now there was only this strange sense of peacefulness, of aloneness, as if she'd been swallowed up by the night, the moon. There was no Jesse or Annabel. She had no children. For now, for once, there was only Sarah, a woman, a being, a part of all this. She breathed in and out, watching her breath form into white smoke and then dissipate into the sky. A bird or squirrel moved on the branches above her and a single leaf fell to the ground.

She could not say how long she lay there like that. A few minutes. A few hours. But she was aware that she had to stay perfectly still. The moment she moved, the agony would start, reality would rush in. She tried to close her eyes, let sleep come, but it denied her. She opened her eyes again and a lonely cloud covered the moon. Sarah sat up.

She looked around the park. It was deserted, as far as she could tell. From somewhere far off, she heard music, but then it faded, and she knew it must have been from a passing car. Her dress was soaked through on her back and the wetness chilled her. She stood up.

The tears started then. The despair hit her like a cannon blast in her gut. The air was sucked out of her and she hunched over. In between sobs, she kept saying, "Jesse, Jesse." She stumbled over to the tree and leaned against its trunk.

The tears would not stop. She tried to halt them, get a grip on herself, but it was impossible. She would calm down a little and then the image of Jesse on Annabel, in Annabel, would flash through her brain, in perfect, minute detail, and the sobs would come again. She wondered if she would ever forget. How could a person ever get over something like that?

She could not reconcile the images. Just a few hours before finding them together, Jesse had whispered in *her* ear, kissed *her* lips. In the end, did it not matter who was beneath him, as long as he satisfied himself with someone? Was it the alcohol? Was alcohol an excuse for something like this?

Car headlights shone into the park and Sarah ducked behind the tree. The car was moving slowly and when it got closer, Sarah recognized it as her own. It came almost to a stop next to the park and Jesse's voice called out.

"Sarah? Sarah, are you there?"

Sarah stood still behind the tree. How horrible it was that his voice sounded the same, that except for that one image, everything else was the same. She could easily show herself, go to him, pretend it hadn't happened, and to the world everything would be as it always was. The difference would only be in her heart, in the part of her Jesse had decimated.

She waited and did not move. In a moment, Jesse drove off. She watched the car go, saw it swerving slightly. She moved out from behind the tree.

She knew what would happen next. Jesse would be sorry. He would blame it all on the drinking. He would tell her he didn't know what he was doing, that he hardly remembered any of it.

And then it would be up to Sarah. Because that was the thing about infidelity. After the secret was out, the betrayer was no longer the main player. It was the betrayed who had to deal with the horror, the destruction, the choices. This would all be put on Sarah's shoulders and she would be the villain if she couldn't forgive him. She would be the woman who put one little incident ahead of years of marriage and family.

Sarah shook her head, trying to clear it. She was still crying, though she hardly noticed it; tears had become an indelible part of her tonight. She thought of Patrick and the tears came harder. What was he feeling? What would happen to him? How could such a good man be dealt such a rotten hand?

And then, finally, Sarah thought of Annabel. Her tears stopped abruptly and she stood up straight. In one instant, when Patrick flung open the car door, everything about her had become clear.

Annabel had never been her friend. She had planned for this to happen from the very beginning. Everything she had done, every smile she had given, every secret she had shared, had merely been a prelude to that moment when she could steal Jesse away. Oh God, Sarah could not believe how gullible she had been. She had told Annabel everything! About what Jesse liked, about their relationship, about their difficulties. She had practically handed Jesse to her on a silver platter.

Sarah clenched her fists. She thought of their talks, that drive through the mountains, the way Annabel had grabbed her chin that night after dinner and said "Watch out." She had meant to say "Watch out for me." She had one small bit of morality, one tiny speck of humanity, and in that instant she had known full well that the rest of her was despicable and she should warn Sarah away.

But Sarah had not listened. Annabel was her best friend. Before this night, she would have defended her to any jury. She would have trusted her with every secret.

"Idiot!" Sarah screamed at the sky. Everything was so obvious now. The flirting, the way Annabel had always been after Jesse, the way Sarah had merely been used as a bridge to him. Three years of friendship and every scrap of Sarah's loyalty was turned to hatred in an instant.

Sarah let the rage infuse her, let it burn the tears away and harden her heart. It was more intense than what she felt toward Jesse even. He was a man, a husband. Men did these things. But Annabel was, *had been*, her friend. It was an unspoken rule that women did not betray each other. Women had to be each other's champions. Men simply were not reliable enough to count on.

Sarah and Annabel had shared confidences, secrets, dreams. Annabel had done worse than turn on her; she had taken her heart, chewed it up, and spit it out.

Sarah did not know what to do with the rage. She tried screaming, but that would not release it. She gripped the tree and shook it, but the rage was still there inside her, rumbling like the beginnings of an earthquake. It was so foreign, so alien, so intense, that for a while it scared her.

But then she began to grow accustomed to it. It had a power all its own, a strength behind the fire. She twisted her neck from side to side and loosened her fisted hands. She did not censor the images of horrible deaths that might befall Annabel that flew through her brain. She smiled as each one became more gruesome.

She started walking through the park again. With every step, the anger grew and the sadness abated. As long as she kept moving, she was in control. If only she could keep walking forever. If only it could stay night forever, and she would never have to face the day. If only she could guarantee that the anger would still be there when she had to face Jesse and Annabel again.

Patrick was thankful for the drive while he took the baby-sitter home. He concentrated on his breathing while he listened to the young girl rattle on about things she and Adam had done. He even managed to smile at her, to make believe that everything was all right.

He dropped her off, paid her, and drove away. He took a circuitous route home, forcing himself to drive below the speed limit. He would be calm.

He had been surprisingly composed until he opened the car door on his wife and Jesse. He hadn't gotten upset or said a word, even an hour earlier when he'd seen Jesse slip his hands over Annabel's rear while they were dancing. Fifteen minutes after that, when he was standing at the top of the stairs in the darkness and saw them slip out the front door like a couple of runaway teenagers, he had forced himself not to make anything of it. They were both drunk and just playing around. He wouldn't believe that it would go any further than that.

But then Sarah had come along, looking for Jesse. He could see that she knew nothing and that made him angrier than he'd ever been. He held it back until he heard laughter in the car. Then it was like being someone else for a moment, someone who didn't look away, but who faced his adversaries head-on. For once in his life, Patrick didn't think first. The anger impelled him to open the car door, even though he knew what he'd find.

If it had been a movie scene, he would have laughed.

It was comical, Jesse on top of Annabel, their bodies contorted in the small confines of the back seat, their faces still smiling, the smell of sex permeating the air. Patrick almost laughed, in fact, until Jesse said "Sarah," and then all the humor left him and the anger rushed back in.

He had stood over Sarah while she retched. He had listened to Jesse and Annabel arguing in the car, stumbling over each other to get their clothes back on. And then Sarah stood up and looked at him. He saw her, but didn't see her. He was thinking about how he could have called Annabel on her relationship with Jesse sooner, maybe even stopped this from happening. Because he had known all along that she was intensely interested in him, that Jesse was the kind of man who turned Annabel on, who brought out that desire in her that bordered on obsession. He was intriguing, moody, a passionate loner. He was all Patrick was not.

Then Sarah ran off and Jesse stumbled out of the car. He was about to take off after her when Patrick grabbed him.

"Let her go," he said. His voice did not even sound like his own. It was tougher, harder; he liked it.

"I can't," Jesse said, but he made no move to evade Patrick's grasp. Annabel stepped out of the car then, her dress on, but ripped at the thigh. She looked at Patrick. Even then she did not turn her eyes away. Patrick couldn't help admiring her courage.

He looked back at Jesse. He was watching Sarah disappear around the corner and then his shoulder sagged beneath Patrick's arm. Patrick pushed him away in disgust.

"You're a fool," he said and then walked over to Annabel. Her chin was up, but this time she kept her eyes averted. Patrick opened the car door.

"Get in," he said. "And this time in the front seat."

She looked over at Jesse, and the rage surged through Patrick. He shoved her into the seat, not caring that he bumped her head against the top of the car. He strapped the seat belt over her roughly. She was crying, something he couldn't recall ever seeing her do. He slammed the door in her face.

Jesse was still standing there, looking at where Sarah

had been. Patrick clenched his fists, aching to feel Jesse's bones cracking beneath them, but then Annabel's sobs cut through to him. One traitor at a time. He walked around to his side of the car and got in.

Annabel was still crying as Patrick peeled out of the driveway. It took them only a minute to get home. Patrick got out of the car, and when Annabel still sat there, he opened her door, unfastened her seat belt, and yanked her out.

He pulled her into the house. The baby-sitter was watching television and she smiled at them. Annabel turned and ran upstairs. Patrick made apologies for her behavior and then took the girl home.

Now, as he drove back to his house, he did his best to calm himself. He had never felt violent before. He had never wanted to hurt anybody. Yet now he thought he was capable of almost anything. It wouldn't bother him at all to slap Annabel around, to pinch those breasts she'd let Jesse touch, to make her wish she'd never laid eyes on Jesse.

Patrick pulled up into the driveway. He looked up at the light in their bedroom. Was Annabel frightened of him? Was she capable of fear? He would like to know what she was feeling, what inspired her to do the things she did.

He stepped out of the car and walked to the house. The rage was still there, bubbling. He went inside and up the stairs. He opened the bedroom door. Annabel was sitting in the center of the bed, her dress still on, crying into her hands.

At the sight of her, the anger went out of him, along with everything else. All the love, all the caring; everything was gone. Partly it was because of Jesse, but mostly because he'd never really been allowed to love her. He had held his feelings in for so long, he had suffocated them.

Except legally, she was not his wife anymore, if she had ever been. He thought he should like it, finally being free of her, but the emptiness was worse even than the fury. It made him less than human somehow, without anything inside him.

He walked to the dresser and took out her nightgown.

He threw it at her and it hit her in the face before falling into her lap.

"Put this on."

She didn't move and Patrick sighed. He walked over to her and reached for the zipper in the back of her dress. She flinched as he touched her and Patrick smiled slightly. So she did have a little fear. He unzipped her dress and slid it down her.

"Put this on," he said again.

This time, she did as she was told. She slipped the dress off and the nightgown on. Her cheeks were still wet, but her crying had quieted.

Patrick walked out of the room and into Adam's. He looked down at him in his bed and lifted a dark curl off his forehead. Which was worse, to live in a house with parents who don't love each other, who even border on hate, or to live with only one parent and be cut off from the other? He couldn't say. He only knew that it was miserably unfair that Annabel's mistake and Patrick's decision should so profoundly affect a boy who had done nothing wrong. What Annabel had done tonight was so goddamn selfish it made him sick.

Patrick touched Adam's forehead. He closed his eyes as he ran his fingers over the smooth, warm skin. His son. Whenever things got really bad in the lab, Patrick had only to say "My son," and the frustration would ease. Adam made everything simple. Clear. Or at least he had, until tonight. Now, not even he could balance the scales back toward this marriage, this life. It mattered that walking out of this house, walking away from Adam, was the hardest thing Patrick would ever have to do. But it didn't matter enough.

Patrick leaned over and kissed Adam's cheek. Adam twitched in his sleep and then settled in again. Patrick thought momentarily of stealing him away, or of fighting Annabel for him, but then the idea receded. Annabel had many faults, but ignoring Adam was not one of them. She loved her son. It was the only love of Annabel's that could truly be counted on.

Patrick walked back into the bedroom. Annabel had wiped away her tears and she was ready for him.

"Let me explain," she said. Patrick walked to the chair in the corner and sat down. He stared at her. She seemed uncertain for a moment, as if she had expected protests or anger, but then she continued.

"We both had too much to drink. We were dancing, flirting, just like everybody else. Then, I don't know. It just happened. Maybe I thought he was you. Maybe I wasn't thinking. Next thing I know, we're in the car. I don't even remember most of it."

Patrick watched her for a long time. She was still beautiful to him. He thought she would always be beautiful to him. But her voice did not touch him now. He didn't give a damn about her discomfort or tears. It was amazing, really, that he could lose so much in so little time.

"Well," he said finally, "at least you didn't say he raped you."

Annabel jerked back a little.

"It wasn't rape."

Patrick stood up and stretched out his neck. He was tired, but he knew it would be a long time before he slept.

"What would you like me to say?" he asked her.

Annabel looked away.

"I don't know. I really don't."

"Let me ask you this," Patrick said suddenly, stepping forward. "Do you want me to forgive you? To take you back?"

For a long time they just stared at each other and Patrick knew that whatever she said, he already had his answer in her eyes. He walked to the window and looked out.

"I don't want a divorce, if that's what you're asking," she said.

The moon was three-quarters full, and Patrick wondered where Sarah was, if she was all right. He had wanted to go after her, but that was Jesse's job, or had been until tonight. God, it was all so confused.

"I don't think I love you anymore," he said. There was a hushed silence behind him and Patrick turned around. Annabel's face was pale and she wouldn't look at him.

"It's not just tonight," he said. "I admitted it tonight,

but I think I've known for a while. I don't love you because you don't love me. You never have."

She didn't deny it and Patrick's last hope that maybe he was wrong, that maybe he was blowing this all out of proportion, was lost. He thought of his son, and tears came to his eyes. Maybe he should slow down, think this through.

"You love Sarah," she said at last.

Patrick jumped a little.

"Don't turn this around, Annabel. Sarah and I were not the ones fucking in the car."

Annabel cringed. "It wasn't like that."

"Oh, I suppose it was all fireworks and romance. Like you two were made for each other."

Annabel looked up at him and Patrick thought she might as well shoot a thousand bullets through his heart, she was hurting him that much.

"He won't leave Sarah for you," Patrick said. "He loves her. You can see it in his eyes."

Annabel closed her eyes. "Everyone loves Sarah. Good, wonderful, kind Sarah."

"If that's true, it's only because she knows how to love back. My God, Annabel. How could you do this to your best friend?"

Annabel lay back in the pillows and cried again. Patrick ran his hand through his hair. How easy it was for them to hurt each other, to say the things they knew would cut each other the deepest. They had so many weapons; they knew each other's fears and desires. They could destroy each other, if they wanted to.

"I don't know," she said through her tears. "I couldn't stop myself."

Patrick walked over to the bed and sat down next to her. He put his hand on Annabel's forehead and wiped the hair out of her eyes. She quieted a little.

"I've never seen you cry," he said.

Annabel struggled against her tears. She lifted a finger up and wiped the last of them away.

"Why do you do that?" Patrick asked. "Why won't you ever let me in?"

"It doesn't matter now," Annabel said. "You want to punish me for one mistake."

Patrick grabbed her face and turned her toward him. He looked into the eyes he'd seen so often, but never penetrated. After eight years, he still had no idea what Annabel was about.

"I'm not punishing you. You do that enough yourself. I'm only pointing out what we both know. This marriage is over. It's been over a long time."

He let her go and she slipped back onto the pillow. Patrick stood up and walked into the closet. He took out a suitcase and threw a few clothes in it. He felt a pressure on his shoulder and turned to see Annabel standing behind him.

"Where will you go?"

"I don't know. A motel."

"What about Adam?"

Patrick closed the suitcase and stood up straight.

"All I ask is that you don't say anything to him yet. We should do it together."

Annabel nodded. Patrick watched her struggle to hold herself together, and then fail. He pulled her into his arms and held her. She was shivering and he fought the urge to forget everything, to climb back into bed with her and go on as always. Instead, he simply buried his nose in her hair and drank her in one last time.

He pulled away finally. He kissed her forehead and then her lips, just once. Her eyes held him and for once he could read them perfectly.

"I'm sorry," she said.

He nodded. "I know you are."

Then he took his suitcase and left the house.

Jesse jumped awake when the front door opened. He'd been camped out on the living room couch, plying himself with coffee, trying to sober up. He was almost there now, with a throbbing headache to remind him of more than a dozen drinks last night.

Sarah walked in just as dawn was suffusing the room with a purple glow. She stopped short when she saw him and then closed the door behind her.

They stared at each other for a long time. Jesse knew what he'd done. He almost wished he'd blacked it out, but it was there, as fresh as if he were still in the back of that car with Annabel and Sarah was staring at him, horrified. But the thing was, Jesse didn't feel like he'd done it. The one thing he could not remember was *why*. Why, after that fleeting bit of happiness when the party first started, when he'd kissed Sarah, when he'd realized he could make love with her again, did he end up with Annabel?

He couldn't make the connections. He couldn't get from point A to point B, from Sarah to Annabel. He knew he'd done it. He knew he'd wanted to do it. He knew there hadn't even been a moment's hesitation or guilt. He knew alcohol did not explain away everything. He knew there was no defense for what he'd done.

"Are you all right?" he asked.

Sarah nodded. "Yes. Just a few blisters on my feet. I went walking. I couldn't come back."

Jesse tried to pick his coffee cup off the table, but his hands were shaking too badly to lift it. He tried to hide them in his pockets.

"I'm going to go lie down for a while," Sarah said. "I'll go pick the kids up at eight."

She started up the stairs.

"Sarah . . ."

She held up her hand and Jesse stopped. He tried to move toward her, but he felt huge and clumsy.

"Don't say anything. I don't think there's anything you could say that will make things any better."

She took two more steps.

"I love you," he said.

Sarah turned to him. There were tears in her eyes.

"If it had been anyone but Annabel. Anyone."

Jesse looked away. He could hear Sarah struggling for breath just as he was. He had never thought heartache could be physical, yet that was what it was. The hangover, this lack of breath, a heavy pain in his stomach and chest. He turned back to her.

"Will you let me stay?"

The words came out as soft as a whisper, yet they

echoed through the house, up the stairs. Sarah closed her eyes. He watched her face, studied it, tried to hold off the tears. Finally, Sarah just nodded. Jesse let out his breath as she turned and walked up the stairs. He fell back onto the sofa, put his head in his hands, and cried with relief.

# 12

❧

THERE WAS A certain hush to the house. As if it were insulated with foam and high-tech sound barriers. As if someone lay dead in the next room and the two of them whispered out of respect. As if they were strangers thrown together and expected to make conversation.

Sarah sat on the couch working on the needlepoint pattern she'd been plodding away at for years. Jesse sat at the table, looking over paperwork from the office. The kids were in bed. Sarah wished she'd turned the television on, so at least there'd be some noise in the room, but it would look too obvious if she turned it on now.

Out of the corner of her eye, she could see Jesse watching her, but she did not look up. She had not met his eyes since she came back to the house after that long night spent walking. She really hadn't been sure what her decision would be until she saw his face, and then she knew she didn't have the courage to tell him to leave. He'd shot holes through her love for him, but he hadn't killed it. At that moment, more than anything, she wished he had. She wished her love had shriveled up and gasped its last breath and left her free.

But instead, she let him stay and they went on. Jesse went to work, sometimes stayed late to work on a project, came home, played with Carolyn and Sam, ate dinner, watched television, and went to bed. Sarah watched the kids all day, made the meals, cleaned the house, ran the errands. She asked Jesse about his day. She did his laundry. She slept in the same bed with him, although this time she was the one sleeping at the very edge. She did all she was supposed to and, frankly, she was amazed that they could look so normal and be such a sham. It made her wonder if all her preconceptions about marriage and family were wrong. If maybe everyone were faking it.

Jesse walked on eggshells around her. He was considerate, self-effacing, kind. He started giving the kids baths each night. He cleaned up the dinner dishes. He vowed, when football season started, that he would only watch one game a week. Yet the kinder he was, the worse it got. Every gesture, every forced smile, only reminded Sarah of how and why they had reached this point. It would have been better if he had simply gone back to being the way he was before, more interested in football than in her. Perhaps then she could forget.

"Need anything?" Jesse called out to her.

Sarah gritted her teeth. He was just being nice, but the phoniness of it all made her angry. She would have liked him to be nice to her because he wanted to, not because he was trying to get her to forgive him.

"No, thanks."

"Sure?"

Sarah set her needlepoint down and turned to him. Still, she didn't look right at him, but at a point just to his right. She knew, too well, what he looked like, that his eyes pitied her for her embarrassment and himself for this predicament he was in.

"Yes, Jesse. I'm sure. I don't need anything."

He tried to catch her gaze, but then finally gave up and turned back to his paperwork. Sarah steadied her breathing and picked up her needlepoint again. Later that night, when Jesse turned in for bed, he hesitated as he walked past her on the couch. He took a step toward her and Sarah stiffened. She heard him sigh as he turned and went upstairs. She would give him at least an hour to fall asleep and then she would join him.

• • •

That was last night, but it could have been any night during the past three weeks. Sarah couldn't differentiate between any of them as she waited at a corner table in the university cafeteria. This place was loud and colorful, filled with the scent of hamburgers and coffee and cigarettes. Students talked and studied, laughed and argued. The moment Sarah had walked in the door, she yearned to be a part of this place. It was the one thing she regretted, that she never went to college, became something. She wanted a title after her name. Sarah Bean, Teacher. She wanted to have an answer when people asked her what she did.

She looked up and saw Patrick come through the door. She had spoken to him a couple of times on the phone, but it had been three weeks since she'd last seen him at Jesse's party. He had gone through a metamorphosis in that time. He had lost weight and his suit hung on him. He had let at least two days' worth of stubble accumulate on his chin, something Sarah had never seen him do before. His hair was unkempt, his glasses slightly askew on his nose. And behind them, his eyes were bloodshot, with dark circles beneath them.

Sarah stared at him when he reached the table.

"I'm not looking my best, I know," he said.

Sarah bridged the gap between them and wrapped her arms around him. She felt him hesitate for a moment, but then he held her. He rested his head on hers briefly and then pulled away.

"I'm really all right, no matter how I look."

Sarah nodded, though she didn't believe him. They walked over to the cafeteria line and each took a tray. When Patrick reached only for a salad, Sarah shook her head. She ordered two hamburgers, french fries, and milk shakes. Patrick was laughing as they took their weighted-down trays back to the table.

"Think I can eat all this?" he asked.

"I will if you will."

For a while they ate in silence. Sarah just enjoyed the diversity of the people around her, the hum of voices, the music someone had turned on in the corner. This place was bristling with energy and new ideas, the very antithesis of her house. She turned and found Patrick watching her.

"You'll be here someday," he said.

She smiled. "You're amazing. You read my thoughts."

"It wasn't hard. You eat this place up. I know a few students who could benefit from your enthusiasm."

He took another bite of his hamburger and then set it down. He took off his glasses and cleaned them with his shirt.

"Are you all right?" Sarah asked. "Really all right?"

Patrick put his glasses back on. Sarah noticed a few freckles around his nose that she hadn't paid attention to before.

"I'm hanging in there."

"You loved her," Sarah said.

Patrick hung his head. "Yes. Once. But I was never comfortable with that love or with her. I think I always knew, deep inside, that it would end this way."

"And Adam?" she asked, touching his arm.

"He's the hardest part. Annabel was the only one who held herself together while we tried to explain divorce to him. I told him it didn't mean he would never see me, but I don't think he understood."

He tried to smile at her, but couldn't manage it.

"You can't imagine what it's like to have to walk out the door and know you can't come back," he went on. "I watched his face fall when he realized that I wouldn't be there anymore. The only way I could describe what was in his eyes was terror. He kept reaching out for me, hanging on to me so I couldn't leave. Finally, Annabel had to pick him up and take him away, screaming."

"God," Sarah said.

"I got in the car and cried. I've never cried like that in my life. More than anything I wanted to run back in the house and tell him everything would be okay, I'd always take care of him, but I couldn't do it."

Sarah thought of Carolyn and Sam and what it might mean for them if she and Jesse couldn't work things out. What does divorce do to a child?

"Adam's strong," she said, more for herself than for

Patrick. "Once he gets into a new routine and realizes he can see you whenever he wants, he'll be all right."

Patrick nodded. He picked up his hamburger and then set it down again.

"The hardest thing is I feel I had to make a choice between my own happiness and Adam's. How can I live with myself knowing I chose my own?"

"But you didn't," Sarah said, sliding her chair closer to his. "Adam wouldn't be happy if you stayed with Annabel even though you don't love her anymore. Your unhappiness would have rubbed off on him."

Patrick ran his hands through his hair. It was longer than Sarah had ever seen it, almost to his shoulders. She reached out and touched a strand.

"You're taking on the absentminded-professor look," she said, smiling.

Patrick laughed. "I haven't been paying much attention to myself, that's true. Suddenly being single after eight years of marriage is quite an adjustment. But, strangely enough, I feel better. Stronger. Angrier. Something clicked in me when I saw them together."

Sarah shivered, remembering. "How's the apartment?" she asked, hoping to change the subject.

"As good as an apartment can be. It's noisy. There are some kids upstairs who play their music until two in the morning. But I try not to be there too much, except to sleep. I'm working as much as I can."

"Any luck on your research?"

"No. Nothing new. I keep hoping, though. And I've still got my feelers out at MIT and other places. If anyone shows an interest in me now, I won't have anything holding me back."

They finished their lunches, every bite, and then sat back in their chairs, stuffed.

"Good God," Patrick said. "I haven't eaten that much in weeks."

"It's good for you. I, on the other hand, should have stopped after my second bite. This will add another five pounds to lose."

"You don't have to lose anything, Sarah. You're beautiful the way you are."

Sarah turned away, embarrassed by his compliment. She was becoming deaf to compliments because of Jesse. He said so much, so often, that she didn't believe anything. He didn't realize how obvious he was, how thinly veiled his motivations were. He was merely trying to make things up to her and he would do anything, say anything, to accomplish that. It was no wonder she assumed all his words were lies.

But this was different. She didn't think Patrick was capable of lying.

"Would you like to go for a walk?" Patrick asked. "I can show you the campus."

"I'd love it."

They went outside into the warm early-summer afternoon. The University of Washington was beautiful in the sunshine, with its mix of Gothic and contemporary buildings. Patrick led her through the Quadrangle, with its formal layout and gargoyle sculptures. He pointed out the Aerospace and Engineering Research Lab, a stark concrete structure that Sarah didn't particularly like. Then he took her past Hutchinson Hall, with its brick walls covered in ivy and huge windows, and Sarah felt as if she were back East, at Harvard or Yale.

They walked through the campus, passing students asleep on the lawns, reading books, writing notes. Sarah and Patrick blended into the crowd, and Sarah experienced a giddiness she hadn't felt since before Jesse, when she still had plans for herself. It was all possible here. This was where dreams started. Impulsively, she reached out and grasped Patrick's hand.

"I envy you so much," she said. "Being here. Even though you're not doing exactly what you want. At least you're surrounded by all these people who want to learn, by professors who have stores of knowledge in their brains."

Patrick smiled and did not release her hand. They walked along a quieter, tree-lined avenue between two brick buildings.

"You haven't told me about yourself," Patrick said. "All I know is that you're still there. And so is Jesse."

Sarah looked down at their hands entwined together.

Perhaps she should pull away, but she didn't want to. Patrick's hand was smaller than Jesse's, but still strong. It made her feel warm inside, holding it.

"That night, I just kept walking," she said. "I wanted to get as far away as I could. I kept going over everything again and again in my mind. What had I done wrong? Why wasn't I enough for him?"

Patrick squeezed her hand tighter and Sarah smiled.

"And I thought about Annabel," she went on. "My friend."

Sarah squinted up at the sun. It still hurt to think about it, just as much as it had three weeks ago, the night she found Annabel and Jesse together. For the sake of the children, Sarah had to curb her anger and tears around Jesse. But when she thought of Annabel, she couldn't curb anything.

"I trusted her," she said. "Maybe even more than I trusted Jesse. I opened up to her in a way I never had to anyone. I told her things about us and she used that against me."

Patrick stopped and turned to her. He put both hands on her shoulders.

"I'm sorry. I feel as though it's partly my fault. As though I were responsible for her."

Sarah shook her head. "That's senseless. Annabel is her own person. The truth is, I didn't want to see what she was, what she was after. I wanted to believe she was my friend and so I was blind. She even tried to warn me, I think. When we went out to dinner down on the waterfront. She told me to watch out."

"For her?" Patrick said.

"Yes. It was as if she were two people and the good one knew what the bad one was up to."

They walked over to a stone bench and sat down.

"I've never understood her completely," Patrick said. "I don't think she understands herself completely. She does these things and she doesn't know why."

They were quiet a long time. Sarah closed her eyes and tried to forget. But the image of the two of them was always there, stained red on the inside of her eyes.

"And Jesse?" Patrick asked.

Sarah opened her eyes and looked off over the campus. "I couldn't just say goodbye," she said. "I realized that during the night. I loved him. Though I wanted what he had done to me to change that, it didn't. So I went home. I let him stay. And now we're at a standstill."

They were both quiet. A light breeze picked up and ruffled the trees around them. In the distance, a bell tolled two o'clock.

"Will it ever be normal between you two again, do you think?" Patrick asked.

Sarah laughed, but the sound came out bitter and hard.

"Normal," she repeated. "What is normal? I don't think I ever really understood what Jesse and I were about. I thought he loved me. I thought he would always be faithful to me. The really ridiculous thing is I never thought this could happen to me. It wasn't even in the realm of possibility."

"That's not ridiculous," Patrick said. "You believed in him."

They sat for a while longer in silence and then, reluctantly, Patrick stood up.

"I have to get back to the lab. I'm sorry."

Sarah stood up quickly. "No, I'm sorry. I shouldn't have kept you this long. I—"

Patrick leaned over and kissed her. It was a chaste kiss, held only for a moment, but it disarmed Sarah completely. She stepped away.

"You deserve better than him," Patrick said, not taking his eyes from her face. He turned and walked back toward the lab. Sarah watched him go, bringing her fingers to her mouth, still feeling his lips there.

Annabel reached for the phone and then pulled her hand away. She reached for it again and then stopped. Finally, she turned away from it in disgust.

"Look at you," she said to herself. "Afraid to make a silly phone call."

She walked purposefully through the living room until she realized she had nowhere to go. Adam was at summer school and not due back until twelve-thirty. She had two hours to kill until then. The house was clean, or at least clean enough that she didn't want to bother with it. And now that it was just her and Adam, there wasn't much preparation for dinner. She'd just grill up some hamburgers and potatoes.

Annabel stopped walking suddenly and listened. A car passed down the street, but once it faded, all was silent. She could hear the clock ticking, the hum of the refrigerator. She thought she could hear her own heart beating.

Quickly, she went to the stereo and turned it on. She found the blues station Patrick had hated and cranked up the volume. She sat down on the couch and put her feet up. She closed her eyes, tried to let the music in.

After five minutes, her heart was racing and she stood up. She turned off the music and walked around the house.

"Nothing's changed," she said. "Not a damn thing has changed since he's been gone."

And it hadn't. Patrick was never home this time of day anyway. Yet before he left, she had never been bored and lonely like this. Somehow she always managed to fill her days with shopping or Sarah or outings with Adam. But, at least for now, until she and Patrick worked out alimony and child-support payments, she had no money to spend. When Adam came home from school, he only wanted to be with her, at home, to prove that she wouldn't leave him too. He had no interest in going out. And Sarah, well . . .

Now, when Annabel woke up in the morning, she realized there were sixteen hours to kill until she could go to sleep again and she had no idea how to go about it. It was as if Patrick took her appointments, her courage, her very life with him when he left.

Annabel walked upstairs and into Adam's room. He was taking this hard. For some reason, she had expected him to bounce right back, to realize that he was staying with her and that was the better part of the deal. But instead, he had difficulty sleeping. He crawled into her bed and would scream if she tried to get him back into his own room. He clung to her every second. He had wet his pants a few times at school and, to both her own and Adam's embarrassment, she'd had to send along an extra pair of underwear and pants with him these last few days.

Annabel sat down on his bed and fingered his teddy

bear. Just a couple of months ago, she had taken down the clown wallpaper and put up a pattern with race cars on it, Adam's favorite. And it occurred to her that he had made the leap from baby to boy and she had been too caught up in her own life to notice.

Annabel laid her head in her hands. She tried to cry. God knows she wanted to cry. But there were no tears. Not since the night Patrick left. The instant she heard the front door click shut, her tears shut off too, like a valve. She listened to Patrick's car drive away and kept waiting for it to return, for him to have changed his mind and realized he couldn't live without her. She waited the whole night for that sound, but when dawn came, the driveway was still empty and she knew he had left her.

She tried to gauge her own feelings. Sadness? Regret? Guilt? A mixture of them all? She couldn't say. She knew for certain that she was curious. About Sarah and Jesse. Whether they had survived. She wanted to know when Jesse would call her. What Sarah thought. How long it would take them all to forgive her.

Because they would forgive her eventually. They always did. This was not the first time Annabel had strayed, or hurt someone she loved. Granted, this was a little more dramatic than most, but it was certainly not out of character. No one could accuse her of giving false signals, or surprising them with her actions. Everyone had known who she was going in, so they would simply have to forgive her and accept her again in the end.

The worst part was, Annabel had no link to them anymore. It had become second nature, picking up the phone and calling Sarah. Walking over there for lunch. Buying extra food for Friday night, because the Beans would be over. Although the circumstances had changed, Annabel could not stop herself from going through the motions, from waking up and thinking, *This is Friday. I'll buy extra wine and two packs of spare ribs.* Or picking up the phone when she saw something funny on television, ready to tell Sarah all about it. Or actually stepping out the front door at lunchtime, like always, and looking down the street to see if Sarah was on her way.

And then it would hit her. Those days were over. She

had been expelled from their lives. From Patrick's, from Sarah's, from Jesse's. She assumed that Jesse was an outcast too. That Sarah had walked out on him the way Patrick had walked out on her. Was he suffering as much as she was? Were any of them experiencing these same withdrawals, as if their friendship had been an addictive drug they'd had to stop cold turkey.

Annabel got off her son's bed and walked into her own bedroom. She did not hesitate this time, but went straight to the phone. She dialed the number she had memorized, although she'd never called it until now. He answered on the second ring.

"Jesse Bean," he said.

Annabel took a deep breath.

"It's me. Annabel."

There was only silence. In the background, Annabel could hear Jesse's coworkers laughing. It made her heart feel tight.

"What do you want?" he said finally.

Annabel sat down on her bed. "Just to talk. To see how you are."

"I'm fine."

Annabel waited for more, but there was nothing. She twirled the cord around her finger.

"Are you still . . . you know?"

"At home? Yes. Sarah and I have worked everything out."

Annabel felt her breath leave her. She had avoided walking over to their house, even just to check if Jesse's car was there. She was better than that, she told herself. And she couldn't bear the thought of Sarah catching her lurking around like a fugitive, like the villain she was sure they were all making her out to be. Besides, she had believed, however naïvely, that Jesse would call her and tell her what they would do now.

"Oh," she said. She was shaking and she had to grip the receiver with two hands.

"If that's all," Jesse said.

"Jesse, please. I—"

"Look, I don't think we should talk to each other anymore. We've already done enough damage. Why don't you just get on with your life and I'll get on with mine?"

"But I don't have a life," Annabel said before she could stop herself. Her lungs had collapsed, or stopped working. This had all been some kind of game until now. Even Patrick leaving hadn't been real, not really. It hadn't reached her heart; it hadn't stopped her from going on, from getting up, from breathing. Because there was always Jesse. At some point, she would talk to Jesse and everything would be all right. She didn't know what she had expected. For Sarah to have left him. Or for them to be together, but struggling. Whatever it was, she certainly hadn't prepared herself for his antipathy, his dismissal of her. She remembered his party as if it were the only memory left in her brain. She remembered every touch, every kiss, every moment. It had meant something. It had meant everything.

Still, she could not cry. She knew it might help her cause, it might melt Jesse the way Sarah's tears always did. But she could not do it. She was dry inside.

"Is Patrick gone?" Jesse asked.

"Yes."

"Look, I'm sorry. But I can't jeopardize my marriage anymore. I'm going to make it work."

Annabel looked out the window. The clouds were moving in and it looked as though five days of sunshine were over. There were so many things Annabel wanted to say. If she were any other person, she would tell him she needed him, that he had done something to her, penetrated her soul in a way not even Patrick had, that she would do anything if he'd just come over and see her, talk to her, tell her she was worth something and not just a drunk fuck in the back seat of a car. But she was not any other person, she was Annabel Meyers. That had been both her downfall and pride all her life.

"Good luck," she said.

Jesse sighed in relief. "Thanks. Goodbye."

Annabel hung up the phone. She sat perfectly still, not even blinking. She stared at the same place on the wall until it blurred, until it was gone. The silence of the house swallowed her up.

• • •

That night, Annabel brought a brand-new whiskey bottle upstairs with her. She had put Adam down two hours earlier and so far he had not woken up and come to her. Annabel closed the door to her bedroom and crawled into bed.

She did not bother with a glass now. She unscrewed the cap and drank straight from the bottle. The liquor didn't burn as much as it used to, and she had to get halfway through the bottle before it dulled her senses to the extent she wanted. She did not pause between swallows, but kept drinking and drinking, wishing she could get her hands on a pill that would work faster and with fewer calories.

She laid her head back onto the pillows and closed her eyes. She felt the whiskey slide through her, numb her, loosen her muscles, trip off all her breakers. After fifteen minutes or so, she was willing to set the bottle down on the nightstand in between drinks.

She looked over at the phone. Maybe she could call Sarah. Tell her she was sorry, that it wasn't really her fault. She'd just been drinking, Jesse was looking so good, and how was she supposed to resist him? Sarah would give her a chance to explain. That was the great thing about Sarah; she was so forgiving. She had taken Jesse back, hadn't she? And he was her husband, the man she had trusted more than anybody. Surely, she'd have a little room left in her heart for Annabel.

Annabel was leaning over to pick up the phone when she heard the scream. She jumped up, confused for a second, but then realized it was coming from Adam's room. She ran down the hall and threw open his bedroom door. He was sitting up in bed, his dark hair plastered to his forehead with sweat, his mouth wide open, still screaming.

Annabel went to the bed and held him.

"It's okay. It's okay."

His screams turned to cries and he gripped her so tightly she couldn't breathe. His tears soaked through her nightgown and into her skin. Annabel rocked him back and forth, saying soft things.

"Daddy," Adam said and Annabel stiffened. "I want Daddy."

Annabel rubbed her cheek against the top of his head. "I know. I want him too."

She picked him up, her six-year-old son, marveling at the weight of him. He clung to her, his lithe little arms around her neck, his eyes still wet. She took him into her room and pulled him up on the bed with her. She cradled him in her lap, as she used to when he was a baby.

She didn't know when she started crying. She wasn't even aware that she was; it seemed as if her tears were merely an extension of Adam's. They clung to each other and Annabel realized he was the only person in the entire world she trusted not to leave her. He was the only person she believed when he said he loved her.

"Oh Adam," she said. "I'm sorry. I didn't think."

"Daddy. Daddy." He kept repeating "Daddy" until his tears trailed off and his body got heavy. Annabel lifted him off her and down onto the bed beside her. He stayed close to her body, as if he were feeding off her warmth. Annabel brushed his hair off his forehead.

She reached over for the whiskey, making sure Adam was asleep before she took another swallow. And then another. She lay down beside him, pulling him into her chest, hoping to drown in him. His cheeks were still wet and she dried them. She reached up to her own and dried those as well.

The silence came again, but this time it was tempered by Adam's breathing, the twitching he made in his sleep. And Annabel realized it wasn't so bad; her life was at least endurable. The whiskey dulled the madness and Adam reminded her she still had a soul.

# 13

❧

JESSE KNEW WHAT was happening the moment he walked into the office, back from his sales circuit south of Seattle. The desk of the department secretary was empty, a few of her picture frames and pencils already cleared away. And there was a hush to the place that he'd noticed in other departments and offices after the axe fell.

He stood for a moment in the entry, waiting for the horror or shock or even anger to set in. When it did not come, when instead he felt he could breathe again, as if he had been holding his breath for years and had finally exhaled, he smiled. He moved to his desk in the corner.

"Jesse," his boss, Walter Stevenson, said as he came into the room. The department secretary, Mary, came out behind him, wiping away her tears. She would not meet Jesse's eyes.

"I had a good run," Jesse said. "Pitkin put in a new order. Henderson probably will too."

"That's great," Walter said. "Look, can I see you in my office?"

He turned and walked back down the hall without waiting for a reply. Jesse took a quick look at Mary. She was sitting at her desk, with her head in her hands. Jesse took a step toward her and then stopped. What could he say? He walked into Walter's office and closed the door behind him.

Walter was standing near the window, one of the few in the building, looking out into a cloudless, bright blue afternoon. He didn't turn when Jesse walked in.

"It's been bad," Walter said.

"I know."

"The whole industry. Aircraft. Electronics. Those damn idiots in Washington are finally willing to call it a recession." He took a breath, then went on. "You know we've been laying people off for months now, trying to trim the fat. The economy is killing us."

Jesse remained silent. He still waited for the anger to surface. Any man in his position, with a wife and two kids to support, a mortgage and car to pay off, and credit cards charged close to their limits, should be scared to death of this situation. And yet Jesse felt, strangely, the way he had when he was eighteen, when he was the bad kid on the motorcycle who didn't give a fuck about anything. All the rules adults played by didn't apply to him. He had no fear of the future. Life was an easy enough game to master.

"There's nothing we can do," Walter was saying. "The layoffs are getting more extreme. Our division is being shut down entirely. They'll get some kids from the main plant, who don't demand as much salary, to take over our sales circuits. There will be three months' severance pay. They're keeping the insurance benefits going for three months and you can get it at a discounted rate after that if you haven't found anything else. It's not much to offer, I know, but it's the best I can do."

Walter turned now and looked at him. Jesse could see the sweat on his forehead and around his armpits. How strange, that the boss should be the one suffering and not him.

"It's all right," Jesse said. "I saw it coming. For a while I thought we might be spared, since we're the ones bringing in the money, but I guess they can get by without us too."

"It's a bureaucracy," Walter said. "They've got to cut fat where they can cut it. It's nothing personal."

"Of course not," Jesse said.

"You can stay on for another week or two, if you want. But we won't be doing much. Just closing down. The severance pay starts immediately."

Jesse waited for something more, but when Walter was silent, he turned and walked to the door.

"Jesse?"

He turned back.

"Will you be all right?"

Jesse smiled. It made no sense, and yet the truth was that he felt lighter than he had in years. For just a moment, he wasn't thinking about his problems with Sarah. He wasn't thinking about what he would do, the résumé he'd have to update, the interviews he'd suffer through. The only thing on his mind was this breathtaking sense of freedom, of being out of a job he hated, a shit job he had taken because he had to do something, be an adult. For just a moment, the whole world was open to him and it was like being born again.

"Not to worry," he told his boss. "I'll be just fine."

Jesse cleaned out his desk that afternoon. There was no way in hell he was going to hang around for two weeks, listening to people cry. Besides, suddenly Jesse could not wait another second to be out of there.

He said his goodbyes without a tear, without a regret. And it occurred to him that his four years there had not made a dent in him, had not affected him in any way. He had met people, had a few drinks with them, shared a few laughs, and he knew without a doubt that that would be the end of it. They all said they would keep in touch, but they would not. Aside from the sales he'd brought in for the company, it had been a wasted four years, with nothing to show, nothing lasting to come out of it.

Jesse walked to his car. God, how he longed for his bike now. If he still had it, he would hop on, loosen his tie, and spend the rest of the day getting lost in the woods. It would be only him, Jesse. No wife. No kids. No boss. No responsibilities. When was the last time he'd had that kind of freedom?

Instead, he slipped into his predictable Toyota and dumped his box of four years' worth of nothing on the seat beside him. He looked at the clock on the dashboard. It was three-fifteen. He had at least three hours to kill before Sarah would expect him home.

He turned on the engine and headed north. There was a place he knew, about twenty miles north of Seattle, that would be perfect now. The sky was clear, bright blue, a perfect early autumn day. He drove without music. He didn't need anything but his own thoughts.

He got off the freeway and headed up the hill. It was lined on either side by pines and firs. A few houses were back among the trees, but they thinned out as he crept upward. Finally, he reached the top, a bluff that was devoid of trees. A developer had cleared this site for a new housing development, but for now it was empty, with a striking view of the Sound.

Jesse parked on the dirt and got out. He walked toward the edge of the cliff, first loosening his tie and then removing it completely. He threw it on the ground and stepped on it as he passed.

He reached the rim of the bluff and looked down at the water. The wind was up and the waves were choppy. In the distance were the buildings of downtown Seattle, the restaurants and offices, the bustling port, the ferries, the yachts. But here, all was silent except for the wind.

Jesse sat down on the ground and lifted his face to the sun. He was thirty years old, an age he'd never thought he'd be. He had believed that he was so far from his parents and their friends in temperament and ideas that he would stay young forever.

And yet, from the moment he was born, he wanted to be grown-up. Not old, just grown-up enough to live his own life. He had bristled against his parents' rules and chipped away at them until they were almost happy to see him leave the nest at sixteen.

He remembered walking out that day. He could see that small pile of his possessions he'd crammed onto the back of his bike so clearly, he could almost reach out and touch it. He could hear his mother sniffling behind him as she stood on the porch, watching him go. His father's voice rang out: "Once you're gone, you can't come back." Jesse had turned then and smiled. "Thank God," he said.

Getting on his bike, roaring the engine, feeling the neighbors' eyes on him; that had been the greatest moment of his life. He had stolen the show, had had his five minutes of fame, proved that he was somebody special, different. And he'd had that same sense of freedom and exhilaration today, as if the world were open to him, as if he'd been living under martial law until now.

At sixteen, he hadn't been afraid of what he might encounter. From his parents, he had gone to a friend's house and then to another. He had found a few odd jobs, made enough to get by. He stayed in school, graduated because it meant something to *him*, not to his parents. He had lived, completely, wholeheartedly, his own life.

He had looked at people in their thirties—married, with kids and houses—with scorn. He would never fall into that trap. He would never be predictable. He knew he wasn't as smart as the next guy. He wasn't as ambitious. But Jesse Bean was someone special. He was unique. He marched to his own beat.

And then he met Sarah. He didn't plan on loving her. He sure as hell didn't plan on marrying her. But there was something irresistible in her innocence, in the way her parents objected to him and thereby made their relationship into something more than it was. He thrived on stealing her away after they'd gone to sleep. It became his very existence, finding ways to steal her from them, from her safe, sane life.

The ultimate challenge was to marry her. It would prove that he was the stronger one, the smarter player. It had never occurred to him that by marrying her, he would become what he scorned.

Little by little, he settled in. Times were rough in Spokane, so they moved to Seattle. He took the job at Boeing because it was the only one that was offered. It paid well, he was surprisingly good at it, and that was that. Sarah had Carolyn and then Sam. They bought the house. And all along, Jesse hardly noticed that he was living a life he hated, that the grandness of his existence had vanished, that he had buried all thoughts of uniqueness under the surface of domesticity.

There was one moment, however, when he broke

away, when he stopped caring so much about conventions and rules. Jesse closed his eyes. He stopped censoring his thoughts and let Annabel back in. He remembered every second of that night with her. He could re-create her smell, her taste, the vibrancy of her that somehow seeped into his veins and invigorated him. For a moment, she brought him back to life, she resuscitated him. She made him feel young again, and alive, and strong, and full of hope and daring.

Jesse opened his eyes. The veil came up again and he pushed the thoughts of Annabel away. She aroused him sexually, certainly, but that was all. He didn't particularly like her. She was too brash, too aggressive. She had bullied Patrick for years and, in the end, he had gotten the hell out. Jesse felt sorry for her, being all alone with Adam to take care of, but she had brought it on herself.

As for his own marriage, Jesse thought it was getting back on track. He was doing his best, God knows. He complimented the hell out of Sarah. He was trying to take the kids off her hands more, help her more around the house. She knew how he lived for Sundays, yet he had vowed to watch only one game this fall and spend the rest of the time with her. There was nothing more she could ask of him.

And yet Jesse felt that she was asking for more. He wasn't sure what she wanted, but he could see in her eyes that she wasn't satisfied, that she was still angry, that he would probably have to pay for that one night with Annabel for the rest of his life. Of course he'd been wrong to do it, but it didn't seem fair that one moment's mistake should be held against him forever. He was no longer holding that night she was out with her man from the park against her. Hell, he'd never even brought it up, not even lately when he could have used it to even their scorecards. He had forgiven her, so why couldn't she forgive him? What the hell did she want from him? He'd already given up everything for her. He'd become an entirely different person for her.

Jesse took off his shoes, the ones he'd paid a fortune for, and threw them out over the water as far as he could. He watched them fall, one after the other, and then make only a small, insignificant splash in the water below. He found his cigarettes in his pocket and took one out. Sarah had mentioned lately that he should quit and so Jesse sat and smoked the rest of the pack, one after the other, as a show of opposition.

He lay back on the ground, a cigarette in his mouth, and watched the smoke curl upward. Soon, the blue sky turned to yellow, then orange, then a vivid red, then black. And still Jesse lay there, smoking. He knew he should leave, and yet this was a place where shoulds didn't exist. In this place, there was only Jesse. He had no one to report to. No explanations were required.

At eight-thirty that night, Jesse got back into his car and drove down the hill. He stopped at a local market, picked up another pack of cigarettes with the remaining change in his pocket, and laughed when people stared at his shoeless feet.

He drove home and pulled up in the driveway. The lights were all on and Jesse knew there would be hell to pay for being late. Still, he could not feel guilty. He had done what he needed to do for himself. Just this once, Sarah would have to understand that.

When he walked inside, Carolyn ran into his arms. She was already bathed and smelled of soap. Jesse closed his eyes when he held her. It wasn't fair that there were moments like these, moments when a hug from his daughter seemed like the most beautiful thing in the world, a thing worth dying for. If it were only crying and crapping and ear infections, it would be so much easier to walk away.

"How's my girl?" Jesse said, putting her back down.

"Great. Mommy and I made cookies. Want some?"

She pulled him into the kitchen. Sarah was there, cleaning off the counters. The smell of chocolate-chip cookies flew into his nostrils and Jesse smiled.

"Smells great."

Sarah nodded. She did not look at him, or come over to greet him. She rarely did anymore. She did not make any move before he did, as if she could only respond to him and not initiate an action. Carolyn lifted her hand up onto the counter and found a cookie. She handed it to him.

"I put the chocolates in," she said proudly.

Jesse mussed her hair and ate the cookie. It gave him an excuse not to kiss Sarah, or tell her he was sorry. He didn't know if he could do it today, pretend a regret he didn't feel.

"It's wonderful," he said.

Carolyn clapped her hands. Jesse smiled at her, wishing they all could be more like her, pleased by so little, delighted by the slightest compliment. He realized, quite suddenly, how lucky he was to have a child like her. She could very well be moody or hyperactive or any of the things all the other parents complained about. Instead, she was an adorable, almost always happy little girl.

He scooped her up.

"I'll tell you a story. How's that? Little Red Riding Hood, maybe?"

"Oh no. Not that one. Rapunzel. Tell me Rapunzel."

"You've got it."

Jesse started walking up the stairs with her.

"I'd like to talk to you after she's in bed," Sarah called after him.

Jesse stopped and felt the rigidness creep into his spine again. How strange, that she could do that. She was almost like a mother that way, and he the child. It didn't even matter what she said, he bristled against it as if it were a punishment.

"Of course."

Jesse took Carolyn upstairs and got her into bed. He sat beside her and she looked down at his feet.

"Daddy, you have no shoes. Did you forget to put them on this morning?"

Jesse laughed. "No, actually after work I went to a beautiful place overlooking the ocean and I threw them in the water. What do you think of that?"

Carolyn's eyes widened and then she clapped her hands.

"That's great! Can I do it? I hate my red shoes."

Jesse brushed her hair off her forehead and smiled.

"You can do whatever you want to do. Don't let anyone tell you differently."

Carolyn clasped her hands around his neck and

brought him down to her. She kissed his forehead with wet lips.

"What was that for?" Jesse asked her when she lay back down.

"Just because," Carolyn said, with a look that was much older than her four years. He shook away the thought of her growing older, bestowing that same kiss and look on some other man, and searched his memory for the story of Rapunzel.

"Okay. Let's see. Once upon a time there was a young woman with long, long, long blond hair who was shut away in a tower."

"Rapunzel!" Carolyn said.

"Yes, Rapunzel. You see, there was this evil witch . . ."

Half an hour later, Jesse closed the door to Carolyn's bedroom. She was sound asleep, still smiling, probably dreaming of letting her own blond hair grow out enough so her prince could climb up it. Jesse checked on Sam and then went back downstairs. Sarah was sitting at the table, drinking a glass of wine.

Jesse took out a cigarette and lit it. Sarah raised her eyebrows, but said nothing. Jesse sat down beside her.

"I called your office when you were late," she said. "Walter told me what happened."

For the first time, Jesse had a hint of what this layoff might mean to them. Not just to him, but to all of them, as a family.

"I figured that's why you didn't come home right away," Sarah went on. "Where did you go?"

Jesse shrugged. "Nowhere in particular. I just needed time to think."

That wasn't really a lie. Sarah would interpret it her way, to satisfy her own image of what he should be, and perhaps that was nothing new for them anyway.

"I wish you'd told me right away," she said. "We should work this out together."

She didn't look at him when she spoke. Jesse couldn't recall a time since his party when she had looked at him. It was as if she didn't want to see who he was. She'd rather live with her own fantasies and memories than face him head-on.

"There's nothing to work out," he said. "They fired me and I'll have to find something else. The end."

"We have to work out what we'll do in the meantime. How we'll pay the bills."

Jesse stood up. His father had been laid off once. He hadn't heard the actual conversation afterward, but he was certain his parents had worked off the same script. Anything that had to do with money and adults was so intense, so serious. What a bunch of fools, placing so much stock in silly green slips of paper.

The truth was, it would all work itself out somehow. If they couldn't pay the bills when they came, they'd cut back, or sell something, or borrow from Sarah's parents. Why couldn't they just let things happen? Why did everything always have to be so planned, so goddamn structured?

"Look," he said. "I'll handle it. I always have before."

"Why are you angry at me?" Sarah said. "I didn't do anything."

"Of course not," Jesse said. "You never do anything. Not good little Sarah."

The moment he said it, he wished he could take the words back. She was right. He was angry at her. It didn't make sense, but he was. He'd been angry at her since that night with Annabel. She had taken him back and then played the put-upon, betrayed wife and he was sick of it. Every day, with the tears she just barely held back and her hurt, pouting little mouth, she made him beg her forgiveness. She made him plead just to be with her. He was angry at her for turning him into a spineless little man.

He waited for her tears, but they didn't come. He looked at her, still sitting in the chair, staring at the wall.

"Sarah . . ."

She held up her hand. Jesse sat back down in the chair beside her.

"You've always known who I am," she said quietly. "I haven't changed."

"Neither have I."

This time she did look at him. She held his gaze for so long, he had to turn away.

"You have," she said. "It's not just that night with Annabel. You've been changing since the day we got married. I thought you'd be my knight, like you were when we were dating. But now you're . . . I don't know. Somewhere else. It's like I don't have the main part of you here with me."

"Look, if you're worried about the money, don't be. I'll find something. I always do."

"It's not that."

"What the hell is it then?"

Sarah jerked back as if he'd slapped her. There was no reason for Jesse to snap at her, and yet he felt so impatient with her words, with the way she had to make everything so complex. Nothing meant what he thought it meant. Every word to her had some deeper meaning, every gesture carried some greater weight. She interpreted things one way, taking in all the subtleties, and he interpreted them another, seeing only the surface. He was tired of all the mixed-up communication.

"It's that," she said.

"What?" Jesse said, running his hand through his hair. It was like talking to a person from another country. He had to pull everything out of her and then try to interpret it.

"Your tone. You don't respect me anymore. You see me as this weight around your neck."

"Come on, Sarah. That's not true."

She turned away and crossed her arms. Jesse knew the rules. He was supposed to plead with her now, tell her he was sorry, debase himself enough so that she felt righteous again. Instead, he stood up.

"Let's not do this," he said.

"Do what?"

"Get into an argument. We should talk about this tomorrow."

"I don't want to talk about this tomorrow. I want to work it out now. I have a right to know about my own life, how I'm going to survive, if I'll have enough food to feed my children, if—"

Jesse slammed his hand down on the table and Sarah jumped.

"I'll tell you what I did today," he shouted. "I drove to this place I know, threw my shoes into the Sound, and smoked a pack of cigarettes. I felt good, dammit. Better than I have in weeks. And do you know why? Because I didn't have a wife making me feel like filth because I got too drunk one night for my own good. Because I didn't have to sit in a goddamn office I hate doing shit work. Because I was just me again. Just Jesse. Something I haven't been since the day we got married."

Sarah was still sitting there, but now there were tears rolling down her cheeks. Jesse had watched them start falling while he spoke, but he couldn't stop. There were words in him that had to come out.

"You're really a hypocrite," he went on, finding some kind of sadistic pleasure in watching her hunch over, recoil from his words. She did not give in to her tears as she usually did. But this was worse somehow, the way she cried without sound, the lines of tears slipping down off her chin onto the table. "You did the same goddamn thing. Maybe you didn't fuck the guy, but you went out with him. It's no different than what I did except that I never called you on it or made you pay for it."

Sarah looked up at him.

"What are you talking about?"

"Come on, Sarah. Don't deny it now. I know all about your little escapade with the man from the park. How he listened to you and I didn't. How I was ignoring you and you decided to be with somebody who paid attention. Annabel told me everything."

Sarah stared at him, confused.

"That night you weren't here when I got home," he went on. "I know what you were doing."

"You thought I was having an affair?" she asked.

"I called Annabel to see if you were there. She didn't want to tell me. She'd promised to cover for you. But she broke down. She tried to soften it, to say you were only having lunch and nothing else."

Sarah shook her head. "So she did that too," she said. "I shouldn't be surprised, but I still am somehow. I wonder how she lived with herself, how she faced me and still managed to lie so smoothly. All that time I thought we were friends, she must have hated me."

"So you're still denying it?"

Sarah glared at him. "Use your head, Jesse. There was no man in the park. Annabel made the whole thing up. She convinced me to surprise you with a romantic night. I got a sitter, made reservations at a restaurant and hotel. She was the one who told me not to be here when you came home. She must have had it all planned from the very beginning."

Jesse walked around the table. He wanted to deny it, to hold on to the anger so that he wouldn't have to be the only villain in the house, but Sarah's words rang too true. Had Annabel done it for him, because she wanted to be with him? Or simply because she couldn't stand to see anyone else happy?

"I can't believe you never said anything," Sarah said.

"I forgave you. I could accept that you'd made a mistake."

"I didn't make a mistake," Sarah said. "If you'd just thought about it, you would have realized Annabel was lying. But you wanted to believe her instead of me."

"At least I was willing to put it aside. I didn't let this one betrayal ruin everything, the way you have."

"It's not the same thing," Sarah said. "Even if Annabel's story was true, I didn't throw another man in your face. I didn't screw him in the car outside our house, like it was some kind of carnival show and everyone could come and watch."

"Goddammit, Sarah. It's over. It's never going to happen again. What's the point of me even saying I'm sorry if you're never going to accept the apology? You've done your job, you've made me feel like shit. When the hell are you gonna let this go?"

Jesse started toward her, but she leaned back in her chair, away from him, and he stopped.

"It's come to this then," she said. "To blaming each other for our lives."

"That's not what I meant to say."

Sarah stood up. She finished off the last of her wine and walked past him.

"I'll sleep with Carolyn," she said.

"Sarah, no."

She said nothing and walked out of the room. Jesse picked up her wine glass and threw it. The last drops of Burgundy stained the wall like blood.

# 14

PATRICK ALMOST OPENED the door and walked in before he remembered he was required to knock now. He rapped against the door and smiled when he heard Adam bouncing down the stairs inside. His son flung open the door and threw himself in his arms.

"Right on time," Adam said, hugging him.

"Of course. I wouldn't miss a second of our time together."

Patrick walked into the house, the one he still paid for but did not belong in. It looked the same except that Annabel had taken their wedding picture off the mantel and replaced it with a school picture of Adam. Patrick realized, for the first time, that their wedding picture had been the only photograph of the two of them in the house. How strange that they had never bothered to get out the camera and take snapshots of their lives, as if none of it were worth remembering. How easy it had been for her to erase him.

"Where's your mom?"

"Upstairs, brushing her teeth."

Nothing new, Patrick thought. Even for an almost exhusband, Annabel had to be picture-perfect. Patrick looked down at his son, who still clung to him. They had every Saturday and Sunday together. Annabel had been more than fair about visitation. The whole divorce settlement, in fact, had been remarkably cordial. Patrick was willing to go on paying for all the expenses he had covered before. Annabel could not deny Adam anything, so she was liberal with the time he could spend with his father. They were better to each other as divorce partners than they ever were as husband and wife.

Patrick picked up Adam and swung him over his shoulder. He was getting heavier every time he saw him. He was in second grade now and had even been known to talk of girlfriends in his class. It was amazing, the changes children went through in so short a time, from infant to toddler to child to teenager to adult, in two decades. An adult, in that time, could stay almost exactly the same, in the same place, surrounded by the same people. Stagnant.

"You're so big," Patrick said, swinging him around, soaking up the sound of Adam's laughter. It was as if he had to reacquaint himself with his son every weekend, refamiliarize himself with his features, his gestures, his sound and smell. He would try to hang on to all the images of him during the week, but by Thursday or Friday, the clarity of his vision of Adam faded and he could hardly wait to see him again, to replenish his supply.

He swung Adam up and down and around, getting them both dizzy. Finally, they collapsed on the floor, laughing, and Annabel was standing above them.

"Having fun, children?" she asked.

Patrick looked up at her. He could tell immediately that she'd been drinking. She was an expert at hiding her liquor, but there was no masking the redness in her eyes, the slight sway of her legs. The smile left Patrick's face instantly and he stood up.

"Son, why don't you go upstairs and get your things?"

"Okay," Adam said, running away.

Patrick stared at Annabel and she smiled. He could smell the toothpaste meant to mask the whiskey. He grabbed her hand and pulled her around the corner, into the kitchen.

"Just what the hell are you doing?" he asked. She tried to pull her hand away, but he held on.

"I don't know what you're talking about."

She still spoke clearly, if more slowly than usual.

"Drinking," he said. "It's not even ten in the morning, for God's sake. How are you supposed to take care of Adam if you can't even wait until you're fully awake to have a drink?"

Annabel yanked her hand away and glared at him. She stomped over to the sink, but found nothing in it to busy her hands. She turned back around and looked at him.

"I take care of Adam just fine, better than you could. It was just one drink, and I'm entitled to that."

"It's no way to deal with your problems."

"What problems?" Annabel said, waving her hand around. She staggered a little and gripped the counter. "Didn't you know I'm happy as a clam? I love it that the phone is silent all day. It's the best feeling in the world to be treated like some kind of pariah by the people who used to be my friends."

Patrick almost put his arm around her to comfort her, but then that good, solid anger he'd had since he found her in the car with Jesse kicked in again. She'd brought this heartache on herself.

"You've got to get it together," he said. "Adam needs you now."

Annabel walked to the back door of the kitchen and leaned against it. She was hunched forward, her hair was slightly out of line, and Patrick was surprised at how vulnerable she looked. Could it be that there really was a tenderness inside that shell? Or was she only acting this way for effect? With Annabel, it was impossible to tell.

"I've got it together," she said, squaring her shoulders. All traces of her vulnerability vanished, as if they had never been there at all. She turned and stared at him. "I had a drink because I wanted one. I didn't need it; it just sounded good. I knew you were coming for Adam, so I didn't see any harm in it. And if I want to get drunk, I'll get drunk. It's no business of yours anymore."

"Adam is my business," Patrick said.

"Only on Saturdays and Sundays. I don't have to be as lenient with your visitation rights, you know. My lawyer said once a month would be fine with the judge."

"And I don't have to be as lenient with my wallet,"

Patrick said. "There's no way I'm going to cut back on child support for Adam, but I don't have to keep paying for your whiskey."

They stared at each other and then Adam walked back into the kitchen.

"Ready, Dad?"

His hand crept into Patrick's.

"Sure, sport. Say goodbye to your mom."

"Bye, Mom," Adam said and then turned and ran out the front door to Patrick's car. No kiss. No hug. Patrick watched the pain flicker in Annabel's face, but then it was gone.

"He loves you," she said.

"He doesn't see me as much," Patrick said softly. "He's just excited, that's all."

She nodded. Patrick stepped toward her and awkwardly touched her arm. She still felt the same, yet it was strange now, like taking a liberty that didn't belong to him.

"Maybe you should talk to someone," he said.

She jerked away from him and tossed back her hair. Patrick knew that whatever contact he'd made with her had been lost.

"I don't need to talk to anyone. I'm doing fine and I don't need you to tell me how to live my life."

Patrick turned and walked out of the room. Before he reached the front door, he heard her open the cabinet in the kitchen. She was taking out the whiskey.

Sarah met the two of them inside the high school gymnasium. Patrick was teaching Adam how to dribble a basketball when she arrived with a picnic basket and blanket.

"I bring supplies," she said.

Adam dropped the basketball and reached her first. He put his arms around her.

"Aunt Sarah," he said. "I've missed you. How come you don't come over anymore?"

Sarah looked over his head to Patrick. Patrick shrugged and Sarah looked back down at Adam.

"I've been really busy, sweetie," she said. "But I've missed you too."

Adam seemed appeased by this and took the basket out of her hand.

"What have you got?"

Sarah laughed. "Sandwiches and sodas. Some homemade cookies too."

"Great."

Patrick came to her side.

"Thanks for coming," he said.

"You don't have to thank me. Anything to get out of the house."

They laid down the blanket and took out the food. Adam dug into everything with relish.

"Where's Carolyn?" he asked.

"She and Sam are at home with their dad."

"That's good," Adam said. "She's such a baby."

"Adam!" Patrick said.

"Well, she is. She always wants to play baby games with me and I hate it. She's not even in school yet."

Sarah smiled and ate her sandwich. She looked around the empty gymnasium and listened to the rain beating down on the roof. It was a cold January day and the forecast was for the rain to turn to snow sometime this evening.

"How are you?" Patrick asked softly.

Sarah looked over at Adam, but he had found something to interest him beneath the bleachers and had taken his sandwich with him on his hunt.

"I've been better," she said. "Jesse hasn't found another job yet and things are tight. My parents just gave us a loan."

"That should help."

"Financially, yes. But Jesse can't stand taking money from them. He thinks it makes him more like them, and he hates that."

They were quiet while the rain beat down and Adam's feet scuttled on the floor.

"Does Jesse know you're here with me?" Patrick asked.

Sarah looked at him. "Of course. I'm not doing anything wrong."

"I know that, but—"

"But nothing. If Jesse got even mildly upset about me having a harmless lunch with you, I think I'd walk right out the door and never come back."

"Would you really?"

Sarah set her sandwich down. She reached for her soda can, but then changed her mind.

"I don't know," she said softly. "Sometimes, when he refuses to even call about a job because he says it's not 'right' for him, or when he acts like I'm the one who was in the back seat of that car, like I'm the one who changed everything, I just want to leave. I want it to be over."

"And other times?"

"Other times, he's Jesse again. I can look at him and get a shiver up my spine just like I did when I was sixteen years old. And then I would give anything to keep him, to make him love me like he used to."

Adam came out from under the bleachers, proudly showing off two quarters.

"You should see all the stuff under there," he said. "Trash and clothes, even an old hot dog. I didn't eat it though."

"Good thing," Patrick said.

Adam picked up the basketball.

"Can we play some more?"

"Give me a chance to finish eating," Patrick said. "You go ahead."

Adam dribbled the ball down the length of the gym and tossed it almost to the base of the hoop.

"You're getting there," Patrick called out to him. "Just give it a little extra push."

Adam retrieved the ball and tried again. Sarah watched Patrick's eyes as he urged on his son. This was a side of him she had never really seen before. His love for Adam was intense, almost hungry. Annabel had never given him a chance to show that love. She had always taken charge of Adam, just like she took charge of everything. Sarah stiffened. Just the thought of Annabel made her body go rigid. In her dreams, she and Annabel went on as always, best friends, sharing secrets and driving fast cars and laughing. But as soon as she woke up, the vision faded and she remembered the lies, the betrayals. All she was left with was this anger that she doubted would ever go away.

And then there was Patrick. Wonderful, kind Patrick who had stepped into Annabel's shoes and become her best friend. He listened better than his wife ever had. He called her faithfully, no matter how busy he was. From the moment he opened the car door, there had been a bond between them. The two of them, the betrayed.

Adam threw the ball and it hit the rim of the hoop and bounced off.

"Whoa-ho!" Patrick shouted. "Did you see that? You were almost in there! Great shot, Adam!"

Sarah picked up her sandwich again. It was almost possible to erase her other life, her other family, and pretend that this—a man, a woman, a boy, having a picnic, shooting baskets—was all there was. How nice it would be if that were true, if there weren't any hidden meanings beneath their words, the way there were with her and Jesse. If no one were trying to hurt anybody.

"Will you come back to the apartment with us?" Patrick asked, without looking at her.

Sarah's hand trembled for a second and she hid it in her lap.

"No, I don't think so. I've got to get back home."

Patrick nodded and stood up. He raced down the length of the gym and stole the basketball away. In one smooth, easy motion, he made a jump shot and landed the ball through the hoop.

Annabel downed her fourth whiskey sour and ordered another one. The bartender didn't hesitate. She was the life of the place. Not a single man had left since she arrived.

"Okay boys," she said, "who's next?"

Annabel looked around the smoky pool room. She had already raked in fifty dollars beating these poor fools in eightball. Still, they were lining up to play with her.

"I'll do it," a young man, no more than twenty-one, said. He had curly blond hair and a thin mustache he was trying to grow in. Annabel walked over to him and put her fingertip under his chin.

"Does your mama know where you are?"

The boy and all the other men laughed. Annabel winked at him and stepped back to the bar.

"Break," she said.

She could sip her drink now. It was a routine she followed. First, she had to get Adam out of the house with Patrick for their weekend together before she could open up the liquor cabinet without feeling watched. She kept pouring out the booze and gulping it down while she slipped into her black dress, the one that pushed her breasts up and out the top. Then, at five o'clock, she headed for a bar. Every weekend, she tried a new one. It wouldn't do to see the same faces and bodies.

Once she arrived, she steadily drank down three more whiskeys. It took that much to make her feel something now. After that, she could relax, sip her drink, and flirt a little.

This particular bar tempted her because of its pool tables. She hadn't been a bad player back in her teens, when her parents had a table. It would be easy to make a little money. None of the men were playing to win. They just liked to see her bend over to make her shot.

The young man broke, but nothing went in the pockets. Annabel set her drink down and sashayed over to the table. The men cheered her on and Annabel gave them her biggest smile. She liked these men and they liked her. It was as simple as that. At the end of the night, as always, she planned to choose one to go home with. They'd find somewhere interesting to do it, maybe under his dining room table or out on the balcony, and she'd squeeze her eyes shut and pretend he was Jesse. Then she'd wait until he fell asleep before she sneaked out. By the next morning, his name would be forgotten.

Annabel lined up for the five ball in the corner pocket. Even with the whiskey coursing through her, she made it easily. The men cheered. Annabel looked back at the young, handsome man she was playing.

"What's your name, boy?" she said.

He swallowed twice.

"James."

"Well, James, did you put your money on the table? It's up to twenty dollars a game now."

James reached into his pocket and took out his wallet. With shaking hands, he reached in and got out a twenty. As he was leaning over to place it on the rim of the table, Annabel traced her fingertip along his arm. She watched the gooseflesh rise on his skin.

The other men were all complaining, telling her not to waste herself on jail bait, but Annabel had already made up her mind. She smiled at James and grazed his ear with her lips.

"Later," she whispered.

He swallowed again and Annabel laughed. She turned and concentrated on the game.

For the first time, Annabel brought a man back to her house. James was not even twenty-one; he was nineteen. A fake ID had gotten him into the bar. He still lived at home, with his parents. They could have gone to a hotel, but there was something exhilarating about bringing him home, to where Patrick used to be.

"Wow, you live here?" James said, when Annabel pulled up into the driveway. She had been lucky to make it home at all. The road was swerving all over the place, but she had given James her address and then listened to his instructions of "Turn left" and "A little more to the right," and somehow they had gotten here. They stepped out of the car.

"Yep, this is home sweet home."

"Cool."

Annabel laughed. It was snowing and she had no jacket. Now that was a stupid thing to do. She laughed harder. She kicked off her shoes and stood in the snow in her stockings.

"Are you crazy?" James said, coming over to her.

"Yep. Crazy as a . . . as a what? What's crazy, James?"

He shook his head and tried to pull her toward the door. Instead, Annabel pulled away from him and tilted her head back. She tried to catch snowflakes on her tongue.

"Mmmm," she said. "Try it."

"No. Snowflakes aren't what I'm interested in."

Annabel giggled. Her feet were cold, yet she didn't

mind. They felt detached from her. She looked down at her body, saw the gooseflesh thick and pimply on her bare arms, but didn't care. It felt wonderful to be so cold. She felt alive again.

"Oh James, isn't it wonderful? Don't you love the snow?"

"Yeah. I guess so."

James kept trying to walk to the door, but Annabel would go nowhere. She twirled around in the snow and ended up on her rear. James ran back to her.

"Are you all right?"

Annabel was laughing. The concern in this boy's eyes amused her. Who was he anyway? Oh yes, the bar. He was the one she'd chosen.

"Kiss me," she said. "Kiss me in the snow."

James leaned forward and kissed her. Annabel quickly put her arms around his neck and pulled him down on the snow. She opened her mouth and sampled the wonderful, sour taste of him. She could feel his penis pressing against her.

"Katie," he said. "Please."

Annabel pulled away.

"Who's Katie?"

"You are, remember?"

Annabel laughed. That's right. That was her name for the night. Katie Melody. A ridiculous name no one had questioned.

"Katie, that's me," she said. James helped her to her feet and this time managed to get her to the front porch.

"Where's your key?"

Annabel smiled at him.

"Guess."

His eyes instinctively went to her breasts. Annabel pulled him closer and she could feel his hot breath on her cheek. He lifted his trembling fingers and placed them on her neck. Annabel leaned back against the house and lifted her knee up between his legs.

"You're getting warmer," she said.

She giggled as his fingers slipped down between her breasts. She thought she heard movement in the bushes outside her house, but she wasn't paying attention. This boy's fingers were working miracles.

Jesse slammed the front door on his way in. The lights were already off in the house and he knew Sarah would be tucked away with Carolyn. She had been sleeping with their daughter since the day he lost his job.

He stomped through the house and went to the refrigerator. He took out a beer and drank it quickly, with the refrigerator door still open. Then he slammed it shut and walked up to the bedroom.

He stared at the bed. Sarah had not gone near it for months. She had even refused to take the bed and let him sleep on the couch. She wanted to be a martyr, as usual. Make him feel like shit.

They could hardly stand to be under the same roof together. She wanted him to take a job, any job, no matter how unhappy it made him. She wouldn't try, for even one second, to understand his point of view. He wasn't going to do just anything again. This was his chance to find out what he really liked. And that would take time. But of course, time was something Sarah couldn't stand to waste.

Jesse took off his jacket and flung it across the room. Then he followed that with his shoes, flinging them against the wall. All thoughts of Sarah vanished.

It was the first time he'd given in to himself, satisfied his curiosity, and snuck over to Annabel's. And look what it had gotten him! The nerve of that bitch. Annabel was practically doing it in the snow, for everybody to see. He should have known that was what she was, just a casual whore. Their screw in the car hadn't been anything new for her.

Jesse marched to the bookshelf and, with one swipe, threw everything to the floor. He was looking around for something else to throw when the door to the bedroom opened.

"What's going on in here?" Sarah said.

Her eyes were still red with sleep and her hair messy. She looked around the room and then back at Jesse.

"What's going on?" she said again.

Jesse looked at her and felt the anger overwhelm him.

She knew damn well what was going on. She knew exactly what she had done to him. She had sucked the life out of him. Annabel had done the same thing years ago to Patrick, made him into nothing, a timid little boy doing his wife's bidding, and now it had happened to Jesse.

Jesse crossed the room in less than a second, before he could think. He yanked her head back by the hair and kissed her before she could cry out. He rammed his teeth against hers and thrust his tongue into her mouth. He could feel her trying to pull away, but she was no match for him. He felt his erection growing, finally feeling her body against his after all these months.

He pulled away only long enough to pull her over to the bed.

"Jesse, stop," she said. He didn't care what she said. For once, he didn't give a goddamn what she wanted. He'd had it with her and Annabel and all their games. He'd had it with pleading and asking her forgiveness and doing everything Sarah's way. He'd had it with her sleeping like a queen in Carolyn's room. Sarah was his wife, dammit. He had a right to her.

He shoved her down on the bed and yanked her nightgown up over her face. While she struggled to pull it off her eyes, Jesse loosened his pants. He was holding her down with the weight of him.

Sarah got the nightgown up over her head and looked up at him. He could see the terror in her eyes and that only intensified his erection. She was scared of him now, was she? He would teach her to be scared of him, her own husband. He would teach her to keep him out of her bed. He would let her know who he was, a man she couldn't browbeat with her demands and tears.

He got his pants off and didn't look at her face as he rammed himself inside her. She only cried out once and then he didn't hear anything else. He thrust himself in and out, as hard as he could, thinking of his time with Annabel in the car and then thinking of her in the snow with that teenager. Thinking of the early days with Sarah, when he still had a little self-respect, and how her hard face lately and the way he had bowed and scraped to her had stripped all his pride away.

He thrust himself inside her and hated her. She still did not accept his explanation, that he was drunk, that he didn't know what he was doing, that it didn't mean anything. She didn't give a damn anymore about anyone but herself, and certainly not about him. She would keep punishing him until his dying day. It was only fair that she got a little bit in return.

Jesse kept ramming himself at her until all the thinking stopped, until it all built up into one painful ball and squirted out of him and into her. He came as he never had before, but instead of clinging to Sarah, he pushed off on her, arched his back up and pressed his hands down hard on her breasts so that he got the maximum effect.

When it was over, he collapsed on top of her. His ears were ringing and his arms shaking. As his body started to normalize, he heard Sarah's crying. He noticed her tears were soaking his shirt.

He slipped off her and sat on the bed. Sarah lay there, naked, not even making an effort to cover herself. There was blood on the blanket between her legs. Her cheeks and neck were covered with tears.

Jesse stood up. He found his pants and slipped them back on. As he reached for Sarah's nightgown, she flinched away from him. Jesse handed her the gown.

"Put this back on," he said.

Sarah took the nightgown from him and slipped it over her head. She looked down at the blood between her legs and cried harder. Jesse went into the linen closet in the hall and got a washcloth. He took it into the bathroom, soaked it under hot water, and then handed it to her.

She put it between her legs. She was still crying and he noticed now that her whole body was trembling. He wanted to stay angry, to keep the same fury he'd had when she first came in here, but it had all gone out of him. Yet, he could not comfort her either. He was empty inside. He stood there, watching her cry, and knowing that he had just ended it all. In less than one minute, he had severed the last thin strands of their marriage.

When the bleeding stopped, Sarah crawled back up on the bed. She curled into a ball. She was still crying.

Looking at her, something did move Jesse's heart. But as he took a step toward her, her crying intensified.

"Go," she choked out. "Just go."

Jesse hesitated a moment and then nodded. There was nothing left to say with words that he hadn't already said with his body. He turned and walked down the stairs and out the front door without looking back.

# 15

❦

PATRICK LEFT THE lab and walked the streets to Washington Park. He wasn't getting anywhere in his research, which was nothing unusual. But today, for some reason, the frustration was too much. He couldn't concentrate. He couldn't see his way around the problem or come up with any new approaches for studying the cell structures. He was so disillusioned with it all that he couldn't see any alternative but walking away completely and never coming back.

He reached the park and headed through the arboretum. He had to calm himself, find the positive in all this, regain some of his enthusiasm and hope. He'd just walk until his mind bottomed out, until he could go back to the lab and start over, again.

It was March and everything was drenched. A light mist fell through the sky and fogged up his glasses. Patrick took them off and slipped them in his coat pocket. Everything became a blur, which, for once, he found strangely appealing. He couldn't tell exactly what was what, if that green mass was a shrub or a tree. He couldn't make out the details of what he was stepping on.

He ran his hand over the plants at his side, ferns and moss-covered fir trunks. The leaves were cool and wet; the textures spongy and soft. He lifted his fingers to his nose and sniffed; they smelled faintly of mint. He managed not to think of work, but he was unable to stop his thoughts completely. Nothing in his life was the way he wanted it to be.

The divorce was final now. All the papers had been signed and processed. Annabel had kept his name, because she was used to it and she didn't want to go through the hassle of getting a new driver's license. But other than that, it was over. Almost nine years wasted. Except for Adam.

They had fallen into a routine, Patrick and his son. Weekends were spent doing things, going to the museum, or out on a ferry, or playing cards, or seeing a movie. It was as if they had forgotten how to just be together. Every minute had to be action packed and fun filled to make up for the time they were apart.

It was exhausting, being with Adam. Every Friday night, when Patrick picked Adam up at Annabel's, he was full of anticipation and energy. But by Sunday night, when Patrick dropped him off again, he had only enough energy to drive home to his silly little apartment and plop down on the couch. He would look back over the past two days and remember only a blur of zoos and arcades and restaurants and games. Entertaining Adam and giving him everything he wanted was the goal; *being* with Adam became only secondary. It was not what he wanted, but there seemed to be no way around it. This was what divorced fathers did. They took their children places. They bribed them into thinking that divorce really wasn't so bad, they weren't losing all that much.

Patrick would have liked things to be different, slower, more meaningful. In his fantasies, he and Adam simply came to his apartment, sat around together, talked and laughed. But in reality, Patrick felt this overwhelming need to make things up to Adam, to prove he was still a good father even though he had walked away. If he could do that with an extra scoop of ice cream or another ride on the roller coaster, then he would. He would do anything at all to release this guilt from his soul.

Every night, in his apartment, Patrick wondered how a man like him had gotten to a place like this. He had been so certain that his life, except for his work, would be humdrum. A marriage, babies, a house with a front porch and swing. He never would have guessed that he'd be involved in melodrama. He hated being part of the growing group of divorced men. He didn't want to be part of a trend.

He avoided the eyes of the other newly single men in his apartment building, the ones who, like him, had rented furnished apartments and had nothing personal on their walls. The ones who were trying to readjust to living alone. He didn't want camaraderie. He wanted his life to change. He wanted back what he had had, only with someone different from Annabel.

It was amazing, really, that he had ever attracted a woman like Annabel in the first place. Or that they had lasted as long as they had on so little. And especially amazing that he had the nerve or stupidity to leave her.

Patrick turned a corner and came into a picnic area of the arboretum. A man was sitting on one of the farthest benches, but Patrick could only make out the outline of him. He turned and was heading into the forest section of the park when someone called out to him.

"Patrick."

Patrick stopped. He knew the voice, knew who the man sitting on the bench was. He didn't need his glasses to recognize the shiver up his spine. He turned around slowly.

Jesse was walking up to him. As he got closer, he came more into focus. Patrick could make out jeans and a tattered sweatshirt. He could tell that Jesse's hair was all over the place, and perhaps a couple days' worth of stubble blotted his face. Patrick fished into his pocket and took out his glasses. They were spotted with water, but clear enough to let him see that Jesse was a mess. As much of a mess as Patrick had been when he left Annabel.

"Hey, Jesse," Patrick said. The shiver had disappeared and he found, strangely, that he was not nervous. Every emotion was turned off except for that anger that had sustained him through the separation and divorce. It had been his salvation, that alien, hard rock of fury in his stomach. It had blotted out most of the pain. It had made him feel like another person entirely.

He knew that Jesse had left the house, finally. Patrick hadn't seen Sarah for a couple of months, but she had told him over the phone that it was over, they were filing for divorce. She did not explain why, and Patrick did not probe. Sarah cried whenever Jesse's name was mentioned, and he did not want to distress her.

"Fancy meeting you here," Jesse said.

He ran his fingers through his long blond hair. He looked thin and pale and cold. Patrick could see him shivering.

"You should get inside. It's cold out here," Patrick said, even though the idea of Jesse freezing to death was not so unappealing.

Jesse shrugged. "I don't notice."

Patrick stared at him. In the months after he found Jesse and Annabel together, he had not let himself think about Jesse at all. It had been alien to begin with, having a friend like Jesse. Patrick had never had close friends in high school or college; his work was the only thing that mattered and young men with raging hormones did not understand that. And once he got the job at the university, the research took over. He had colleagues, yes. And acquaintances. And people he saw in groups. But never just one man he called up and said "Let's go out" to. Never anyone like Jesse.

Before he even had a chance to appreciate what he had, Jesse threw their friendship back in his face. Patrick knew Sarah was hurt about Annabel's betrayal. Now as he watched Jesse shiver, he recognized his own hurt. Their friendship had not been deep, but there were moments when it was perfect. Moments when Jesse's laughter or slap on the shoulder was all he needed. Moments when a single word from Jesse was worth thousands from Annabel.

Jesse had killed it so easily. Still, when Patrick thought about Jesse's character, the kind of man he was, his escapade with Annabel made sense. That was the problem with Patrick, he could find the sense in senseless things.

"You're out of the house," Patrick said to him now.

Jesse nodded and looked up at the bland covering of gray over their heads.

"She told you."

"No details. Just that you'd left and she filed for divorce."

"It was bound to happen, I guess," Jesse said. "Life goes on."

Patrick clenched his fists. How dare Jesse be so casual about the whole thing? Didn't he know he had ruined Sarah's life, ruined Patrick's life, and, actually, ruined Annabel's? Was there even one speck of his soul devoted to anyone other than himself?

Again, as when he found Jesse and Annabel in the car, Patrick no longer felt like himself. Someone harder, tougher, without a scientific, controlled bone in his body, stepped forward.

"I didn't get to tell you," Jesse said, not noticing the change in his eyes, "after it happened ... after ... well, I'm sorry."

The apology was so late, so insignificant, that Patrick almost laughed. Instead, for the first and only time, he let go of restraint and rationality, and pulled back his fist. He let it go with every ounce of his strength and hit Jesse square on the jaw. Jesse stumbled back, started to lose his balance, but then righted himself. He took a step forward, his own fists clenched for battle, and Patrick readied himself. But then, surprisingly, the fight went out of Jesse's eyes and he only rubbed his jaw.

"I guess I had that coming," Jesse said, opening and closing his mouth, making sure all the parts worked.

Patrick looked down at his fist. It was still clenched and red where he had made contact. He knew it was crazy, but for a moment he was sure that he and Jesse had switched places, that Jesse's fist had somehow attached itself to his arm, that his spirit had seeped into Patrick's soul. What else would explain how far each of them had come from what they used to be? What else would explain Patrick throwing a punch and Jesse backing down from a fight?

Patrick opened his hand. He came back to himself and realized that his fist belonged to him; Jesse wasn't the only man who could throw a punch. He felt no regret. He liked the hardness of his skin, the sting in his knuckles, the welt that was rising on Jesse's chin. He should have punched Jesse the night he found him in the back seat. He had held himself back too long.

"You're a son of a bitch, Jesse Bean," he said.

Instead of getting angry, Jesse flashed him a smile.

"Ain't it the truth."

The smile was still there when Patrick turned away. He would not be sucked in again. He thought of where his loyalties lay now, and he knew they were with Sarah. For a brief, wonderful while, he had had both of them, Jesse and Sarah, male and female, silence and sympathy. But now it was on to new times.

"Have you got a place to stay?" Patrick asked.

"Sure. Here and there until I can find the right job. You know how it is."

The truth was, Patrick did not know how it was. He did not know a damn thing about Jesse and he probably never would. He walked away without saying another word and didn't look back. He heard the scrunching of gravel behind him, and by the time he turned around, Jesse was gone.

Jesse looked in his car's rearview mirror and smoothed back his hair. He had borrowed a friend's razor and shaved off his stubble. He had found some change and gone to a laundromat. His clothes were clean and his eyes were white. He was what Sarah wanted him to be.

He got out of the car and walked to the door. He heard both laughing and shouting inside and peeked in through the glass. Sarah was chasing after Carolyn, who obviously thought it was hysterically funny to take an expensive crystal decanter and run around the house with it. Sarah finally reached her halfway up the stairs and scooped her up with one arm. Jesse laughed.

Sarah heard him and looked at his face, smashed up against the glass. She jumped a little and then set Carolyn down. She took the decanter away and shooed her up to her room. She walked down to the door and opened it.

"What are you doing here?" she asked.

Jesse tried not to show his unease. It was still amazing how reversed everything was, how she could make his stomach feel sick and his legs wobbly instead of him doing that to her. He couldn't believe how badly he wanted her, now that he had thrown her away.

"I was just in the neighborhood. I thought—"

"Jesse, we talked about this. If you want to see the kids, you should call first."

"I don't want to see them. I mean, of course I do, but I'm really here to see you. It's a gorgeous day. I thought . . ."

Sarah was shaking her head and Jesse stopped. Since that night he walked out, he had wanted nothing but to come back. He had sent her letters, called her, stopped by, sent flowers, chocolates, lingerie. He had found a job to please her, and then quit when she told him that wasn't enough. Then he got another one and quit that one too. He had tried to charm her with his smile, his jokes, and then tried to move her with tears. He had gone through his entire repertoire of emotions and reactions and still he could not change her mind. She wanted a divorce. He found it difficult to believe she could be so adamant.

"Jesse, please don't make this harder than it is already. After that night . . ."

She did not let him in. Jesse stood there, with the sun at his back, looking in on the house that was once his own. He still owned it. Technically, he could push her out of his way and step inside. Instead, he took a step backward, away from her.

"I've made a lot of mistakes," he said. "I did the best I could. I really did."

He looked up to see if she was responding to his change in tone. He did not see any moisture in her eyes. She still gripped the door, as if she might slam it shut on him at any time. Jesse clenched his fists.

"I know I shouldn't have forced you," he said. "But I was so angry. I couldn't see straight. The moment it was over, I regretted it."

Sarah met his eyes.

"You know, I really don't care what you felt," she said. "You violated everything that night. Me, our love, my trust in you. It's over, Jesse. You can stop by here a million times and it will still be over."

She started to close the door, but Jesse shoved his body into the gap. He gripped her arm and stared at her.

"I love you, Sarah."

Sarah shook her head. "No you don't. You haven't got the slightest clue what love is."

"Sarah, please."

Sarah stepped back, out of his grip. Jesse looked around the room wildly. He was searching for something, anything to make her understand. If he could just show her an old photograph of the two of them when they were happy. Or some present they got on their wedding day. If only . . .

He looked back at her and knew it was no good. He stepped out of the doorway. He had been bumming around for weeks now, staying with one friend for a while and then another. He had taken on and lost two jobs since he left this house. He really didn't think he had it in him to keep trying.

He only wanted Sarah. It had taken over every atom of his body and mind, the way the motorcycle and football had, only twenty times more intensified. She was the reason he got up in the morning. He didn't think it through. He didn't analyze why he felt it now, after she was gone. He could not see past the point of getting her back in his life.

And now he knew it wouldn't happen. The divorce would go through, he would be painted as the bad guy, and that would be that. They had been married seven years ago this summer.

He looked up at her.

"I never thought you could be like this," he said.

Sarah nodded.

"Neither did I." She closed the door.

Sarah sat with her lawyer in his office. He was a cool, calculating man who did not understand her in the slightest.

"He has to pay, Sarah," he said. "It's his duty. It's required by law."

Sarah shook her head.

"You don't understand. He has no job. He has nothing to pay with."

"And you don't understand that he will have to get a job. He has to take care of his children, and you. It's been four months since he moved out of the house and you haven't seen a dime of child support."

"I have savings," Sarah said.

The lawyer stood up and walked to the window. She could see the angry tic working in his jaw.

"Let me explain this to you one more time," he said. "Jesse is still legally your husband and your children's father. For the whole seven years of your marriage, he has supported you. He has paid the mortgage and car payments and put food on the table. Simply because you decided to get a divorce does not give him the right to let you starve. On top of that, he was the one to bring about the dissolution of your marriage. He had the affair. He raped you. We could suck him dry, Sarah."

Sarah closed her eyes. She was shivering badly, even though the room was warm. She really didn't know how long she could listen to this man talk about her and Jesse as plaintiff and defendant. It was never what she wanted, this mean-spirited attempt to bleed each other to death. She only wanted it over. She only wanted to stop crying, to stop hurting, to get on with things.

"I understand what you're saying," Sarah said, her voice trembling. "But you've got to understand that my intention is not to annihilate Jesse. Of course I want and need child support. But right now he's not able to pay any. As soon as he gets a job, I'm sure he'll be more than willing to take care of his children."

The lawyer came back to his chair and sat down. He gave her a look that made her feel incredibly stupid and naïve.

"In court, I'm going to go for the highest payment and I'll tell you why. You'll never see a dime from this man. He'll always have an excuse for not paying. Either he won't have a job, or he'll be getting back on his feet, or the check got lost in the mail. I want the payments to be high enough so that when you finally decide to prosecute him for lack of support, you'll get what's coming to you."

Sarah left the office tired and shaken. The lawyer made this whole thing into some kind of war game, with strategic maneuvers and secret weapons. He seemed to have totally forgotten that there were people involved, people who had once loved each other, who still loved each other in a crazy kind of way.

Sarah drove to the sitter's and picked up the kids. Carolyn was rambunctious in the car on the way home. Sam was crying.

Sarah was getting by on three hours of sleep a night, an ever-shrinking sliver of determination left inside her, daily support calls from Patrick, and checks from her parents. Jesse called too, to tell her that he'd gone on an interview and it looked promising, and as soon as he could he'd send money. But promises did not pay the bills, as her lawyer liked to say.

Still, Sarah could not fault him for that. She knew how miserable he'd been at his last job, even though he thought she didn't understand. And she knew how devastating it was to him for her to give up on them. She had always been the one holding them together. It was the one thing Jesse depended on; her unwavering love, no matter what he did.

Then, in one night, when he rammed himself inside her and would not look at her face or listen to her crying or acknowledge that she was a person, his wife, and not some faceless, mindless body he could punch out his aggressions on, he killed her love. Not all of it. She didn't think it was possible that she would ever stop loving him completely. But he killed the tenderness she had for him, the part of her that trusted him, that was comfortable around him, that wanted him near her.

Still, it was not easy to tell him to go, to continue telling him to go every time he stopped by or called. But she did it. It was as if, when he raped her, he transferred all of his anger to her. In a strange way, she became stronger from his abuse. It was not worth it; she would rather still be weak and not feel this incredible sense of violation, as if he had ripped her open and taken what she had inside. But she could not change things. There was a hard part inside her now, a part that managed to slam the door in Jesse's face every time he came by.

Sarah drove up in her driveway. She was busy getting

Carolyn and Sam out of the car, so at first she didn't see the figure on her doorstep. Then she heard Carolyn squeal.

"Aunt Annabel! What are you doing here?"

Sarah went rigid. Of course Carolyn had to be wrong. Annabel would not come now, after so long, after all her opportunities for making things better had come and gone. Sarah picked up Sam and looked at her front door. Annabel sat on the stoop, hugging Carolyn.

Sarah tried to straighten up, to square her shoulders, but this time she couldn't. She was not up to this. Every day she had to stay strong enough to deal with Jesse and the lawyer and her kids. But not Annabel. She took one look at her and broke.

She tried to take a step, but her legs remained frozen. Sam started to cry in her arms.

Annabel stood up and looked at her. Carolyn was tugging on her dress, but she ignored her. They looked at each other and Sarah felt the tears slipping down her cheeks. Sam still cried and fought her embrace. She put him down and he waddled off toward the lawn.

It had been so long since Sarah had seen her. A full year. At first, Sarah had been sure that Annabel would call, that she would try to make things better. Sarah knew what she would say to that. She had it all planned. She'd be stoic and cool and indifferent. She would sting Annabel with the one thing she knew would devastate her. Nonchalance.

But Annabel never gave her the chance. She did not call or write or attempt to make things better. And Sarah wondered which was worse, having her best friend betray her, or the silence of the days afterward, when Annabel did not care enough to say she was sorry.

Carolyn finally gave up trying to get Annabel's attention and followed Sam onto the grass. Annabel walked toward Sarah and Sarah stared at her. She looked good. It was impossible that Annabel would ever look anything less than perfect. But still, Sarah was surprised that everything that had happened had not taken a toll on her.

Annabel reached the front of the car and stopped, still three feet away from Sarah. The tears welled up in Sarah's eyes and then the sobs rose in her chest. She had tried so hard for so long to be strong, to hold everything in. All at once, that was impossible. It hurt so much. It was all so damn unfair. She did not deserve the hand she'd been dealt.

Annabel did not try to soothe her. Sarah leaned against the car and cried until she was exhausted. She gasped out the last few sobs and then quieted. When she looked up, she could see that Annabel's eyes were red too, that she had shed a tear for every one of Sarah's.

Sarah waited for Annabel to start her explanation. There was no other reason for her to be here and Sarah had waited so long to hear it. But every time Annabel opened her mouth, she shut it again. Finally, Sarah was the one to speak.

"I always thought you'd try to patch things up some-how," she said.

Annabel lifted her chin a notch.

"Would that have been possible?"

"No."

Annabel nodded. She did not take her eyes from Sarah's face. Sarah felt transparent again, as if she weren't complex at all. She wished she had more defenses; she did not want Annabel to know how deeply she had hurt her.

"I've gotten halfway down the street hundreds of times," Annabel said. "But I couldn't take another step. I couldn't bear your eyes."

"Why today then?"

Another tear slipped down Annabel's cheek.

"I couldn't bear the silence anymore."

Sarah broke away from her gaze and looked over at her children. Carolyn was doing somersaults and Sam was clapping every time her head disappeared into the tall, uncut grass.

"What do you want from me?"

Annabel leaned against the car.

"I don't know. I'm not foolish enough to ask for forgiveness."

"Why would that be foolish?"

"Because you wouldn't give it to me. It would always be this thing between us, something you had that I wanted. You'd keep it just out of my reach."

Sarah looked at her.

"You are so jaded," she said.

Annabel smiled slightly.

"Yes. I am."

"And you're wrong. At first, when I was so angry, I thought I'd never forgive you. But later, when I was only sad for what we'd lost, for what you threw away, I would have listened. Only you never gave me a chance."

Annabel closed her eyes and Sarah looked at her. It had been so long since she'd seen her and yet it could have been yesterday.

"Today," Annabel said, without opening her eyes, "Adam went to school and the silence of the house just about killed me. I started walking down here, like I always do. It's like a pretend game a child might play. I pretend that everything is as it was. I'm welcome here."

Sarah looked down at Annabel's hands. They were trembling so badly she tried to hide them behind her. Sarah could not recall ever seeing Annabel nervous before.

"Usually I stop halfway," Annabel said. "But today, my feet kept going. I wanted to turn around. My mind was practically screaming at me to turn around, but my feet kept going. I reached your porch and knocked. I almost turned and ran away then, but something held me. When you didn't answer, I thought you were standing on the other side of the door, laughing at me."

"I don't think I have it in me to laugh anymore," Sarah said.

Annabel opened her eyes. They looked at each other and Sarah thought about pushing the past aside, throwing herself into Annabel's arms, hugging her until all the pain in her eyes evaporated. She could put an end to this now. She knew Annabel was not faking her despair. Despite the perfect exterior, her eyes were hollow. Until this moment, it had not occurred to Sarah that Annabel was hurting too.

But the moment passed, the insight passed, and Sarah knew she would keep her distance. She could still be moved by Annabel. She might even still love her. But she did not trust her. Every tear might only be a ploy to gain Sarah's sympathy. Every word might be spoken only to twist Sarah's heart.

"You told Jesse I had an affair," Sarah said. "That was why you told me to be out of the house when he got home, so you'd have time to lie to him."

Annabel looked away.

"I didn't plan it," she said. "Jesse called me to see where you were and the words just came out. I couldn't believe I was doing it, that I could be so bad."

Sarah breathed deeply. She had hoped for some kind of explanation that would prove Annabel was not guilty of this too. But Annabel did not even try to deny it. At every step, Annabel had outfoxed her, manipulated her, betrayed her.

Sarah stared at her and let the anger overtake the pain. Annabel watched her eyes and saw Sarah's expression harden. She stood up from the car and smoothed down her hair. She tried to pull herself up straight, but then she collapsed back in. Her face fell and she hugged herself. She cried without sound and Sarah could not help it, she took a step toward her.

"Annabel, don't."

"I'm lost," Annabel said, her shoulders heaving up and down.

Sarah touched her arm once and then let go. At one time in her life, Sarah would have buried Annabel in her arms and soothed her. But Annabel herself had taught her how to play with the big boys, to watch out for herself and no one else.

Sarah gathered her children and guided them into the house, forcing herself not to look back at Annabel.

# 16

JESSE PACKED UP what little he owned and put it in the trunk of his car. He had been gathering canned food and crackers and sodas for weeks now, although he had never admitted the reason why, even to himself. He told anyone who asked that you just never knew when a few supplies would come in handy. Like when you were short of cash. Or after an earthquake. Or to take on a sudden camping trip.

Jesse had been staying with a friend of a friend for a week, and he knew he had worn out his welcome. He had run out of people to turn to.

The divorce was final. Sarah had not responded to any of his pleas. She had not answered a single one of his letters. She would not let him inside his own house unless he called first for an appointment with his children.

Even his friends who, for a while, had understood about his unhappiness with the working world were on his case to get a job now. There was a limit to how long they allowed someone to be irresponsible and still be their friend. It was coming up on a year since Jesse's layoff. They all thought that was enough time for him to find something new, something that made him happy. They didn't understand.

He did not want to be happy. He did not want to find

a new job, go on, get himself back together. He had lost Sarah, lost his kids, lost his home. He was miserable and, in a perverted way, that misery appealed to him. It gave him an excuse for not getting up in the morning, for not shaving, for wandering through the park instead of pounding the pavement looking for work. He wanted to wallow in it. He wanted to curse God for his fate for the rest of his life.

And if he couldn't have what he wanted, if people wouldn't leave him alone to disintegrate, then he would prefer to be nothing, faceless. He wanted to walk a street where no one knew him, where no one gave a shit what he did. He only wished that he could disappear completely, erase every trace that he had ever been here at all.

This town had taken him down. Ever since he and Sarah moved here, it had given him nothing but heartache. First the crap job, then the fiasco with Annabel, then the layoff, then the divorce. He thought about going back to Spokane, but there wasn't anything there for him anymore. His friends would be all grown-up now, probably with wives and jobs and lawns to care for. His parents didn't want anything to do with him.

This morning, when he woke up, Jesse knew what he had to do. The answer had been there all along, he just hadn't been ready to face it yet. But today, he met the solution head-on. He was not afraid. If anything, he was exhilarated by the possibilities of losing himself, of forgetting, of setting himself free.

He got in his car. He had already had a tune-up, filled the tank, and gone to the bank. He left Sarah enough money to get by for a few months. He didn't think he'd be gone longer than that. Besides, she had her parents to look out for her. Jesse was on his own now. It would be hard enough to survive, without a few bucks in his pocket.

He drove through his old neighborhood. He went first past Annabel's house. The curtains were all drawn although it was a beautiful summer day. Annabel's car was there. He tried to picture her inside, but couldn't. Amazingly, he could not see her face at all, as if her memory had faded to gray. Until now, the memory of her face was even more detailed and precise in his mind than Sarah's.

He turned the corner and drove to Sarah's. He parked across the street and stared at the house. He knew his children were in there, knew that they would not understand why their daddy had left. He had written a dozen notes to them and torn them all up. There was nothing he could say that would soften this. He knew the kind of man who deserted his family. Selfish, cruel, hard-hearted. Even though Jesse was walking out, he still didn't think he was that kind of man. He loved them. The crazy thing was he loved all of them more than anything.

He just wanted . . . relief. He was so tired of trying and failing to win Sarah back, of seeing the hatred in her eyes. He was so sick of these same streets, the same people, the same life. Every morning when he woke up it was the same. He wanted to get away from this godforsaken rain forest and hit the desert. He wanted to drive through the plains at a hundred miles an hour and see only corn fields. He wanted to flatten himself against the land until it sucked him up, until he became part of it.

Why was it such a crime to be different? Why was there only one set of rules, with strict guidelines, and if you didn't follow them, you were an outcast? Jesse had always known he was different. He couldn't settle in the way other men could. He did not have science to excite him, the way Patrick did. He could not spend nine hours in an office he hated and not be adversely affected. He did not like the feel of a house he owned over his head. It only reminded him of how anchored he was, how hard it would be to run away if he had to. He wanted the sky and stars as his ceiling. Packing up his things, screwing everything that was respectable—it felt as if he were breaking out of prison, gasping at the first breaths of freedom he'd had in years.

But his children would not understand that. Nor would Sarah. Jesse could only imagine what they would think when they realized he was gone. It saddened him, but it did not change his mind. He was breathing again, free again, just Jesse again, for the first time since he got on his bike and rode away from his parents.

Three times, he put his hand on the door handle, ready to get out of his car and tell Sarah what his plans were, try to explain. Three times, he released his hand and settled back into the seat. There were no explanations. At least none that someone like Sarah would understand.

Even in his own mind, with all his rationalizations, it didn't make sense. You didn't just leave, cut out on your family, what was left of your friends. You played by the rules, lived in today's society, got a job, paid your bills, did the right thing.

But Jesse didn't know what the right thing was anymore, at least for him. He thought if he went on one more job interview and shrank beneath the glare of a snot-nosed kid in a three-piece suit sitting behind an oversized desk, he would kill someone. He'd just go out and buy a gun and go crazy, pummel bullets into every moving object.

He thought if one more person told him he owed it to Sarah, to his kids, to twist his soul inside out and scrape out a living flipping hamburgers or delivering newspapers or whatever menial task he could get, regardless of his pride, he would go insane. He thought if he woke up one more morning in this town, knowing Sarah was lost to him, he'd turn that gun on himself.

The only thing that gave him any peace was the thought of leaving. Getting lost. He'd just slip through the cracks, become a mere speck on the highway. He couldn't think about what this would do to Sarah or Carolyn or Sam. He was so goddamn tired of thinking about what everyone else was feeling. Now, finally, he had to do what was right for him.

Jesse turned on the engine again. He took one more look at his house and then pulled into the street. He said no goodbyes and did not look back. He turned the radio on loud and headed for the freeway. He wasn't sure why he was crying.

Sarah called all over town. It had been a week since Jesse had come by to see the kids and he hadn't called. He was never easy to get a hold of, but usually someone knew where he was.

"No sign of him," they all said. Jesse went from friend to friend, staying until he wore out his welcome and then moving on. It was an alien life, one Sarah did not understand in the slightest. But then, lately, she didn't understand Jesse either.

"You have no idea where he might be?" she asked Bill Davidson, the last person Jesse had stayed with.

"Nope. He packed up his car a week ago and left. I figured he was going camping or something. He had all that food stored up."

"What food?"

"Canned goods. Cookies. Tuna. Anything that will save a while. Didn't he tell you where he was going?"

"No."

Sarah spent two days on the phone and then she went out looking. She drove past all the parks where Jesse liked to spend his days. She went to the waterfront. She talked to the bartenders in his favorite bars. Every time they gave her the same response, that they'd had no sign of him, the fury settled in deeper.

With more calm than she felt, she called the police. This time he had been missing more than twenty-four hours. The police wrote out a report and made an investigation. They got back to her in two days.

"Looks like he cleared out," the detective said. "You happen to notice he made a thousand-dollar withdrawal from your savings account the last day anyone saw him?"

Sarah sucked in her breath.

"No."

"Well, he did. He got a tune-up, too. It's pretty clear he hit the road. That's not unusual with newly divorced men. He probably just needed to cut loose for a while. You're probably glad to get rid of him, huh?"

She waited until the detective left, and then she slammed her fist against the wall. She waited for the worry and sadness to set in, but they did not come. She pounded the wall twice more, wishing that it was Jesse's face, that she could tell him exactly what she thought of him.

How dare he do this, just leave without a word. If he didn't care about her, what about his children? What explanation could he possibly give her for deserting them? Had he simply had enough of Seattle, of his job quest, of all of them, and so he hit the road? His free spirit that had been so appealing when he was a teenager was despicable now that he was a father. If something happened to them while he was gone, would he care then? Or would he just shrug it off to coincidence and go on, as completely selfish and self-sustaining as always?

Sarah waited two days to tell Carolyn and Sam. She tried to work out the words in her head, soften them, but in the end she merely sat them down on the couch and knelt in front of them.

"Your father won't be around for a while," she said.

Sam fidgeted with the threads on the couch. Carolyn stared at her.

"Where is he?" Carolyn asked.

"I don't know. He didn't tell me where he was going. I only know that he plans to be away for a while."

"Will he be home in time for Christmas?"

Sarah inched closer to them. She put one hand on each of their knees. Carolyn was almost five years old now, just starting kindergarten. Sam would be three in December and was finally developing his own personality; he had a tendency to pull back from the rest of them.

"I don't know," Sarah said. "I wish I could do better than that, but I just don't know."

Sam reached into the couch and pulled out a crayon. He laughed and Sarah knew she hadn't reached him. She wasn't sure whether that was good or bad, if he would be better off hating his father for leaving, or not having a concept of a father at all. She let him get down and play.

Sarah looked at Carolyn. Her chin was trembling and the tears pooled in her eyes. Sarah grabbed her to her and held her close. She rested her chin on top of her daughter's head and cursed Jesse from the bottom of her soul. How could he do this? It wasn't enough for him to cheat on her, to rape her. No, he wasn't satisfied until he destroyed his children. Was he really willing to sacrifice Carolyn's adoration? Or to let Sam grow up not realizing there were such things as fathers?

What a completely selfish act, to take off without a word, to leave them to their own devices. What kind of a man was he? How had she ever thought she'd loved him?

How would she cope? She hadn't even begun to think

of the bills she'd have to pay. She had been borrowing from her parents ever since Jesse's layoff, but she couldn't depend on them forever. Had he thought of that? Did he think she would just go out and get a job? What about Carolyn and Sam? What would she do with them?

Did he think at all? Or, as usual, were there only his own desires, his own needs, in his mind? Was it hard? Or did he just drive away without a second thought? My God, how could he leave her like this?

Carolyn cried out in pain and Sarah realized she had been squeezing her. She pulled away and stood up. She tried to regulate her breathing, to slow her heart. It was so alien, this fury, like a monster unleashed inside her. She turned away from Carolyn, so she wouldn't see it.

"Daddy just had to go away for a while," Sarah said, focusing on every word, trying to make each one sound plausible. She felt as if she were betraying herself, sticking up for Jesse, yet she would not berate him to his children. They loved him. They should love him.

Carolyn cried harder and Sarah turned around. She sat on the couch and pulled Carolyn into her arms. Carolyn pressed her face into Sarah's chest, crying so hard her little body convulsed in tremors. Sarah clung to her and felt her daughter's pain through her own body, ten times worse than anything she'd ever felt on her own. She knew she would die right then, give her own life, if only to make her happy again.

"It's because I didn't pick up my things," Carolyn said, in between sobs. "He yelled at me and I still didn't pick them up. And then he left."

"Oh no, honey," Sarah said, tilting her face up to hers. "I swear to you, it had nothing to do with you. I swear it."

"What was it, then?" Carolyn asked. Sarah leaned her forehead against Carolyn's. It was a question she might never know the answer to. Still, she grasped at what she did know, to try to make sense of it.

"Daddy left because he'd lost so much. He and I couldn't live together anymore, and he couldn't settle on a job he liked. He probably just felt that he needed to make a fresh start somewhere."

"But what about us?" Carolyn cried.

*Yes, what about us?* Sarah thought. How do you explain to a child that her father had left her alone? That he did not care one way or another how they survived, or whether they did at all.

"I don't know," Sarah said. She squeezed Carolyn tightly. Over her shoulder, she saw this house, the one she had thought symbolized all she had achieved; a husband, a family, a home. Now, all it symbolized was a payment she couldn't make, a place where, more often than not, one of them was crying, a place where dreams died.

"Come on," Sarah said, standing up. "I'll take you two to bed."

Sam ran up ahead of them, oblivious to tears. He hopped into bed with his teddy bear and Sarah tucked him in.

"Are you all right?" she asked him.

He smiled. "Okay, Mommy," he said.

Sarah leaned over and kissed him. She took Carolyn into her room and slipped her into bed. She kissed her forehead and was about to turn off the light when Carolyn bolted upright.

"Maybe he's lost. Or hurt. Mommy, we've got to find him."

Sarah walked back to her daughter and put her hands on her shoulders.

"Your father is not lost. He left willingly and hopefully he will return willingly. But right now, he doesn't want us to find him."

Tears pooled in Carolyn's eyes again as she lay back down.

"Then I hate him," she said, turning her face toward the wall. "I hate him and I don't ever want him to come back."

Sarah sighed. She could not defend him when Carolyn's words matched her own feelings exactly. Besides, there was nothing left inside her to defend him with. She was empty except for this boiling rage. She didn't know how to stop it, or how to express it. It was just there, sizzling, eating her up.

She walked out of the room and downstairs. She stared

at the bills on the counter, wondering which she could put off paying the longest.

The alarm clock went off and, as always, Sarah waited for Jesse to turn it off. Then, as always, she remembered that he wasn't there, that it had been almost a year since he had been there to turn off the alarm, and she reached over and snapped it off herself.

She pushed off the covers and shivered against the cold. Winter was here again. It seemed it was always winter here now.

She went into the bathroom and turned on the shower. Once under the hot water, she stood still. She followed a ritual every morning of motionlessness, of trying to reach a state where there were no more thoughts. But she never achieved it.

At least the fear was gone now. Those first few weeks after Jesse left, Sarah had felt paralyzed, afraid to take another step. She could not think what to do. Should she wait for Jesse to come back, or should she assume he never would, and try to go on?

It was Patrick who said she had to go on. They spoke on the phone one night and he said, "Sarah, you can't count on him now. Don't you see that? Even if he does come back, he probably won't have a job to help you pay the bills. You've got to figure out a way out of this."

"But how?"

"Sell the house if the mortgage is too high. You could take the profit and—"

"No, I can't sell it. It's our home."

"Can you borrow enough from your parents, then, to help you make it?"

"Yes, but not forever. Oh Patrick. I'm not ready for this. All I'm good for is being a wife and mother. I can't do this—"

"Stop it, Sarah. Give yourself some credit. You'll do what you have to do, if not for yourself then for Carolyn and Sam. You'll have to get a job, that's all. It's not so terrifying."

But it was terrifying. It was a world she had never entered before. And yet, somehow she passed through that unfamiliar doorway and came out standing on the other side. She did what she had to do; she got a job. She was making it.

The most ironic part was that once she picked up the phone, once she went on the interview, once she got the job, working became one of the easiest things she'd ever done, easier than taking care of her own kids or trying to make ends meet.

Sarah closed her eyes and let the water rush over her face. This was not how she had planned it. Once Sam reached kindergarten age, she was supposed to go back to college, get her degree, then her teaching credential, then be a student teacher, then get her own classroom. Instead, when she was not prepared in the slightest, she found herself in a work force she had never been in before.

It took her two weeks after that talk with Patrick to gather enough courage to look at the newspaper classifieds. When she lifted up the paper, her hands were shaking so badly, she could barely read the ads. Then once she steadied herself, she realized it had all been for nothing anyway; she was not qualified to do anything. She was a high school graduate, a mother, an ex-wife. She could not be a communications specialist, or an accountant, or a drug-abuse counselor. She had no experience or expertise.

Every morning for the next ten days, Sarah read through every ad carefully and then set the paper down and put her head in her hands. She had not gotten involved in Jesse's job search. She'd had no idea that it was not easy. She had assumed he just wasn't trying hard enough.

At least he had some experience. Sarah had nothing. She hadn't even worked while she was in high school. But she had to do something. It didn't matter how menial or degrading. She had children to feed and an ex-husband who had left her to die. Her parents could not support her forever.

So she started calling. Restaurant hostess. Telephone sales. Receptionist. Either the jobs were filled or the hours were wrong or she was not right for the position. For weeks, she called every minimum-wage, no-experience-required job and came up empty. She took Sam with her and walked into every store and restaurant, pleading for anything. It was always the same response. They took one look at Sam, saw baby-sitter problems and extra sick days to take care of him, and told her they had no position to offer.

Close to two months had passed when she saw an ad for a day-care center worker, hours nine to five. Sarah wasn't going to call, because it would mean she wouldn't be at home when Carolyn got out of kindergarten, but she was desperate. She phoned the center and they asked her to come in that afternoon.

There was no question that she could do the job. She'd been doing the same thing since Carolyn was born, changing diapers, breaking up fights, cleaning up food, telling stories. Sarah sat down with the owner and was immediately offered the job. The center was desperate too and needed someone that day. Sarah had brought Sam along, because she couldn't find a sitter, and the owner agreed to let her bring him with her to work, for a slight cut in salary. For a bigger cut, Sarah could pick up Carolyn at lunchtime and bring her also. Those trade-offs brought the salary down to the bare bones, but Sarah took it. What else could she do?

That was a month ago. Now, Sarah stepped out of the shower, dried off, and opened the closet. She had ruined most of her good clothes in the first two weeks. She had thought, however naïvely, that she was a working woman and working women dressed in skirts and blouses. She had not wanted to take into consideration that she was working in a day-care center where the children spit and urinated on her, where they touched her silk blouses with chocolate-covered hands. Today, she reached for jeans and an old sweater.

She only had time to put on a little makeup before the rush began. Carolyn awoke and wanted Captain Crunch. Now. Sam fell out of bed and started crying, did not want to eat or get dressed, and peed on the carpet as soon as he managed to wiggle out of his pants. Sarah dealt with all this, trying not to cry, or to simply curl up in the corner and let sanity go completely. She got Sam dressed while he screamed, fed Carolyn her cereal, got her ready for school, walked her out to the bus, got her on, then took Sam back inside and tried to get herself ready for work.

She saw the bills on the counter as she stuffed Sam's bag full of extra clothes and food. They were stacked more than two inches thick now. Her parents had just given her another thousand, "to tide her over," but it would not last her out the month. There was the mortgage, the car, the insurance, Sam's doctor bills for his ear infection, the clothes she had had to buy Carolyn for school, the dishwasher to fix, food. It seemed impossible that they had ever been able to make ends meet before, even when Jesse was here.

Jesse. The name still sent waves of fury up her spine. He had cheated on her and raped her, yet it was this total lack of regard for his children, for how they would survive, that had destroyed her love for him completely.

"Mommy, I have to pee," Sam said. Sarah closed her eyes. Amidst all this, there was the horrendous battle of toilet-training Sam. And it was funny, but it was the little things, the daily grind, the toilet-training and spilled milk and temper tantrums that really wore her down, that were even more debilitating than Jesse leaving. Because this was her world now. From six o'clock in the morning until nine at night. Feeding, peeing, screaming, crying. Babies everywhere. And no one to help her out.

Sarah took Sam to the bathroom and pulled down his pants. He sat on the toilet and Sarah leaned against the wall. In a few minutes, she would take him with her to her job, deposit him in a circle of ten other two- to five-year-olds, and there would not be another moment's rest until she went to bed. And somewhere out there, probably lying in the sun in Malibu, or skiing in Aspen, was Jesse. Without a care. Without a thought for his family. Sarah had never hated anyone as much.

# 17

❦

PATRICK CLENCHED HIS fists as he waited for the call to go through to Boston. His lab assistant, Terry, had taken the message and scribbled it out almost illegibly. A Mr. Browhurst or Browhunt or Bowhurl or Bowman had called from MIT. Patrick ordered everyone from the lab and made the call.

When the secretary there picked up, her voice was difficult to hear through the static.

"Hello. Cancer Research Center."

"This is Patrick Meyers. A Mr. . . ."—he hesitated a moment—"Browhurst called me."

"Mr. Browden, you mean."

Patrick looked at the note. Not even close. He would have to teach these students how to print.

"Yes."

"Just a moment."

Patrick waited again. The MIT Center for Cancer Research had had his résumé and known about his interest for two years now. He had kept in touch consistently, but he knew that getting in was a long shot. He had spent his entire career at the University of Washington, and while it was a prestigious college, it was a minor player in the cancer-research field. Patrick was a good scientist, he had a solid reputation in local circles, but he had done nothing outstanding. MIT was for the outstanding. Along with the National Cancer Institute, it had the best equipment and facilities and got most of the grants in the field. In Patrick's mind, it was the only place to do cancer research.

A man came on the line and, through the static, Patrick recognized the name of Clarence Browden.

"Thanks for calling me back," Mr. Browden said. "I wanted you to know that Mike Wiley passed your résumé on to me. As you may or may not know, we have an opening in our research center. Dr. Feinstein passed away and we are looking to fill the niche. He was studying chemical carcinogens and bacterial mutations."

Patrick said nothing. He couldn't say anything even if he tried. His tongue had swollen and clamped his mouth shut. He felt too human all of a sudden, with too many human emotions.

"I was looking over your résumé and I spoke with some of your colleagues out there in Washington," Browden said. "They all had very nice things to say about you."

This time Patrick did find his voice.

"Thank you."

"But you see, the more I spoke to them, the more I realized you're not quite what we're looking for. You're more a classical geneticist, and we really need to fill the void here with someone more trained in chemical analysis. I wanted to talk to you personally because we really do value your interest in MIT. I want you to know we'll keep you in mind for any openings that might come up in the future."

Patrick looked around the lab. It was all the same, all exactly the same. Nothing had changed except that the last shred of hope of getting out of here, of actually doing something important, had left him.

"Mr. Meyers? Are you still there?"

"Yes," Patrick said.

"I am sorry. There are so many good scientists and so few openings. It seems a shame, doesn't it, to waste all that talent when the stakes are so high?"

"Yes, it does. But I appreciate you telling me personally."

"Tell me something," Browden said. "There are rumors that you're getting into immunology there. Is that true?"

Patrick leaned back in his chair. His fists were unclenched; all the fire had gone out of him.

"I'm trying. The only grant we've gotten recently is for more classical studies, but I've been working up a prospectus on monoclonal antibody technology. Right now, the odds for getting the grant aren't in my favor."

"The odds are never in our favor," Browden said. "But we're scientists. We find a way around odds. Let me know if you get it, will you?"

Patrick said he would and hung up. He was thinking of a lifetime here, on the periphery of what he loved, what he lived for. He'd never be allowed in the ring.

He walked outside and got into his car. He played the game of driving around aimlessly for a while, but eventually he tired of it and headed for Sarah's. He knew all along that he would end up there, as he always did. Stopping by was something he had fallen into after Jesse left, when Sarah needed someone to turn to.

She had called him soon after she realized Jesse was not coming back, at least for a while. Patrick was over at her house in ten minutes and stood silently while she cursed her ex-husband. He did not tell her about that day he ran into Jesse in the park. It would not help her find him, and it would only multiply his own guilt. Patrick had noticed Jesse's unkempt clothes and hair that afternoon, but he had been too busy throwing punches to see the desperate look in his eyes. It was obvious then that Jesse was on the verge of doing something dramatic. If Patrick had only calmed down, reached out, helped him, then Sarah would not be alone.

But he had not done that. Patrick was partly at fault for Jesse's leaving; they were all at fault for each other's problems. The four of them had been so wrapped up in their own injustices. Annabel felt they had all abandoned her. Patrick and Sarah could not forgive being betrayed. Jesse thought they could not possibly understand him. They were all so caught up in themselves, they couldn't stop for even a second to see each other clearly.

It wouldn't have taken so much for any of them to give

in, just a little, to understand that there were always two sides, or three, or four, to a story.

At least Patrick understood Sarah's side. He was the only person who could come close to understanding what she was feeling, and so they formed a bond. After Jesse left, he would have come to her every day, if he had been able to think up enough excuses. He told himself he was there for her, but really he just enjoyed her company. Even when she was sad, he loved being with her. It was the only time the pressure behind his eyes eased, the only time he didn't feel there was somewhere else he should be.

When she cried, he listened. When she got angry, he let her rage. He did not defend Jesse. He was as much at a loss as she was trying to figure out why Jesse had done what he'd done, how he could have walked out on his family. It went against everything Patrick believed in. A man, a father, a husband, was the last line of defense between his family and the world. It was a duty, like fighting for your country, which you did not run away from.

Patrick and Sarah had gotten together once a week during these last few months. As the weeks passed, Patrick found himself absorbing her emotions. He'd spend a couple of hours with her and then go home furious at Jesse's callousness. He'd wake up in the middle of the night in a cold sweat, shouting for her. Every nightmare followed the same theme: Sarah was calling out to him in the darkness, but he couldn't find her. Or he would catch a glimmer of her but not be able to reach her. He was left with the same sense of inadequacy every time, as if he weren't doing enough.

But he helped her out as much as he could. Over the weeks, Patrick had watched the energy drain out of her while she put in her eight hours at the day-care center and then came home and put in another eight taking care of the house and kids. Every time he came by, he offered to help out. She refused at first, but then, when she was so exhausted she could hardly stand, she gave in. He mowed her grass, took out the trash, and did some of the repairs around the house. It gave him a good feeling, to be working on a house again.

When he pulled up today, he was not surprised to see

the For Sale sign on the lawn. Even though she had refused to even consider selling the house right after Jesse left, it was only a matter of time before she faced reality. She did not make nearly enough to pay all the bills. Every month, she fell further and further behind, even with the help she got from her parents. The only surprise, and hurt, was that she hadn't told him it had come to this, that she hadn't asked for his opinion or help. She never asked him for anything. He always had to offer and then plead with her to let him help her.

Patrick got out of the car and walked to the door. Sarah let him in immediately.

"You look awful," she said.

He looked at her, with her clothes covered in paints, her hair a mess, and laughed.

"You do too."

"I have an excuse. You don't have fifteen kids smearing you with their dirty fingers all day."

She smiled and he followed her into the kitchen. She was cooking up hamburger patties on the stove while the kids watched television and made a mess on the floor with blocks and Legos and paper and crayons.

"Hi guys," Patrick said.

They smiled up at him and then went back to their toys. At first, they had been wary of him. Especially Carolyn. She did not want any man in the house if it wasn't her father. But after Patrick brought Adam a few times to smooth things over and slipped her an opportune sucker or chocolate bar, she warmed up to him. It was bribery, he knew, but he had to take advantage of whatever worked.

For the first three months after Jesse was gone, Carolyn asked Sarah every night when her father was coming home. Then she asked less and less frequently and her eyes stopped watering when she didn't get the answer she was looking for. Now, Carolyn sometimes went days without bringing up Jesse at all. If only adults could readjust so quickly.

"You're selling the house," Patrick said to Sarah.

"Yes. There's no way around it."

She didn't look at him, but he could see the sag in her shoulders.

"Where will you go?"

"I . . . I'm not sure. An apartment near the day-care center probably."

Patrick nodded. He wanted to say "Let me help you. Let me pay the mortgage for a while." But even if he could have afforded it, which he couldn't, he realized there was a boundary he couldn't cross. They were friends and nothing more. And Sarah still considered Patrick connected to Annabel, a detriment he might never be able to shake. Sarah had all these rules about what they could say to each other, how they should act, even now that Jesse was gone. At some point in the last few months, all of Patrick's rules about her had disappeared.

"I'm sorry," he said finally.

"Yes, me too. Mostly for the kids. I wanted them to grow up here."

"They'll probably bounce back quicker than you," Patrick said.

"Maybe. But Carolyn is afraid to move, afraid Jesse will come back and won't be able to find us."

Patrick looked over at the kids. He felt a need to protect them, just as he wanted to protect Sarah. It was stronger than anything he'd ever felt at home, with Annabel and Adam, but then Annabel hadn't needed protecting, and she took care of Adam just fine on her own.

"Can I help with dinner?"

Sarah asked him to make a salad and Patrick found everything he needed in the refrigerator.

"Aside from the house, how's finances?" he asked.

Sarah shrugged. "I got my three-month raise. It's not much, but it should cover another bill or two. I'm still borrowing from my parents. They want me to come back to Spokane where they can watch over me personally."

"You can't go," Patrick said, setting the vegetables on the counter. He surprised her with the intensity in his voice. He surprised himself too. He went on, more quietly.

"I mean, this is your home now, isn't it?"

"I suppose. Part of me almost said yes, but then I realized that would be copping out. I've got to give myself a little longer to make it work on my own. A year ago I would have gone to them immediately. But things are different now."

Patrick turned back to the counter and started on the salad. For the second time today, he'd felt as if he couldn't breathe. A life here without Sarah. Without making up a chore to do for her just so he could see her. Without pulling out every joke he knew to make her smile. It wouldn't be bearable.

As he broke up the head of lettuce and felt her presence beside him, it was clear to him that he loved her. She was the kind of woman he'd always thought he'd love, before he met Annabel and was trapped in her sensuality. Sarah was soft and kind and gentle. She had no secrets, or plans, or hidden agendas. Everything about her was on the surface, where he could read it easily.

Patrick thought of the job at MIT he had almost gotten and then lost and knew it must be fate. How could he have considered leaving Sarah? At least not before she had a chance to clear her heart of Jesse. Not before he got an opportunity to tell her how he felt.

He loved her. How perfectly simple it was. It was not wrapped up in jealousy and domination, the way it had been with Annabel. It was just there, like a river of overwarm blood that ran through him, like light, like arms that came around him and comforted him. For now, it didn't matter if she returned even a flicker of love. For now, Patrick was content just to feel it, to know he was capable of love again. For now.

He turned to her, smiling.

"What?" she said. "You look like you just told yourself a joke."

"Not a joke," he said. He laughed out loud. He couldn't help it. All the pressures, all the regrets and disappointments, were gone. There was only Sarah. He laughed harder, and pretty soon Sarah was laughing with him. He thought that was beautiful, the way she could be picked up and carried away in joy, even when she didn't understand it, even when it wasn't hers. He reached out for her hand and held it tightly.

"I'm just glad I'm here," he said.

She looked down at their hands together. For a moment, he thought she might pull away. But she didn't. She cooked with one hand and he tried to cut vegetables with one hand, and neither one let go.

This morning, Annabel was not going to drink. Last night, when she could hardly find the bed in the spinning bedroom, she had vowed this would be a nonalcoholic morning. It was Saturday and for once Patrick was not claiming Adam's time. With more enthusiasm in his voice than she'd heard in a long time, Patrick had said he had some kind of prospectus to work on at the lab. Not that she cared. All that mattered was that he was giving her a chance to spend some quality time with Adam, take him to the park, or the miniature golf course, or wherever he wanted to go.

Annabel got out of bed and walked into the bathroom. She had a hangover from last night. She'd mixed things up a little, started with beer, then switched to whiskey, then vodka, then those wonderful tequila shooters to top off the night. She'd gotten a good, early start and hadn't let up once until she fell into bed. She'd bought a special mug for her whiskey that Adam couldn't see into. Not that he knew what whiskey was, but she still felt better knowing she could drink without being watched. And it opened up hours and hours of drinking time she wouldn't have had if she was still hiding it from Adam.

Annabel looked at herself in the bathroom mirror. She was jolted a little by what she saw, but then she realized she was still a little bleary-eyed and dizzy. It was a trick of the lighting that made her look so pale. All her hair needed was a little combing. That blackness around her eyes was probably just smeared mascara that she'd forgotten to take off. And she'd had that flu last week, vomiting up practically everything.

She walked into her closet and took out a pair of jeans and a sweatshirt. Already, she was beginning to think about what she would drink, what it would taste like. She was running low on whiskey and beer; she'd have to stock up today. She looked at the clock on the wall. It was nine-thirty. The morning technically consisted of the hours until noon. That meant she only had to get through two and a half more hours before she could have a drink. Annabel felt a tightness settle over her. She'd have to keep busy.

She pulled the jeans up over her hips and went to zip them up. She thought for a minute that she had the wrong pair, that maybe these were the ones she'd been saving for when she lost a few more pounds, but as she looked down at them, she knew that was not the case. These were her favorite jeans, the ones she wore almost every weekend. And yet, she could not zip them up even a quarter of the way.

Annabel let the jeans fall to the floor and leaned back against the wall. She had not been eating. She knew it was not that. Basically the only thing that had gone through her system in the last week was booze. And she had thrown up most of that.

"Oh God," she said. She crawled to the bed and got back under the covers. She pulled her legs to her stomach. That awful curved part of her beneath her belly button jutted out and touched her thighs. How could she have been so stupid? How could she not have known this, or prepared for it, or taken precautions? Where had her mind gone?

She did not even bother to try to figure out who the father was. The array of possibilities was dizzying. She couldn't recall her last period. She couldn't remember when she'd put her diaphragm in and when she hadn't. There was only this great, black abyss in her mind when she tried to recall the last couple of months. The only things that were clear were the bars. And strange men. And enough booze to make her life seem like the greatest in the world. God, what a lot of booze.

Annabel reached over to her nightstand and opened the drawer. Inside was a flask of whiskey and she opened it. She drank it down quickly, practically choking to get the liquid into her system where it would do some good. She hardly braced against its heat at all anymore. Oh God. Oh God. Oh God. Oh God.

The door opened and Adam stepped inside. Even then, when all she was was so obvious, Annabel could not put the flask down. She cried as she kept drinking, gulping at the liquor without coming up for air. Her eyes met Adam's over the top of the bottle and she could see that he was crying too. The last drop slipped into Annabel's mouth and she dropped the flask to the floor.

She fell back on the bed. The tears stopped. She felt nothing really. No panic. No regret. The alcohol had numbed her. She heard Adam's footsteps and then felt his weight settle on the bed. She looked at him, sitting on the edge.

He was in third grade. The one night in the last six months for which Annabel had stayed sober was his Parent-Teacher Meeting. That day, she created things to do, anything to keep her hands busy and her mind off the liquor cabinet. She cleaned the house from top to bottom, cleared out closets, hosed down the outside of the windows. When she could think of nothing else to do, she arrived at the school much too early, but the teacher had been willing to see her.

It was one of the best nights of her life. Mrs. Crandall could not say enough about Adam. She was always a little more concerned about children from broken homes, but Adam had recovered brilliantly. He was intelligent, sensitive, articulate. He studied hard and helped the other children. He made teaching a joy.

And all along, Annabel had thought, *That's my boy. He's that way because of me. I have done something right.* For an hour, she had not wanted a drink. Listening to Mrs. Crandall was like downing three whiskey sours all at once. It was a rush, a burst of excitement and joy through her veins. As soon as Annabel got home and got rid of the sitter, she pulled Adam to her and held on as tightly as she could. "I love you. I love you. I love you," she said. He pulled back and looked at her with an expression she couldn't identify then, but understood perfectly now. He had been looking at her with pity, just as he was now.

"I can't stop," Annabel said.

"Mr. Richards says it's an addiction."

Annabel sat up. "Who's Mr. Richards? Who have you been talking to about me?"

Adam cried harder and Annabel pulled him to her. He was her tears. She could hardly cry anymore, so he did it for her. Sometimes, she felt suffocated in this house, in this life, and he breathed for her. She knew it was wrong, she knew she placed too heavy a burden on him, but what else could she do?

"It's okay," she said. "I didn't mean to yell." She liked comforting him. It brought back memories of how it used to be, when she was still the adult and he the child. It gave her hope that there was still some part of the old Annabel left in her.

Adam calmed himself eventually, but he didn't leave her embrace. Annabel pulled the covers up over both of them.

"He's Eddie's father," Adam said. "I didn't mean to tell him, but he sort of got it out of me. Once I started talking, I couldn't stop."

Annabel was quiet. She felt sick inside again, whether from this alien thing in her womb or from knowing people were talking about her, she couldn't tell.

"And what else did he say?"

"He said he knows a psy . . . psy . . ."

"A psychiatrist?"

"Yes. He knows one of those who help people stop being addicted. He said he thought he might call you."

Annabel jerked away from her son. She did not want strange men calling her and telling her what to do. She started to move to the edge of the bed, but then the nausea came on and she threw the covers off and ran to the bathroom. The vomit came out in two spurts and still she felt sick. She laid her head on the side of the toilet and the cold of the tile floor seeped up over her bare legs.

"What's wrong with you, Mom?" Adam asked. He had come in and was standing behind her. He put one hand on her shoulder, more like a friend than a son.

"I'm pregnant."

He didn't even flinch and Annabel could not decide if that was good or bad, if it was better to just grow up and be done with all the fantasies right away, or to stall a little in childhood and suck every pleasure out of it while you still could.

"What are we going to do?" he said.

Annabel lifted her head off the toilet. He had said we. Not you. She had been sitting there, waiting for him to tell her he wanted to go live with Patrick in his nice, sane, little apartment where everything was as it should be. She should have known that Adam would not betray her. In the midst of all the crap thrown her way, there was Adam, like a gift, like her salvation. She turned and looked at him.

"We certainly aren't going to have it," she said.

There was a moment of childlike uncertainty and then his face hardened into a replica of Annabel's. He nodded.

"Good," he said.

Mr. Richards did call. Two days later, at ten in the morning, the phone rang and, after finishing off the last of her beer, Annabel picked it up.

"Ms. Meyers?" he said.

Annabel dragged the phone with her to the refrigerator and took out another beer.

"Yes."

"This is Cal Richards. I'm Eddie's father."

Annabel had her hand on the can, ready to open it. Instead, she set it down on the counter, behind some dishes she had yet to clean.

"My son told me he'd spoken to you."

"Look, I know this might seem way out of line, but I want you to know, I'm a recovering alcoholic. I know what it's like to be alone, with no one to turn to. I thought—"

"Whatever my son may have told you, I am not an alcoholic, Mr. Richards. You know how children are. They exaggerate everything. Adam hears about alcoholism from you, sees me with one drink, and thinks I'm an alcoholic. Really, if you would just stop filling his head with all of this drunk stuff, we'd all be better off."

"He came to me. I didn't broach the subject of alcoholism. He was concerned."

"He is a child," Annabel said loudly. The sweat on her neck was slipping down her back. More than anything, she wanted to hang up on this man, but she couldn't, not before she settled this.

"Look, I can see I upset you," he said. "I was just trying to help."

"Well, you're not helping. I don't even know you and you don't know me."

"But I do, Ms. Meyers. That's just the point."

Annabel felt a pain in her hand and looked down to find blood where her fingernails had dug into her palm. She walked to the sink and ran her hand beneath the water.

"I am not an alcoholic," she said slowly. She turned her eyes away from the beer, sitting on the counter.

"Have you already had a drink today?"

"That's none of your business."

"You're right, it isn't. But it is your business. And Adam's business. Believe me, I know better than anyone how hard it is to admit there's something wrong and to get help. But you've got to get help. That stuff will kill you, if you let it. If not physically, then mentally."

"You seem to be doing just fine. You're well enough to pry into other people's business."

Cal laughed softly. "True. But you didn't know me three years ago."

Annabel leaned against the wall. She was staring straight at the beer, wanting it more than she'd ever wanted anything, and yet still listening to this man. It was as if he were a force in the room, holding her back.

"How bad did it get?" she asked.

Cal sighed. "Bad. Rock bottom. I got violent when I drank. After two six-packs, I threw my wife into the wall and broke one of her ribs. I never took another drink after that."

Annabel closed her eyes.

"So it's easy, then," she said.

"Easy? I lost my job during one of my drunk days, when I told off my boss. My wife left me for six months, until she was convinced I would never drink or abuse her again. For years, my son cowered whenever I came near him. My insurance wouldn't cover all the doctor visits it took to get me sober and I went into debt so bad I'm just now climbing out of it."

"But you quit. You did it."

"I still think about drinking," Cal said. "A deal falls through and I want a beer. I have a fight with my wife and

I'm inches from a vodka martini. Three years and I'm still addicted."

"That's encouraging," Annabel said.

"It's not meant to be encouraging. It's meant to be truthful. It's an uphill battle and not everyone makes it, but the alternative is to let the booze own you."

"Let's just say I did have a problem," Annabel said. "Which I don't. But if I did, what would I do about it?"

"Write this number down," Cal said. "Dr. Walinski was my psychiatrist for three years. He specializes in drinking disorders." He gave her the number and, for some reason, Annabel wrote it down. "Or you could try AA, or one of the other support groups. Whatever you feel comfortable with, and whatever works."

"Do you drink at all now?" Annabel asked.

"No. I don't think alcoholics can drink at all once they stop."

Annabel hugged herself. The thought of never having a drink again was too much. It severed whatever loose connection this man had made with her.

"Well, I have to go," she said.

"Just think about it, will you?"

"Yes, of course."

But as soon as she hung up the phone, she opened the beer. She drank it quickly, until his words were forgotten.

Annabel left the construction worker's house at three in the morning. She had felt sick most of the night, but she hadn't asked him to stop. His touch partly offset the stomping in her head. When he was inside her, the churning in her stomach subsided.

After he was sound asleep, she slipped out of bed, pulled on her clothes, and walked unsteadily to the front door. Every now and then, a piece of furniture jumped out at her and she stumbled against it. Finally, she made it outside. She did not look back.

She had forgotten the man's name by midnight. It got lost beneath the drinks and weed and sex. By one o'clock, she only wanted him to fall asleep so she could get out.

She figured she should take advantage of this safe time when she could have sex with no contraceptives. Her appointment for the abortion was not for another two weeks. Her gynecologist was out of town until then, and she didn't want anyone else performing the procedure. That gave her four weekend nights when Adam would be at Patrick's to live it up. After that, she'd get a new diaphragm and wear it religiously.

Last night, she had gone home with a rather shy man named Bill whom she'd met at a bar. He had wanted her to take charge, which was fine, except that he never reciprocated. She was left feeling frustrated and angry.

Tonight was a different story. Gary, or Larry, or maybe even Terry, was a construction worker, with stamina and muscles unlike any she'd seen before. He'd been more than willing to try out new techniques on her, and for once, Annabel had been the one who was worn down. She was raw and achy when he'd finally had his fill. They'd been drinking all along, and he brought out a joint in the middle of it all and they smoked it. Now, as Annabel gobbled up the night air, she swayed as she walked to her car.

She got behind the wheel and fumbled for her keys. Once she found them, she could not locate the ignition. It moved every time she thought she had it right. Finally, with two hands, she got the key in and turned on the engine.

She forgot about lights until she was at the end of the block. She turned them on and tried to remember where she was going. Oh yes. Home. Where was home? She giggled a little, pressed down hard on the accelerator, took a guess, and turned right.

She did not see the lamppost. She smashed right into it, her head slammed into the steering wheel, and the post buckled. The lamp at the top swayed and Annabel watched it through her windshield. It seemed to move in slow motion, the thin thread of metal supporting it growing weaker and weaker. Annabel listened to it creak and then crack with a hypnotic kind of peace. It broke apart and fell toward the car like a feather in the wind.

The lamp shattered the windshield with a loud scream and Annabel was flung back by the bombardment of glass. Pieces flew all around her and lodged in her face and arms. She did not feel the shards sticking out of her cheeks and arms, but the sight of them horrified her. The only pain she noticed was in her stomach, where a part of the lamp had slammed into her, but even that was unreal, far away.

The night was foggy and the clouds closed in around her. She heard the far-off sound of a horn, and then she realized it was her own, that she was leaning on it. There were footsteps and then someone was pounding on the car door.

"Are you all right?" the man said. She could only stare at him. She did not know where she was anymore, or why she was here, or where she was going. But as a contraction swept through her stomach and a wave of warm blood slipped down her leg, she knew one thing. She had lost her baby. And instead of being happy that this had saved her the cost of an abortion, Annabel's mind cleared, the pain rushed in, and she started to scream.

# 18

A NURSE ASKED Annabel who they should call. Annabel's parents were out of town, and since the drinking began, her friends had dwindled. Only Adam mattered, and he was with Patrick.

"My ex-husband, I suppose." She lay back in the hospital bed and gave the nurse the number of Patrick's apartment. The woman dialed and let it ring, but there was no answer.

"He must be out," the nurse said.

It was six in the morning and Adam was with him. He could not possibly be out.

"Call his lab. He always leaves a number where he can be reached."

The nurse called the new number Annabel gave her and the answering service at the lab gave her yet another number. The nurse wrote it down and then dialed it.

A groggy woman answered the phone.

"Hello."

"Yes, I'm calling on behalf of Annabel Meyers. Is Mr. Meyers there?"

"Just a minute."

"Who was that?" Annabel asked her.

"Some woman."

Annabel grabbed the phone from the nurse. The nurse

shrugged her shoulders and left the room. A second later, a hoarse Patrick came to the phone.

"Yes?" he said.

"Where are you?" Annabel said immediately.

"You should know where I am, Annabel. You're the one who called me."

"I didn't call, the nurse did."

"What nurse? What's wrong?"

But Annabel wasn't listening. She had picked up the number the nurse wrote down and was looking at it. She knew it well, even if it had been years since she'd called.

"I can't believe this," Annabel said. "I cannot believe you would do this to me."

"I didn't do anything to you. Now will you tell me what's wrong?"

"Where's Adam? Don't you dare tell me he's there with you."

"Of course he is."

Annabel wanted to scream. She wanted to rip the damn IV out of her vein and throw it across the room. She wanted to flip over the bed, rip the sheets, let the violence out of her system. This could not be happening. First she lost the baby and now Patrick was at Sarah's, had probably been at Sarah's all night. They were in bed together right now, their skin touching, Sarah's hair falling over him. It was too much. No one should be expected to bear so much.

But Annabel could not move. The pain in her stomach held her down and the rage simply churned in her.

"It's not fair," was all she could say. Patrick sighed.

"Look, let's not get into this now. Where are you?"

"At the hospital. They asked me who to call and you were the only one I could think of. The lab gave the nurse your number. Oh, Patrick. How could you do this to me?"

"I don't have anything to do with you anymore, except for Adam. Now what happened?"

Annabel placed her hand on her stomach, on the empty space there. Suddenly, more than anything, she wanted the baby she'd lost. She didn't care who the father was. She didn't care that she had probably poisoned the child with alcohol. She only wanted something else that was hers.

Because she wouldn't have Adam forever. One day he would grow up and leave her and then she would be alone. And then how could she face another empty morning, or the thought of Patrick and Sarah together?

"A car accident," she said.

"Are you all right?"

"I'm talking to you, aren't I?"

In the background, Annabel heard Sarah's voice. She said something like "What's going on?" and Annabel could not stand it.

"Sarah!" she shouted. "Sarah, you get on this phone right now! How could you sink so low? At least I had the decency to keep what Jesse and I did away from the kids. Do you have Adam there in the bed with you? Are you screwing right in front of him? Sarah! Sarah, you little—"

The nurse ran back in when Annabel started screaming and she jerked the phone away. She put it to her ear and then set it back down.

"There's nobody there. You're screaming at nobody."

Annabel picked up a pillow and threw it across the room. Then she did rip the IV out of her vein and screamed as it tore her skin. The nurse ran out of the room and then back in with an orderly. Together they held Annabel down and someone gave her a shot. Soon, thankfully, there was nothing.

When she woke up, Patrick was there. He was sitting in the chair by the side of her bed, like an ordinary husband. He didn't realize she was awake yet, and she looked at him. He looked well. Too well. He'd gotten his hair cut short and it suited him. He'd also gotten a new pair of glasses. For a moment, the memory of him and Sarah together did not come to her and Annabel was simply proud that he had been hers once. But then the conversation with him this morning came bursting in, and she gasped.

Patrick looked up. He did not smile or move closer to her.

"You were pregnant," he said.

Annabel looked away. She had no secrets anymore. They had taken even that away from her.

"The nurse told me," he went on. "She probably assumed the baby was mine."

Annabel did not look at him. She heard him get up and walk over to the window that looked out on the other wing of the hospital.

"I'm sorry you had to find out about Sarah and me that way," he said.

It shouldn't matter. Annabel knew it shouldn't matter. She didn't love Patrick anymore. If it had been any other woman, she didn't think it would have affected her in the slightest. But it was Sarah. Jesse's Sarah. Pretty, sweet, good Sarah, whom everyone wanted. It reinforced the fact that nobody wanted Annabel.

"I don't want Adam there, when you two are together," Annabel said. She could still act calm, which was surprising because she hadn't had a drink today. Funny, but she didn't even want one right now; she hadn't wanted one since she realized she'd lost the baby.

Patrick nodded. "I can understand that. I don't want you to think that it's been happening all the time. Actually, last night was the first time."

Annabel turned her head away again. She did not want to hear this. It was like hearing fingernails on a chalkboard, listening to him talk about Sarah.

"Please," Annabel said.

Patrick walked to the side of the bed and looked down at her.

"The nurse also said your blood-alcohol content was high enough to cause cardiac arrest. It's amazing you haven't killed yourself yet."

He spoke so calmly, so coldly, that Annabel felt as though she were no better than one of his lab experiments, and certainly not anyone he had ever cared about. She felt an overwhelming sense of loss, not just of his love, but of his tenderness and concern.

"It wouldn't matter if I did," she said.

He grabbed her face roughly and turned her toward him. Annabel blinked back tears as he squeezed her. His eyes were hard.

"Pull yourself together, Annabel. If not for yourself, then for Adam. He would be devastated without you."

He shoved her head away. He walked back to the window and stood with his back to her.

"You disappoint him," Patrick said. "Every time you take a drink, you disappoint your son. You become something less in his eyes."

The words were like arrows and Annabel jerked back with each of them.

"Stop," she whispered.

Patrick turned around. "No, you stop."

He left the room. Annabel's tears came then, hard and strong and full, like Adam's tears. She gave in to them fully, painfully, and so did not hear Patrick crying outside her door while he clung to Sarah, who had heard every word.

The market is flat, the realtor told her. Nothing is moving.

Sarah knew he was right, but that didn't help her pay her bills. It didn't make it any easier to keep the house clean for the rare buyer who passed through. Or to remain optimistic about her future, and that of her children. It didn't stop the realization that if she lowered the price any more, she would actually lose money.

And yet, Sarah could not be sad. She knew her finances were in ruin. She knew that a job at a day-care center did not pay for a house like this. It did not put enough food on the table for her and two children. She knew all that and still she was happy. She was a fool, but she didn't care.

Sarah knelt down in the front garden and weeded out the early-summer dandelions. The clouds and rain had been whisked out with the night and it was a stunning June day. This was when she loved the Seattle area, when Mount Rainier was visible in the distance, when there was a hint of a sea breeze, when the air smelled of salt and trees and the first brush of roses.

Sarah hummed as she worked. She could hear Carolyn and Sam in the backyard, laughing, playing with the new puppy. The dog had been Patrick's idea. Sarah had been resistant to it at first, not needing anything else to take care of, to housebreak, to feed, but the three of them wore her down. Patrick came home with a bright-eyed cocker spaniel yesterday.

Came home. Funny how she always referred to this place as Patrick's home. When she called him at the lab, she said, "Try to come home on time, I'm making spaghetti." Or when they went out to dinner, she said, "I wish we could go home together." It was not what she had planned. She had certainly not wished for it. But it had happened, just the same.

Sarah piled her weeds up and then moved to the next spot. She could hear Patrick's voice over those of the children. He was saying something about being gentle. Gentle. In one word, that was how Sarah would describe him. Gentle enough that she never once felt rushed, or pressured, or unsure. Gentle enough that her longing to have Jesse back had ebbed and then disappeared completely.

Sarah had not seen it coming. Perhaps she should have, but she had been too busy trying to survive her first months on the job, trying to get over her anger at Jesse. Patrick had simply been there, to help around the house, to take the kids off her hands once in a while. It was always in her mind to refuse him, to point out that it just wasn't right, him being there, but by the time it came around to doing so, she was too tired.

He became one of them. Sarah and Carolyn and Sam would leave the day-care center at six o'clock, and Carolyn would want to know if Uncle Patrick was coming around. Sam would ask her if he could go over to Uncle Patrick's apartment building and float on the raft Patrick had bought him to use in the swimming pool. If some toy needed fixing, they would simply set it aside until Uncle Patrick came by.

At least twice a week, Sarah began setting a place at the dinner table for him. The first time, it was because he had helped fix the kitchen sink and worked until dinnertime. Then the shingles on the roof. Then getting the lawn ready for spring. Pretty soon, Sarah realized Patrick was simply there, without a reason or the pretense of housework. And by that time, the thought of him staying away was too uncomfortable to think about.

In the beginning weeks, she never thought of him romantically. He was like an old friend she felt completely comfortable with. She didn't have to pretend with him. She didn't have to dress up. If he came over after work, she still washed off her makeup and slipped into her sweat suit. He was not in any way like Jesse, who wanted her to always be picture perfect for him, whose love seemed to have so many conditions, or at least that was how Sarah saw it.

One Saturday, a couple months ago, Patrick had brought Adam over. When he first suggested they all go for a ferry ride, Sarah was reluctant. She was exhausted and Saturday was her only day to catch up on some sleep. But when all three kids pleaded with her, she saw no way out of it.

They drove to the dock and Patrick got them on the half-day ride around Orcas Island. Sarah thought he was crazy, trapping them on a boat with three children for four hours, but it turned out he knew exactly what he was doing.

They had a wonderful time. The ferry was surprisingly empty and Patrick entertained the kids with magic tricks and stories. After an hour or two, Sarah found herself relaxing. She closed her eyes, let the Sound's breezes wash over her, and listened to their laughter. She sat next to Patrick on one of the benches, with the children on the floor at his feet staring up at him, and she let her head fall against his shoulder. When his arm came around her and held her there, she saw no reason to pull away.

They reached the island and had a short stopover. The kids ran off the boat and laughed when their land legs wobbled like jelly. Patrick kept his arm around Sarah's shoulder.

They had just stepped off the boat when Patrick said "I love you, you know," as simply and easily as if he were talking about the weather. Sarah stopped abruptly. She looked up at him, but he only smiled and then hurried after the kids, chasing them around the dock and finally closing in on Sam. He picked him up and swung him over his shoulders, and Sam squealed with delight.

Sarah stood there, trying to reconcile the warmth in her chest with the hesitancy in her mind. But she could not.

She only knew that a part of her had come alive again when he said it. There had been no remembrances of Jesse's declarations of love. Patrick made her happy. He was her friend and would remain only her friend unless she asked for more.

She moved finally and caught up to the others. They had a quick bite to eat in one of the restaurants and then got back on the ferry.

"Can we hear more stories?" Carolyn asked.

Patrick looked over at Sarah. She smiled at him tentatively, and then more broadly. She held out her hand and she saw a look of relief pass over his face. He grasped her hand tightly.

"Once upon a time . . ." he said. The kids all sat at his feet again. Sarah knew the three of them had noticed her and Patrick holding hands, and the way they leaned together, but they said nothing. Perhaps it seemed as natural to them as it did to Sarah.

When they got back to Seattle that evening, they were all exhausted. They piled everyone back into the car and drove home. They had a quick dinner and then Sarah put Sam and Carolyn to bed. There was no question of sending Patrick and Adam back to the apartment.

"I'll make up the guest room for Adam," Sarah said. She put sheets on the bed, and a moment later, Patrick came upstairs with Adam in his arms. Together, they tucked him into bed. As they were walking out, their shoulders brushed and Sarah shivered. She did not look at her own bedroom as they passed it to go downstairs.

"Coffee?" Sarah asked.

"That would be great."

She went into the kitchen and made the coffee. In the living room, Patrick made a fire. While Sarah waited for the coffee to percolate, she cleaned up the counter, set out cream and sugar, rearranged food in the refrigerator—anything to stop the shaking that had come over her suddenly.

When the coffee was done, she poured them each a cup and put a heavy dose of cream and sugar in Patrick's, the way he liked it. She took it out to him.

He was sitting on the couch by the fire. There was no

other light on in the living room, and his skin shone like copper in the firelight. His brown hair turned to gold and his glasses reflected the dancing flames. Sarah handed him his cup and then sat beside her.

They were quiet a long time, and as the minutes ticked by, Sarah's shivering stopped. There was nothing to be afraid of, after all. This was still Patrick and it was a given that he would never hurt her. How strange, to be so secure with someone, to trust him so implicitly. With Jesse, everything had been so uncertain—his feelings, his fidelity, his stability.

"What are you thinking about?" Patrick asked.

Because she couldn't lie to him, Sarah said, "Jesse. I wonder if he's all right."

Patrick looked into the fire. The steam from his coffee rose up and fogged his glasses and he moved the cup farther away.

"Where do you think he is?" he asked.

Sarah shook her head.

"I don't know. On the street somewhere. Someplace where there's no responsibility, where he feels anonymous."

"I don't think he's frightened of the streets, the way you or I would be," Patrick said. "I think, in a strange way, he likes it. He likes being out of the loop."

"I'm still so angry," Sarah said. "How does a man just leave like that? What about his children?"

A muscle twitched in Patrick's jaw.

"I was angry too," he said, "but it's fading. It's impossible to sustain that kind of fury forever, even if you want to. Besides, Annabel blames herself enough for all of us, and Jesse, well, I think he just needed to be by himself. That's no excuse, but it looks like he's trying to get himself together. He couldn't do it here, with all of us watching him."

Sarah looked at him. She could see the tension in his face and hands, the way he made sure he didn't touch her, even by accident. And suddenly, it was all very clear. She would never love Patrick the way she loved Jesse. She had been waiting for it to happen, for sparks to fly, for it to grip her almost like hysteria the way it had with Jesse. But that would not happen. Patrick, and everything about him, was too grounded in reality. He couldn't offer her the world, the way Jesse could, but only a small, safe part of it to build a home in.

Sarah put her coffee cup down on the table. Then she took Patrick's out of his hand and set it down too. This time, it was Patrick who was shaking. She reached over and turned his face toward hers.

She smiled at him. She touched his face with her fingertips, smoothing out his lines, memorizing his freckles. She took off his glasses and set them on the table.

"Come closer," he said. "Where I can see you."

She moved next to him, so their faces were only inches apart. He lifted his fingers to her face too, and they touched each other like the blind, like people who had seen each other for years but never really looked before. Sarah was still smiling, and then Patrick was too, and then their smiles turned to laughter. Patrick leaned his head against hers.

"You're wonderful," he said.

"So are you."

The fire crackled. Patrick slid his hand down from her face, to her neck, to her breast, to her ribs, to her stomach. And for once, Sarah was not thinking about ten extra pounds, or flab where it shouldn't be. She was only reveling in his touch, in how good it felt to be wanted again, and to want again. She reached out and stroked his arm and then slipped her hand around to his back.

When he finally kissed her, Sarah knew this was where she wanted to be, forever. In his arms, by his side. Jesse was impulsive and daring and dangerous and made her heart race. Patrick was calm and considerate, and if her heart wasn't racing, at least it was not skipping in fear either.

Sarah pulled away and they stood up. Sarah did not lead him, and Patrick did not lead her. They walked up the stairs together and closed the bedroom door behind them. In the darkness, Patrick took her in his arms.

"God, I love you," he said.

Sarah smiled. There was no doubt, or worry that it

would end or that he would leave her. Patrick made it all so easy.

"I love you too."

Sarah smiled now, remembering. She turned her face up to the sun. That night was the night Annabel was in the car accident and lost the baby. Everyone had changed after that day. Annabel, according to Patrick, had come home from the hospital and thrown all the liquor out of her house. She had even started seeing a psychiatrist to help her through the rough times, although Sarah had a hard time imagining Annabel letting anyone help her.

And, of course, Sarah and Patrick had changed. Friends to lovers. All the boundaries shattered by that first kiss. Since that night, though, they had not made love when the children were around. Which meant that they hardly made love at all. Which meant that she wanted him more than ever, and she knew he wanted her too.

The side gate opened and a very happy cocker spaniel ran into the front yard and directly into Sarah's garden. He smashed the daylilies with his first step and was heading for her daisies when she caught him. He licked her face and Sarah laughed. Patrick and the kids followed after.

"Have you named him yet?" Sarah asked, setting the dog down.

Adam threw up his hands. "I tried to get them to name him Floppy, after his ears, but Carolyn won't do it. She says it's dumb."

"It is dumb," Carolyn said. "And besides, he's not your dog."

"My dad got him."

"So? He's not staying with you. You don't live here, you know. He's our dog and—"

"Carolyn!" Sarah said, standing up. She walked over to her daughter and cupped her chin in her hand. "The dog is every bit as much Adam's as he is yours. You had better start acting a little nicer to him, young lady."

Carolyn stuck her tongue out at Adam.

"All right, enough of that," Sarah said. "We'll think of a name at some point."

They all turned to look for the dog and found him in

the corner, digging up Sarah's flowers. They all ran for him, but Patrick reached him first. He picked the dog up and was about to hit him when the dog turned his big brown eyes up at him and licked his face. They all laughed.

"Well, go ahead, discipline him," Sarah said.

Patrick looked down at the dog and then marched him back to the gate. He put him in the backyard.

"We should call him Digger," Patrick said, slamming the gate shut.

"Yes. Digger!" Carolyn and Sam said, clapping their hands. Adam turned his head away in disgust, but the name stuck. Digger it was.

It was one of those rare times when they were alone. Sarah had found a reliable baby-sitter and Adam was at home with Annabel. Sarah and Patrick went out to dinner and then decided to take a walk through the park.

Patrick reached over and held Sarah's hand. It was still incredible to him that he could touch her whenever he wanted to, that he could lean over and kiss her and she wouldn't pull away. That she reciprocated his feelings. That she loved him.

With his free hand, he toyed with the box in his pocket. He had been waiting for the perfect moment. He could have asked her at dinner, but he had frozen. More than anything, he wanted her to say yes. He couldn't imagine what he would do if she said no. He had not been nearly this nervous when he asked Annabel to marry him. Then, there hadn't been any uncertainty. He had known she wanted to marry him, that a scientist fit well in her plans. Nonchalantly, over dinner one night, Patrick asked her and, with a nod of her head, Annabel answered him. And then they were married in a whirl of fanfare and little emotion, as if a wedding was just a well-hosted party and the day merely another one marked off the calender.

"You're awfully quiet," Sarah said, leaning against him. He loved the feel of her. Not just her breasts and curves, but every part of her. Her shoulders, her fingertips, the slight indentation of her spine. Annabel was so tall and strong, but Sarah was smaller, softer, with more flesh. He could lose himself in her.

"I'm just enjoying being with you," he said.

She lifted up on her toes and kissed his cheek. They walked among the trees. It was another warm summer night. The spring had been exceptionally dry for Western Washington and this July night was no different.

"I keep expecting one of the kids to tell us to hurry up."

Patrick laughed. He and Adam spent every weekend with Sarah and Carolyn and Sam now. He still went back to the apartment at night, which frustrated the hell out of him, but at least he got to be with her.

"Sarah, I—"

He stopped abruptly. What an idiot he was. He was acting like a schoolboy. Yet this was so important. So much more important than it had ever been with Annabel.

"Tell me," Sarah said.

They were standing beneath an elm tree, its branches fluttering softly in the breeze.

"I want to marry you," he said.

There. It was done. He watched Sarah's face, but he could not read it. She was certainly not horrified or shocked, but she was not delighted either. She had yet to throw herself in his arms and say yes.

She turned and looked out over the trees. He could tell she was thinking, considering, debating. Debating what? Whether or not she loved him? Whether or not Jesse was still in the picture?

"Please, Sarah," he said at last. "Say something. You're killing me."

He tried to make his voice sound light, but it came out choked instead. Sarah turned back to him and gripped both his hands in hers. Patrick tried to brace himself.

"These last few months with you have been wonderful," she said. "The best in my life."

The box with the engagement ring in it felt heavy in Patrick's pocket. He could not get air into his lungs.

"But Jesse is still out there somewhere," she went on.

Patrick pulled his hands away.

"He left you," he said. "He walked out without a word, disappeared completely, yet you're willing to put your life on hold for him?"

"It's not that," Sarah said. "But what do I say to Carolyn and Sam? 'Gee, I guess your daddy isn't coming back so I'm going to replace him.'"

"Of course not. But what if Jesse never comes back? How long are you going to wait?"

Sarah leaned back against the tree trunk. She looked tired all of a sudden, completely worn out. Patrick had been so happy with her these past few months, he had hardly even thought about Jesse. After a while, they stopped bringing him up altogether. It was as if he didn't even exist anymore. But he did. To Sarah. To her children. They had a whole other life that did not include him.

"I can't say," Sarah said. "I just know that, for now, no matter how much I love you, I can't marry you. This isn't something I'm doing for Jesse. It's something I'm doing for Carolyn and Sam."

Patrick fought the anger down and walked over to her. He put his arms around her and felt her collapse against his chest.

"If he comes back, what then?" Patrick asked, not sure if he really wanted to know the answer.

Sarah spoke into his chest. "Then I will tell him I love you and that I want to marry you."

Patrick pulled away and looked at her.

"Do you mean that?"

"Of course."

Patrick tried to read her eyes, but he couldn't. She had never been anything but completely honest with him, and yet Jesse was an unknown. They had only dealt with his memory—and a tarnished one at that—not the actual person. This was Patrick's own catch-22. As long as Jesse stayed away, Patrick had Sarah. But not completely. Jesse had to come back for Sarah to marry him. But if Jesse came back, Patrick might lose Sarah to him. Either way, there was fear and the chance for catastrophe.

Patrick held on to her and tried to be content with this moment, having Sarah all to himself now. But he knew she was thinking of Jesse, and what might happen, and he cursed that part of her that Jesse would always own.

# 19

JESSE DID NOT look back. After almost ten months on the road, he felt that there was nothing behind him, that he had seen nothing. As if he had been driving around with his eyes closed.

Everything he wanted was in front of him. He was on the highway to home, having just crossed over the Cascades to the eastern outskirts of Seattle. He reached for a cigarette and then, instead, picked up the whole pack. He laughed as he rolled down the window and threw the pack out. He watched it hit the ground, once, twice, three times, and then skip out of view. It was almost too easy to do the right thing now. He had spent ten months doing everything wrong, making a lifetime's worth of mistakes; it was as if he'd gotten it all out of his system. From now on, there was only one course, the right one, and he would stick to it.

He drove the freeway he knew so well. God, it was as if he'd never left. It was incredible that time could be so warped, that so much experience, so much pain and hunger and self-loathing could be almost forgotten when there was some prize waiting for him on the horizon. Just the thought of seeing Sarah again, of feeling her arms around him, could erase months of misery.

Not that he would ever forget the lessons he'd learned.

Oh no. He knew what it was to be scum, to be the bum people kicked as they passed, the dirty man children ran away from, the homeless man middle-class professionals would not make eye contact with, as if he would infect them somehow. He understood that there were two lives you could lead, one respectable, following all the rules, like the one he'd had with Sarah, and the other apathetic, where you follow nothing and no one, and let life happen to you. The key was to mix them into just the right combination.

Jesse got off the freeway and headed out on the highway through the forests that grazed the northeastern edge of this Seattle suburb. His time on the road was up. He had passed through twenty-nine states, yet seen none of them. He'd worked a dozen jobs, yet could not remember what he'd done. He had lived in the car, in the gutter, in alleys. He had taken himself down to his smallest components, to a man who had no money and no food, and seen himself for what he really was. Just an animal who would do whatever it took to survive.

And he had come out of it better than before. This had been both the worst and best months of his life. He had kept moving, made no friends, formed no ties. He took odd jobs, bought some food, put gas in the car, and then headed out again. He shoved Sarah and Carolyn and Sam to the bottom of his mind and became the opposite of a husband and father; he became a feather on the wind, a speck on the highway, a blight in respectable people's scenery. He cared for no one and no one cared for him.

He had screwed the system, and it had screwed him back. There was no easy ride, even on the streets. You had to fight for the best spot on the beach, beg for more money, race to the shelters before the food ran out. It was competitive as hell. He had felt free, yet he knew he was in chains all along. He had done the worst thing imaginable, deserted his family, and he had done the greatest, set himself free.

He still didn't understand himself. So much of what he had done did not make sense. He had just followed his feet wherever they led him. He'd met all kinds of people. If the tales were true, Jesse had shared the stars with an accountant, a middleweight boxer, an insurance salesman, a housewife. They all had their stories and explanations. Drugs. Layoffs. Divorce. Insanity. It wasn't any different, really, than living in suburbia.

He told his own story and they all nodded. Cheating on Sarah, losing his job, running—these things were not so hard to accept when you were sitting on a park bench in the middle of the night, with nowhere else to go. No one thought he was wrong to have left. No one blamed him. No one told him to go home. Weeks passed, and then months, and he began to wonder if he'd ever find his way home again.

He had a few run-ins. One man had robbed him while he slept on the beach in Houston, taking the hundred bucks he'd made from a job. Another slashed his tires when Jesse wouldn't let him sleep in his car, and he had to work for four weeks to get enough money to replace them. He woke up one morning to a knife at his throat, but when the man could find nothing worth taking in his bags, he ran off.

The streets were mean, but they were open and free. It took ten months for Jesse to work up the will to leave them. He was twenty pounds lighter, more wrinkled and gray than when he started, but yesterday morning, when he woke up, he knew he wanted to go home. There was no gradual change, no slow coming around to what was right. He just woke up, thought of his family for the first time in ten months, and knew he was done running.

He'd had his time alone. He'd proven there was another kind of life out there, that he'd never be trapped again as long as he had a car to drive and a pillow to rest his head on. But he also knew that these last months had been lonely as hell. He couldn't erase Sarah's face from his brain. He couldn't pretend his family didn't matter.

They did matter and Jesse wanted them back. He wanted to feel Carolyn's arms around his neck and Sam's wet kisses on his cheek. He wanted Sarah. He wanted his home. A bed would feel good again. A roof would be a luxury.

He'd find some job that kept him outside, where he could feel the breeze and brace against the cold. But at night, there would always be a place to come home to, and people waiting for him.

As he got closer to his house, he drove faster. Ten months had passed and yet now he felt he could not wait another half hour to see Sarah again. There was so much to say. He didn't doubt that she would be angry at first. He had left her without a word, without a cent, except what was left in their savings after he took out that thousand. He was coming back with nothing new to offer, except perhaps peace of mind. But that was what he loved about Sarah, that she couldn't hate anyone completely. She could always see the other side. And she had known how miserable he was during the divorce, how empty his life had become.

He still thought about the way their marriage ended. With that night, in the bedroom. The second it was over, he knew it was a mistake, he shouldn't have forced her. But at the time, it had been the only way Jesse could communicate what he was feeling. Sarah had all these words, but Jesse had only his fists and his body. He would never hit her, so sex became the only weapon he had. If he had been able to talk, he would have said, "Look what you're doing to me. Look what you've turned me into. I never promised to be perfect. Why do you have to keep punishing me?" But instead of talking, he forced her legs apart and told her in blood.

What frustrated the hell out of him in those months afterward was that all the good years of their marriage were forfeited for only two nights. One, when he slept with Annabel. And the other, when he forced Sarah. How quickly the good times became meaningless. How much more power anger and hurt had than love.

Jesse turned down the streets of his neighborhood. His heart was racing. It would not be easy, but he would deal with whatever came. He would stand his ground. Because no matter what Sarah thought, he had his side to the story too. This was not just Sarah's story. It was Jesse's story too.

He turned onto his street and saw the house down the block. The lights were on as he pulled up. They illuminated a For Sale sign on the lawn. Jesse's heart slowed a little. The enormity of what he had done to Sarah seeped into his consciousness for a moment and then was gone. Her car was in the driveway. She was still there, so it couldn't have been too bad. Jesse turned off the engine, took a deep breath, and stepped out of the car.

He looked over the grass as he walked. It was cut low and evenly and he wondered if Sarah had done it herself. How had she managed? How had she survived? Had her parents loaned her enough to get through? He wished he'd been able to help her, to send her money or do something, but he hadn't even been able to take care of himself.

He reached the door and stopped. He could hear the television on the other side. It hit him, all at once, that despite the For Sale sign, they had gone on, just like always. Not that he had wanted them to suffer, and yet he thought maybe he would come home to a dilapidated house, to a family struggling to survive without him. He had thought that there would be more signs that his presence had been missed.

Jesse took another breath and knocked. There was no hesitation. In less than thirty seconds, Carolyn opened the door.

Jesse stared down at his daughter. She had grown at least two inches. Her hair was longer and wavier, more like his own. She stared back at him with eyes exactly the same shade as his, turquoise blue. Sweat broke out beneath Jesse's arms as he waited for her to react, to recognize him. Finally, when she said nothing and showed no recognition, he crouched down to her level.

"Carolyn?" he said softly. "It's me. Daddy."

Then she was on him. She threw herself at him and wrapped her arms around his neck. Jesse held her tight and squeezed his eyes shut. The smells of her were all the same, a mixture of grass and crayons and cookies, and a hint of soap to try to mask it all. She was crying. He could feel her hot tears on his neck.

"It's all right," he said. "Daddy's home." He opened his eyes and saw Sarah standing in the doorway to the kitchen. She was holding Sam with one arm and gripping the wall with the other.

Jesse stared at her. He drank her in, wondering how his

memories of her could fall so short of how beautiful she
really was, how much she moved him. She had cut her
hair above her shoulders and parted it on the left instead
of the right side. She was wearing a skirt and sweater that
he didn't recognize. She seemed taller, but he knew that
wasn't possible.

She did not smile or look away from his gaze. He
could not read her eyes. He was ready for her attacks, or
tears, maybe even happiness, but not this. Not nothing.

Jesse disentangled himself from Carolyn, but she still
clung to his hand.

"Look, Mommy," she said. "I told you he'd come
back. I told you. Daddy's home. He's finally home."

Sarah nodded. "Yes, I can see that."

Jesse marveled at the calmness of her voice. Not a
quiver. He looked at Sam, who was burrowing into Sarah's
body.

"Hey, slugger," he said, stepping forward. Sam gripped
Sarah's neck and started crying.

"He doesn't know you," Sarah said. "You're only scaring him."

Jesse stopped in the center of the room. Except for
Carolyn's hand in his, he felt like an awkward stranger. He
didn't know if he could sit or take off his coat or make
himself a drink.

Sarah soothed Sam and Jesse looked around. Things
were all out of place. The books rearranged on the table,
the sofa pulled out from the wall.

He looked up and found Sarah watching him. She had
not moved toward him. She was still standing stiffly in the
doorway, on alert.

"Daddy, come see my room." Carolyn pulled him upstairs. At least there, with his daughter, he understood the
rules. She loved him, he'd come home, and that was the
end of it. They went into her bedroom and she showed
him her dolls and teddy bears. She seemed to have twice
as many as he remembered.

"You've been doing well for yourself," he said, ruf-
fling her hair. He sat down on her bed, which had a new
Mickey Mouse bedspread on it.

She handed him dolls, naming them for him.

"This one's Tudy," she said. "Mommy gave it to me for my half-birthday. How come you weren't at my party? I asked Mommy if I could have a party when I turned five and a half and she said yes. Why weren't you there?"

Jesse pulled her up on his lap.

"I'm sorry, honey. Daddy had to go away for a while. But I'm back now. I promise I won't ever miss another party."

She studied his face and then smiled.

"Good," she said and then jumped off. She went into her closet and found more dolls.

"This one's Rebecca. Uncle Patrick gave it to me. He said it's nice to be able to buy girl things instead of just stupid boy things for Adam. And this one's . . ."

Jesse picked up the Rebecca doll. It had black hair and blue eyes and was obviously expensive. He did not like the thought of Patrick walking through a toy store, thinking about what Carolyn might like, and then picking out this doll. It was an intimate thing, buying a little girl a doll.

Still, Jesse said nothing. He let Carolyn show him everything she owned. It seemed almost normal, sitting there on his daughter's bed. He listened for sounds of Sarah and Sam, but couldn't hear anything below him. Every now and then, Carolyn stopped showing him things and came over and touched his face.

"You're really here," she said. Jesse blinked back tears and covered her hand with his own.

"Yes, honey. I'm here."

Sarah set a place for him at dinner. The only difference was, she set it across from herself, instead of next to her, the way it used to be. He asked her if he could help and she said no. She made a meat loaf that tasted better than anything he'd had in months.

Only Carolyn spoke during the meal. She had almost a year's worth of information to tell him. She had to explain about her kindergarten teacher and where she sat and the work she did and homework assignments and how she was the best kick-ball player in the class, even better than the boys. Jesse ate and smiled and tried not to stare at Sarah, who sat rigid and silent across from him.

Sam had a booster seat now and would not look at Jesse. He hardly ate anything and then cried until Sarah let him get down from the table. He hurried into the living room and lost himself in the television. And still Carolyn went on.

"And Daddy, you've got to come to my play. I'm going to be the witch, you know. I wanted to be one of the fairies, but no one wanted to be the witch and then Mrs. Olsen said I should do it since I'm the best actress and the witch is the best part. Mommy's making me a costume with a great hat and I get to cackle. Hee-hee-hee-hee."

Jesse watched as Sarah smiled. She could not hold it back. He almost reached over and touched her as she did it, wanting to hold the moment, but he knew she would pull away.

"You're a good witch, sweetie," Sarah said.

"Na-ah. I'm the bad witch. It's Sleeping Beauty. Did I tell you that, Daddy? I get to make Sleeping Beauty prick her finger on the spinning wheel. Then she sleeps and sleeps until Jeremy wakes her up. But he says he's not really gonna kiss her 'cause that's gross, but Wendy said she's gonna kiss him anyway and see what happens."

Sarah still smiled, although she tried to hide it by lowering her head. Carolyn told Jesse more about the play, but he found it hard to concentrate when Sarah was sitting so close. There had been times, when he was out of money and hope, when he didn't think this day would ever come. And yet now it had come, and Jesse wondered why there weren't fireworks or rockets going off to mark the occasion.

Jesse cleared the dishes and noticed that Sarah did not come into the kitchen to help. He heard her walking up the stairs and then running the bathtub for Carolyn and Sam. Jesse finished up the dishes and then walked back into the living room.

He tried to find traces of himself left behind. There was still a picture of him, along with the rest of them, on the hall wall, but that was it. Everything had been rearranged. The sofa, the wing chairs, even a new shade put on the lamp. Jesse wondered how Sarah had done it. How could she have gone on so easily without him while he had crumbled to almost nothing without her?

Carolyn came down the stairs a few minutes later, newly washed. She threw herself at him again and Jesse laughed. This, he thought, could make up for almost anything. He remembered how in the beginning he had thought she was more Sarah's child than his. How strange now that Sam hid behind his mother and Carolyn was the one to love him, to forgive him.

He took her upstairs and tucked her into bed. She grabbed his hand tightly.

"You'll be here in the morning, won't you?" Her eyes were wide and teary and he kissed her sweet-smelling forehead.

"I don't think I'll be sleeping here tonight, but I'll come over first thing tomorrow morning and we'll spend the whole day together, just you and me."

"Promise?"

"Promise, sweetheart."

He kissed her again and then walked to the door.

"Daddy?" she said. He turned around. "Adam says Mommy and Uncle Patrick are gonna get married. Mommy says that's not true, not yet, but if they do, will you still be my daddy?"

Jesse did not lose the smile on his face. The funny thing was, on the outside, he looked the same as always. Only he could tell that his veins had frozen, that none of his muscles were working, that he could not find his voice. He heard a sound behind him and turned to find Sarah in the hallway, coming out of Sam's room. She looked at him with eyes that cut him more than harsh words ever could because in them he saw nothing, not anger or bitterness or love. Nothing.

He turned back to Carolyn.

"I'll always be your daddy," he managed to say. Then he closed the door and turned to Sarah. Her hands were on her hips and she held her ground.

"Will you please tell me what the hell is going on," Jesse said.

•    •    •

Sarah was so angry, she couldn't stand still. She stomped past Jesse down the stairs. She eyed the expensive figurines on the mantelpiece her parents had given her, aching to pick them up, one by one, and smash them against the wall. But she did not. Instead, she watched Jesse walk into the kitchen and sit at the table, as if he still belonged there. She followed him.

"How dare you," she said, pacing around the room. "How dare you just show up like this and then have the nerve to ask me what's going on."

"Carolyn told me you were going to marry Patrick," Jesse said. "How the hell do you expect me to feel?" He too was angry, she could see. His neck and cheeks were red, and his fists clenched. The idea that he could be mad at her enraged Sarah further.

"Why shouldn't I marry him?" she shouted at him. "He's been here for me this past year. He's loaned me money when I was desperate. He's mowed the lawn and fixed the roof and given the kids baths. Where the hell were you?"

Jesse opened his mouth, but then said nothing. He unclenched his fists and sat back in the chair.

"Well?" Sarah said, putting her hands on her hips and glaring at him. It was all so unbelievable, Jesse sitting there, just like always. He looked only slightly different, thinner, with more gray in his hair. She had wanted him to come back, wanted to know that he was all right, and yet now that he was here, she could feel nothing but an intense rage. From the moment she walked out from the kitchen and saw him standing in the doorway, hugging Carolyn, she had been filled with it. How dare he just walk in without warning? How dare he not be sick or destitute, the only explanations for his disappearance that she would even partly accept. How dare he smile at her, and expect her to smile back, after all he had done?

"Sarah, please," he said softly. Sarah gritted her teeth, waiting for some lame excuse, some long-winded speech about needing to find himself or live without responsibility for a while. Jesse looked up at her. She knew the gesture. He used to use it to melt her, to remind her that he was irresistible. But that was just it. She could resist him now.

In fact, as she looked him over, she didn't find him in any way attractive. It was as if his actions had disfigured him to her, made him somehow disgusting.

"Maybe we could have some coffee," he said.

Sarah just stood there. She would not make another pot of coffee for him if her life depended on it. When he realized this, when he saw in her face that she was not moved by him, Sarah's heart soared. All those years she had loved him, given in to him, she had never felt a need to assert herself. And yet now, when it happened all on its own, when she found herself standing there, completely untouched by him, it was like being brought to life. She moved her shoulders a little, accustoming herself to this new freedom. She'd had no idea that she had been chained by him. She had assumed her love for Jesse was the best kind, the all-consuming kind. Now that it had left her, she saw all its entrapments, all its shackles, the power it had to suck the substance right out of her.

She realized all of this as the anger went out of her, as she found that she really did not care very much at all what Jesse's explanations were. He could have been kidnapped by aliens or forced to work in a South American prison camp, and she wouldn't have cared.

"You're not making this very easy," he said.

"Did you think it would be?" she replied, sitting down opposite him. She stared at him objectively for the first time. He was handsome, in a rough-edged way. He looked thinner than she recalled, which only enhanced his bone structure. His gray-streaked blond hair now fell to his shoulders in waves. The idea came to her suddenly that he really did look better suited to Annabel, and she to Patrick. Both Jesse and Annabel were striking, unforgettable, a bit hard-edged, while she and Patrick were ordinary faces in the crowd. She thought the idea would hurt her, but instead it made her smile.

"I thought you'd give me a chance to explain things," Jesse said.

Sarah rested her chin on her hand. "Explain."

Jesse stood up and walked to the window. He laid his head against it.

"I didn't plan to leave," he said. "I figured I'd eventually find a job that I could live with. Not another sales job, or the shit work I took afterward just to make it through. But something I could be happy with."

"Whenever you got a job, you quit," Sarah said.

"I know. Working at those places ate me up inside. You've got to understand, I couldn't do something I despised eight, ten hours a day. It made me despise myself."

The thing was, Sarah did understand, though she didn't tell Jesse that. All of a sudden, she understood Jesse better than she ever had when they were married. He had a wild, selfish heart. To restrain it was to kill it. It didn't make him very responsible or easy to love, but it was part of who he was. All those years at Boeing, he had tried to be who she wanted, who he thought everyone wanted him to be. And every day he got further and further from his true self, until he looked in the mirror and didn't recognize the image.

"One morning," he said, "I was looking over the want ads and I felt dead inside. One more day like that and I knew I would kill myself. That's when I knew I had to go."

"Why couldn't you tell us?"

"Tell you what?" Jesse said, turning around. "That I wasn't going to live up to my end of the bargain? That I was going to lose myself in the streets, become everything you hated? I loved you, Sarah. I'd rather you thought I was dead."

Sarah saw the agony in his eyes, but it did not reach her. She was still awed by her sudden apathy, as though someone had swooped down and stolen her soul away.

"And your children. You didn't care what they thought either?"

Jesse ran his fingers through his hair. Sarah wondered where his cigarettes were. She thought he could use one now.

"I thought it was better to stay hidden. Out there, I wasn't the same man. I was nobody. I woke up in my car one morning in South Carolina and some kid had his face pressed up to the window. You should have seen his eyes. He was looking at me like I was some freak in a carnival show, and that was what I looked like too. Unshaven, dirty, with everything I owned in that car with me. That kid could have been Sam in a few years. Would any man want his kids to see him that way?"

"They didn't understand," Sarah said, still not caving in to his bid for sympathy. "None of us understood your need to go out and punish yourself."

Jesse turned away. "I suppose it was that. A punishment. But also a relief. This house, finding a job, trying to pay for all of you . . . I couldn't take it."

"You're a selfish man, Jesse," Sarah said.

Jesse nodded. "I know you won't believe me," he said, "but I love all of you. It killed me to do what I did to you. But I didn't have any other choice. This is who I am."

Sarah nodded. "I believe you," she said.

He turned and looked out the window again.

"I lived in the car, on the streets, wherever. I was in twenty-nine states, though I couldn't tell you which ones or anything I've seen. It wasn't like a vacation, Sarah. I got a few jobs and then quit when they started to take the life out of me. I tried not to remember this life, or you. I lived from day to day, and the truth is, that kind of life almost appealed to me. It took all the pressure off. All that mattered was eating and getting through the night without getting knifed by someone who liked my spot beneath the bridge better than his. It was all reduced to the basics, something even I could understand."

Sarah stood up suddenly and walked over to him. She put her hand on his shoulder.

"You survived," she said. She could feel him trembling beneath her touch. Funny how he seemed so weak now, when it was his strength that had attracted her to him in the first place.

"Yes, I survived. I don't know why. I came just as close to letting go. I finally ended up in Phoenix where I got a job I liked, as a construction worker. I saved a little money, pocket change really, but it's for you. I know it won't make up for anything, but it's all I've got to offer."

He turned around and Sarah saw the tears in his eyes. She wanted to respond to him, to help him despite everything, but still she felt nothing. She released her hand and turned away. She walked back to the table and sat down.

"You can put the money in an account for the kids," she said, "if that will make you feel better. But I don't want it."

"Sarah, you need it. I saw the For Sale sign. I know the bills on this place. And the car and—"

"I've survived too," she said loudly. "I got a job, just in case you're interested. It doesn't pay much, but I've learned how to cut corners and make it last. I could have sold the house weeks ago, if I'd taken a low offer, but I decided to hold out until I got something respectable. My parents help me and so does Patrick, whether you want to hear that or not. I don't want to be indebted to you."

"I still owe you child support," he said.

"Yes. And you can start paying that back now. But I'm telling you, it's for the kids. Not for me."

Jesse walked around the table and stared at her.

"You hate me, don't you?"

Sarah shook her head. "I thought I did. When you walked in here tonight, I hated you so intensely I thought it would swallow me up. And then, all of a sudden, it vanished. To tell you the truth, Jesse, I don't feel a damn thing for you."

Jesse turned his head away. An hour ago, Sarah would have taken pleasure in hurting him, but now she simply stood up and walked to the front door. Jesse followed her and watched her open it.

"Go," she said. "I've heard your explanation and I accept it. I won't stop you from seeing your kids, even though I think you'd better tread carefully with Sam."

"What about us?" Jesse said.

"Us? There is no us. There was never really any us. There was only Jesse and his wife."

Jesse shook his head.

"How can you be so cold?" he said.

This time, Sarah did react. She walked over to him and pointed her finger at his face.

"This coldness is only directed at you," she said. "If it's there, it's because you put it there."

"Tell me you won't marry Patrick," Jesse said. "That would kill me, Sarah."

Sarah shrugged and walked back to the door.

"I don't know what I'll do. And frankly, I don't think anything can kill you, Jesse. You're indestructible."

He looked at her for a long time and Sarah knew he was searching for the woman he had loved, the timid girl he'd married. She was pleased when he couldn't find even a trace of her.

He walked to the door and hesitated. He turned back toward her.

"I always loved you," he said.

Sarah sighed. "I know, Jesse. Now go."

He walked out and she closed the door behind him. She waited until she heard his car start and then drive off down the road before she let out her breath. She was free.

# 20

❧

LATE THAT SAME night, Annabel was sitting at a table with five men. The six of them had polished off four bottles of whiskey and were hard at work on the fifth. Annabel's body felt wonderfully loose and flowing, but she was crying as she drank. She could not believe that she had given in so easily after the weeks of struggling for sobriety. She had taken the first drink that was offered to her. She was run-down, completely depleted of energy. She knew she would never be able to pull herself out of this hole again.

Someone knocked on the door and the men all looked at her.

"Get that," one of them said. She looked around, but could find no door. The knocking came louder and louder, and there was shouting too, and then the dream fell away. Annabel opened her eyes and saw her bedroom. She was tight and anxious, but still sober.

It took her a moment to realize the knocking was real. She glanced at the clock, saw that it was almost one o'clock in the morning, and then threw off the covers. She grabbed her robe and hurried down the stairs. She was grateful that Adam was a deep sleeper.

She reached the front door, but didn't open it.

"Who is it?" she said.

"Me. Jesse."

Annabel stood still. She thought maybe she was still dreaming. Jesse had appeared to her often enough in her dreams. He was the hero in every fantasy, riding in just in time to save her from booze or the horror of Patrick's love affair. No one had asked her, during this past year, if she was worried. If Jesse's disappearance affected her. It never occurred to anyone that she had feelings too.

"Will you let me in?" Jesse asked.

Annabel turned around and looked in the mirror. It was a reflex action, smoothing down her hair, pinching color into her cheeks, wiping the smeared mascara out from under her eyes. She had gotten the stitches out of her forehead a month and a half ago and there was a white scar there. The rest of her scratches had healed. She did not look good, not even close to what she could look like with a couple hours of primping. But Jesse was here now, and when would she get another chance?

She turned the lock on the door and opened it. Jesse stood there, in Levi's and a flannel shirt. She hadn't seen him since that night they were in the car together, but he was still familiar to her. She stepped back and let him inside.

Annabel locked the door behind her and then turned around. Jesse stood just inside the door, within touching distance. They stared at each other without speaking. Annabel drank in the sight of him and managed to hold off her tears of relief. *Thank God,* her mind was saying. *Thank God he's all right.* A world without Jesse in it was not a world she wanted to contemplate.

He looked haggard and run-down. She noticed the gray streaks in his hair and longed to reach out and run her fingers through it. She forgot, for a moment, that she had her own problems, that lately it was she who needed to be comforted. She wished she could pull Jesse to her breast and hold him there.

He was watching her too. Annabel was certain that her recent life was written all over her. First the booze, then the brief pregnancy, then the crash, then that awful day when she came home from the hospital. Adam had welcomed her home, checked on her bruises and stitches, and then proceeded to tell her everything about his ferry ride to Orcas Island with Sarah and Patrick. And all the while, Annabel was imagining what Sarah and Patrick looked like in bed together, how Sarah's hair fell over Patrick's chest, how she fit into the crook of his shoulder better than Annabel had. She tried to imagine what they had done after Annabel called Patrick from the hospital. Had he come to her bedside right away, or had he stayed on for one more quickie before tending to the needs of his ex-wife?

"The boat was cool," Adam had said. "We were practically the only ones on it. And Dad told us stories. Great ones about dragons and kings and knights. Aunt Sarah laughed more than she ever had and took us home and let me stay overnight."

Annabel put her hands on her empty stomach and closed her eyes.

"Your dad and Aunt Sarah are pretty good friends now, aren't they?" she said, not knowing why she said it. She didn't want to know. She really didn't.

"It's gross," Adam said. "They were holding hands and making goo-goo eyes at each other on the way back on the boat. Carolyn kept jabbing me with her elbow, trying to get me to look at them, but I just ignored it."

As soon as Adam went off to a friend's house, Annabel marched into the kitchen. She had the cap off the whiskey bottle before she stopped.

With the bottle still in her hand, she walked to the mirror in the entry and looked at herself. There was a bandage on her forehead, covering up the stitches she'd had to have. Her left eye was swollen and bruised. There were scratches where the glass from the windshield had penetrated her skin. She was achy and stiff, like an old woman.

But it was not the surface bruises that bothered her. They would heal; she would grow strong again. But when she looked at her eyes, she did not recognize them. The pupils took up the whole space, two big, ugly marbles of black outlined in red. She could not see into them, or through them, to what was inside. She had no idea who was looking back at her.

Annabel looked down at the bottle in her hand. So harmless. Only glass and liquid. She squeezed it, wanting to give in to it, to just keep on drinking until she really did die, until she got into a car and crashed into a brick wall instead of a lamppost, or went home with a psychopath instead of a construction worker, or lost Adam to Patrick and Sarah and killed herself. She did not want to fight, or pull herself together, as Patrick had told her to.

But when she looked back in the mirror, she knew she would fight. Because although her eyes looked foreign, she knew that behind them, somewhere, was a sliver of the woman she used to be. She had not been able to stop drinking for Adam. Or for Patrick. Or even for herself. But she would stop to prove to Sarah that she had not won. Because if there was one thing still alive inside of Annabel, it was her vanity, her pride. If there was one thing she had relied on all her life, it was the belief that she was irresistible to men, that she was the one they wanted.

Annabel laughed strangely, bitterly, as she stared at herself. Love could not save her. Or motherhood. Or friendship. How ironic, how completely typical of her that only this competition, this need to avenge herself on Sarah, could give her the courage to try.

She walked back into the kitchen and took down all the bottles. She had so many of them. Vodka, gin, whiskey, wine. She looked them over lovingly, as if they were her children. And then, one by one, thinking of Sarah and Patrick in bed together as she did it, Annabel smashed the bottles against the wall. The glass flew everywhere. Booze ran down the wallpaper and seeped into the hardwood floors. Even now, Annabel could still smell it. It took every ounce of willpower she had not to lick the floor.

But she did not lick it. Instead, she avoided bars, avoided television shows where people were always drinking, and went day by day. It was the only way she defined herself these days, by the fact that she still had not taken a drink. She tried to control the shaking. She took up smoking and was hooked instantly. There were minutes, even, when she did not think of liquor at all. But there were still the dreams, and the sporadic cravings that threatened to overwhelm her. There were still the nights when she sneaked into Adam's room and held his hand while he slept, trying to infuse his peacefulness into her. There were still the twice-weekly sessions with Dr. Walinski, the psychiatrist Cal Richards, Eddie's father, had recommended to her. Annabel had called him after she smashed all the bottles, before she could stop herself. She started crying as soon as the receptionist said hello.

"I need help," Annabel had said. It was the first honest thing she'd said in months. The receptionist got her in that day. And since then, twice a week, sitting in that chair in Dr. Walinski's office, listening to him tell her that she was going to be all right, was the only relief Annabel got.

Now, Jesse stared at her. "You look good," he said.

Annabel smiled at the ridiculousness of the statement. She did not look anywhere near good. She walked past him to the couch and motioned for him to follow her.

They sat down next to each other. He still wore the same cologne, she noticed.

"Where have you been?" Annabel asked. Jesse looked at her and then they both smiled. It was such an innocent question when compared to his actions. She could have asked it of a child who had been out playing for a few hours, or of a friend who hadn't been home for her calls.

"Everywhere," Jesse said. "Nowhere at all."

Annabel nodded. This time, she could not help herself. She reached out and touched the hollow in his cheek.

"You've lost weight," she said.

He did not push her hand away. He turned his eyes to her and Annabel did not blink while he studied her. She wanted him to see her the way she really was. It was the first time in her life she wanted someone to really see her.

"You've been struggling," he said.

Annabel dropped her hand, but Jesse caught it in his.

"I gave up booze," she said.

Jesse stared at her. Annabel remembered all the drunken nights and, recently, all the painfully sober ones, and for a moment it seemed as if Jesse were scanning the memories with her, as if he had been with her all along.

"I never thought it was a problem for you."

"It was. It got to be. That's my whole life now, every second is another second I can't take a drink."

Jesse dropped her hand and Annabel was sure that

she'd lost him. Her breath left her. What a fool she was, being honest, wanting him to see her as she really was. If only he'd come back before the accident. She could have been what he wanted. She could have gone on drinking, getting wild. It all would have been worth it, if only to keep the admiration in Jesse's eyes.

Now, she had ruined it all. She gripped her robe tighter and leaned away from him. She might as well tell him the whole truth now. He wouldn't stay with her anyway.

"I go to a psychiatrist twice a week," she said. "Mostly he helps me stay sober, but we deal with other things too, with Sarah and Patrick, with you."

Annabel waited for him to leave. She could see in his eyes that she had disappointed him, that she was more than he'd bargained for. He hesitated. He started to stand, but then, so quickly she could not prepare, he pulled her to him and held her with a force that made her lose her breath. He buried his face in her hair, and she lost herself in his skin and scent. She hardly noticed she was crying.

"Annabel," he said, and her name sounded like music on his tongue. She gripped him tighter, until she really did lose her breath, and then she released him.

"I'm not me anymore," she said.

"You are."

He kept hold of her hands and Annabel searched his eyes for sarcasm. Instead, she saw only acceptance, even, perhaps, concern. There were a million questions to be asked. Where had he been? Why did he leave? Did he still love Sarah? But none of them seemed of much importance now. Now, there was only Jesse, and he was touching her, and she was happy. She had never realized things could be so simple.

"Let's get married," he said.

Annabel jumped a little. She waited for him to start laughing, to tell her he was kidding. When he only stared at her, his eyes serious and calm, she sat back in the couch.

"I don't understand."

"What's to understand? I went away and got myself together. And while I was gone I realized you were the one for me. We're right together. You know we are."

The thing was, Annabel did know they were right together. She had known it since the day she met him, when he was still firmly Sarah's husband. But something did not fit. Things had ended bitterly between them, after that night in the car. Jesse had insisted they not see each other anymore. Then, even after Jesse and Sarah's divorce, he had not contacted her. He had disappeared for ten months without a word, without a goodbye. And now, she couldn't be what he'd expected.

There was a missing piece somewhere. Yet Annabel didn't want to question it. She ignored the absent declarations of love. More than anything in the world, she simply wanted to marry him.

"Have you told Sarah?" she asked. "Does she even know you're back?"

Jesse stood up. He walked across the room, then turned around and stared at her.

"Forget about Sarah," he said. "She doesn't mean anything to me anymore. It's you I want."

"Adam will have to agree," Annabel said. She wanted Jesse more than anything, but she would not go against Adam. Not after all he had done for her, everything he had been to her. She deferred to her son on so many things now. She let him choose the movies they went to see. He searched the *TV Guide* and picked out the shows they'd watch for the evening. Annabel had never been able to do that with anyone else, give up her options and control, but Adam made it easy for her. He had become so strong in these last few months. He was hardly ever a child anymore. He came home from school, did his homework, and moved close enough past her to make sure there was no scent of liquor on her breath. Annabel had long ago stopped trying to right the ship, to make him the baby and her the adult again. The truth was, it was a relief to let him run things, to not have to make any choices.

Jesse stared at her.

"All right," he said. "If that's what you want."

Annabel did not think anymore. What good was thinking when her heart was already lost, when her body wanted him so badly? She stood up and walked over to him. She kissed him the way she had wanted to kiss him since that long-ago night in the car, with feeling instead of precision. And when she was done, and he was panting, and his hands were all over her body, she knew she had at least won the first battle. If she could make him want her body, she was certain she could eventually make him want her soul.

"When?" she asked as he untied her robe and slid it off her. Then he slipped the straps of her nightgown over each shoulder and it slid to the floor. She shivered as his fingers traced patterns over her breast.

"As soon as we can," he said. "We can get the blood tests tomorrow, register for a license, and then find a justice of the peace."

Then his lips were on her and Annabel forgot all her questions.

Adam took only a little persuasion.

"He hasn't even been around," Adam said after Annabel came into his room the next morning and told him Jesse wanted to marry her.

"I know. But before he left, he and I . . . We felt something for each other. It never died, I guess."

Adam looked at her and Annabel forced herself not to turn away. He was just a boy, after all. He couldn't read her soul, he couldn't sense deception. He had no idea what had happened between her and Jesse in the car.

"Do I have to call him Dad?" he asked.

Annabel sat down beside him.

"Of course not. Whatever you're comfortable with."

Just a few months ago, Adam might have crawled into her arms at this point, let her soothe his fears and trepidations. But now he just stiffened and then stood up.

"Dad's gonna marry Sarah," he said. "He won't admit it, but he's going to."

Annabel nodded. It didn't hurt quite as much today.

"Yes, I think you're right."

"It's weird," Adam said. "It's weird for me and Carolyn and Sam."

Annabel looked at him.

"I'm sorry," she said.

Adam shrugged. "You don't have to be sorry. You

can't help what you feel, I guess. But it's still weird for us. I thought you should know."

Annabel toyed with the bedspread. Adam knew so much more than she did. He had a grasp on things she wasn't even close to figuring out. She wondered if he would always be this perceptive, or if wisdom was a consequence of childhood, and he would lose it, as the rest of them had, as he aged.

"Well, I guess if you guys love each other . . ." he said.

Annabel took a deep breath and smiled.

"Of course we do."

Jesse had stayed the night and sneaked out early in the morning, before Adam could see him. He came back later in the day, after Adam had left for a friend's house, and the two of them went for their blood tests and filled out a request for a marriage license. Afterward, they pulled up into Annabel's driveway and stood beside the car.

"I have to tell Sarah," Jesse said.

Annabel lifted her chin a notch. "She and Patrick are probably going to get married."

Jesse did not tell her he had already heard that. Instead, he looked her over. Annabel was not as perfect as he remembered. Physically, she was the same. She had the same flawless makeup and hairsprayed hair and perfumed skin. But today he noticed that her hands shook almost constantly, that she turned away from every liquor store they passed. She had taken up smoking and was agitated if she didn't have a full pack.

She was a far cry from the woman he'd been with in the back seat of the car. When she told him about her alcoholism, he almost got up and walked out. *He* was the one with the problems. He didn't have the energy or desire to take on anyone else's.

But then he'd looked in her eyes, seen a vulnerability there she'd never exposed before, and decided to stay. When they made love last night, she clung to him and cried when he was inside her. It both repelled and attracted him. She seemed to be two different people, one strong and one weak, and Jesse wasn't sure which one he liked better. He looked away.

"At least you haven't had to be here to watch them," Annabel said.

He turned back to her and took her hand. He had come to her last night directly from Sarah's. He hadn't thought about what he was doing. But when he had seen her, when he had seen what was in her eyes, the adoration, the respect, every emotion the very opposite of Sarah's, the marriage proposal had jumped right out of him. The funny thing was, he had no regrets now. She'd beat this booze thing soon enough and then he'd have the Annabel he remembered by his side, every night. And, better than that, their marriage would be a knife through Sarah's and Patrick's hearts.

He smiled.

"Don't think about them," he said. "Think about us. Think about what you're going to wear to our wedding."

He leaned over and kissed her and then got back in his car. He was still smiling when he knocked on Sarah's door.

She was not happy to see him, but he didn't care. He brushed past her, into the house, and scooped up Carolyn.

"How's my girl?" he asked.

"Great! Where are we going today?"

Jesse laughed and made sure Sarah was still behind him.

"Today we're going to find a suit for your daddy's wedding."

Carolyn clapped her hands and kissed him. But it was Sarah's intake of breath that made him smile. He turned around and faced her, with Carolyn still in his arms.

"Hooray!" Carolyn said.

"You went to her," Sarah said softly.

Jesse nodded. He put Carolyn down.

"Go to the bathroom before we go, sweetie," he said.

"But I want to hear about the wedding."

"You will in a minute. Just go now, okay?"

"Oh, okay."

When she was out of the room, Jesse looked back at Sarah.

"Does Annabel know you were here first?" Sarah asked.

Jesse shrugged. "She knows I want to marry her. That's enough for her."

Sarah shook her head as she walked past him. Jesse followed her into the kitchen where she was cleaning up.

"I can't believe you'd get married just to spite me," she said.

"It isn't to spite you. You're not the center of everything, Sarah."

Sarah put her hands on her hips and turned to him.

"Are you telling me you love Annabel?"

Jesse flashed her his smile.

"Of course I do."

"Then why did you try to get me back last night?"

"I was trying to do the right thing. But when you acted the way you did, I went where I should have gone in the first place. To Annabel. To a woman who's got some passion in her."

Sarah looked away and Jesse felt a surge of triumph. It was like winning a round by knockout. Carolyn came out of the bathroom and slipped her hand into his.

"I told Adam he was wrong," she said. "I told him you'd come back and Mommy would marry you, not Uncle Patrick."

Sarah's and Jesse's eyes met. Jesse crouched down beside her.

"I'm not marrying your mom, sweetheart," he said. "I'm marrying Annabel."

Carolyn pulled her hand away. She backed up until she hit the counter.

"Why can't you marry Mommy?" she said.

Jesse looked at Sarah, but she remained silent.

"Your mommy and I already tried that," he said, "and it didn't work. Besides, you like Annabel, don't you?"

Carolyn pulled away from him and ran to Sarah. Sarah picked her up and rocked her.

"I hate Annabel," Carolyn sobbed. "Adam says he has to do everything for her now. She's crazy. He says first she was sloshy all the time and then she was mean to him and now she hugs him too much. I hate her!"

Jesse took a step toward her, but Sarah waved him off.

She took Carolyn into the living room and sat down with her on the couch. She dried her tears.

"Adam loves his mother," Sarah said. "You know that. Annabel went through some hard times and Adam helped her and now she's getting better."

"But I don't want Daddy to marry her. I want him to marry you."

She started crying again and Sarah closed her eyes. Jesse watched them, feeling that all his great plans were not so great anymore. He had not expected this. The worst part was, he hadn't thought of his children at all when he asked Annabel to marry him. He had been shocked when Annabel told him she'd have to talk to Adam first. He hadn't realized their children had turned into real people while he was gone.

"That's not going to happen," Sarah said. "I know that's hard to accept, but it's true. Your father has a right to be happy now with someone new, and that someone he wants is Annabel. This will make Adam your stepbrother. That will be nice, won't it?"

"Yuck!" Carolyn said, her sobs turning to sniffles. "Adam's gross. He opens his mouth with food in it. And he spits into his milk and drinks it."

Sarah wiped the rest of her tears away.

"Come on now," she said, "I've seen you do that too."

Carolyn pulled away from Sarah. She glanced over at Jesse, who gave her a big smile.

"I'd like you to be part of the wedding, honey," he said. Her sniffles stopped abruptly and she jumped off Sarah's lap.

"Really?"

"Yes, really. Maid of honor, even. We can pick out a dress today."

"And can I have a hat?"

"Of course."

"And flowers?"

"Sure."

Carolyn threw herself at Jesse and he laughed. It was bribery, sure, and it probably wouldn't last, but at least he'd gotten her to stop crying.

"Does Annabel know about her maid of honor?" Sarah asked.

"Not yet."

Just briefly, they smiled at each other, and then Sarah looked away.

"I hope you know what you're doing, Jesse," she said. Jesse nodded.

"I hope so too."

August was a busy month for weddings, but Annabel pushed and prodded and managed to get their license within a week. They set a date for the following Sunday and Annabel called Patrick to let him know.

"It's none of my concern when you have your wedding," Patrick said.

Annabel gripped the phone tightly. Even now, he wouldn't satisfy her with a reaction. She could call him a dirty, rotten pig and he would respond calmly that no, he wasn't, he was a man, and she should get her facts straight.

"I know that," she said. "But this is a major change for all of us and I wanted to give you some warning."

"Consider me warned."

"You can be with your precious Sarah now."

Annabel held her breath through the silence. Finally, Patrick said, "Sarah and I have nothing to do with either of you. If we do get married, it will be because we want to. This isn't a competition."

After he hung up, Annabel wondered what made her say the things she did, why she wanted to hurt the people she had once loved.

At the wedding, it was Annabel and Jesse, Adam as best man, Carolyn as maid of honor, two witnesses pulled off the street, and a justice of the peace. Jesse had wanted to bring Sam along, but Sarah had refused, saying Sam was still confused over exactly who Jesse was. The ceremony took six minutes. Then they signed the license, Adam and Carolyn threw rice on them, and it was over. Annabel was Mrs. Jesse Bean.

They took the kids out to dinner to celebrate. Annabel would have preferred a quiet and romantic restaurant, but with two quarreling kids they decided it would be better to go for hamburgers. So their wedding-night meal was burgers and fries and milk shakes and plenty of noise. But it hardly mattered because Jesse held her hand beneath the table and she was happy.

Sarah had agreed to keep Adam for the night. Annabel tried to ignore the knot that twisted in her stomach as Jesse drove them to Sarah's to drop off the kids. Her mind replayed the words *I am Jesse's wife. I am Jesse's wife. I am Jesse's wife* again and again. She had gotten what she wanted. This was her moment of triumph. Yet the joy was not pure; doubt and guilt gnawed at it.

It was almost laughable when they parked the car in the driveway and walked up to the door. Almost. It was amazing to Annabel how calm and normal people could appear on the surface while they were nervous as hell inside.

Jesse glanced at her when they reached the door.

"Ready?" he said, with a smile.

Annabel did not betray herself. She smiled back.

"Of course."

Jesse knocked. Sarah opened the door quickly, as if she had been waiting on the other side.

"Well," she said, staring at them. Annabel was surprised by how good she looked, how tall she held herself. She was surprised too by the violence of the nausea in her stomach. She knew she was holding all the cards, that she had won, that she had Jesse. Yet it still seemed that Sarah was a step above her.

"We did it," Jesse said.

"I guess you did."

Sarah did not invite them in. Adam and Carolyn squeezed past them into the house, leaving the three of them facing each other in the doorway. Annabel had a desire to push her way in, to refuse to leave Sarah's house until they had all gotten back what they had lost. But she didn't do it. It was a crazy idea anyway. Nothing could penetrate the hardness in Sarah's eyes.

"How's Patrick?" Annabel asked. It was all she could think of to say. Immediately the absurdity of the situation hit her. Here she was married to Sarah's ex-husband, asking Sarah about her own ex-husband.

Sarah lifted her chin up a notch.

"He's fine. There's been some rumbling going on at MIT. One of the professors there is retiring, and Clarence Browden called and told him he's in the applicants' pool for the job. He said I should wish you well when I saw you."

"Really?" Annabel said, although she knew it was true. Patrick would deny her the jealous outburst she longed for. He would be calm and rational and say that Annabel and Jesse were better suited than he and Annabel ever were.

Annabel looked at Sarah. There was still hostility in her eyes, but not as much as there had been that day in the driveway, when Annabel exposed herself completely and Sarah walked away. Did Sarah have any idea how much courage it had taken for Annabel to come to her, and how humiliating it had been to be left there, crying, in her driveway? She had held out an olive branch and Sarah had sliced it in half. That day, whatever faith Annabel still had in friendship had been shattered. She would not trust it again. She would never let Sarah or anyone else see her that vulnerable again.

"Yes, really," Sarah said at last. She looked over her shoulder to make sure Adam was out of earshot. "He's a little concerned about the kids, of course, how confusing this will be for them. He's planning to take a little extra time with Adam next week to talk to him."

Annabel frowned. She didn't like hearing about Adam from Sarah. Sarah might be involved with Annabel's ex-husband, but that didn't make Adam any of her business.

After an awkward moment Jesse put his arm around Annabel's shoulder. It occurred to her that he had refrained from doing that until now for Sarah's sake.

"Well, we'd better be off," he said.

Sarah nodded and started to close the door.

"I'll expect Adam after school tomorrow," Annabel said.

"Fine."

Sarah shut the door a little too loudly. When Jesse and Annabel looked at each other, she saw the humor in his eyes and the knot in her stomach loosened. She would not talk to him of pain and loss. She would keep it light, the way he liked it.

Simultaneously, they both laughed.

"God," Annabel said. "How weird."

Jesse pulled her close as they walked back to the car.

On the other side of the door, Sarah heard their laughter. She leaned against the door and gulped air into her lungs. *Oh God,* she thought. *Oh God. Oh God. Oh God.*

It shouldn't hurt. Of course it shouldn't hurt. But it did. To see the man you'd loved so much, the man who had sworn to be with you forever, standing in front of you with another woman. Actually touching another woman. To see your best friend glorying in beating you, flaunting the fact that your friendship meant nothing to her, that getting what she wanted was all that mattered. It had been all Sarah could do not to scream at them to get away from her.

It was petty and juvenile and completely irrational, but even though she had lost all of her love for Jesse, Sarah still thought of him as hers. She didn't want to be married to him. She didn't wish him a lifetime of loneliness. But the thought of him with someone else, the sight of him with someone else, especially Annabel, was too much. For seven years, *she* had been Jesse's wife. It was how she defined herself. Annabel had stolen not only her husband, but also her title, her definition.

Sarah shook her head. She made sure Adam and Carolyn were playing nicely, then went upstairs to check on Sam. After she was certain that he was still sleeping soundly, she walked into her bedroom and lay down on the bed.

Sarah closed her eyes. She remembered her wedding day, and the early days of marriage, and a happiness she hadn't come close to since then. She knew that, probably very soon, Patrick would ask her again to marry him. She also knew that she would be happy with him, but it wouldn't be that ecstatic kind of happiness she'd had with Jesse. But what she couldn't say, with the sound of Annabel's and Jesse's laughter still ringing in her ears, was whether or not that little bit of happiness with Patrick would be enough.

# 21

S ARAH LEFT THE kids and rushed back downstairs. She had a roast in the oven and a bottle of wine
breathing on the table. She lit the candles and turned the
classical station on low. She hurried into the bathroom and
looked at herself. There were circles under her eyes, but
she had managed to cover up most of them with concealer.
She looked as good as she could, considering everything.

The doorbell rang promptly at eight. Patrick was always precisely punctual. Sarah smoothed down her dress
and walked to the door.

Patrick smiled and kissed her cheek absently. Sarah
tried not to let her dissatisfaction show. It had been this
way ever since Jesse and Annabel got married three
months ago. She and Patrick didn't know how to be together anymore. That proposal he had made in the park a
few months before Jesse came back hung over them heav-
ily. The condition for marriage then had been that Jesse
had to come back. He had. He had even married Annabel.
There were no more excuses.

But Sarah wanted an excuse. She did not want to simply follow Jesse and Annabel's lead. Jesse and Annabel's
marriage tainted everything, including Sarah and Patrick's
love. What had seemed pure and beautiful a few months
before now seemed seedy. Sarah had always thought that

she and Patrick had come together on their own, out of mutual love and respect, but now it seemed they were merely the other half of the straight switch, a by-product of that back-seat quickie Jesse and Annabel had shared years ago. It galled her to be linked with them. Jesse and Annabel's marriage had turned this whole thing into some kind of game or competition, and they were winning.

Sarah did not want to get married and then have people say to her, "Now let me see if I have this straight. You were married to Jesse and Annabel was married to Patrick, and then you swapped? How strange! What do your kids think? Doesn't it make you feel just a little bit incestuous?"

The truth was that it did make her feel incestuous. It also made her feel manipulated and out of control.

On the other hand, she hated this distance between her and Patrick. She hated his casual kisses, the way he avoided her eyes. It was obvious that Jesse and Annabel's marriage had had the same effect on him that it had on her.

Tonight, she didn't know what she'd been hoping for. Maybe for him to break the stalemate. To talk to her, really talk to her, about his fears, about Jesse and Annabel, about them. But instead, she only got the usual: an indifferent kiss and faraway eyes.

After the usual small talk, they sat down to dinner. Patrick poured the wine and Sarah served the roast and salad.

"Clarence Browden called me," Patrick said. "He wants me to come to MIT for an interview."

Instantly, the tension evaporated. Sarah gripped his hand.

"Oh Patrick. This is what you've dreamed of."

He smiled and for a moment Sarah was sure everything would be all right. They would work things out, the sting of Jesse and Annabel's marriage would fade, and they would find a way to be together.

But then Patrick said, "I don't know how I could bring myself to leave you and move to Boston."

And that's when Sarah knew. This was the beginning of goodbye. Patrick would not propose again. He pretended that he was happy for Annabel and Jesse, and that he felt no jealousy. But it wasn't true. He hurt as much as she did.

"Well," Sarah said, "let's cross that bridge when you get to it. When do you leave?"

"Thursday."

They ate the meal and spoke about MIT and all its virtues. They spoke of Adam, but never of Jesse and Annabel, and how their happiness stung. How, every time they thought of them, they remembered the night of Jesse's thirtieth birthday party, and the two of them in the back seat of the car.

When they were through and Sarah got up to clear the table, Patrick pulled her back down. He let his hand linger on her wrist and Sarah's heart picked up its pace. *Now*, she thought. *Now he'll say something.*

"Are you all right?" he asked.

Sarah nodded.

"Yes. You?"

"Yes. I think so."

The silence lengthened and Sarah watched a bead of candle wax fall onto the table.

"It's been tough," Patrick said. "Ever since their wedding, everything seems different."

Sarah looked at him.

"Not everything."

But he did not understand her meaning. "No. We all live in the same places, wear the same clothes. But everything has changed. Every time I go over there to get Adam, I have to face them, face them together . . ."

Sarah's heart slowed its pace again. They were winding down, distancing themselves. She didn't know how it had happened in so short a time. It was as if there were a screen between them, and only certain words got through.

"It will get easier," Sarah said, because that was what she always said, the nice thing, the right thing.

"Yes, I suppose."

Sarah stood up then and cleared the dishes away. Patrick helped her clean up, but Sarah felt none of the old camaraderie when they worked side by side. Now, she was only aware of how stiff they both were, how the classical music was the only sound filling the void.

When they were through, Sarah took out the coffee.

"Regular or decaf?" she said.

Patrick looked at a spot over her right shoulder.

"Actually, I'm kind of worn out. All the excitement, getting ready for the interview. And I promised Adam I'd be over first thing tomorrow morning."

Sarah turned quickly so that he wouldn't see her shaking. She put the coffee away and waited until she had her smile firmly affixed before she turned back around.

"Okay, then," she said. "We'd better get you home."

She walked him to the door. All at once, she just wanted him to go. It was too hard to pretend to be indifferent.

"Sarah," he said. He leaned over and kissed her lips softly. She held her hands down with sheer will, not clinging to him the way she wanted to. She could feel his love through his lips; she could hear his confusion in his sigh. He pulled away.

"Well, I'm off."

Sarah's shoulders slumped a little, but she still managed to smile.

"Drive safely," she said.

Patrick nodded and walked out. Sarah waited until he was in his car before she closed the door. She turned off the music and ran upstairs.

Annabel smoked the cigarette down to its stub and then reluctantly extinguished it. She quickly pulled another one out of the pack she kept on the table beside her and lit it. She sucked the air deeply into her lungs, let it burn her, and then exhaled.

"You seem more nervous than usual today," Dr. Walinski said. He was very small, with black, wavy hair that never stayed in one place and thick dark glasses. At first, Annabel had laughed at him. She didn't think a man like this could help her. But she had been very wrong.

"It's a bad day," Annabel said. "I keep getting the shakes."

Dr. Walinski nodded. He sat in the chair opposite her, with a notepad and pen in his hand. There were no couches here, which surprised her at first but then made her grateful. The chairs were leather, and comfortable. Actually, the room was very pleasant, painted dark green and stuffed with books and lush plants. Like a wealthy man's den.

"Any particular reason for them that you can think of?" he asked.

Annabel shook her head. Since when did she need a reason? Six months without a drink and it was as bad as the first day. Every morning, she woke up and knew she couldn't make it through all those hours without a drink. Every minute, she was on the verge of grabbing her purse and running to the liquor store. Every second she didn't break down and drink was like a miracle. Annabel puffed hard on her cigarette. She shook her head.

"No reason. Just everything," she said. "I shake almost all the time."

The doctor nodded. "But you're still making it," he said. "Do you realize how brave you've been? How much you've accomplished?"

Annabel tried to smile, to accept the compliment, but she knew it wasn't true. She was not brave. All that courage she used to have, that ability to stand up to anything, anyone, had deserted her. It was as if the alcohol had dissolved it.

"I would drink if I had booze in the house," she said.

"But you don't have it there."

"But I would still drink it if it was there."

"But Annabel, the point is you have not gone out and bought it. Every day, you make the decision not to drink. And every day, you're getting stronger."

"I'm not," Annabel said, sitting forward. Her hand was shaking so badly, she flicked ashes all over her pants. She brushed them away before they burned her. "I don't feel strong. I feel worse than I did at the beginning, and that doesn't make sense because I have Jesse now."

"Did you really think that Jesse would solve all your problems?"

Annabel fell back in her chair.

"Yes."

"But he had nothing to do with your drinking," Dr. Walinski said. "Your drinking came from inside you."

"For months, he was all I dreamed about," Annabel said, sucking hard on her cigarette. "I imagined that if he came back to me, I'd get my confidence back. I wouldn't need to drink because I'd have him."

"And what is the reality?" the doctor asked.

Annabel shrugged. "The reality is he doesn't love me. At least, he doesn't love me the way he loved Sarah. He leaves me alone. He spent the first month getting over the shock of seeing my face every morning and the next two looking for work. Now that he's got the construction job, I hardly see him."

"How does he respond to your alcoholism?"

Annabel jerked away. Even after all this time, she could not stand that word.

"It's not what he wants. I can see that. But he married me knowing it, so he can't complain. He knows I come here. I've asked him to come with me, like you said, but so far he won't do it. He doesn't bring liquor in the house. I suppose that's all I can ask for."

Dr. Walinski made a note and Annabel smoked down the remainder of her cigarette. The smoking had started on her third sober day, when she thought she would rip her hair out if she didn't do something with her hands. She went out and bought the cigarettes and never looked back. She didn't care about lung cancer. Or heart disease. Or stinking up the house. She only wanted to stop the pain.

"What about Adam?" Dr. Walinski asked. "How's he managing the stress?"

"I lean on him too much," she said.

"He loves you."

"He's nine years old and I treat him like he's an adult. It's just that when I hold his hand, I feel stronger somehow. I've tried to turn to Jesse more, but I can't be weak with him. That isn't how he wants to see me."

"Jesse married a woman," the doctor said, "not a mannequin. He knows you're not perfect."

Annabel said nothing and Dr. Walinksi tapped his pencil on his pad.

"Does Adam understand what's going on with your alcoholism?" he asked.

"Yes. That's the sad part. I almost wish he wasn't so

smart, that he didn't see so much. Most of the time, he treats me like a friend he's comforting. But then sometimes, he's just a boy again. He goes the other way when he sees me coming."

Annabel lit her third cigarette and took two deep drags.

"I try to calm down before I speak to him," she went on. "I really try not to jump on him. I know it's not his fault I feel this way. In fact, he's probably the only reason I'm still sane. But . . ."

"But you're on edge. You feel like you're ready to explode."

"Yes. Oh God, yes."

The trembling eased up a bit and Dr. Walinski smiled.

"I believe you're going to make it, Annabel. I don't say that lightly. Believe me, I have some alcoholic patients who I know will not be able to pull through. They just don't have the resources. Their personalities cannot stand the strain. But you are . . . different."

Annabel tried to straighten her back and found it sore. How long had she been hunched forward? she wondered.

"I am not minimizing how hard it will be," the doctor went on. "You've gone through the same physical withdrawals as everyone else. And now you're going through the emotional ones. You will not have an easier time of it than anyone else. But I think if you stick with our one-day-at-a-time principle, if you take a moment every day to look at yourself, to remember who you used to be and who you want to be, you will make it. You'll come out the other side."

"And Sarah and Patrick?" Annabel asked.

"There is not a limited amount of happiness in the world so that every person's share cuts into your own," he said. "When you're stronger, we'll deal with your animosity toward them, but for now, you have to concentrate only on you."

Annabel looked away. "And Jesse?" she asked.

She asked it during every session, and every session Dr. Walinski gave her the same response.

"You knew who Jesse was when you married him. You can't ask for more from him than he's capable of giving."

"I try to let him be who he is," she said. "I don't say

a word when he watches football all Sunday. I didn't complain once all the time he was looking for a job."

"Don't get me wrong," Dr. Walinski said, "he has to do his part. You should never allow him to abuse you or take advantage of you. But you've said yourself that he's not demonstrative, that he's selfish. Most people do not change. If you want a man who will shower you with love, you're probably in the wrong marriage."

Annabel nodded, although inside she was already plotting her next move. Dr. Walinski talked of patience and understanding, but what he didn't understand was that it was her need to win that gave her strength, that stopped her from going to the liquor store and buying the place out. It was this quest to make Jesse love her, this need to avenge herself on Sarah, this desire to prove to Patrick that she was the better woman, the more desirable one, that made her open her eyes in the morning and start breathing.

Patrick sat on the plane on his way home from Boston. The world, or at least his world, had been altered drastically in the past four days. He was going to work at MIT. His dream had finally come true.

He had flown in last Thursday, met with Clarence Browden for dinner, and then first thing Friday morning gone on a tour of the campus of the Massachusetts Institute of Technology. He and Clarence had walked past its one-of-a-kind stone building with a giant columned portico and green dome, the building Patrick had seen in his dreams for years. Then they went to the Research Center, an unimposing building on a side street, to visit its labs. Once through the door, Patrick felt as if he were entering another world. The equipment was first-rate; the labs were twice as large as those back in Washington. Clarence went over the experiments being run and Patrick was speechless. The researchers were taking on challenges that he'd never get to do back home. They just weren't given the grants for things like this. Comparative cell cultures, redundant virology experiments, even his simplistic immunology tests, yes. But all the grants for studying oncogenesis and bacterial mutations and tumor specific antigens went either to the National Cancer Institute or MIT.

Clarence introduced him to Robert Weinberg and David Baltimore, the leaders in the cancer research field, and Patrick felt like a kid meeting his favorite movie stars. These were the men he had based his whole career on. He read their work the way an aspiring writer reads the classics.

Then Patrick and Clarence went to lunch at a restaurant just off campus. It was loud and stank of cigarettes and burgers.

"You haven't said much," Clarence said. "I'm worried that you're no longer interested."

Patrick laughed out loud. It was so ridiculous a thought, he couldn't help it.

"I've been interested since the day I was born. I shouldn't say it, but this job would be like a dream come true."

Clarence nodded. They ordered hamburgers and sodas for lunch and then sat back in their chairs.

"The position will open up in three weeks," Clarence said. "That's not a lot of time, I know, but we need you. Carl Ubanks is retiring for health reasons, although I have a feeling he'll be hanging around quite a bit. It seems none of us can leave this place completely. Even when we're on vacation, we're always calling in, checking on the results. I often wonder if it's something in our blood, some virus we can't shake."

Patrick nodded. He still felt as though he were dreaming.

"You'd have your own lab," Clarence said. "It's the smallest we've got, but it's got all the facilities. You can pick your own graduate students. You'll finish up Carl's experiments first. He'll fill you in on everything and stick around a while to help see you through. After that, when you've got a feel for the place and where you want to go, it's up to you."

That's when Patrick understood that he had the job. A completely selfish surge of joy went through him. This had nothing to do with Sarah or Adam or Annabel. This was all about him, and what he had worked for, and how hard he had tried to do something important. This was his chance to be more than just a name on someone's payroll. This was his chance to be great.

The food came and Patrick bit into his hamburger. It was thick and juicy and absolutely perfect. He wiped his chin and smiled and Clarence extended his hand. Patrick gripped it tightly.

"Welcome to MIT," Clarence said.

Saturday and Sunday, Patrick had toured Boston with a realtor. Prices were high, but with the increase in salary Clarence had promised him, he'd be able to swing it.

It wasn't until now, when he was on the plane, that Patrick realized he was visualizing himself alone in his new house. His son would still be in Seattle, with Jesse and Annabel, and Sarah would be there too.

Sarah . . . Patrick did not know what had happened to the two of them. He still loved her. She still was the only woman he wanted for his wife. But he hadn't come close to proposing again. The words had just stuck in his throat.

He gripped the armrest and looked out the window. They were somewhere over the Midwest, over square chunks of farmland.

It wasn't fear that stopped him from proposing. Patrick closed his eyes, but that didn't hide the truth. He knew it had always been his way to just let things happen without getting involved, to let life play him. He had done the same thing with Annabel. She had chosen him, gone after him, caught him. He proposed, but it was as if she were pulling his strings.

The captain announced that they were approaching the Rocky Mountains. Patrick looked down, but instead of seeing the mountains, he saw Sarah's face. The air rushed out of his lungs and he squeezed his eyes shut. He had missed her these last three months. He'd been with her, but they never really connected. They never really talked.

He thought back to the night he found Jesse and Annabel in the car together. His skin had toughened in an instant. He remembered that day in the park, when he punched Jesse. On both of those occasions, he'd surprised himself with his strength. He wasn't the same, gawky boy Annabel had strung around her finger. He wasn't the love-sick husband with blinders on. He'd grown up, he'd matured. He felt passion; he could fight for what he wanted as well as Jesse could.

The past was behind him. It shouldn't stop him from going on. He was tired of associating everything he and Sarah did with what Jesse and Annabel had done. They had nothing to do with each other anymore. He wanted to marry Sarah because he loved her. Not for revenge, or because Annabel had married Jesse. But simply, purely, for love.

Impulsively, Patrick turned to an older woman sitting beside him.

"I want to ask a woman to marry me," he said.

The woman was surprised for a second, then she smiled.

"Good for you."

"You've got to fight for what you want, don't you?"

The woman nodded. "When it's worth fighting for."

Patrick smiled and looked out the window again.

"Oh, she's worth it all right."

Sarah was waiting at Sea-Tac International, nervously clenching her fists. She knew what she wanted to do, what she had to do, but that didn't make it any easier.

These last four days, while Patrick was gone, had surprised her. She expected to miss him, to worry that he would get the job and leave her. What she didn't expect was to be so angry. The second Patrick stepped on that plane, it hit her. They had all deserted her: Jesse, Annabel, and now Patrick, and she was sick of it.

She was angry, at Jesse for leaving and then coming home and turning to Annabel, at Annabel for betraying her yet again and marrying him, at Patrick for letting things die between them, as if it meant nothing. And she was angry at herself, for not being stronger, for not speaking up, not fixing things.

She had never understood the power of anger. Jesse had been the one with the temper. One of the biggest obstacles between them was that she simply could not understand him when he flew off the handle. She got upset, yes. And depressed. And anxious. And scared. But angry? She didn't even know what that was until now.

She liked it. That was the strange part. It intrigued and excited her to feel the way she did. The first time she banged a pot on the stove, she was afraid one of the kids would come around the corner and tell her to be quiet. But neither of them did. If anything, they liked the extra noise. When she screamed for the first time, it was as if the shout broke through to her soul and let the rest of her frustrations out. Carolyn came into the bathroom once, heard her screaming, and imitated her. For a minute, they both stood there with their faces tilted up toward the ceiling, howling like coyotes at the moon. Then they both broke out laughing.

The anger reached her in a way nothing else had. It made her wake up, see her future, realize that if she didn't act, she would lose the most precious thing in the world.

Patrick was the sixth man off the plane. For a moment, he didn't see her, and she drank him in. Then their eyes met.

He walked over to her slowly and Sarah heard nothing but her own heartbeat. When he finally reached her, he set his carry-on bag down. Other passengers shuffled past, but Sarah ignored them.

Patrick had already called to tell her he had the job. He would be leaving in three weeks. Now was the time to turn that anger into something more productive. Now was the time to start being the woman she wanted to be.

She took a step toward him, he took a step toward her. At the same time, they both said, "We have to get married."

Sarah looked up at him, stunned. He laughed and pulled her into his arms.

"We've been idiots," he said.

"I know."

"Do you mean it? You'll come to Boston?"

"Of course. I love you."

Sarah buried herself in him. This was right. More right than it had ever been with Jesse. She'd go to Boston and be happy and someday this whole mess of people and marriages and love and hate would work itself out.

• • •

Patrick had all the words planned, yet still he was dreading this day. Everything had been so simple while he was in Boston, getting the job. Then his relationship with Sarah fell into place. Why, then, hadn't he foreseen the heartache of this day? Why hadn't it occurred to him that leaving Adam would be the hardest thing in the world?

Patrick walked up to Annabel's door and knocked. It only took a moment, and then Jesse opened the door.

The two of them stood there, staring at each other. Jesse was thinner than he remembered, but he looked surprisingly good. The anger came on again, but not as strongly, and Patrick realized he was verging on forgiveness now. Soon, when he thought of Jesse and Annabel, he would wish them well. Soon, thankfully, the past would no longer sting him and he would be free of it.

A blink of the eye, it seemed, and he and Jesse were standing on opposite sides of the portal. This had been Patrick's house once. It had been his hand on the doorknob. Patrick was a logical man; he understood that he and Annabel did not love each other anymore, that she had loved Jesse from the moment she saw him. He understood and accepted that this house, and everything in it, was not his any longer. And yet, against all logic, losing it all cut to the core of him. He felt violated, seeing Jesse there, standing in his place.

"I came to see Adam," Patrick said at last. Jesse nodded and stepped aside. Patrick walked in past him.

The television was on loud, something Annabel could never tolerate when Patrick was here. Jesse walked over to the stairs and shouted up to Adam.

"Hey, Adam! Your dad's here."

In a second, Adam was bounding down the stairs, saving Patrick from making conversation with Jesse. Patrick hugged him tightly.

"Hi, sport. How does ice cream sound?"

"Great!"

Adam flung open the front door and was gone. Patrick looked back at Jesse.

"Thank Annabel for letting me tell Adam about the job myself."

"She's out shopping," Jesse said. "But I'll let her know."

Patrick nodded. He wanted to say more. God, there was so much to say. Yet there were no words that could do justice to how he felt. Perhaps Annabel and Sarah could just say what they felt, but it was different with men. Patrick would not expose his discomfort, or apologize for hitting him in the park, and God knows Jesse was too proud to bring up his struggles and his reasons for marrying Annabel. And Patrick knew, with sudden clarity, that this would never change. No matter what happened, or how many opportunities they had to talk, they would never clear up all the misunderstandings. They would never understand each other's point of view.

"Well, that's it then," Patrick said. He turned and walked out of the house. He had already stepped off the porch when Jesse called after him.

"Take care of Sarah, will you?"

Patrick stopped and turned around. There was no sarcasm in Jesse's eyes. Patrick loosened his fists and nodded.

"I will."

In the ice cream parlor, the jukebox was turned on loud and kids from someone's birthday party were running around like monkeys. Patrick had hoped for a quieter setting, but he knew that Adam was comfortable here. The waitress brought them two banana splits with extra hot fudge.

Patrick stared at his son. His soul. All the very best parts of himself in another person. He reached across the table and mussed his son's hair.

"I want to tell you about a new job I got," Patrick said, shouting a little to be heard. Adam giggled as a dot of whipped cream smeared his nose. He wiped it off and Patrick went on.

"You know how I've always wanted to work at an important cancer research center, don't you?"

Adam nodded. He scooped up fudge and put it all in his mouth.

"Well, I got the chance. MIT, the Massachusetts Institute of Technology, one of the best places to do cancer research, offered me a job and I took it."

Adam continued eating, but he dropped his eyes from Patrick's face. Patrick went on, his voice becoming a little unsteady.

"You know where Boston is, don't you, son? Sure, it's on the other side of the U.S., but it's only a six-hour plane ride away. I'm going to work it all out with your mom. Summer vacations. Maybe Christmas. Easter. I told you about me and Sarah. She'll be there too when you come. And Carolyn. And Sam. Think of all the things we can do there. Boston has so much history. So many things to see. I'm sure—"

Patrick stopped. His voice was crumbling and there were tears in his eyes. He thought, *Please don't let me break down here*. He took a deep breath and the tears subsided. Adam set down his spoon and looked up.

His eyes were watery, but he wasn't crying. He reached across the table and took Patrick's hand.

"I understand, Dad," he said.

Patrick closed his eyes. He hadn't thought about this. Hadn't thought about it at all. He would be leaving his son. How on earth could he have believed that a job was more important than Adam? And yet, he knew he had. And he knew he would believe it again as soon as Adam was out of his sight. It was awful, really, that it was so easy to forget how much he meant to him.

He opened his eyes and Adam was still there, doing his best to smile at him. Patrick squeezed his hand. Nine years old and he was doing a better job of this than Patrick. He had grown up so much this past year.

"You know I love you, don't you?"

Two tears slipped out of Adam's eyes and then he squeezed them shut, just like Patrick had, until the tears stopped. He opened them wide again.

"I love you too, Dad."

Patrick nodded. They both looked down at their sundaes, which neither was going to finish, then out the window, then at the monkey kids, anywhere but at each other. Then Patrick clapped his hands.

"Hey, I know," he said. "It's sunny out. Let's go play miniature golf."

With a look of relief, Adam jumped up. They left the sundaes behind and went outside. Patrick knew there was more to say, but he left it alone for now. They drove to the miniature golf course and didn't mention Patrick leaving again.

Three weeks later, Patrick, Sarah, Carolyn, and Sam arrived at the airport. When they reached the gate, they spotted Adam, along with Jesse and Annabel, standing in the corner. A judge had decided how much the children could see their fathers from now on. A week at Christmas, a week at Easter, up to six weeks during the summer. The lawyers had agreed that it was fair, but for Patrick it would not be nearly enough time with Adam.

For a moment, none of them moved. Then Sarah pretended to busy herself with the children so she wouldn't have to face Jesse and Annabel, while Patrick took them in one last time. Their bodies leaned together, as if they were holding each other up, and Patrick thanked God that at least this new job would save him from having to look at them.

It was the children who broke the spell. Adam rushed toward Patrick and Carolyn ran to Jesse. Only Sam stayed back, clinging to Sarah, eager to get on the plane.

Patrick knelt down and held his son. He could see, out of the corner of his eye, Jesse holding Carolyn, drying her tears. Patrick closed his eyes and held Adam tighter.

"I'll see you soon," Patrick said, although the words were hollow. Adam nodded. He was crying, but he pulled away first. They looked at each other once more and then Adam walked back toward Jesse and Annabel, his shoulders shaking but his head held high.

Carolyn would not let go of Jesse. She held on until Jesse was crying, until Annabel bent down and whispered something in Carolyn's ear that made her smile. Jesse gave Carolyn one more hug and then turned away as she walked back. When she and Adam passed each other, they reached out their hands and grazed their fingertips.

Carolyn was crying again when she reached them, and Sarah picked her up.

"Adam will always be your son," Sarah said, leaning against Patrick.

Patrick nodded. He watched Jesse put one arm around Adam's shoulders and the other around Annabel's waist. The three of them walked away without another word, without a final goodbye. Patrick took a deep breath and led his new family onto the plane.

# 22

THE LIGHTS IN the restaurant were dim, and in the shadows Annabel looked exactly like she did the first time Jesse saw her: perfect. But when he leaned closer, he could smell the smoke from her cigarette. The candles on the center of the table illuminated her face and he could see her eyes. They were tired and heavy. She'd been fighting the booze for a year and a half now and it was still hard for her. What a fool he'd been back when they first got married, thinking it would take a couple of months and then she'd be over it. Jesse was just beginning to understand that she would never be over it.

"God, I'm nervous," Annabel said. Jesse nodded. For a moment, he had forgotten why they were here, at this restaurant they couldn't really afford. Now he remembered. Annabel's psychiatrist, Dr. Walinski, had encouraged her to get a job and she had finally taken him up on it. Today she got the call from Farrar, Farrar, and Parterri, a prestigious law firm that had an office only a few blocks from their house. They had offered her a job as their receptionist.

"You'll do fine," Jesse said. The waitress arrived and he noticed that Annabel's gaze kept falling on the wine list. He slid it away, beneath the menus.

"Could we have a bottle of sparkling cider?" he asked.

"Certainly."

When the waitress went away, Annabel reached over and touched his hand.

"It will be nice to have some money, won't it?" she asked.

Jesse looked away. After Sarah and Patrick got married, the two couples agreed to stop swapping child support payments. But now Jesse was out of work. Again. He and Annabel had been married just over a year and he had gone through three jobs. He kept waiting for her to complain, to tell him to show some responsibility, but she did not. Even now, she wasn't complaining. She was only stating facts. It *would* be nice to have some money.

"Yes," he said.

She dropped her hand, and when the waitress came back, they ordered. Jesse picked the inexpensive chicken breast, although he hated children. Annabel, however, went all out and ordered crab legs. She stubbed out her cigarette and raised her glass of cider.

"To me," she said and then laughed.

Jesse looked at her. This was the woman he remembered, the woman who had consumed his thoughts while he'd been married to Sarah. This woman was confident and sexy and wild. But the woman he'd been married to this last year was someone else. She was a woman who couldn't keep her eyes off the wine list, who depended on her son to make decisions for her, who held Jesse a little too tightly every night before falling asleep. And yet, she admitted to no weaknesses. She swore she was the same as always, that pretty soon she would stop seeing Dr. Walinski and they would be fine, just fine.

Jesse remembered that one session she had dragged him along to. For months, she had begged him to come along, saying that the shrink wanted him there, that he thought it would do Annabel some good to hear Jesse's point of view. Jesse had made excuse after excuse not to be there until finally Annabel wore him down.

He was uncomfortable as hell the whole fifty minutes, sitting in those damn leather chairs, watching that doctor scribble notes every time he said a word.

"Could you just tell Annabel," the doctor had said, "what you feel about her alcoholism. How it affects you."

Jesse had looked at Annabel, but she had tilted her body away from him, as if she were scared to see what he looked like. She had seemed smaller in that office. She smoked constantly. She pulled her legs up beneath her in her chair. She seemed like a child, really, and Jesse resisted the urge to take her hand.

"It doesn't affect me. She's still Annabel."

"Of course she is," Dr. Walinski said, "but her alcoholism must affect you. Does it bother you not to have liquor in the house, not to be able to drink around her, to avoid bars, places that you used to go?"

Jesse looked at the psychiatrist. When he put it that way, of course it bothered him. What did this man expect him to say? The truth? That he hadn't bargained for this? That he'd thought he was marrying that woman who pulled him into the back seat of the car, a woman who liked to drink and party and who had control of herself? Instead, he'd gotten a woman who smoked too much, shook too much, and tried too hard to pretend everything was as it used to be.

Jesse looked at his wife. *His* wife. That day in the doctor's office, they had been married six months exactly. And yet every morning, he still woke up surprised to find her beside him. He still expected to see a head of blond hair disappearing around the corner instead of a dark one.

But that blonde was in Massachusetts now, with Patrick. Jesse would always remember the day Patrick called to make his announcement. Annabel had been out of the house at the time, and when Jesse answered the phone, Patrick said, simply, "Sarah and I are getting married and moving to Boston."

Jesse had dropped his head in his hands.

"Jesse? You there?"

Jesse had known this was coming. He and Annabel had even laughed about it, made a joke about how mixed up they all were. But none of those jokes had prepared him for the reality of Sarah leaving him for good. Even though he was married to Annabel now, it had been comforting to know that Sarah was still close by, that she had held off marrying Patrick, that there might still be a shred of feeling left in her for him.

Finally, Jesse found his voice.

"Yes. Congratulations."

"Thanks. I'd like to talk to Adam myself."

"Of course. I'll have Annabel call you when she gets back."

He hung up then and stood in the silence of the house. So it was done, then. Over. Sarah would marry Patrick and forget all that Jesse had ever meant to her.

He was surprised by how calm he was, how he didn't cry or try to break anything. He felt empty, more than anything. He'd lost Sarah a long time ago, but now he would lose his children too. Sarah would take them to Boston and pretty soon Carolyn and Sam would start calling Patrick "Dad" and Jesse would only be a stranger in their lives.

By the time Annabel came home an hour later, Jesse was ready. He told her the moment she walked in the door and he was surprised that her only response was a smile.

"Well, at least we did it first," she said.

Jesse laughed and kissed her. Thank God she was the way she was. She always made things so easy for him. In the psychiatrist's office, three months later, he wished he could make things easier for her.

"Look," he said to Dr. Walinski, "Annabel's doing her best. I'm doing my best. Leave it alone."

Dr. Walinski stared at him without speaking and Jesse knew then that he would not come back, that his being there did not help Annabel in the slightest. He could not be honest with her. Once, perhaps, he could have. He could have told her, straight out, that he was disappointed, that he'd thought she was stronger. But not now. Not since he'd seen her struggle, seen her eyes fill with tears when he made some stupid remark about missing those evenings at the bars, not since those nights when she thought he was asleep and she pressed herself against him and said, "Oh Jesse."

He understood, he sympathized, and he didn't want to set her back. He could just as easily have been the alcoholic, the one who let go into booze. But instead he had lost himself in the streets. They both had their own addictions. They both had found a way out.

The doctor wrote something on his pad, and without looking, Jesse reached out to Annabel. She hesitated, and then her hand slipped into his. He held it tightly; it was all he could do. He still had no words. He wasn't verbally adept enough to tell her that although he was disappointed, he was also relieved. She was human, she made mistakes, and she accepted his mistakes as well. He admired the way she was fighting it, the way she got up every morning and faced another day without what she wanted most in it. He was awed by the way she loved and supported him, no matter how bad things got for her.

"Annabel, do you have anything to say to Jesse?" the doctor asked. She tried to pull her hand away, but Jesse would not let go. He turned to her, but she avoided his gaze.

"No," she said softly.

The doctor leaned forward.

"Are you sure?"

Annabel ground out her third cigarette and, this time, did look at Jesse. She met him head-on with those hazel eyes that still took him in. She opened her mouth, but then closed it and smiled. She turned back to the doctor.

"Jesse knows how I feel," she said. And the truth was, he did. She loved him. No strings. No pressure. No requirements. She simply loved him.

Now, at the restaurant, Jesse stared at his wife. He could hardly see the alcoholism at all in her now. There were little signs, but only he knew her well enough to notice. She still turned her head when she heard the clinking of ice. She still avoided looking at bars they passed while driving. But her day-to-day life was easier. She could laugh again. She'd released her grip on Adam a bit and started making her own decisions. She found the ad for the receptionist job on her own and got the position without any help from him.

"It'll be so strange," Annabel said. "Getting up in the morning to go to an office. God, I hate the mornings. But once I get through that, I'll be somewhere, doing something. And while you're still at home, Adam won't have to fend for himself in the afternoon."

She said it without any hint of malice, but still Jesse tightened up. He was so used to criticism about his joblessness that he couldn't help it. He kept waiting for her to start shouting, to tell him to go out and find a real job and stick to it. Every day he waited, and every day she was silent.

"I'll find something," he said.

"Sure. But until then, this works out perfectly. Oh Jesse, say you're happy for me. Say you're proud of me."

Jesse stared at her. She was still the most beautiful woman he'd ever seen, despite all she'd been through. Just once, he'd like to say the right words, to tell her how he felt, to make it all come out right. But when he opened his mouth, he knew it wasn't to be.

"You don't need my approval," he said.

She turned away and he watched her take in her breath. But when she turned back to him, she was smiling again.

"Ah," she said, "here comes our food."

Six months later, when Annabel was firmly entrenched in her job at the law firm, Jesse walked into a bicycle shop in the local mall. He had called earlier that day about the ad they ran for an assistant manager. He had an appointment for three o'clock.

When the manager walked out of the back room to greet him, Jesse knew two things. One, that he could do this job, that there was nothing too demanding or demeaning about selling bicycles. And two, that he and the manager were going to be friends. The man was short and stocky and wore his black hair too long. He was wearing Levi's and a sweatshirt and he was sweating.

"I'm Jonathan Rivera," he said. "I just got back from my ride, so you'll have to excuse my appearance."

Jesse extended his hand.

"Jesse Bean," he said.

They shook hands and Jesse followed him into the back office. Its walls were covered with pennants and posters and pictures of various girlfriends, no doubt.

Rivera looked close to forty years old, but it was obvious he'd never grown up. Jesse smiled.

"You said over the phone that you were looking for a job to settle into," Rivera said.

Jesse sat down. Settle into. Would those two words ever stop chilling him? He didn't think so. Yet he had said the words over the phone. They'd come out of him before he could stop them. During these last six months, he'd watched Annabel settle into her job. She came home every night with law books and case studies and even copped out of sex sometimes to study.

"Mr. Farrar thinks I've got a head for law," she'd say as an excuse when he touched her. Then she'd dig her head back into the books. "There might be a future for me after all."

Jesse could only take so much of that. He couldn't sit around the house while Annabel forged ahead on a career. He had to find something to do. There had to be some job out there that inspired him the way law had inspired Annabel.

"The truth is, Mr. Rivera—" Jesse said.

"Call me John."

"All right. The truth is, John, I've been through a lot of jobs. I know I shouldn't say that, but it's the truth. I'd like something I can sink my teeth into. Something that isn't such a grind to come to every day. Something that's maybe even a little bit fun."

John studied him. He toyed with a pencil on his desk.

"You like to ride?" he asked.

Jesse shook his head. "I used to ride motorcycles."

"Half of this job is testing out the new bikes. I go every day, from two to three, and then for half-day treks on Saturday and Sunday. It's better than riding a motorcycle. You're using your body, your legs, your arms. I get lost in the motion of it. I get lost completely, and that's what I'm after."

They looked at each other and Jesse thought, *At last there's someone who understands.*

"Will you give me your word that you'll stay at least a year?" John asked.

Jesse took a deep breath, thought of where he'd been and where he wanted to go, and then nodded.

"Yes."

He left his car in the mall parking lot and rode home on one of the Schwinns from the store. He was awkward at first, not having ridden a bicycle since he was a teen-ager, but after a few blocks, his body adjusted, and he picked up speed. He even took a roundabout route home, changing gears, playing with the brakes, marveling again at the wonderful feel of the wind against his face. He had missed it, missed the moist Seattle air stinging his eyes, his hair flapping against his cheeks.

He knew, at once, that this would be his new passion, that he'd have to have all the gadgets, the helmets and toe clips and water bottles and cycling pants. He could already feel himself giving in to it.

He rode up into his driveway and carefully leaned the bike against the garage. He tensed as he walked to the door, anticipating Annabel asking him where his car was and then grilling him about this new job he hadn't even bothered to tell her he was going after.

He went inside the house. Adam was sitting in front of the television, watching *I Love Lucy*. He was ten and a half, but sometimes he acted more grown-up than Jesse and Annabel put together. He looked up from the show, smiled, then returned to it.

"You have a good day at school?" Jesse asked.

Adam nodded.

"Learn anything?"

"Sure," Adam said, without taking his eyes from the screen. Lucy climbed out onto the fire escape and then got locked outside. Adam laughed.

Jesse shook his head. He still did not know what to say to Adam. He still thought of him as Patrick's child, even though Patrick was three thousand miles away in Boston, with Sarah and Carolyn and Sam. Jesse stiffened. He still could not tolerate the thought of Sarah and Patrick and their life together. Even after all this time, Jesse could not accept the fact that it was over, that Sarah would never love him again.

Jesse headed into the kitchen. Annabel was still in her

high heels and slim skirt and blouse, and she was whipping up a casserole. For a moment, she didn't notice him and Jesse watched her. The job had done wonders for her. That doctor had been right; she needed the self-esteem boost, she needed to feel appreciated for something other than her looks.

The funny thing was, the more studious she became, the more appealing she was to him. She still spent hours fixing herself up in the morning, but at night she sometimes washed off her makeup and climbed into bed with her hair a mess. She had been reading so much, her eyesight had suffered, and the doctor prescribed reading glasses. After a few nights of hiding in the den so Jesse wouldn't see her, she eventually came out and asked him what he thought. Jesse had taken one look at her, the tortoise-shell rims resting on the tip of her nose, and pulled her up to the bedroom. It was like being with another woman since Annabel took the job. Every time he thought he had her figured out, she changed the game plan.

Now he stepped forward and Annabel turned around. He waited to be interrogated about where he had been, why he hadn't been at home to take care of Adam while Annabel was still at work. But instead, she only smiled.

"I've missed you," she said. "Dinner will be ready in half an hour."

Jesse stepped back, confused. He still did not know her. She never did anything expected and she followed none of Sarah's old rules.

"I got a job," he said. "At Pendleton's Bike Shop in the mall. It'll be bad hours, nights, weekends."

Annabel did not hesitate or stop working. She finished her casserole and slipped it into the oven. Then she grabbed a sponge and started mopping up the mess she'd made.

"That's fine. Do you think you'll stay?"

If there had been even a hint of sarcasm in her voice, Jesse would have walked out right then. But she was only asking. He shifted his weight to his other foot.

"I promised the manager I'd stay a year. I'll keep my word."

Annabel nodded. She put her dirty dishes in the sink and then dried her hands. She walked over to him and hugged him.

"Congratulations, then," she said.

She started out of the room toward the stairs. Jesse went after her.

"No questions about salary? About how this will affect us?"

Annabel stopped and turned around.

"Would you like to tell me about your salary? About how this will affect us?"

Jesse ran his fingers through his hair.

"Sarah would have wanted to know."

Annabel looked out the window. The sky was already black, although it was only five-thirty. Jesse knew he'd hurt her, knew he was not acting right, that he had not been acting right since the day they got married a year and a half ago. He kept anticipating fights that never happened, preparing rebuttals for arguments she never made. It was all so different now. Annabel was so incredibly different.

"I'm sorry," he said.

She nodded and then smiled at him.

"I understand. But you know I'm not Sarah. I only want you to be happy, Jesse. I won't put any pressure on you."

"Why not?"

She took a step toward him and touched his cheek.

"Because I love you."

She hesitated a moment, and he knew she was waiting for him to say it back. But the words, the emotions, everything stuck in his throat. Love was what he had felt for Sarah, once. He didn't know if he ever wanted to feel it again.

"I've got to go change," she said. She started up the stairs.

"I think I'm going to take up cycling," he called after her. "I left the car at the mall and rode one of the bikes home."

He almost wanted to hear her complain, so that at least he would know how to respond. He could fight fire with fire, but her nonchalance, her acceptance of everything he did, was alien to him. But, as he'd known she would, she only nodded.

"Sounds good."

She disappeared into the bedroom upstairs and Jesse turned around. Adam was still sitting on the couch, but his eyes were no longer on the screen. They were on Jesse.

"What?" Jesse asked.

Adam shrugged. "Nothing. Just watching you two."

"And what did you see?" Jesse asked, stepping forward.

Adam turned back to the television. "Nothing you can't see for yourself," he said.

Annabel looked up at the clock. She jumped a little when she saw that it was six-thirty, that she had been working nonstop on the research for this disability claim for three hours. She stood up, stretched, and looked around her office.

This was her office now. No longer was she the pretty receptionist out front. She was now the respected legal assistant with a small but very workable office in the back of the building.

She gathered her things together. Jesse was off today, so he'd be at home now, taking care of Adam. He had been at the bicycle shop for fourteen months, two months longer than his promise to John, the manager. He was beginning to feel a little penned in, but he had told her that he wanted to stick it out, to learn a little more, and then maybe to think about opening up his own shop someday. He probably wouldn't want another bicycle shop—he was bored with that—but perhaps a health food or sporting goods store. When he told her this, while they were lying in bed two months ago, Annabel had seen a spark in him for the first time. He finally had a dream for himself. He wasn't quite sure how to get there, or if he could even do it, but the dream was the first step.

Annabel stuffed all her papers into her briefcase and snapped it shut. She'd had her own dream. The day she started working here, she knew it could lead her into something more, if she were willing to put in the effort. She was fascinated by all the cases, by the attorneys' discussions, by the arrogance of the profession. She wanted to be a part of it.

It was Henry Farrar, one of the partners, who suggested she study to become a legal assistant. It was Henry who encouraged her, who helped her, who gave her the job as soon as she was ready. It was Henry Farrar who came into her office now, just as she was getting ready to leave.

"Staying late again," he said.

Annabel smiled. Henry had taken an unusual interest in her from the very beginning. She knew he'd hired her based on her looks alone; she had no experience to offer him. But he had watched her growth as if she were his own personal Eliza Doolittle. He had advised her on her business wardrobe, pushed her to stop smoking, which she had finally done two months ago. He seemed to think that her burgeoning intellect was his own creation.

He walked over to her desk and sat on it. He was a handsome man, with stark white hair and laugh lines around his eyes. He wore no wedding ring, although he was married. He did not hesitate to tell her that his vows with his wife were very loose.

"I'd better be getting home," Annabel said. "Jesse will be wondering where I am."

"Not so fast," Henry said. "Let's talk a little. You need to unwind before you go home to the hubby and kids."

Annabel set her briefcase back down on the desk. She could not say no. He was the boss and, besides that, he was her friend. She sat on the desk beside him.

"That's better," he said. "Tell me what you did today."

Annabel started talking about the brief she'd been working on, but she hadn't said three words before Henry lifted his fingers to her neck. He traced a pattern from ear to ear and Annabel's words fell away. Henry leaned forward and kissed her neck where his fingers had been. Annabel sat perfectly still.

He moved his lips around her neck and Annabel looked down at her body. For the first time in her life, she was leaning away from, not toward, a new man. She was flattered, his kisses chilled her, but her body just did not want this. How strange. How wonderful and strange to know that when it meant something, she could be faithful.

She knew all about the thrill of an affair, the eroticism of a new man's fingers. But none of that could compare to being with Jesse.

She stood up. Henry pulled away and raised his eyebrows.

"I love my husband," she said quietly. Henry was about to protest, but Annabel raised her hand. "That's not why I pulled away. This has nothing to do with either of you, really. It's about me. I just don't want this."

Henry studied her, but Annabel was miles away. She was thinking about all the men she'd been with, the ease with which she'd cheated on Patrick. She had loved him too. But it was different with Jesse. Jesse had come to her, seen her at her worst, as an alcoholic who could barely control her urges, and he had wanted her anyway. Something had changed in her the night he proposed. There was no thrill in infidelity anymore. The thrill was in wearing her reading glasses and still turning Jesse on. The thrill was in washing off her makeup and hearing Jesse say she was beautiful. The thrill was in coming home every night and seeing Jesse's car or bike in the driveway, knowing that he had chosen to stay with her another day.

She came back to the room, to Henry. She touched his hand.

"I'm flattered," she said. "At another time in my life, the answer would have been yes."

Henry stood up. "You're sure?"

Annabel nodded. "Yes. Surprisingly."

"Can we pretend this never happened?" Henry asked.

Annabel nodded again, this time with relief.

She drove home quickly and found Jesse's and Adam's bikes in the driveway and the two of them asleep on the living room couches. Jesse had been introducing Adam to the art of cycling and the two of them were often gone for hours. Annabel did not know what they talked about, or if they talked about anything while they were cycling. But the awkwardness between the two of them was gone. They might never be father and son, but they could at least be friends.

Annabel walked to her son first and wiped his hair out of his eyes. He was a young man now, with Patrick's in-

tellect and her looks. He had given her more support than
any friend, more love than any husband. She didn't deserve him, and she thanked God every time he came home
to her from a vacation with Patrick and Sarah. It amazed
her that he hadn't seen his mistake yet and gone to live
with Patrick.

She walked over to the other couch, to Jesse. He was
spread out and dirty and a grease stain on his pants would
leave another mark on the sofa. He'd left his soda can on
the coffee table, and when Annabel lifted it up, she saw it
had left a ring. He might quit his job tomorrow and never
get another one. Or he might withdraw all of their savings
and pump it into this dream of his to open his own store.
He might do any number of things and, believe it or not,
that was what she loved about Jesse, the fact that he could
surprise her, that he was still a mystery.

Her love for him twisted her heart, and she knew there
was no cure for it. She had to believe that he loved her
back, even if he'd never said it, because believing anything else was unbearable.

She bent over him and kissed his lips.

"You love me, Jesse," she said. He sighed in his sleep
and turned on his side. Annabel smiled at him and walked
upstairs.

# 23

❧

S O HERE THEY were, fifteen years after Sarah and Patrick had left for Boston. At a place where none of them, except perhaps Patrick, wanted to be. Sarah looked at herself in the hotel room mirror. No amount of makeup could disguise the fact that she was getting old. Jesse must have noticed that when she ran into him by the lake this morning. Yet, when she looked at him, it was like looking at the man she had married twenty-four years ago, not the man he was now. She didn't see the gray or the wrinkles. Perhaps it was the same with him.

While Sarah was running this morning, she'd had the strangest feeling that she was being watched. And then, when she stepped out of the trees and into the light, Jesse was there. She had not seen him since she moved to Boston. The closest she ever got to him was when she took the kids to the airport for their summer vacation in Washington and knew he'd be at the other end, to pick them up. Or the occasional times when she had to call him, to talk about something Sam, or more likely Carolyn, had done.

Yet today, she had recognized him instantly on his bicycle. Sam had said that Jesse was still obsessed with cycling, the way he had been with football and motorcycles. But even without that information, Sarah would have known him. After all this time, and despite her love for

Patrick, he was still her Jesse. Every one of his features, the way he held himself, the way he moved, was familiar to her.

She walked up to him rather awkwardly, not knowing what to expect. But then he smiled and the tension broke. It was wonderful, really, to see him again. She had not allowed herself to miss him. That would have been like a betrayal of Patrick. But she was filled with pleasure at seeing him now, betrayal or not.

He touched her face and Sarah didn't pull away. It was like coming full circle, allowing him to touch her again. She instantly recognized his fingers.

He told her she looked beautiful and, strangely, Sarah believed him. He made her laugh by saying, "Long time no see," as if they were merely children who had been separated a few weeks. In an instant, he made her remember why she had loved him.

She held that feeling now and smiled. Time did soften the pain and enhance the pleasure. There were good times to remember, for all of them. Perhaps they could search those good times out today and let the rest go. Perhaps everything would be all right.

She could hear Patrick humming in the shower and she smiled. A little over fifteen years ago, Sarah had finally sold her house in Seattle and moved to Boston with Patrick, taking Carolyn and Sam and Digger with her. She remembered the day they boarded the plane clearly, because she considered that the beginning of the second half of her life.

Their wedding had been small. Just a few people Patrick had met at MIT, Sarah's parents, who flew out from Spokane, and Carolyn and Sam. The organist had played "We've Only Just Begun," Sarah and Patrick recited their vows, and then it was over. Patrick had turned to her and smiled.

"That's it then," he said.

"Kiss her," Carolyn said. "Kiss. Kiss. Kiss."

Sarah smiled and tilted her head up. There was only a brief moment of recollection of other lips, other vows, and then Patrick blotted out everything.

Sarah was happy in Boston. She made friends there

more easily than she had in Seattle. She had adjusted to the climate, the customs, and even developed a touch of a New England accent over the years.

The city was hers. She walked through the Common and felt as if she owned it. She took the kids for ferry rides in the harbor and felt as if she'd lived there all her life. She had come to Boston to be with Patrick, but the break had done wonders for her. She was forced to get out and meet people and this time she rose to the occasion, joining an art class and the PTA. She was frightened at first of the congested downtown streets, but in no time she learned to maneuver through them like a pro. The city was louder than Seattle and Sarah found that she welcomed the noise, the life, the greater variety of people.

Boston held no memories. There was no chance that she would run into Annabel or Jesse at the store. There were no restaurants to avoid because the four of them had eaten there once. Everything was new and exciting and hers.

She went back to school. Patrick brought it up one night after Sarah mentioned that she was thinking about trying to find a job.

"You don't need to," he said. "I make enough."

They were lying in bed together, in their new house that was still furnished mostly with unopened boxes. The house in Seattle had closed only two weeks earlier and the furniture had just arrived.

"I know that," she said. "It's just that—"

"You were at your best then," Patrick finished for her. "When you had to do it all."

Sarah cuddled into his shoulder. It was so different, being like this with Patrick. It was warm, soothing, unpressured. With Jesse, there had always been an undercurrent of sexual desire, an unstated but no less obvious understanding that if she touched him, he would want her. It was both good and bad, always being wanted.

"I'd like to be able to spend more time with Sam," Sarah said. "In Seattle, he was always being rushed around somewhere."

"Have you thought about college?"

Sarah pulled back and looked into his eyes.

"For me?"

"Of course for you. Don't you remember all those talks we had about it? How you wanted to teach. Well, now's your chance. Go to college. Get your degree. Do it."

Sarah opened her mouth and then closed it. The blood was rushing through her. She had not mentioned how difficult it was to watch Patrick walk out the door in the morning and know he was going to MIT. She could imagine him in his laboratory every day, his hands itching to get started, his mind focused on one goal. God, how she envied his purpose.

"Where?" she finally managed to say.

"Anywhere. You're in university heaven around here. You could go to MIT. Boston College. Hell, Harvard."

"It'll be expensive."

"So? It's worth it, isn't it? It's what you've always wanted."

Sarah sat up. She could see it all; the lectures, the studying, the coffee and discussion with classmates. Coming home and having something to say to Patrick about what her day was like instead of letting him do all the talking. Being relevant. Going somewhere.

"I can use the proceeds from the house," she said. "It's not a lot, but it should at least get me part of the way through."

"There you go," Patrick said. "You can organize your classes around Carolyn's school time and they've got day-care on campus for Sam. Even with your studying, you'll be able to spend a lot more time with him."

Sarah leaned over and kissed his cheek softly.

"You are so different," she said.

Patrick nodded. He knew who he was different from. He wished they all didn't compare themselves and their spouses to each other, but he supposed it was logical that they did.

"So are you," he said.

Sarah went to Boston College and got her bachelor's degree in liberal arts and then went on to get her elementary-school credential the following year. She became something. Now, when she thought of her life, she always thought of her students first, even before her own children. The students were the real measure of her success. When they went on to junior high and high school and did well, Sarah couldn't help taking just a tiny bit of credit for it.

Strangely, she didn't feel the same way about her children. Sometimes she didn't think she'd had the slightest hand in shaping the kind of people they had turned out to be. Sam was nineteen now, in college at Michigan, interested only in the Wolverines' record. He was here in Denver only because Jesse had called and threatened to personally come to Michigan to beat the life out of him if he didn't attend his sister's wedding.

Somewhere along the line, Sarah had lost him. She knew Sam loved her as much as he could love. But he had simply drifted away over the years, into sports, into his friends. He had placed himself on the periphery of the family and seemed to enjoy it best there. The divorces meant nothing to him; he had been too young to understand the heartache involved. The switch meant only that he had summer vacations in Washington and two Christmases. When he won a baseball scholarship to Michigan, he left without shedding a tear.

Carolyn, on the other hand, had always kept herself in the thick of the family. She had changed from an adorable toddler to an emotional, somewhat melodramatic child. She had always loved Jesse. Sarah had to accept that early on. She was a daddy's girl and Jesse did nothing to stop her adoration. Seeing him at Christmas and Easter and during the summer was what she lived for. If anything wonderful happened to her, it was Jesse she called first. The less she saw him, the more majestic he became.

Then, when she reached her teenage years, Carolyn became a different person altogether. Overnight, it seemed, she turned surly, unresponsive, even downright hostile. She got into trouble almost constantly and never once apologized or admitted that she'd done anything wrong. If Sam was only going to float in and out of their lives, without turmoil, Carolyn seemed to think she'd better make up for it.

She did all the usual things. Smoking. Prying open the liquor cabinet and swallowing enough vodka to make herself sick. Staying out past curfew. Sneaking out to see friends and boyfriends.

Sarah was the disciplinarian. It wasn't a role she liked or wanted, but there was no getting around the fact that Carolyn was her child, not Patrick's. Oh, they pretended he was an equal partner. When Carolyn made her blindingly angry and she needed time to cool down, she'd say "Go talk to your father," meaning Patrick. But they all knew that there was a difference, that no matter how good and kind and fatherly Patrick was, Jesse was the *real* one.

But still, Patrick adored Carolyn. Even when she openly defied them, lied about where she was going and who she was seeing and then sneaked out again when they grounded her, Patrick could not stay angry at her. She's just rebellious, he'd say. She's spreading her wings. Getting a taste of life. All the clichés. Carolyn's teenage years were the worst time in their marriage. It was as if Carolyn had built a wall between them and forced them to stand on opposite sides.

Then, one morning when Carolyn was fourteen, Sarah knocked on her door to call her to breakfast. When there was no answer, she opened the door. The bed was empty. There was a note on the pillow.

> *I couldn't stand it anymore. Dad understands me better than you ever will. I went to live with him and I'm not coming back.*
>
> Carolyn

Sarah had sat down on the bed and cried. She had tried to do everything right and had succeeded in doing everything wrong. Over the years, she had tried to do what all the parenting books said. When Carolyn stole money out of her purse or came home four hours after curfew, Sarah forced herself to take a deep breath before she spoke to her. She thought, *Stay calm. Don't yell. Explain the situation.* But the second she opened her mouth, she started screaming. "Don't you have a considerate bone in your whole body? Look what you're doing to me! How can you do this, Carolyn? How?"

Patrick was no help. He was too logical. He told her it

was a phase and that Carolyn would grow out of it. He said, "Better now than later." And in the end, it all came down to Sarah saying "She's not your daughter. You don't understand." Then Patrick would turn and walk out of the room and they would be silent and cold to each other for a few days until a new crisis arose.

Sarah had fingered the note Carolyn left on her pillow. She felt a presence in the room and lifted her head. Patrick stood in the doorway.

"She's gone," she said. "And I'll bet Jesse paid for her ticket and didn't even bother to give me any warning."

Patrick looked out the window at the early-morning sunlight.

"You wouldn't have let her go, if he had."

"Damn right I wouldn't. This is her home."

Patrick came to Carolyn's bed and sat down beside his wife. He didn't touch her. Sarah suddenly realized they had not made love for months. Every day had been filled with responsibilities. Her job. His job. Getting Sam to baseball practice. Making dinner. Dealing with Carolyn. They were not romantic at all anymore. She didn't even remember what romance was.

"Maybe this is for the best," Patrick said.

Sarah stood up and paced the room. The tears still slipped down her cheeks.

"How can you say that? She's gone. She somehow got herself to the airport, probably with one of those hoodlum friends who drive, and is going to live with Jesse and that . . . that wife of his."

Patrick bristled. It was still not allowed, this former-spouse bashing. And for the umpteenth time, Sarah had a profound urge to be married to someone with no ties or loyalties to Jesse and Annabel, someone who would let her say whatever was on her mind, someone who was totally supportive of *her*.

"She's angry," Patrick said. "She thinks we don't understand youth."

"I don't understand it!" Sarah shouted at him. "It's alien and terrifying to me. Every day I have to live with the fact that she could sneak out and get hit by a car and I'd never be able to find her. I'm afraid of drugs and booze and little boys who think they're men who could either rape her or get her pregnant or both. She's just a baby, Patrick. She's my baby!"

She sobbed and Patrick went to her. They heard Sam shuffle past in the hallway, but he did not come in to see what was wrong. In another ten minutes, the front door opened and closed and Sam was gone.

Patrick spoke softly in her ear.

"You were young once," he said. "If I recall correctly, you defied your parents' orders and sneaked off to meet one of those little boys who thought he was a man. You even married him."

"I was wrong," Sarah said.

"But no one could have convinced you of that. Not then. Not when you had so much passion and conviction."

Sarah pulled away from him. She took a deep breath and steadied herself. She wiped the tears off her face.

"This is Jesse's fault," she said. "He goes behind my back all the time with Carolyn. He's the hero and I'm the villain. I'll bet he ate this up, swooping in and saving her."

Patrick sighed. "Perhaps. And perhaps once Carolyn's been living there for a while, granting that you let her live there, he'll get to play the villain a little too. I mean, come on Sarah, we both know Annabel. She's not willing to share the spotlight with anyone. Do you think she'll let Carolyn grab all the attention?"

Sarah smiled, the first real smile in weeks. Patrick put his arm around her again.

"I say I make us some coffee and then, together, we call Jesse."

"You think I should let her stay?"

Patrick leaned his head against hers. "Yes. Because that's the only way she'll ever see that this is her home and that you're doing your best. Right now, she thinks you're the world's worst mother. Let her get a taste of Annabel."

Sarah laughed.

"You're vicious," she said.

"I know."

•     •     •

Of course, with twenty-twenty hindsight, Sarah could look back and see that those weeks Carolyn spent in Seattle were the foundation of her love for Adam. She was four-teen then, Adam was seventeen. Annabel was working at the law firm, Jesse had left the bike shop he'd been at for years and was working in a health food store, gathering experience so he could open up his own shop someday. It was summer time and there was no one in the house all day except for Adam and Carolyn. Sarah shuddered even now when she thought of what might have gone on be-tween them then.

Perhaps it was nothing, only friendship. After all, Carolyn did come home, as Patrick had predicted, in a lit-tle over six weeks. Annabel, who was more lenient but also less responsive, was definitely not the kind of mother Carolyn wanted and Jesse was not quite as heroic up close. So Carolyn called and asked if she could come back and Sarah did her best not to gloat. She welcomed her daugh-ter at the airport with open arms, stuffing the anger and hurt over the way Carolyn left down into the pit of her stomach.

"Welcome home," she said. When Carolyn ran to her and held her tightly, she knew it was worth it. Everything—all the pain and anger and fighting until dawn—was worth just this one thing, this one moment of holding her beautiful daughter.

After that, there were letters for Carolyn from Adam and phone calls to Seattle that neither Patrick nor Sarah nor Sam had made. But at the time, Sarah had thought lit-tle of it. If Carolyn had taken up a friendship with Adam, that was fine. It was better than them fighting, the way they used to. Sarah had had no idea that they would come so far from those fighting days, that seven years later, she would be waiting in a hotel room on their wedding day.

Patrick came out of the hotel bathroom, a towel wrapped around his waist.

"You'd better get ready," he said. "Carolyn's going to be here soon and I have a feeling the bride will want all the mirrors to herself."

Sarah nodded and stood up. She was dizzy for a moment and she gripped the edge of the dresser. Patrick came to her and held her arm.

"Are you all right?"

Sarah nodded. What good would it do to tell the truth? She couldn't say, *I'm scared. Carolyn is marrying Annabel's child, and I don't know what that means. And I'm not only scared for her; I'm scared for us. Can we really stand to be connected to Jesse and Annabel in yet another way?*

Patrick wouldn't understand. He would tell her that this would simply bring the four of them back together. Carolyn and Adam's wedding would make them whole again.

Sarah could talk until she was blue in the face and that would still not change the past or stop this wedding or help her avoid confronting Annabel again. It would only make her look weak, something she had given up being years ago, after Carolyn left for the second time, for good, for Adam.

So instead, she just said, "I'm fine," and pulled away from Patrick. She went into the bathroom. The wedding was only three hours away.

# 24

❧

ANNABEL SAT UNDER the hair dryer in the hotel beauty salon. A woman was polishing her nails and another was blending colors for her makeup. Annabel had offered Carolyn the same treatment, her treat, but the girl had insisted that she wanted to get ready herself. Annabel had never been able to understand her.

Annabel looked at the clock on the wall. Three hours to go. Tack on another five or six hours for the wedding and reception, and then it would be over. Thank God.

You had to have been a fool not to see this coming, and Annabel was no fool. She knew way back when Carolyn ran away and came to live with them that something like this could happen. She and Adam had been together before, of course, but never for any length of time. Those few weeks that summer had changed things.

If Annabel recalled correctly, that was the summer before Adam left for college in Denver. Carolyn couldn't have been more than fourteen or fifteen at the time.

When Carolyn called, crying, saying she wanted to come live with them, Annabel had resisted the urge to say no. For Jesse, there was no question of refusing Carolyn. Carolyn was his little girl, his baby, his pride. This was his chance to really be her father, to have some influence in

her life. Annabel had swallowed her jealousy and welcomed Carolyn as warmly as she could.

It had been awkward at first. Fixing up Carolyn's
room, accommodating her into a family that was complete
without her. She stretched the limits of their already tight
budget. She wouldn't eat a scrap of meat and Annabel had
to stop at the health food store once a week to pick up
tofu. Whenever the rest of them had steaks or chicken,
they had to suffer through one of Carolyn's tirades about
the slaughter of helpless animals.

By then, Annabel was well entrenched in her job as a
legal assistant. She did all the research and hard work and
the lawyers got all the glory, but that was all right. She
was considering becoming a lawyer herself someday, and
then it would be her turn.

One afternoon, she had to come home for lunch to pick
up a file she'd forgotten. The office was only a few blocks
from the house and it was a bright, warm day, so she decided to walk. With the music blaring, the kids must not
have heard her when she let herself in.

Annabel did not have to go upstairs. The folder was on
the counter in the kitchen. She could simply have grabbed
it and left. But the moment she opened the door, a strange
sensation prickled her skin. Adam and Carolyn were almost always parked in front of the television downstairs.
She had assumed they watched it all day while she and
Jesse were at work. So if they weren't doing that, what
were they doing?

Annabel tiptoed up the stairs, although even she
couldn't hear her own footsteps over the music. She
walked to the door of the master bedroom, which was left
open, and peeked through.

She sucked in her breath when she saw them. Their
clothes were scattered all over the floor. Carolyn was on
top of Adam, naked, the smooth lines of her thin body
practically melting into the harder ones of Adam's. They
were laughing. Then, with a look Annabel had never seen
before, Adam slipped his hand behind Carolyn's neck and
pulled her face down to his. He kissed her hard and long,
as if kissing were everything. Annabel backed out.

She turned and hurried down the stairs. Her pulse was

racing and she felt hot. She grabbed the file and let herself out. She tried to steady her breathing as she walked back to the office.

Annabel couldn't blame them. She would have done the same thing in their position. Alone all day together. At that age when sexuality is a miraculous discovery, when your body itches to be touched. And, of course, the master bedroom. The thrill of being in Mom and Dad's bed, play-acting that they were adults.

Annabel reached the office and leaned against the wall outside. If Jesse had seen them, he would have strode into the room and pulled his precious little girl out of Adam's grip. Sarah would have screamed. Patrick would have . . . Annabel wasn't sure. Probably gone in and explained about pregnancy and condoms and responsibility.

But Annabel was Annabel and they were lucky it was she who saw them. She would keep their secret. She was wise enough to know that forbidding sex was the best guarantee that they would find a way to do it. She had to let them be, let them discover each other and themselves, and then hope that the passion would die.

She thought it had died when Carolyn decided to go back to Boston. She saw the look she and Adam exchanged at the airport, the agony in both of their eyes, but if Carolyn was willing to leave him, then their relationship couldn't have meant that much.

Annabel was wrong. The letters started as soon as Carolyn left. And then the phone calls. And then as soon as Carolyn was out of high school, she got in her car and drove from Boston to Denver, to Adam, for good. There were angry calls from all sides, demands that she not give up her life, that they not *live* together. At the end of every conversation, when everyone was hoarse from screaming, it was Adam who got on the line.

"I love her. Can't you understand that?"

Annabel could. She never told him that. But she could.

Now he would marry her. Adam already had his career started as a journalist. He was a man now. A brutally honest one. He sought out the truth in everything. Sometimes, Annabel thought he was the antithesis of her, and yet she loved him. God, she loved him.

The hairdresser lifted the dryer and Annabel moved to a new chair. The woman brushed out her hair until it shone. The dye Annabel had gotten the week before hid the gray completely.

"There you are," a voice said behind her. Annabel turned around and saw her son coming toward her. She had let Adam go off to college with a smile. He had never known how hard it was for her to lose him, how the house had seemed empty without him. He had never realized that he was the only conversation within those walls, that she and Jesse found so little to talk about when he wasn't there.

Annabel smiled as he kissed her cheek. During those months when she was getting off the booze, Adam had been her conscience, her strength. But once Jesse came into their lives, she stopped depending on him so much. And it was obvious then how relieved Adam was. He pulled away quickly, replacing her with friends, with school, with his first attempts at writing that would form the basis for his career later on, and Annabel never got him back again.

Now, she knew what he wanted, a mother who did not dote on or coddle or suffocate him. He did not want a mother like Sarah. So she held all the feelings in. And, in a way, her love for him became more special, more pronounced, hidden away where only she could find it.

"How do I look on my wedding day?" he asked.

Annabel looked at him. It was like looking at herself, only masculinized. The dark hair, the hazel eyes, the tall, still lanky body. He was smoking, something he did almost constantly.

"You look perfect, as always."

"Aw, Mom."

She laughed and turned back toward the mirror. The woman went back to work on her hair.

"Have you seen them yet?" he asked, sitting in the chair beside her.

Annabel closed her eyes for just a second. Then she smiled.

"No. But there's plenty of time for that."

"Don't you think you guys should get together before the ceremony, so it won't be such a shock?"

Annabel turned to him.

"We're all adults, Adam. We can handle this."

Adam scanned her face, looking for that honesty he demanded, but she was older than he was, more experienced. She could hide things better than he could find them.

"Okay." He stood up. "I'll be up in your room, getting ready."

He started to walk out of the salon.

"How's Carolyn?" Annabel called after him. She should have asked it right away, of course. Sarah would have.

Adam's face lit up. It was the same look she'd seen on him so many years ago, in her bedroom. She was awed by the depth of love he had for this girl.

"Perfect," he said, and then turned and walked out.


Patrick sat on the edge of the hotel bed, watching Carolyn smear rouge over her cheeks.

"Adam won't even recognize me," she said. "I never wear makeup."

"You should," Sarah said. She was laying out Carolyn's satin wedding dress on the bed, smoothing out the wrinkles. She was already dressed in her light blue satin and lace dress. She did not look like any mother of the bride to Patrick. She was still his bride.

"Every woman can stand a little makeup," Sarah said.

"Mom, you're so out of it. Nobody wears makeup anymore."

"Then why are you putting it on now?" Sarah asked.

"For the photographs. I don't want to look totally washed out. But as soon as the reception's over, I'm taking it off."

Sarah looked over at Patrick and rolled her eyes. He smiled. He was perfectly content here, wrapped in feminine perfume and giggles. These were his two favorite women. Sarah was his love, his soul mate. She still listened with rapt attention when he spoke about his work. She had stood by him through the disappointments, the failed experiments. She was there to cheer his successes, the small victories and the amazing breakthrough in tumor-specific antigens. Amazingly, not once in their entire marriage had she disappointed him. Oh, she made him angry. She could be stubborn. She didn't fight enough for Sam and fought too much for Carolyn. But he was never surprised by her actions. She acted as he always knew she would, like a wife and mother doing her best, like Sarah.

As for Carolyn, it was a cliché, but he really couldn't have loved her any better if she were his own. She was twelve when she first called him Dad. He had been working in the yard when she stepped out on the porch.

"Dad, lunch is ready," she had said.

For a moment, Patrick didn't move. He thought maybe Jesse was standing behind him, but then he knew that was silly. He looked up and his eyes met Carolyn's. It was her style just to say it, not to make a big deal over the change but to simply move to a new level without any fanfare. He wanted to run up and hug her, tell her how much it meant to him, but he didn't. He only smiled.

"I'll be right in," he said.

Patrick had been there through all her metamorphoses. When Carolyn suddenly realized she had a voice and could disagree with people, he felt as if he were rebelling with her. Not that he condoned what she did, all the trouble she got into, but it was impossible not to understand. All you had to do was look at the fire in her eyes, the need to go out and *experience* things. To kill that passion would have been senselessly cruel.

If only he had held on to that logic. He had been so analytical about everything until the summer Carolyn graduated from high school. Then, in the span of one morning, he made a complete turn the other way.

Patrick and Sarah and Sam had been sitting at the table having breakfast. It was already a hot, sticky morning, and Sarah had opened up all the windows. The sunlight fell in big, chunky squares on the floor. A few flies buzzed above their heads.

Carolyn walked into the room, already dressed in jeans and a T-shirt that ended above her belly button. She put her hands on her hips and stared at them.

"I've decided to go," she said.

The three of them looked up at her.

"Go where, honey?" Sarah asked.

"To Denver. To Adam."

Sam sneaked a quick look at them and then took his bowl of cereal to the sink. He was out of the room and upstairs in a flash.

"I beg your pardon?" Sarah said. Her voice had quivered slightly and Patrick reached over and gripped her hand.

"Look, I don't want a big scene about this," Carolyn said. She walked through the room, touching the curtains that hung listlessly in the heat. "I love him. You must know that."

"Why must I know that?" Sarah said, pushing back her chair and standing up. Patrick could feel a headache coming on. "You never confided in me about him."

"Come on, Mom. Nobody confides in their mother."

Patrick watched Sarah's face fall. He threw his napkin down on the table and stood up.

"That's it," he said. He walked over to Carolyn and stood face to face with her. "I've had it with the way you treat your mother. She's done everything in the world for you and you throw it back in her face every chance you get. You act like a spoiled little brat."

He could see the surprise in her eyes; he almost never raised his voice to her. But, just as quickly, it was gone, replaced by defiance.

"I'm seventeen years old," she said. "If you stop me from going, I'll just run away. And I'll keep running away until I'm eighteen and you can't do a damn thing about it."

Sarah was crying now. Patrick turned and went to her, but when he tried to hold her, she pushed him away.

"Why?" she said to Carolyn. "Why are you being like this?"

"I'm not being like anything," Carolyn shouted at them. "I'm out of high school and I want to move to Denver. What's the big deal?"

"Your whole life's the big deal," Patrick shouted back. He knew that logically Carolyn had a right to do what she wanted to do. But logic wasn't working this time. There

was only one emotion: fear. Carolyn would walk out that
door and they would never see her again. Or she would
marry Adam and forget she had her own brain, her own
skills to develop. Or things wouldn't work out with Adam
and she would lock herself up in isolation. Or . . .

"What about college?" he said. "And all your friends?
You won't know anyone there but Adam."

"Adam's all I need!"

Carolyn stomped around the room and Patrick could
see so much of Jesse in her. He wondered if Sarah saw it
too, if that's why she was crying so much, because it was
like fighting Jesse, losing Jesse, all over again.

"Will you live with him?" Sarah said, lifting her head.

"Of course. And please don't read me the moral act.
We love each other and that's enough."

"God," Sarah said and walked to the window. She
looked out into the hot sunshine. Patrick took a step toward her and then stopped. He turned back toward
Carolyn.

"Can't you see what this is doing to your mother?"

Carolyn shook her head.

"You guys are unreal. You make yourselves the center
of everything. Can't you see that this has nothing to do
with you? Why can't you let me live my own life?"

She turned around and ran out of the room. Patrick
looked down and saw his fists clenched. He opened them
and stretched out his fingers, trying to get the blood moving again.

He went to Sarah by the window. She had stopped crying.

"We'll have to let her go," she said quietly.

Patrick shook his head.

"No we won't. Not until she's eighteen. We've got a
few months left to change her mind, to—"

Sarah took his arm.

"Is this my Patrick?" she said, smiling. "Think about
it. If we stop her, we'll only set her mind on it more. We
have to let her go. Let her decide for herself if it's right or
wrong."

Patrick shook his head. He didn't want to lose her. It
wasn't that he didn't trust Adam. He knew he had become

a good, decent man. Whenever he and Carolyn were together, though up until now they had tried to hide it, it was clear how much Adam adored her. He would cherish her, make her life wonderful, and Carolyn would never come home. That was the real fear.

"How can you just let her go?" Patrick asked.

Sarah sighed. She turned back toward the sunlight.

"She's already gone," she said.

They let her go. Patrick could clearly remember the day they all packed up Carolyn's VW and then stood in the driveway, saying goodbye. Carolyn was not as strong as she pretended to be. She clung to Sarah, crying.

"What am I doing?" she said. "I don't know what I'm doing."

Sarah soothed her and held back her own tears.

"You're following your heart," she said. "You'll be all right."

Patrick hugged Carolyn the way fathers do, not too tightly and without tears. He smiled at her when he pulled back.

"Drive safely," he said. "Call us when you stop for the night. We want to know where you are."

Sam hugged her awkwardly, told her he'd come out if she could get Bronco tickets, and then Carolyn was off. She honked the horn as she drove down the street. Sam immediately left to meet friends, and Patrick and Sarah stood in the driveway with their arms around each other.

"Maybe if it weren't Adam," Sarah said.

"I know," Patrick said. "I know."

Four years had passed since Carolyn drove away. She had surprised them all. She did not lose herself in Adam. She immediately applied to the University of Colorado and was accepted into the school of business. She would graduate with her degree this June. And she did not desert her family. She came home every year for visits. She became, if anything, stronger through Adam's love.

There were heated debates she never knew about. Annabel had called Patrick once, soon after Carolyn arrived on Adam's doorstep, furious that Patrick had done nothing to stop the girl.

"It's incest, dammit!" she shouted at him.

"Get a hold of yourself, Annabel. You know damn well it's not."

"Well, it's as close to it as you can get without breaking any laws."

"Look, they love each other," Patrick said. "I can't say that I like it very much either, but making a stink about it will only push them closer together."

And there had been that long discussion with Adam, when both he and Carolyn came out for Christmas. Patrick and Adam had walked through Boston Common, more like brothers or friends than father and son. Since that day Patrick left Seattle, he had been little more than a spectator in Adam's life. It was both belittling and rewarding to see Adam grow into a fine man, without his help.

"I want to marry Carolyn," Adam had said, without preamble. He and Carolyn had been living together for a little over a year. Adam had just graduated with a journalism degree and landed his job at *The Denver Post*. It was perfectly normal that he would want to marry the woman he was living with.

And yet the air went out of Patrick's lungs. It had come to what they had all hoped to avoid. This marriage would merge them all closer, as if they were the sides of a cube collapsed on itself. It was not just Adam and Carolyn who would be marrying, but all of them.

"You love her," Patrick said. Their heavy boots crunched the packed snow that had fallen a few days earlier. Their breath flew up in white smoke in front of their faces.

"Yes. I think I always have."

Patrick nodded.

"I know it's weird," Adam went on. "I know none of you really want this. But I can't help what happened to you guys before. I shouldn't have to suffer for it."

Patrick stopped walking. There was no one else around. The air was cold and thin and it hurt his chest to be out in it. He stared at his son, who was now the same size as he. Adam puffed on his cigarette and then crushed it into the snow.

"It's just ... It's just all so confused," Patrick said. "You're mine and Annabel's, but Jesse's too. And Carolyn feels like my daughter, even though she's technically Jesse's. It's like we were all woven through a loom and came out with the strands intertwined."

"You were all friends once," Adam said.

"Once. There's no going back, though. Some things can't be forgotten."

"But Carolyn and I have nothing to do with that. She's all I ever wanted, Dad. I look at her and I see everything good. She's honest and strong. She's this whole, complete person. It's like doubling myself, being with her."

Patrick saw the intensity in his son's eyes. Adam fished into his pocket and came out with another cigarette. Patrick opened his mouth, but Adam stopped him.

"Yeah. Yeah. I smoke too much."

Patrick laughed and they headed back toward the house.

"You're all grown-up," Patrick said.

"Shouldn't I be?"

"Of course. But I just keep wondering when it happened, where I was."

Adam took a deep drag of his cigarette.

"You were a good father," he said. "I always knew you loved me."

There was no sound after that, except for the crunching of their boots, and the beating of Patrick's heart.

"Dad? Dad? Are you listening to me?"

Patrick came back to the room, to Carolyn, who had finished her makeup and was standing over him.

"Of course."

Carolyn laughed.

"You'll be on the left and Jesse-Dad on the right. You'll be able to get along for ten seconds, won't you?"

Patrick stood up. He looked at himself in the mirror. The black tuxedo fit him well, he thought.

"Of course we will. As long as you kiss me first when we reach the altar."

"Oh Dad."

Carolyn disappeared into the bathroom and Sarah came to his side. Patrick could read the sadness in her eyes, the loss, but no nervousness. He was surprised by that.

"Half an hour and counting," Patrick said.

"What do you think she'll wear?"

Patrick laughed. Over the years, Annabel had become just "she." They had made her into much more than she was, more evil and more powerful. Sometimes they forgot that she was just a woman.

"Something low-cut, no doubt," Patrick said. "Black, if I still know her."

"Maybe she's changed."

They looked at each other and started laughing.

# 25

❧

JESSE LOOKED THROUGH the hotel window and watched the wedding guests arrive. They walked around the lake to the gazebo, stopping now and then to chat.

Sam, who was also staying in the hotel, came into the room to complain about his tuxedo.

"It fits funny," he said. Annabel worked on it, while Sam fidgeted.

"You're supposed to be down there, escorting everyone to their seats," Jesse said.

"Nobody wants to sit yet," Sam said. "And there's a World League game on. They've got a big-screen TV down in the bar."

"You're not old enough to be in there," Jesse said.

"Come on, Dad. I'm just watching, not drinking."

Annabel puffed out Sam's sleeves.

"That's as good as it's going to get," she said.

Sam looked at himself in the mirror and wrinkled his nose in distaste.

"Damn monkey suit," he said. He headed for the door.

"Don't forget the wedding!" Jesse called after him.

"Yeah. Yeah."

When Sam was gone, Jesse turned back to the window. Adam was pacing the halls somewhere, waiting for this damn event to happen. Jesse had been the same with Sarah. He had felt as though he waited forever to marry her. With Annabel, it had been different. They made the decision and did it. No messing around. No planning and coordinating for months.

Annabel came to his side. She was wearing a dark blue, almost black, satin dress. It was form fitting, not exactly mother-of-the-groom material, but it suited her. He could tell, from the lines on her face, that she was nervous. He felt a rush of sympathy for her, and put his arm around her shoulder.

"It'll be all right," he said. "We're almost there."

She nodded and leaned against him. He had leaned against her these last few years. She had made the steady money, while he searched out his career. He stuck out the sales job at the bike store for seven years, taking over as manager when John was transferred. Then he found a new job as a manager at a health food store and jumped into that to try to learn the trade. Then, three years ago, he was finally ready to strike out on his own. He took every penny of his and Annabel's savings and plunged it into a health food store. He convinced Annabel that everyone was taking better care of themselves and they would make a fortune on it. Although they hadn't made that fortune yet, he was making a profit. He was his own boss. And, all in all, he was happy.

He squeezed Annabel tighter. When he had seen Sarah earlier today, it had been like reversing time. She was his again, Annabel was forgotten. He had wanted to rush up to her and crush her in his arms, but instead he only smiled. When Sarah reached him, he said, "Long time no see."

They both laughed. He reached out and touched her cheek. It was as soft as he remembered. Yet her eyes were different. Like they saw more. He told her she was beautiful. She blushed, but didn't avert her gaze.

"Our daughter's getting married," Sarah had said.

"Yes. Adam's a good man."

She nodded and then looked back toward the hotel, as if they were being watched.

"Sarah . . ." He couldn't complete the sentence. He wasn't sure what he wanted to say.

"I've got to go," Sarah said. "But I'm glad to see you."

Jesse nodded. "Me too."

He got back on his bike and rode away.

Now, it was funny, but in that short span of time with Sarah, when they had said nothing really, he felt he had actually managed to say goodbye. When he had looked into her eyes, he saw a stranger, not the woman he married. That stranger was Patrick's wife. For the first time, Jesse accepted that she was Patrick's wife.

"Are you ready to go down?" Jesse asked Annabel.

She nodded, although he could see in her eyes that she was still unsure. She checked herself once more in the mirror and walked to the door. He watched her go, watched her put on that facade of strength and bravado, and knew that beneath it, she was the softest one of them all, softer even than Sarah.

"I love you, Annabel," Jesse said. Annabel stopped. Her shoulders hunched forward. Over fifteen years of marriage and he'd never said it. He wasn't even sure that he'd felt it, until the words sprang out. It had never occurred to him that she needed to hear it, that deep down, she was like any other woman.

He watched her back, could see her breathing, and then she pulled herself up straight again. By the time she turned around, her facade was back in place. She smiled at him.

"It's about time," she said.

Sarah and Patrick were standing near the fireplace in the hotel lobby when Annabel and Jesse walked in. There was a moment of silence, of taking each other in, and then Patrick broke it.

"Good to see you both," he said, extending his hand. Jesse took it and they shook, once. Patrick took a step toward Annabel and kissed her cheek.

"Hello, Patrick," she said. Sarah took in her dress, low-cut as Patrick had predicted, but not quite black. Annabel had not lost her figure. Her hair was still jet black, although that could be dye. She was wearing more makeup than Carolyn would wear in a lifetime, and yet on her it looked just right. She smiled at Sarah. Before Sarah could prepare for it, Annabel had leaned over and kissed her cheek.

"Good to see you too, Sarah."

For a moment, Sarah couldn't speak. All the images came back, the scene in the back seat of the car, the quick marriage after Jesse came back, the way the two of them had laughed, after they came back from the justice of the peace. But then, just as quickly, the images switched to their good times, their laughter, their drive through the mountains. There was an equal dosage of both good and bad. She smiled.

"You too."

Sarah looked over at Jesse. As she had noticed earlier this morning, he looked fit and healthy. The gray in his hair suited him, defined his eyes better. The two of them, Jesse and Annabel, were still the most striking couple she'd ever seen.

"Well," Jesse said.

Annabel laughed a little and Sarah could feel her nervousness. Of all of them, Sarah would have thought Annabel would be the least nervous. She wondered if she had gotten anything right about her.

Sarah looked down and noticed that Jesse's hand was around Annabel's waist, protectively. She wished Patrick would do the same.

"Yes, well," Sarah said.

"It's a beautiful day for a wedding," Annabel said.

"Yes, it is."

They were quiet again. This time, Patrick did slip his hand around Sarah's shoulders. She wondered if he could feel her shivering.

"Is Carolyn still up in your room?" Annabel asked.

"Yes," Sarah said. "She won't come down until Adam is out at the gazebo."

Annabel nodded. There really was nothing to say, Sarah realized. They were far past small talk. Yet all other subjects were off-limits. It was ridiculous, like the kind of second-grade fight she tried to break up between her students. Yet she couldn't make a move to stop it. She looked at Annabel, at her cool beauty, and all the anger came back tenfold. She wanted an apology. After all these years, she still wanted an apology.

Then the anger faded and she felt that pull of friendship again. She longed to know what Annabel's life had been like, how she was, what she felt. Her right foot wanted to take a step forward, while the left kept inching back.

"Listen," Sarah said. "I think we should just—"

"Mom. Dad," Adam said, rushing into the lobby. All four of them looked around and Adam laughed. Sarah took a deep breath and knew she would never complete the sentence. She would never say, "I think we should just sit down and talk, not about the past, but about the present. We should let it go, finally." Perhaps it was fate, that the words would never be said. Perhaps she wouldn't have been able to finish the sentence anyway; the words would have just died there, on her tongue.

Adam looked wonderful in his white tuxedo with tails. He had the height to carry it off. He looked so much like Annabel it was startling.

"We're ready," he said. "Sam will walk Annabel down the aisle first, then Sarah. Then Carolyn will walk in with you two on either arm. Everyone got it?"

"Yes," Annabel said. "But put out that cigarette first."

Adam took a last puff and then crushed it in the ashtray. Sarah watched as Annabel fixed his collar and straightened his jacket. She couldn't help smiling. She remembered how happy it had made Annabel when she told her she was good with Adam. As if she hadn't realized it on her own.

"Still a mother," Sarah said, before she was able to stop the words.

Annabel abruptly pulled her hands away. Sarah could see that she'd upset her, that she'd taken the words as an insult instead of as a compliment, as she had intended. Sarah reached out and touched her shoulder.

"We're not so different," she said. "I'm the same way with Carolyn."

Annabel smiled at her tentatively, and then Adam got their attention. He ushered them out the door.

"Let's go. Let's go," he said. "I've waited long enough."

Sam escorted Annabel to the right side of the aisle and Sarah to the left. Deciding which aisle was whose had been one of the stickier issues of the wedding. Annabel glanced out of the corner of her eye at Sarah. Even before she'd seen her, Annabel had known she would opt for a lacy dress. It suited her. After all these years, she seemed to have finally found what suited her.

Carolyn came down the aisle with both of her fathers. Patrick was smiling, Jesse was stoic, and Carolyn was on the verge of tears. Still, she managed to hold them in and Annabel felt a twinge of pride. No one would give her any credit, but Carolyn was partly her daughter too.

The ceremony was beautiful, with the brush of the wind stroking Carolyn's dress, with the smell of flowers and evergreens swimming past their nostrils. Jesse sat beside her, his hand in hers, tightly. He loved her. The years had passed, jobs and children had come and gone, and they had learned how to live together, how to make each other happy. She accepted his eccentricities and let him cycle whenever he wanted to.

She never insisted he love her. She knew, when she married him, that it was not in his game plan. He had loved Sarah and that was enough. And yet, as the years passed, getting his love became everything to her. Sarah aged and grew stronger; Annabel aged and softened. She wanted Jesse's love. More than anything in the world, she wanted it.

After Adam left for college, they learned how to be alone together again. They had candlelight and sex in the living room, and every night Annabel waited for Jesse to say "I love you." Every morning she woke up and thought this would be the day.

She had thought she was getting close to it until this morning, when she saw Jesse and Sarah out by the lake. In those few minutes they were together, it was obvious that he still loved her. The way he had reached out and touched Sarah's face told the whole story. He felt a tenderness for her that he had never felt for Annabel.

And yet only a few minutes ago, he had said he loved her, Annabel. Annabel had not expected it. When the words came, it was almost as if he'd hit her, sucked all the wind out of her. He loved her. He hadn't just said "I love you." He'd said "I love you, Annabel," so that she would be sure.

She looked at him now, while the minister spoke of eternal love. Jesse turned his head and their eyes met. He told her all she needed to know now, without words. *You love me,* she thought. She told him back, through her eyes, that she loved him too.

The guests clapped loudly when the ceremony was over and followed the couple back into the hotel. Hors d'oeuvres had been set out, champagne was flowing, and the band had already struck up the first song.

Carolyn and Adam made their way through the guests, laughing, accepting congratulations. Patrick and Sarah stood near the appetizers, sipping champagne.

"Okay?" Patrick asked.

Sarah smiled up at him.

"Yes. Surprisingly."

Patrick leaned over and kissed her forehead.

"Not surprising to me. You just needed to see them to realize they don't mean so much anymore."

"They've been the villains in every one of my nightmares," she said.

"And us in theirs, I imagine."

Sarah sipped her champagne.

"I realized earlier that I'm still waiting for an apology. I never got one, you know. Not from Annabel or Jesse."

"It's at the point now where they probably think they can't bring it up without hurting you. It was so long ago, Sarah."

Sarah looked up at him. More than anything, Patrick wanted her to forget. It was the only thing that infringed on their happiness now. The past. Jesse and Annabel. The betrayal, as Sarah called it.

Yet it meant nothing to Patrick anymore. As he had known it would, all of his anger had faded with the years. He had no desire to punch Jesse again, or to make Annabel suffer. It was a mistake, yes, the way they had come together at the party. But they were drunk, and unhappy, and only the most moral person would have been able to resist the temptation. Jesse and Annabel were only human, after all.

It just didn't matter anymore. Patrick had Sarah and he knew that was the better end of the bargain. The hurt had stopped years ago.

Patrick knew what Annabel had gone through to get over booze. What she was still going through. He saw her across the room, as far away from the champagne as possible. And he could only imagine what Jesse's life had been like that year he was on the road.

They had both made it back and, frankly, Patrick admired them for it. And now, with Adam and Carolyn's wedding, he and Sarah and Jesse and Annabel would be more connected than ever. He didn't want another repeat of the awkwardness they'd had in the lobby. Somehow they would have to find a way to get along.

Sarah was watching Jesse and Annabel too. Jesse had just taken Annabel's hand and was leading her to the dance floor. Sarah watched as Jesse slipped his arm around Annabel's waist and she leaned against his body. They were right together. Anyone could see that.

"He loves her," Sarah said softly.

"Yes. I think he does."

Sarah set her champagne glass down and looked up at him.

"Can I have this dance, Mr. Meyers?"

Patrick quickly led her to the floor. When she came into his arms, he felt complete again, the way he always did when he was with her. The song was slow and long, and Patrick savored every second. Almost at the end, Patrick bumped into someone behind him. He looked around and Annabel and Jesse were standing there.

"Sorry," Patrick said. They were quiet for a moment and then they all laughed. Why couldn't they, after all, be friends? Not best friends as they used to be, but four peo-ple who could laugh a little, get along.

Patrick looked at Jesse and Annabel and, with a smile, wished them well. Then he swung Sarah around, away from them, and danced.

## About the Author

CHRISTY COHEN was born in southern California and graduated with a degree in Psychology from California State University at Northridge. She began her writing career as an editorial assistant at an entertainment magazine in Los Angeles, and then went on to free-lance work, placing short stories, articles, and poems in a number of national publications. She lives with her husband and Labrador retriever in Boise, Idaho.

# Don't miss these fabulous Bantam women's fiction titles on sale in July

☐
## CRY WOLF
56160-X  $5.50/6.50 in Canada
### by Tami Hoag
Author of STILL WATERS

*A juicy novel of romantic suspense set in the steamy Louisiana Bayou by the author* Publishers Weekly *calls "a master of the genre."*

☐
## FANTA C
56274-6  $5.99/6.99 in Canada
### by Sandra Brown
Author of TEMPERATURES RISING

*A single mother struggles to balance the needs of work, home, and the passionate desires of her own heart.*

☐
## TWICE IN A LIFETIME
56298-3  $4.99/5.99 in Canada
### by Christy Cohen
Author of PRIVATE SCANDALS

*A gripping story of two women who find their friendship threatened when they each fall in love with the other's husband.*

☐
## THE TESTIMONY
29948-4  $4.50/5.50 in Canada
### by Sharon and Tom Curtis
Authors of SUNSHINE AND SHADOW

*"[THE TESTIMONY] is one of the finest books I've ever read."* —Romantic Times.

**Ask for these books at your local bookstore or use this page to order.**

☐ Please send me the books I have checked above.  I am enclosing $ _____ (add $2.50 to cover postage and handling).  Send check or money order, no cash or C. O. D.'s please.

Name _____

Address _____

City/ State/ Zip _____

Send order to: Bantam Books, Dept. FN109, 2451 S. Wolf Rd., Des Plaines, IL  60018
Allow four to six weeks for delivery.

Prices and availability subject to change without notice.

FN109 8/93

# Don't miss these fabulous Bantam women's fiction titles On sale in August

## • THE MAGNIFICENT ROGUE
**by Iris Johansen,** author of THE TIGER PRINCE

*From the glittering court of Queen Elizabeth to the craggy cliffs of a Scottish island, THE MAGNIFICENT ROGUE weaves a passionate tale of two lovers who must risk their lives to defy the ultimate treachery.* ____29944-1 $5.99/6.99 in Canada

## • VIRTUE
**by Jane Feather,** author of THE EAGLE AND THE DOVE

*"An instantaneous attention-grabber....Well crafted...with a strong compelling story and utterly delightful characters."*
—<u>Romantic Times</u> ____56054-9 $4.99/5.99 in Canada

## • BENEATH A SAPPHIRE SEA
**by Jessica Bryan,** author of ACROSS A WINE-DARK SEA

*The passionate tale of a beautiful scholar who encounters a race of rare and wondrous men and women under the sea who face a grave peril.* ____56221-5 $4.99/5.99 in Canada

## • TEMPTING EDEN
**by Maureen Reynolds,** author of SMOKE EYES

*The passion between a beautiful aristocrat and a famous private invistigator nearly kills them both when they pursue her missing twin.* ____56435-8 $4.99/5.99 in Canada

**Ask for these books at your local bookstore
or use this page to order.**

❑ Please send me the books I have checked above. I am enclosing $ _____ (add $2.50 to cover postage and handling). Send check or money order, no cash or C. O. D.'s please.

Name _____

Address _____

City/ State/ Zip _____

Send order to: Bantam Books, Dept. FN110, 2451 S. Wolf Rd., Des Plaines, IL 60018
Allow four to six weeks for delivery.
Prices and availability subject to change without notice.　　　　　FN110 8/93

# THE LATEST IN BOOKS
# AND AUDIO CASSETTES

## Paperbacks

| | | | |
|---|---|---|---|
| ❏ | 28412-6 | A SEASON OF SWANS  Celeste de Blasis | $5.95 |
| ❏ | 28354-5 | SEDUCTION  Amanda Quick | $5.99 |
| ❏ | 28594-7 | SURRENDER  Amanda Quick | $5.99 |
| ❏ | 29316-8 | RAVISHED  Amanda Quick | $4.99 |
| ❏ | 28435-5 | A WORLD OF DIFFERENCE  Leona Blair | $5.95 |
| ❏ | 28416-9 | RIGHTFULLY MINE  Doris Mortman | $5.99 |
| ❏ | 27032-X | FIRST BORN  Doris Mortman | $5.99 |
| ❏ | 27283-7 | BRAZEN VIRTUE  Nora Roberts | $4.99 |
| ❏ | 27891-6 | PEOPLE LIKE US  Dominick Dunne | $5.99 |
| ❏ | 27260-8 | WILD SWAN  Celeste De Blasis | $5.95 |
| ❏ | 25692-0 | SWAN'S CHANCE  Celeste De Blasis | $5.95 |
| ❏ | 27790-1 | A WOMAN OF SUBSTANCE  Barbara Taylor Bradford | $5.95 |
| ❏ | 29761-9 | THE WILD ROSE  Doris Mortman | $5.99 |
| ❏ | 28734-6 | WELL-SCHOOLED IN MURDER  Elizabeth George | $5.99 |

## Audio

| | | | |
|---|---|---|---|
| ❏ | SEPTEMBER by Rosamunde Pilcher  Performance by Lynn Redgrave  180 Mins. Double Cassette | 45241-X | $15.99 |
| ❏ | THE SHELL SEEKERS by Rosamunde Pilcher  Performance by Lynn Redgrave  180 Mins. Double Cassette | 45183-9 | $15.99 |
| ❏ | COLD SASSY TREE by Olive Ann Burns  Performance by Richard Thomas  180 Mins. Double Cassette | 45166-9 | $15.99 |
| ❏ | WELL-SCHOOLED IN MURDER by Elizabeth George  Performance by Derek Jacobi  180 Mins. Double Cassette | 45278-9 | $15.99 |

Available at your local bookstore or use this page to order.

Send to:  Bantam Books, Dept. FBS
2451 S. Wolf Road
Des Plaines, IL  60018

Please send me the items I have checked above.  I am enclosing $_____ (please add $2.50 to cover postage and handling). Send check or money order, no cash or C.O.D.'s, please.

Mr./Ms._____

Address_____

City/State_____Zip_____

Please allow four to six weeks for delivery.

Prices and availability subject to change without notice.          FBS 6/93

# The Very Best In Contemporary Women's Fiction

## Sandra Brown

| | | | |
|---|---|---|---|
| _____ | 29085-1 | 22 INDIGO PLACE | $4.50/5.50 in Canada |
| _____ | 56045-X | TEMPERATURES RISING | $5.99/6.99 |
| _____ | 28990-X | TEXAS! CHASE | $5.99/6.99 |
| _____ | 28951-9 | TEXAS! LUCKY | $5.99/6.99 |
| _____ | 29500-3 | TEXAS! SAGE | $5.99/6.99 |
| _____ | 29783-X | A WHOLE NEW LIGHT | $5.99/6.99 |

## Tami Hoag

| | | | |
|---|---|---|---|
| _____ | 29534-9 | LUCKY'S LADY | $4.99/ 5.99 |
| _____ | 29053-3 | MAGIC | $4.99/ 5.99 |
| _____ | 29272-2 | STILL WATERS | $4.99/ 5.99 |
| _____ | 56050-6 | SARAH'S SIN | $4.50/ 5.50 |

## Nora Roberts

| | | | |
|---|---|---|---|
| _____ | 27283-7 | BRAZEN VIRTUE | $4.99/5.99 |
| _____ | 29597-7 | CARNAL INNOCENCE | $5.50/6.50 |
| _____ | 29490-3 | DIVINE EVIL | $5.99/6.99 |
| _____ | 29078-9 | GENUINE LIES | $4.99/5.99 |
| _____ | 26461-3 | HOT ICE | $4.99/5.99 |
| _____ | 28578-5 | PUBLIC SECRETS | $4.95/5.95 |
| _____ | 26574-1 | SACRED SINS | $5.50/6.50 |
| _____ | 27859-2 | SWEET REVENGE | $5.50/6.50 |

## Pamela Simpson

| | | | |
|---|---|---|---|
| _____ | 29424-5 | FORTUNE'S CHILD | $5.99/6.99 |

## Deborah Smith

| | | | |
|---|---|---|---|
| _____ | 29690-6 | BLUE WILLOW | $5.50/ 6.50 |
| _____ | 29092-4 | FOLLOW THE SUN | $4.99/ 5.99 |
| _____ | 29107-6 | MIRACLE | $4.50/ 5.50 |

**Ask for these titles at your bookstore or use this page to order.**